Kit —
& hope you love this!

OVERCOOKED

MARK MCWATERS

ISBN: 978-1-7360868-0-3

For Frances, who keeps my head in the clouds
and my feet on the ground.

THANK YOU!

To all my beta readers, my astounding critique partners in A Novel Group of Writers and the Seminole Writers Group, my deepest gratitude for your varied perspectives, incisive comments and your tireless hunt for typos you are so gleeful to find.

Chapter One

WHAT AM I?

El—short for Eldridge—Montcalm clapped a hand on the hairpiece hugging his misshapen head and pushed outside through the revolving office door. The gush of wind from outside smacked him in the face and he leaned into it as the growl of traffic and crowd murmur of pedestrians welcomed him out onto Marietta Street in downtown Atlanta.

The delicious smell of grilled hot dogs cut through the exhaust stink and he followed his nose to a red and yellow-striped hot dog stand on the corner. He waited behind three people while the harried dog man slapped dogs in buns.

"What you have sir? Polish? Brat? Hebrew National? You make a choice."

"Which is your best?"

"All good. They all good. Choose one. Or two." The vendor eyed Eldridge's skinny frame. "I think two."

"Polish."

"Eggselent choice. The best." He selected a sizzling kielbasa off the grill and plopped it into a bun without looking. "Next." A young blonde pushed to the front and the man greeted her with a gap-toothed smile. "What you have Miss?"

Eldridge took his dogs and handed two dollars to the man's wife standing at the far end of the cart. On a metal shelf in front of her, jugs of mustard and ketchup squatted like fat yellow and red buoys. Pickles and onions congealed in plastic containers beside them. Flies buzzed back

3

and forth between the lot.

He held his hot dog under the mustard pump and almost pushed it before he saw the smear of sticky yellow on the pump handle. *Right. Like he'd ever touch that bacteria bomb.* Fortunately, he didn't have to.

El had certain skills he kept from the rest of the world, abilities he'd yet to perfect. He tapped into one now. Normally he wouldn't, not with all these people around. But he also had no wish to serve as a petri dish for the bubonic plague.

It took minimum concentration, finer movements came easier every day, and the mustard pump pressed down on its own. He slid his dog side-to-side underneath it and thought no more about it until—.

"Holy crap! Did you see that?" The blonde next in line shrieked and stamped a foot. "It pushed down on its own. *OMG*—tell me you saw that."

Something uncurled in the pit of his stomach. *Oops.*

People waiting behind him for their chance at the condiments and e-coli buffet crowded forward. Some added their two cents:

"Hell, yeah. I saw it."

"Pushed down like magic."

"Nah. It's one of them automated thingies. I've seen that."

"Yeah, right." A large guy with three dogs clutched in his mitt shoved forward and lifted the mustard jug. "Where's the plug smart guy?"

It might have been the big guy. Or, maybe he couldn't resist showing off. Or, maybe the devil made him do it.

Screw it. Look ma no hands.

He pushed the mustard pump again.

"Gaaa." Mr. Three Dogs dropped the mustard jug like it had morphed into a rattlesnake. The top popped off. Yellow goo splashed the front of the man's khakis, the blonde screamer's shoes and Eldridge's jeans.

He got a chuckle out of it later that evening, practicing his skills upstairs in his room while he waited for his mom to call him for dinner. Like every session, he started small. Moving pencils held a special place in his heart. An accidental mental push one day during a college paper had been the first clue to his talents. Tonight he blew through his self-described training regimen.

Eyes closed, hands clasped in his lap, he flicked the light switch on and off in his room, straightened the picture on his desk, and slid a clutch of shirts up and back along the closet rod. He opened and shut the blinds for his grand finale. Kid stuff. Boring.

Twenty-four years old and still living with the folks had its perks. But he needed to get out in the world and do something important; make a difference.

"Eldridge, dinner," his mom called upstairs. "It's on the table."

Junior copywriter at a crappy ad agency downtown meant a paycheck. But it didn't exactly have save-the-world potential written into its mission statement.

Mid-way through dinner, his mother's meat loaf changed all that.

"Pass the ketchup, please," his father said.

Ketchup.

El flashed back to lunch at the hot dog stand.

"El? While I'm young?"

What'd that one guy say? *It pushed down all by itself. Like magic.*

"El?" his mother said.

"Never mind, I'll get it myself." His father walked over to El's side of the table and snatched the ketchup bottle. "No problem, Dad. Why thank you, Son." He sat back down and leaned over to his wife. "There he goes again, honey. Your spaceman son."

"Our spaceman, dear."

Magic the guy said, his exact word.

The *Amazing El!* came to life that night between the meat loaf and mashed potatoes.

El jumped up. "Thanks, Mom. Gotta head." He raced upstairs and came clumping back down with the basketball from the back of his closet clamped underneath one arm. "I won't be late." He slammed the front door before his dad replaced the cap on the ketchup.

A short bus ride later, El leaned against the side of his ad agency's glass-front office tower fifty feet down from where the red and yellow hot dog cart had been earlier. Something about *bringing things back to where it all started* felt right to him. Remembering the smell of grilling dogs made his stomach growl and he realized he never finished dinner. Somehow, even that felt right, a starving artist with an empty stomach. In a year or so he'd tell this story on TV talk shows. Embellished a tad for his fans, of course.

He smiled and bounced the basketball. Streetlamps and storefronts lit the night with artificial daylight. Blue, pink and yellow neon fought with the brilliant mercury vapor lamps spaced every hundred feet. Cars shushed by on damp asphalt, the smell of rain fresh in the air. A slight chill made him shiver. From the cold or the excitement of the downtown buzz? Pedestrians hustled in and out of cars, restaurants, nightclubs, and bars. Some singles, mostly pairs, and the odd group passed him without a glance.

They were his people. His audience. Being among them tied his stomach in knots. Adrenaline? Stage fright? Best thing for it was to take the stage.

He started small. Spinning the basketball on a finger, something any teenager could do. The few people who noticed spared him a couple seconds and a pitying shake of the head, one more homeless loser hanging out on the street.

Until he dropped his hand and left the basketball spinning in space.

A couple passing by arm-in-arm were the first to see it. The guy hit the brakes and yanked his date back by her elbow.

"Oww! That hurt. Oh, my god!"

Two more couples plowed into the first pair. "What the fu—holy shit."

El casually cracked knuckles on both hands before re-palming the ball and dribbling it on the sidewalk. Now, he had the crowd's attention.

"Hey. Do it again, man."

"Did you see that? Watch this guy."

"Yeah. Funny dude with the big head."

Eldridge waved the people closer with both hands while the basketball continued to bounce itself.

"Hey y'all, my name's El. Anybody up for a little *magic* tonight?"

He studied the man and woman who'd stopped first. They would be his first in a long line of admirers. The woman looked young, an unremarkable brunette in short dreads. The guy filled out most of a faded Atlanta Falcons football jersey.

El reached out to the woman. Probing her thoughts.

"I know, right?" he said. "My head looks like a big light bulb."

She gasped.

"That's okay. It's how I do what I do. Like this—"

Eldridge held out a hand and the ball stopped bouncing, suspended in mid-air. "Here, take it." The ball moved slightly toward the woman's date. The man reached for it and the ball jogged up, down, side-to-side. Every time he grabbed, the basketball zigzagged out of reach.

"Hey." The man glowered and the crowd, twenty or so by now, laughed. "Freak," he spit.

Falcons jersey forgot all about reaching for the spinning basketball and lunged for El instead. The ball bounced to the pavement as El put out a hand.

6

"Now, now. Norman is it?"

Norman jerked to a stop, like someone grabbed him by the shirt collar and yanked.

"Didn't mean to embarrass you, man," El said. "My bad."

"How'd you know my name?"

"I know all kinds of things, Norman." He tapped his chest. "I'm the Amazing El. It's what I do."

Eldridge crooked a finger at the basketball rolling at their feet and it jumped into his hands. He called to the back of the crowd. "Can everyone back there see okay?"

"No . . ."

"Hell, no . . ."

"Speak up . . ."

"Hold on a second," El said. He rose about six inches in the air. "Is this better?"

"Are you seeing this? Look at that."

"Sucker's floating."

"Nah. It's a trick."

He raised higher, a foot and a half off the ground. "How about now?"

"How's he doing that?"

"That's nothing. David Blaine does the same trick."

"He's an alien, dude. Look at that head."

The sudden shrill of a police siren, followed by a loudspeaker, silenced the crowd for a couple of seconds:

"Everyone on the sidewalk and in the street disperse immediately. You are interfering with street traffic. Disperse immediately."

But the flashing blue and red lights got the crowd going once again. Their murmurs returned and grew louder by the second.

"Five-o's rollin' up."

"Stare and act natural."

"If they ask, I'm driving."

Someone yelled from the back, "Make 'em disappear dude." The crowd laughed and applauded.

Eldridge, watching from his heightened vantage point, saw the black-and-white roll up before any in his crowd. He watched it pull to the curb and the lights flick on and two officers get out. Saw them adjust their gun belts and settle their hats before pushing forward.

Onlookers at the back of El's crowd, especially the ones on tiptoes in the street, were the first to give up their spots. Ranks thinned from back to front as the two uniforms shouldered their way through.

The few lucky ones in the very front grudgingly stepped aside as the policemen pushed into the clear. The crowd closed ranks behind them.

El descended slowly to the ground as one of the officers keyed a shoulder mike, "Car 23 is ten-ten at the 1200-block of Marietta. No backup at this time."

The other officer put his hands on his hips and looked Eldridge up and down. "Well, well. What have we here?"

El cleared his throat. "Good evening officers. What seems to be the trouble?"

One of the officers staggered as people shoved closer. "Maybe you can tell us—hey, back up." Both officers whirled on the crowd as a few in the rear pushed forward for a better view. "*Back up*. BACK UP RIGHT NOW."

One cop waved the crowd back as the other slid his baton from its holster ring and slapped it into his palm.

"Show's over, folks. Be about your business," Baton Cop said. *Slap. Slap.*

"Nothin' to see here." His partner took a step toward the crowd and Baton Cop used his department issue length of mahogany to shove the front rows back a few feet.

"Show 'em El."

"Yeah. Give 'em a taste of magic."

"Levitate their asses."

The restless crowd murmured but kept their distance. Satisfied, the cops turned back to Eldridge.

Baton Cop grinned at his partner. "Told you, Charles. Another friggin' magician. You owe me ten."

Non-Baton scowled and snapped his fingers. "All right magic man. Cough 'em up." He held out a hand. "Come on, come on."

"I'm sorry?" Eldridge had no idea what the man meant.

"Hah," said Baton Cop. "Double or nothing says he has no permit."

"Ah." El nodded briefly. He squinted at Mr. Baton a few seconds before saying, "Don't forget the diapers."

The officer blanched. "Who told you to say that?" He glanced at his partner.

"Don't look at me." Non-Baton glanced from his partner to El and back.

"Seriously," Eldridge said. "Janet will be so *upset* if you forget them again."

"Cut that out."

Eldridge focused on the next cop. "And you, Officer *Crash*? I'd re-think that twenty bucks you put on Detroit."

"How did you—? Who—? Nobody calls me Crash anymore."

"So," The Amazing El mugged to the crowd, "I need a *permit* for that?"

The crowd whistled and applauded. Cell phone cameras waved above the crowd like glowing eyes on alien appendages.

"Show us the permit or we show you to the car," Baton Cop said.

"Officers, you got me." El spread his hands. "I don't have a permit. I didn't know I need—"

"Turn around. Put your hands against the building."

"Can't we be civil about this? I'm sure we can—"

Crash Cop grabbed El's wrist and twisted. Eldridge twisted, too. Anything to avoid a broken arm. He felt a forearm shove hard to the back of his neck and he fell forward, turning his face in time to keep from smashing his nose into the concrete wall. His cheek and forehead took the brunt of the blow.

"Hey, come on guys. What did I do?" El felt the scrape of concrete on his cheekbone.

"Had to do it the hard way, hey magic man?"

Eldridge felt cold steel clamp around one wrist while the officer fished for his other arm.

"Guys, this is all a misunderstand—" The words came out slurred. A consequence of having your face smashed into a wall.

"Pigs."

The shout came from somewhere to El's left.

"Pigs." A different voice, this time from the right.

"Pigs . . . Pigs . . . Pigs . . . ."

Individual cries became a crowd chant in seconds.

"Pigs . . . Pigs . . . Pigs . . . "

Baton Cop squinted at the crowd and reached for the mike on his shoulder.

"Hey, El. Here's how I *make* pigs *disappear!"* The shouted boast came from close behind El, somewhere in the front of the crowd.

Eldridge never heard the gunshot. First came the flash, brilliant white like a flashbulb. Then the acrid stink of discharged gunpowder cleared every other scent from his nose.

"Gun! Gun!"

Women screamed and men yelled. Baton Cop dropped his stick and clawed the pistol from his holster. He stabbed it at the crowd, pointing it, swiveling left and right. People ducked and pushed to get away. The policeman's eyes, big as nickels, scanned for a target as, en masse, people whirled to run, shoving to get clear, tripping, and falling.

The scene reduced to white noise and a kaleidoscope of pictures that flickered in El's head like an old-time movie. The buzz of street panic ebbed and swelled until it all faded into a silent gray fog that left room only for very specific images thrust front and center he relived again and again:

The feel of Crash Cop's hand sliding down El's back, the man's fingers scrabbling for a hold as his legs folded beneath him . . . the geyser of red and the pink spray from the stricken man's mouth as he tried to speak, one hand clamped tight to his neck . . . the man's slow slump to the sidewalk and the frantic calls from his partner on the radio . . . "Officer down. Officer down. Shots fired. Shots fired. Officer down."

Those sounds faded too, into the rasp and wheeze of a frightened, dying man.

Eldridge hit his knees beside the fallen officer and looked into desperate eyes. "Hold on, man, help's coming. Hold on."

He knew the cop had passed way beyond listening or understanding him. The way the breathing slowed. How the man relaxed and sank into the sidewalk told him that.

"Oh, Jesus. Oh, God. Charlie. Stay with us, dude. Stay with me." Baton Cop crouched beside his partner and began ripping buttons and unstrapping Velcro to help the failing man breathe easier. As he did, El watched Charlie's hand fall away from his neck.

He saw the black hole. Perfect, round, like from a hole punch. Blood pulsed from the wound in a slowing rhythm; the geysers were over.

Not knowing what he was doing, El clamped his own hand to the man's wound and pressed down. Hard. The blood seeping against his palm felt warm, like water from a tap. When his hand slipped in the slickness he readjusted and kept pressing.

He barely heard the other cop screaming into his mike, calling for help. Yelling at the crowd. *"You assholes. Goddammit! You assholes."* Imploring his partner. "Come on Charlie, hang in there. Hang in there."

Through it all, El kept his hand clamped to Charlie's neck wound. Heat pulsed under his palm. The warm blood getting warmer, the slickness getting sticky.

His vision tunneled to a round circle; neat and round like the hole in the downed cop's neck. Big enough to hold the injured cop's face, the circle view shifted to his hand on the man's neck, then clicked back to the man's face. Only those two images over and over.

Someone close by spit *"Come on, officer. Come on, officer,"* through clenched teeth. He didn't realize, until the pain in his jaw clued him, the tortured mantra came from him.

Still, he held on and pressed hard, willing the heat under his palm to grow and spread its warmth halfway up his arm.

By the time the paramedics had hold of him, trying to yank him away from the fallen man, his whole left side blazed with heat. Felt like he'd burst into flame any second. Yet, he refused to let go.

The EMTs gave up after a fashion and ministered to the downed officer, working around El. Checking vitals. Looking for other bullet holes. Apparently concluding pressure on the wound is what the man needed. Who administered it was not as critical as keeping it in place.

"Hey, Johnny. I've got a pulse. BP 90 over 60 but steady. And *climbing.*" The paramedic on the monitor looked up with wide eyes.

"Not possible." Johnny halted his check of the wounded man. "Show me."

EMT number one tilted the monitor and called out, "95 over 65."

"Thought you said this man got shot in the neck." Johnny scowled up at the downed cop's frantic partner.

Baton Cop looked at the crouching paramedic like the man had suddenly sprouted wings. "He did get shot. You see him."

"Clear out, mister. Let go. LET GO." Johnny and the other EMT pried Eldridge's arm away from the fallen officer. El fell back on his butt. Handcuffs dangling from his bloody left hand got a couple of weird looks as he clasped his arms around his knees. The two paramedics bent over the fallen man to examine his wound, really examine it, for the first time.

"Give me a saline and some 4-by-4s." Johnny nodded toward the open case beside them.

Paramedic number two dug out a plastic bottle and a fistful of gauze and handed them to his partner who immediately sprayed the downed officer's neck liberally with saline. Dabbed gingerly and squirted more. Wiped more firmly and finally unscrewed the cap from the saline bottle and doused the area.

"Shot in the neck you say? Find me the hole. Give me another read on the blood pressure."

"Holding at 95 over 65."

"I don't get it," the first paramedic said.

Eldridge crawled over to the officer and got close enough to see for himself. No hole. No wound. No spurting blood.

He looked at his bloody hand and at the EMTs and the circle of police and firemen standing around them.

The downed cop coughed a couple of times and spat a gob of dark guck to the side. He struggled to sit up while the two paramedics fought to keep him down.

"What happened?" the officer rasped and coughed again. "What's all the excitement?"

Eldridge had a pretty good idea what had happened. He scooted on his butt to the side of the building and pressed his back against the cold glass. Good-bye street magician and hello—what? Doctor? Healer? *God?*

Fourteen cell phone cameras captured most of the episode. Eight had been recording from the gunshot, on. Three zoomed in to show shaky close-ups of El's face.

Within five minutes, six videos hit the web. In a day, four went viral. He wouldn't find all that out until later. Right now, he stared straight ahead and watched the frantic parade of life rush by on the sidewalk. Cops and medicos and fire personnel tried to control the scene. Pedestrians pushed against the yellow tape barricade for a better look.

A pair of shiny black high heels zeroed in on him with no hesitation. They stepped up to him and stopped, unimpeded. The right foot tapped, not impatient so much as contemplating.

He looked up and saw a black silhouette haloed by a streetlamp. No details except for a pale white hand reaching down, waggling its fingers at him.

"Come on now overcooked. We need to get you out of here."

"I'm sorry? What did you say?"

"We need to go."

"No, before—"

"Overcooked. Tell me you never heard that term before."

"Never."

"C'mon. *Overcooked? Don't make me come out? I'm not ready? Womb wrecker?* These are all new to you?"

"I think you better go."

"Oh my god, Eldridge Montcalm. You don't know what you are, do you?"

"I know you better get going before the cops see you. They're going to want to talk to me. Ask lots of questions. You don't want to be here when they do."

"Eldridge. Take my hand."

"Not to mention that cop. I think I did something." He ran his un-cuffed hand through his hair. "I don't know what I did. Did you see it or—?"

"El. Shut up. Here," she wiggled her fingers, "take my hand."

He felt like a fish contemplating a lure.

"Fish?" she said. "Nice analogy. Not all that flattering."

"Hey, did you read my thoughts just then?"

"You are a babe in the woods, Eldridge Montcalm. Good thing I came along when I did."

She pulled him up and he got a good look at her—petite, trim. No clue about her age. Giant sunglasses and a wide floppy brim hat hid her face. An aluminum briefcase hung by her side. The woman's mouth looked pretty enough; lips not too plump, with curves. Bright pink lipstick glistening. The tip of her tongue came out and licked briefly at her top lip.

"I'm not usually this bold, I assure you."

He gave her a light push. "Now you can boldly go."

"Fine, we'll do this here." She set the case on the ground at her feet. "We're sort of related you know."

"I'm pretty sure my parents would have mentioned a sister."

"Not like that." She took off her glasses and carefully peeled away her hat.

Even the cascade of blonde curls couldn't hide the shape of her head, slightly bulbous, more so than his even, with pasty white skin.

"Oh."

Not the most brilliant comeback in history. But he'd never seen another, what did she call him, overcooked?

"I'm your first one, aren't I? I wondered about that. Newsflash. We're extremely rare, but we're not unique."

"First?" *He felt like a rookie playing catch up. Not a good feeling.*

"For a genius, you tend to be a tad slow don't you? We're supposed to be the smart ones, Eldridge." She fanned herself with her hat. "I've been watching you for awhile. Now you have me worried."

"What do you mean watching me?"

"I know. Creepy, right?" She started tapping that foot again.

"Among other things," he said.

"We overcooked can't be too careful. Your little stunt here tonight will have attracted the attention of some very powerful people and let me emphasize this, they don't like stunts. Hate them, actually."

The crowd of first responders had thinned around them. The ones remaining gathered equipment, snapped cases shut, policed the area for hazardous waste. They paid the odd-looking pair zero attention, as if they didn't exist.

"I won't be able to hold these fine folks off much longer. We need to get this done and get the hell out of Dodge. Quick, grab my other hand."

He stood rock still, replaying her *very powerful people* comment.

Her casual *hold off these fine folks* had yet to penetrate. Every second with this woman brought up more questions. "This is all good, okay? Right now I need to go."

"We don't have time for me to explain. Give me your hand."

"No. Leave me—"

She reached and grabbed both hands. Each one gripped tightly in hers.

He felt her squeeze, hard. He thought they must look like two oddballs at a prayer vigil. She chuckled and this time he knew for sure she'd read his mind.

"That's right, El. You're not the only one who can do that. Shocker. Close your eyes and let it happen."

Images fanned through his mind like fanning a deck of cards. He saw people, lots of people, flick by, all ages, male and female, all with the telltale light bulb heads. Each accompanied by a sharp stab of emotion he actually felt.

Relief . . . fear . . . surprise . . . joy . . . happiness . . . distrust . . . disbelief . . . giddiness . . . curiosity . . .

"Tell me you felt all that. Yes?"

Her words threw cold water on an experience he didn't want to let go of. Literally. *Somebody pinch me. Is this for real?*

"First off, I make it a point never to pinch strange men on a first date. Second, this is most definitely *for real.*"

He snatched his hands away. "Stop reading my mind."

"Why? You do it. I saw you earlier, playing with your audience on the sidewalk." She shrugged. "Stupid human parlor tricks are not what we are about. You have a lot to learn Eldridge Montcalm."

"Who were all those people?"

"You already know that answer. Overcooked. Like you and me. What I played for you were the exact emotions they all felt when they met another one like them for the first time."

"Damn."

"Kind of a head rush, right? More tricks, my boy. You got a lot of stuff up in that shapely noggin of yours you haven't tapped into yet. And it's about time you did. Because we need your help with something." She stooped and picked up her briefcase. "I hope that genius globe of yours is a quick study. We got to get you up to speed fast. It's a matter of life and death and that is also *for real.*"

"We? Who the heck are you? I don't even know your—"

"Beatrix." She stuck a hand out. "Beatrix Goode. Please call me B, everyone does. Whoops." A passing EMT slowed for a second and looked straight at them with a puzzled expression. "We need to go.

They'll wake up and start seeing us soon."

Beatrix pulled and he allowed her to lead him down the sidewalk and away from the busy scene. He had no idea whether he could have resisted had he wanted to. Frankly, he didn't have the energy. The night became a bewildering blur of emotion and memory as he followed meekly behind this young woman he barely knew. Random illumination by car headlights and streetlamps lit them as they scurried from shadow to shadow and blended into the Atlanta night.

Chapter Two

GIRL'S GOT SKILLS

They met at Beatrix's apartment three times that week. It became apparent after the first meeting that Eldridge would be a quicker study than Beatrix anticipated. She called their sessions *pushes*. They were similar to the first handholding episode that night on the street downtown but lasted much longer and went much deeper.

Eldridge described them to her once. "Feels like you're tramping through my head in spike heels." He suffered trip hammer headaches on the days after each push but he couldn't quit. Little Miss B opened dormant pathways in that big brain of his he never knew existed. *Only way this ride ends is if my head explodes.*

Today, he stayed busy polishing his favorite skill. He practiced while Beatrix sat across on her sofa, buried in her laptop. She refused to look at him.

"Bet you can't do this." He floated a basketball in the air between them, positioning it so, if he closed one eye, the ball replaced the head on her shoulders. He so wanted to laugh but something told him that might really piss her off.

She set her laptop aside and closed it deliberately before looking up. "Tell me something, El. Ever wonder *why* we're the way we are?"

He sensed that any answer he blurted out would be wrong. He tried to adopt an earnest, thinking-hard face.

"The thing that makes us different is we overcooked had a longer gestation period than the normals; twelve months instead of nine."

Eldridge nodded. "So you've said." With the lapse in concentration, his hovering basketball dropped and bounced away. "Aw, man. Look what you made me do."

"Concentrate, please? We weren't given these abilities to play games."

"Really?" He crooked a finger and rolled the basketball to the opposite side of the room.

She threw a pillow at him and the basketball smacked into the bookcase and bounced off undirected. "Most of us, the real thinkers in our group, think the extra time in the womb jumped us forward a couple of evolutionary steps."

"Or, it made us freaks with dome heads and gave us extra abilities to compensate us for our troubles."

"You're that shallow? Seriously?"

"Besides, you still haven't told me who *us* is."

"I will, when you're ready. And you are not even close."

"Aliens, right? We come from aliens?"

"You haven't heard a darn thing I've been talking about."

He closed his eyes and struck a pose, touching fingertips to his temples. "I sense that . . . you're mad at me."

"I can't be around you right now." Beatrix jumped up and grabbed her coat. "Lock up when you leave."

"B, come on. I'm only having a little fun. I'm messing—WITH YOU." He yelled the last part as the front door slammed. By the time he decided to give chase and throw it open, the elevator closed on her at the end of the hall.

He reached out to her mentally, a familiar talent by now but still fun, as she descended floors. He got a telepathic slap for it. *Ouch.* The sting on his cheek felt so real he ran to the bathroom to check his image in the mirror. *No shit.* A hand imprint pulsed angry red before fading away. *Girl's got skills.*

He couldn't sit there cooling his jets after such a dramatic exit. *Screw her.* He pulled on an FSU hoodie and jammed his hands in the sweatshirt front pocket. A walk sounded pretty good. A little fresh air, a little contact with the common folk . . .

He returned a couple hours later in time to catch Beatrix throwing her last few things into a suitcase and zipping it closed.

"Hey, what's going on?"

"I'm out," she said. "I thought you had potential, but this isn't working."

"Hold on a second, now."

"You're not getting it, El. And I can't make you."

"I had a lot of time to think while we were both out," he said. "I had a kind of epiphany."

She put her hands on her hips. "This ought to be good. I'm surprised you know the word."

"I figure, instead of sneaking around and hiding our gifts, we embrace them. Come out of the closet, so to speak. Think of what we could do."

"After all I've tried to shove into that pea brain of yours?"

"It's going to take some cash." He planted his feet and spread his arms out wide. "Tell me, what do you see?"

"A dumbass?"

"The Amazing El! Street Magician to the Stars."

"Oh, no. Hell no."

"I was playing before. If I really concentrate, and focus—"

"Abso-frigging-lutely not."

"The money will come rolling in and we can do what we want."

B hefted her suitcase off the bed and left that same day. She apparently couldn't see the genius of his idea *at all*.

On her way out, she bundled the few clothes he'd amassed at her place—he'd stayed over a couple times—and drowned them in the kitchen sink.

"Oh, real mature, B."

"You really want to go there? *Mr. Amazing*? I told you before, no one must know what we can do."

"What does it matter? A little entertainment for the troops. Brighten some lives."

"That's not why you're doing it, El. *For them*? Bullshit. It's for *you*. So you can feel superior. Bring fire to the natives. Play God."

"You're wrong."

"You can't hide things from me, Eldridge. I've been in your miserable excuse for a head. You know I'm right." She stood in front of him with her arms crossed. Tears sparkled in her eyes. "Damn it El. I had high hopes for you."

Every comeback he thought up sounded like it belonged on a schoolyard so he said nothing.

"Have a nice life." She shoved her case and the last of her boxes out the door and turned around. "You be careful Eldridge Montcalm. Some of us out there aren't like . . . *us*. They're smarter, stronger. And right about now, a whole lot angrier. I have to go try to make peace with them."

A familiar noise behind him got his attention and he turned. His basketball began bouncing in the middle of the room. Bounce. Bounce.

Higher. Higher. It hovered there. Chest high.

"See, it's fun, right?"

He turned to see B looking at him, tears streaming down her face.

"Hey, why are you crying?"

She clenched her eyes and the basketball exploded behind him. He whirled in time to see white powder from inside the ball disperse in a cloud.

He turned back and watched her stomp down the hall. Inside his head a tiny nugget of white heat blossomed into a blinding, cataclysmic pain that brought him to his knees. Eyes clenched, hands pressed tight to his temples, he slumped against the doorjamb and waited for his head to explode like the ball.

The rent on her apartment lapsed a week later and he hadn't seen her since. By then, the monster headache subsided to a throbbing drumbeat and back home he went. Not for long, though. All that would change. He didn't know the reasons for B's meltdown but he'd show her. Show his dad. Show them all once the world got a load of his skills and *The Amazing El* got famous. Until then, dues must be paid.

Unbeknownst to him, all during his abbreviated training with B and certainly while he and Beatrix had their dramatic little disagreement, several videos from that night with the fallen police officer torched the internet, approaching record share numbers. A couple of them topped two hundred thousand. One, that showed his face clearest, with handy zooms into the dangling handcuff and the bright red blood dripping down his arm, topped four million with no signs of slowing down.

Over on the sunny California coast, a laptop slammed shut and crashed through a hotel window. It hit the pool deck a hundred feet below and exploded. Shards of computer screen glistened in the sun and computer keys skittered along the concrete like shattered teeth.

Patrons catching rays by the hotel pool swore they heard a woman ten floors up screaming and cussing someone named "El" or "asshole." Accounts varied on that point.

Two of the hotel guests, some described them as having inordinately large, weirdly round heads, stood up from their chaise lounges, grabbed their towels and headed for the lobby.

A third man, same weird round head but standing at least a foot taller than the others, went straight to the parking lot and got into a white SUV. He drove off, squealing tires and narrowly avoiding oncoming traffic.

Chapter Three

MOTHER ON A MISSION

Mother Magdalene cast her eyes heavenward and solemnly intoned, "Forgive this sinner oh Lord, for his grievous transgressions against you and guide my hand as an instrument of your righteous retribution."

Thwack.

The riding crop cut into the flesh of the young man's back. The red welt rose in seconds to join the stack of similar marks, most weeping droplets of blood. The man, in his early twenties, had been an early convert to Mother's religious family. Crisscrossed all over his back, faded pink, shining scars gave evidence of many previous *forgiveness ceremonies,* as Mother called them.

The church of *In His Name* had almost four hundred such disciples in piety but enrollment had stalled. No new blood in over six months. The suffocating weight of her failure to expand His glorious message may have added extra sting to Mother's last strike.

No matter. John, Josh, Josiah, whatever his name, would take it as evidence of her love for him. And Mother Magdalene did love him. She loved them all in her own fashion. God's love formed the very core of her teachings did it not?

"God's love be with you my child." Mother freed the man's hands from shackles mounted strategically to the wall in her office. She caught him as he sagged forward. They often did that. At least this one kept his feet under him. Many a time, she'd had to cradle newly absolved sinners to the carpet and pray over them until they found the strength to stand.

It had never been a problem. Mother had been a farmer's wife in an earlier life and had stacked many a hay bale into a barn loft or truck bed. She had strong hands and a stronger back. The wrung out form of a devout believer caught in the twin throes of ecstasy and pain posed no challenge at all. Especially one like this, a beautiful young man with strength and stamina enough to suffer through his *saving*.

She came around to his front and prodded under his chin with the leather crop. He stiffened and stood straight.

"God has a special mission for you my child. Never forget that. You must stay pure to receive His teaching. As we all must."

"Yes, Mother."

"Go to the kitchen. Ask the cook to swab your back with vinegar. Then swab with olive oil. Tell her I sent you."

"Yes, Mother. Thank you, Mother."

"Now," she shooed him off with the riding crop, "go and meditate on what you have learned today."

After the young man scurried from her office, closing the door behind him, she held the leather crop to her nose and inhaled. The smell of the cowhide mixed with the metallic tang of blood made her swoon so, she had to grab a corner of her desk. She held on as she inched around to her chair and flopped down into it.

Underneath her gold satin robes she felt the cool of a tiny bit of wetness down there. It always happened after a ceremony and she looked forward to it like any schoolgirl anticipating the back seat of her boyfriend's car. To heighten the experience she ran a hand up to her breasts and yes, the nipples on both were hard as erasers. She tweaked them and crept her other hand down to the warm between her legs.

Yes. Oh, YESSS—

Knock Knock.

"Mother?" The voice outside her door spoke through the gravel of a heavy smoker. Reformed, of course. That would be Bernard, her secretary.

"Not now Bernard. I am communing with our Lord."

"You will want to see this, Mother."

Shit.

The moment passed, she dried her fingers on a tissue and threw it into the wastebasket under her desk.

"I suppose the Lord will forgive you this one time." She dripped the exact amount of acid on her voice. "Come in."

Bernard burst through her door before the words died, a skinny ferret-faced Englishman with bad skin and shockingly white teeth. "I wouldn't bother you after a—a ceremony—you know I would not but this is so important, I knew the Lord would want you to see it right away."

She peered at him closely, trying to detect even the slightest hint of snark on his face as he rushed to her desk to unfold an electronic tablet. As always, she could not get a definitive read. Inscrutable as an Asian. May be the only reason she kept him around.

"Fine. Show me what you and our Lord have cooked up for me."

He placed the tablet in front of her like a waiter presenting a fine filet mignon.

"Tap the space bar, Ma'am."

"Thank you for that, Bernard. I would have had no idea how to start a video." Mother made no effort to hide the snark on *her* face.

The picture onscreen showed dark and grainy. The videographer shook at the most inappropriate moments.

But the power of the images, illumined in blue and red flashing lights, brought her heart to her throat.

The videographer kept shifting the camera in his hands, and the sound alternated between scratchy and boomy. But she could hear well enough. She scooted forward and peered close when *"I thought you said he got shot in the neck!"* came through the tiny tablet speakers.

As the scene played out and the injured cop sat up coughing, the picture zoomed into the man's face. Doughy and bewildered, even in the colored lights, the man's face floated above a black stain of blood from chin to neck. It matched the dark of his eyes. Then the camera shifted to zoom in on the face of a young man with an odd shaped head. He sat hugging his knees, handcuffs dangling from one wrist.

Mother played and re-played the video and sat thinking with her hands clasped in prayer position.

Lord, give your poor servant strength.

She slammed the tablet shut and shoved it across the desk at her faithful servant.

"Bernard," she closed her eyes and let the memory of the red and blue-limned scene loop beneath her lids, "do you know what we have here?"

"Um."

"Come, come. You're a smart man, a devout man, are you not?"

Bernard took a second to answer. He'd been caught by her twisty questions in the past and had learned multiple, painful lessons never to offer a quick opinion on anything. She spared him further devilment by answering for him.

"I suppose no more nor less than my other disciples. We are all flawed in His eyes." She paused and cast a pious look heavenward. "Even the most righteous of us has imperfections we carry with us from the Garden.

"But this—this abomination has the stink of sulfur about it. I want you to follow that scent like a hellhound bound for home. We must know more. Surely there are other videos on your MyTube."

"YouT—" he bit back the correction in the nick of time. Mother didn't like being corrected. "You are so right, Mother. Your wisdom is all-seeing."

"I want to know where this happened. When it happened. Who these people are. And most of all, I want to know more about that strange looking spawn of the devil with the deformed head."

She jumped to her feet and the gold robe sagged open, exposing her swaying breasts and furry mound. She took no notice as she leaned forward on her desk, hands balled into fists. "I have been praying for a sign. Something to help lead us out of the wilderness and reach the multitudes with my—our—message. Now, He has answered me."

Mother closed the front of her robe absently, cinching the sash across her middle.

"Bring me everything you learn and fast. Like your soul depended on it. The devil is at work and we will not be caught with our HEADS UP OUR ASSES!" She pounded on her desk for emphasis. She needn't have bothered. Her red face and wild eyes were enough for Bernard.

He scooped up the tablet with alacrity, made a passing semblance of a bow, turned and flew out her office door. He peeked in meekly a second later to close her door quietly, the way she liked it.

Chapter Four

THE AMAZING EL

Beatrix pulled to the curb several houses down the block from her destination and looked around. She spent most time staring into her rearview mirror and checking each car on the street, in front and back. As far as she could tell, every one exuded that comfortable air of suburb that no rental car could match. No unmarked vans. No, God forbid, police cars. And every one of them deserted.

She swiveled the mirror to check herself last. Straight blond hair, sunglasses, and floppy hat. The Beatrix look firmly in place. She touched up her lipstick and exited the car.

The neighborhood sat quiet. At 11:00 in the morning it should be. The worker bees had left for their various hives. Kids were at school filling their spongy little heads with lessons of the day. B walked past three modest stucco homes in yellow, pink and off-white, each with a well-tended yard that might have modeled in a Home Depot catalog.

Her target nestled into its place as dutifully as the rest, a slight tinge of green in its stucco, arched windows on either side. Double doors with beveled glass and a wrought iron plaque mounted on a porch wall announced *Montcalm Residence circa 1991.*

Cute. Exactly like the woman who answered the door after her first ring.

"Yes?" The lady in the tennis outfit looked as well kept as her yard. "May I help yo—oh, my."

Beatrix assumed the woman's double take had everything to do with B's unusual look. She unconsciously raised a hand to pat the blonde tresses framing her face.

"Is El, I mean Eldridge, here?" Jeez, she might as well have said, *Can El come out to play?*

"He's not feeling too well today, dear. Perhaps another time would be better."

"Let me guess. Headache? Massive, blinding headache?"

The woman's hand clenched around the edge of the door. "Why, as a matter of fact—"

"Puking? Please tell me there's been lots of puking."

"He has had a few incidents. Why that's any of your business I'm sure I don't know."

"Serves him right."

"Excuse me young lady?"

"It is imperative that I speak with your son immediately, Mrs. Montcalm."

"How did you know my name?" She looked at the plaque on the wall and stiffened. "I'm afraid my son will not be entertaining visitors for, I don't know, the near future so good morning to you."

Eldridge's mother started to close the door but B stepped forward and stopped it with an open palm. The lady's eyes widened.

"Yes, I know," B said. "I am rude and no, I am not going to hurt you. Thank you, I too like my hat as a matter of fact."

The woman stood open-mouthed as Beatrix pushed the door wide and stepped inside. "Yes, forgive me. I did take a tiny peek inside your mind." B reached forward to touch El's mother reassuringly but the lady recoiled. "No, please do not call the police. That would be very bad for your son. And me."

His mother clapped hands to the side of her head as if for added protection.

"I'm afraid that won't help, Mrs. Montcalm. I know what you're thinking. Please, I beg of you. Your son needs to see me. For his safety and yours."

For emphasis, Beatrix removed her sunglasses, floppy hat and after a slight hesitation, her blond wig.

Seconds later, Beatrix followed the woman up a staircase to a closed door at the end of a hallway. The woman tapped on the door with a polished fingernail. "Honey?"

"Go away, Mom. Please, I told you." The voice came muffled and strained through the door.

"There is a young—lady—here to see you."

Silence. Then, "B?" The voice quavered with self-pity.

Beatrix had enough of the nurturing shit and politely pulled El's mom aside. She barged in and made sure to bang the door on whatever might be on the other side. As it happened, a bookcase, one of many, partially blocked her way.

"Holy crap." B took two steps into El's bedroom and stopped short. Except for the bed up against the windows straight ahead, books took over the entire room. Bookcases lined the walls. Bookcases stood in rank and file, library-style, to fill every square foot of floor space. Books were stacked five and six high on bed tables to either side of Eldridge, who sat propped up on pillows with a laptop and a book light strapped to his forehead.

"Read much?" she said.

"What are you doing here?"

"Saving your sorry, self-centered, stupid ass. That's what. Now get up."

"What did you do to me?"

"Aww. Wittle man got a wittle bitty headache?"

Eldridge scowled. "It's not little."

"What do you expect? I had to get your attention. What we do has consequences, El. That would have been your next lesson."

"This never happened before," he whined and reached for a glass of water beside his bed.

"Saving lives takes more juice than bouncing a damn basketball. Remember the headaches after our sessions?"

He nodded as he drank.

"Sessions? Basketball?" El's mother, hovering in the background, stepped forward. "What kind of sessions?"

"You didn't tell her? Your own mother?" B adopted a look of feigned chagrin and turned to gently usher his mother out of the room. "Kids, right? I promise, he will tell you everything the moment I am through with him."

She pushed the confused woman out into the hall and shut the door. At the same time, she blazed a thought to the center of El's cerebral cortex:

"You tell her anything and you are dead meat. You hear me?"

"Okay, okay. Jesus. Leave me a few brain cells intact."

"Your little stunt that night may or may not die down. These things tend to have lives of their own."

"These things?"

"Internet, El. Ever heard of it? You're frigging viral. YouTube videos of your damn *miracle* are cropping up like zits. The whole world has seen you and your stupid magic show. That means, so has The

Council."

"I didn't know what I was doing."

"No shit, Houdini."

"And . . . what Council?"

"I told you there were others out there like us who are not to be messed with and you needed to lay low. Well, good job with that."

"I should have let the man die? Bleed out? I guess I acted on instinct or something."

"Or something." Beatrix so wanted to pace but the cramped room wouldn't allow it. "You've accelerated this thing far beyond anything we were prepared for."

"What thing and who's we?"

"The good guys, you freak. Now get dressed."

"Turn around."

"What?"

"I'm naked."

"Like I haven't seen—? Fine." Beatrix crossed her arms and whirled around. "Anything I can get you? T-shirt? Calvin's? Fuzzy slippers?"

"You could ask my mom for a Tylenol. It's time for another one."

"Like that'll happen." She snapped her fingers. "Let's go, let's go. We got thinking to do. Plans to make. Disaster to avoid."

"I'm ready."

She turned back around to see El in a pair of shorts, sandals and a t-shirt with *The Amazing El* emblazoned across the front; white type in a red comet's tail.

He shrugged. "My mother found a sketch I made. She thought it would cheer me up."

"Everyone should have a mother like yours. Lose the shirt."

"But—"

"Or, you're on your own. And with what's ahead of you, alone is something you cannot afford to be."

The doorbell rang as they started down the stairs. They froze and let Mrs. Montcalm answer the door. "Might this be the home of a Mr. Eldridge Montcalm?" came a reedy little voice with an English accent.

"I'm sorry, sir," his mother said, "You must have the wrong residence."

"Oh, I see. I'll be off, then. So sorry to bother, mum. Have a nice day."

When his mother turned around and saw them she whispered, "That strange little man had the whitest teeth!"

Chapter Five

MEET THE SPEAKER

C alvin Jones drove his white Escalade 350 miles, blasting down California Hwy.1 at ten miles over the speed limit. Unusual for him. Normally, he minded their group's mantra to never attract notice. Showing out on the radar of CHP's finest had never been a goal of his. It wouldn't do for The Speaker himself to be pulled over and grilled by some bored cop with nothing better to do between donut stops.

He didn't really notice his speed until Date Shakes – 99¢ in giant, faded purple paint zoomed past on his left. The deserted Shake Shack served as his sight cue, prompting an automatic, controlled turn onto a concealed dirt road leading up into the hills.

Shit. That episode at the Monterrey Hotel must have rattled me.

He stomped the brakes and clamped tight to the wheel as the back end of the big SUV fishtailed across the oncoming lane. *Thank god Big Sur PCH is deserted at 3:00 in the morning.*

The Speaker spent the next thirty miles snaking through twisty roads and switchbacks off the Pacific Coast Highway to his compound hidden in the redwoods. The first thirty minutes he spent muttering to himself and pounding his sizable fist onto the dash. The next he composed and discarded plan after plan for how to proceed next. Even the cathedral overhang of mammoth redwood trees and filtered silver light from a full moon did little to soothe his rage.

Finally, he nosed the big, white SUV into its spot beside a cabin carved into the overturned trunk of a giant sequoia. He turned off the engine and sat. The cracks and pops of the cooling engine sounded alien notes in a land so clearly given over to nature. He breathed Zen deep, trying hard to calm down. Took in the clean smell of ocean air trapped by the inland spine of mountains. The pungent cedar/pine tang of the forest wafted over him like perfume. It usually scrubbed his psyche clean of the outside world. Not this time.

Calvin ran a hand over the dent in his dash. Consequences. *What did he keep harping on in Council? What we do will always have consequences.*

He prayed the abortion he witnessed earlier in Monterey would go down easy with them. What had begun as a chance for his favorite Seeker to present her case to The Council ended before it began with a shattered laptop and a rain of curses. Calvin knew in his heart that Beatrix's failure might very well set in motion consequences even he might not be able to fend off.

Calvin stepped up to the wide plank door and waved his hand. The deadbolt slid back with a solid thunk and the heavy door swung open on silent hinges as he entered. Like everything about The Council, their mission and their methods, the primitive wood door masked a much more substantial interior. One-inch metal plate covered the backside of the door. The rustic doorknob and lockset housed sophisticated insides that would never be compromised.

The Speaker stepped inside and the door closed with an automatic clunk behind him. Soft interior lighting at the base of the redwood walls winked on, bathing the interior in a warm orange glow. He whisked his fedora off and hung it on an antique hat rack by the door without looking. No fancy wigs for him. The comforting gray felt with indented crown and wide brim disguised his outsized head in style. He never left the cabin without it.

He splashed a couple drams of Macallan single-malt in a glass with ice and settled in front of a bank of monitors to check out the bad news. It couldn't be good. He'd known that the moment Beatrix's laptop crashed through the hotel window and shattered on the pool deck where he and some of The Council waited.

Two of his most trusted Council members had been with him. Beatrix had asked to make her case to them before presenting to the full Council. She'd shared snippets of her progress on the phone; growing more excited over every new development she described with the young man she called "El." *You won't believe the strength in him. His energy extends ten feet from him at least. He's using it to push a basketball around, doing stupid magic tricks. He has no idea what he can do.*

Calvin gulped his Macallan 1824 and tasted nothing but the glow of smooth fire down his throat. A shame, because his nightly Scotch ritual ranked high on his list of most important things. The effects of the alcohol never touched him, of course. He'd learned to control that decades ago. But the comfort of the familiar glass in his hand and the swirl of the old whiskey over his tongue relaxed him.

Until tonight.

He sat at a desk carved from driftwood. He'd handpicked and hauled the wood up from the Big Sur cliffs himself and paid a master woodcarver a handsome fee to construct the desk to his precise specs. The bleached gray of the wood contrasted beautifully with the warm colors throughout the rest of his cabin. Facing him across the desk were four monitors set in the wall. Each connected to a different Internet feed that scoured cyberspace using specific algorithms of his own devising.

Part of The Council's mission, the easy part, involved simply locating others like themselves. *Overcooked* Beatrix called them, a reference to their twelve-month gestation periods. The unusual characteristics common to them all—white skin, bulbous head, advanced intellect—almost always captured the attention of someone. Invariably that attention wound up on the Internet. A social media post, a newspaper article, god forbid a research paper, buried in a blog or, in this case— Calvin clicked through channel after channel on every feed—a goddamned avalanche of video postings from a crowd of assholes.

He watched every video, some of them several times, and opened a second bottle of Macallan halfway through it all. In his wildest imagining of what might constitute a worst-case scenario, he never would have come up with the scene playing out in shaky images and breathless audio commentary on the screens in front of him.

Several images stuck with him. They played and replayed in his mind like a newsreel of everything he and The Council had been dreading for decades: B's find, *The Amazing El,* as he proclaimed himself on one of the videos, hovering three feet off the ground . . . A mortally wounded and dying cop spurting arterial blood from a neck wound . . . El with his hand clamped tight to the officer's neck . . . EMT's fighting to separate El from the downed man . . . The dead man's return to consciousness—one video titled itself *Death and Resurrection in Downtown Atlanta* . . . and finally, The Amazing El sitting dazed, glassy-eyed and drenched in blood with handcuffs dangling from one wrist. All of it bathed in stark flashing blue and red lights.

Calvin whirled in his chair and hurled his glass at the far wall. It stopped in mid-air, inches from collision, and hovered there while The Speaker buried his head in his hands and tried to still a riot of emotions.

Jesus Christ Beatrix, what have you done?

He and the empty glass of whiskey were still for a long minute, until the push intruded on his consciousness like a flashing red light.

He and every other member of The Council communicated telepathically. They had no need for face-to-face conversation and pushes kept them safe. The government had yet to figure a way to eavesdrop on telepaths. That's what made the meeting set up at the Monterrey hotel so special. Beatrix pleaded with him to set it up. *I need to see their faces when I show them. El is too special to expose to the whole Council like all the others.* He gave in to her like always and agreed. Now, he would pay the price.

The push in his head insisted and he acknowledged. *"What took you so long?"*

"What?" The voice belonged to John Smith, as he knew it would. John Smith had been on The Council as long as Calvin and had made it clear for years he thought he should have been elevated to The Speaker role long ago.

"What do you want, John?"

"Are you seriously asking me that?"

"I'm seconds from convening The Council, if that's what you mean."

"Your pretty little Seeker really screwed up this time." Emotion doesn't carry telepathically the same way it does in spoken words, but Calvin swore he heard the glee in John Smith's thoughts. *"She needs to be punished."*

"You're home?" Calvin resisted taking the man's bait.

"Half an hour ago. Have you seen the Internet? It's blowing up—"

"So, Lucy should be home as well. She doesn't live that far from the coast." Lucy and John were the two with him at the hotel.

"Who gives a crap about Lucy Brown?"

Calvin smiled. John Smith. Lucy Brown. Calvin Jones. Everyone on The Council adopted plain, average names to help in their efforts to stay unremarkable and unnoticed. Something about *Lucy Brown* always made him smile.

"I take it you both went looking for Beatrix at the hotel?" Calvin said.

"When you split, we headed straight for her room but no dice. She vanished. Cut out on us like her mentor."

Calvin let that remark slide. *"What time is it in India?"*

"Again, who gives a shit? We're in big trouble, Speaker. Wake Patel's sorry ass up."

Calvin crossed the room and settled into his Speaker chair.

Really nothing more than a La-Z-Boy recliner, he thought of it that way because the comfy red leather chair helped him concentrate as input from all on The Council bombarded him at once.

He pressed back in the chair and sent out a mass push strong enough to wake Patel in Mumbai and rouse Michelle in Paris. Calvin had more power than any of them, a function of his size and evolution. He also stood a foot taller and seventy-five pounds heavier. Plus, his position as Speaker had honed his skills.

It took a few minutes for them all to chime in. Michelle in Paris. Ramon in Spain. Karla in the Ukraine and the others.

They began the meeting by thinking the shared credo that started every meeting:

The world must never hear us, never see us, never know us. Until The One brings us to the Given Goal. For the good of all mankind.

John Smith, the first to chime in, stepped on the traditional Speaker's role. *"We are convening this meeting of The Council because of certain events that happened recently in Atlanta, Georgia."*

Calvin squelched a chuckle when no one responded.

"As John Smith has stated," he took back the lead, *"I called us to order to address a concern that has arisen in the southeastern United States. Before we go any further, I want to insist that everyone access the Internet immediately and go to—he mentally sifted through several of the URLs he'd visited earlier—YouTube. Search Term: Death and Resurrection. Let me know when you are all up to speed."*

Calvin used the brief timeout to retrieve his hovering Scotch glass and pour himself two more fingers of the amber nectar. His moment of peace lasted a little over ten minutes as Council members across the globe logged in and digested what the Internet had to show them.

"I know this will be extremely disturbing to you," Calvin pushed. *"I want to give you time to air your opinions. Please be honest and do not hold back. Now is not the time for political correctness."*

John jumped in before The Speaker finished pushing out his last thought. *"What you may or may not be aware of is this is all the work of one of Beatrix Goode's charges. We were all urged by The Speaker to elevate Beatrix. If you remember, I voted against her elevation."*

Tanya Patel chimed in next. *"She has put us all in grave jeopardy. The world is not yet ready for us. I fear that her elevation must be terminated."*

Sentiments from the rest of The Council ran along similar lines.

"She talked up this one as different, special. On this, her judgment proved faulty."

OVERCOOKED

"Beatrix developed quickly, became a promising pupil. I am disappointed that she has failed us."

"We knew from her chosen name she would be a problem. Beatrix does not like staying in shadow."

The Speaker let them vent until the griping ran its course. If a sigh could translate telepathically they would have all felt his displeasure.

"Am I the only one of us with the vision to see the big picture?" he said. *"Do not any of you wonder—what if Beatrix is right?"*

Silence. Even John knew when to check his thoughts.

"You want to punish her for her grievous errors in judgment. And they are serious enough that I convened this Council, I agree. But what if this Eldridge Montcalm is indeed, The One?"

The Speaker aimed his next thought at John with enough push to make them all stir uncomfortably on all sides of the globe. If John Smith truly fancied himself Speaker material, perhaps he should feel true power.

"John, it is true you were the lone dissenting voice in Council. I'm sure we all appreciate your insight. Now, you can either sit and congratulate yourself, or you can offer up more of your sage wisdom to guide us to our next course of action."

John missed the sarcasm in The Speaker's thought, as The Speaker knew he would, and could not resist the opportunity to set himself apart from the others. Also, as The Speaker knew he would.

"Beatrix has cast a shadow on our Given Goal and endangered us all. By the way, I lay responsibility for that at The Speaker's feet." John continued after getting no reaction. *"She failed in her mission to mentor this Eldridge Montcalm. Clearly, she could not control him. She did not instruct him properly in our ways. She must be punished for her over-reach."*

"I see," The Speaker felt obliged to speak when no one else stepped up to contribute. *"Then what becomes of, what did he call himself? The Amazing El? Does anyone have a suggestion?"*

The Speaker waited patiently for his trap to close. He could almost hear it slam shut when John again responded.

"I shall take over her duties. I will remove Beatrix and begin an immediate evaluation of this Eldridge person myself. If he is The One—which I doubt—I will know it quickly. I will not fail."

The Speaker cloaked his emotions carefully to keep his pleasure hidden. John Smith had half the skills of Beatrix, if that. Calvin trained that girl himself and knew her capabilities. He didn't blame her for running off. He knew how much her first Find meant to her. He remembered his own. The fact that his turned out to be the biggest pain in the ass on The Council notwithstanding, John Smith had been a worthy Find. Calvin well remembered being excited to discover him.

"*John,*" The Speaker said, "*we are all thankful to have someone of your abilities to entrust with this critical responsibility. I'm sure I don't have to remind anyone how vital it is that John Smith succeeds. He has put himself in serious jeopardy for all our sakes.*"

"*Wait a minute, now—*" John Smith began.

"*For we all know the consequences should the unforeseen happen and John Smith fail.*"

The Speaker felt an unmistakable mental squirm from John as the man began to realize the serious implications of his impetuous action.

"*Join me, all of you, in sending John Smith our sincere thanks for his selfless commitment to The Given Goal.*"

The Speaker cloaked himself off from the rest of The Council, effectively adjourning their meeting. He took a delicate sip of his Macallan and this time, tasted every delicious hint buried in the complex DNA of the world's finest whiskey.

Chapter Six

ON THE RUN

Eldridge would never let her know of course, but his heart felt nine pounds lighter the moment he heard B's voice outside his bedroom door. His relief lasted maybe five seconds, then shifted into reverse the moment she stepped into his room. But she hadn't abandoned him and that thought filled him with a joy he didn't want to examine too closely.

"Jesus, El. Could you move any slower?" Beatrix walked backwards in front of him, taunting with that voice while he struggled with a duffel bag stuffed tight and round as a sausage. "Hey, I got an idea." B smacked the side of her head. "Show me some of your levitation stuff. I couldn't get enough of you on YouTube."

He halted for a second and squeezed his eyes shut. Why not give it a try? How hard could it—?

"Ow." Pain flared in his head like hammers pounding on the inside trying to break out. He dropped his bag and dug fists into both temples. "Goddammit!"

"You idiot. You actually tried it?" Beatrix walked up and grabbed his duffel. It floated beside her as she pushed him up the sidewalk toward her car. "There are consequences to everything we do, El. For everyone, overcooked and normals. Consequences for you? This time?"

They got to her car and the bag floated beside her while she unlocked the lemon-yellow Camaro's doors.

"Remember the headaches from our little sessions? In the

beginning? Those unbelievable headaches the days after?"

He sagged against the car door without opening it, still holding onto his head and breathing through his mouth. He nodded his answer and yelped at the effort.

She opened the passenger side and steered his duffel into the backseat with a finger before letting it drop to the floor. "Those were consequences."

"So. They were worth it."

"I agree. That's why I'm here, in fact. But what you did the other night? I'm not even talking about Amazing El doing basketball tricks or squirting mustard on a Kielbasa—which I can't believe didn't hurt you at all."

"Please, B. No lectures."

"Oh, no. You had to levitate your stupid ass three feet off the ground—"

"Four."

"What?"

"Never mind."

"Then start a freaking riot and THEN," she looked around as if expecting the neighborhood to agree with her, "you practically resurrect a dead policeman. Which half the world has seen by now."

"I don't think he died, really. I don't know what happened exactly, but—"

"Stop right there."

"What?"

"At *I don't know what happened exactly*. You're right, you don't know. How could you? You were so busy being a self-centered jerk we never got to that part of your training. Some of us never get to that part. Hey," she pounded on the top of the car, "how do you feel?"

He cringed and whimpered, "What is your problem?"

"Feel amazing Mr. *Amazing El?*"

"Lay off me, B. That's not funny."

"Correct. It's light-years from funny. Now get in the car and quit whining like a baby."

He opened the door and settled in like his seat held a cushion of eggs.

"I've seen sloths at the zoo move faster. Christ, you know how to milk a moment." B adjusted her rearview mirror.

In reflex, he looked in his side view. A rattletrap Mustang roared to life four cars back and on the opposite side of the street. A cloud of blue-white smoke wafted so thick around it he couldn't make out the driver.

OVERCOOKED

B froze for a second, staring into her mirror. "Spinning a basketball in mid-air is one thing, numbskull." She snapped her seatbelt. "But what we do, what we *can* do, isn't a game. There are reasons we're the way we are, and consequences for what we do. You skipped ahead about ten sessions when you saved that cop."

She tapped him on the head and he swore he felt her fingers push right through to his brain.

"Now you're paying it."

"You know what, B?" *Christ on a pancake, he'd had about enough of her shit.* "If I had to do it all over again? Save a cop's life? I'd do the same damn thing."

"So would I, El."

"So you and your consequences can go f—what?"

"I said, SO WOULD I. Now buckle up. I got a C in *How To Ditch A Tail* in Overcooked School."

He saw her eyes glued to her rearview and checked his side view in time to see the Mustang squeal away from the curb and hurtle toward them.

"There's an Overcooked School?"

Beatrix stomped the clutch, shoved the gearshift into first and grinned at him. "You are too easy, Eldridge Montcalm. I'm *kidding*." She crushed the gas and the back end slewed back and forth as she whipped around the parked car in front of them and shot forward. "Hold on!"

A news van from the local station swerved in time to avoid a head-on collision as they skidded around the corner.

"See that?" B said. "You were minutes from the evening news." They blew through a stop sign and El hit his head on the roof as the car bucked across drainage dips in the road.

"Shit, slow down." He felt all around his head checking for bumps and gashes.

"Getting us up to speed, babe." She double-clutched and he pressed back in the seat.

Cars squealed left and right as they ran more stop signs and avoided one T-bone crash after another.

"You can thank me later."

"If we live."

Traffic ahead of them sat stopped at a red light, ready to feed onto a major four-lane highway.

B got off the gas and Eldridge exhaled in relief as they coasted forward.

Jesus, finally. At least they weren't going to die in a gasoline-

soaked fireball—hey!

He felt the car lurch and glanced at B in time to see her grin. She risked a quick glance into her mirror before she yanked the car down into second. The wheels spun and El felt the car slide as she pulled into the wrong lane.

"WHAT ARE YOU DOING?"

"Saving your sorry ass," she yelled. "Hold on."

They hurtled down beside the line of waiting cars toward the intersection. El watched the drivers in cars facing them across the intersection stare open-mouthed at the idiot rushing straight at them. The light changed while they were still two cars from the front. B leaned on the horn and whipped around and back into line, now in front of a long procession of law-abiding drivers. She glanced into the rearview mirror.

"Hah! Who's your Momma, asshole?"

He turned to look behind them and saw the smoky Mustang at least ten cars back and falling further to the rear.

El wiped sweaty palms on his jeans and noticed his headache had disappeared.

"Hey," he pressed all around his head from the back of his neck to his forehead, "it's gone."

B looked over at him and frowned. "Really? Your headache's gone already?"

"Oh, man." He tapped on top of his head to test it out. *Yep. Not a twinge.*

"Quit that, you dummy."

"I'm telling you. No headache. Nothing. It's like a miracle."

"Yeah," she cleared her throat, "a lot of that going around lately."

Chapter Seven

HURT ME!

B ernard shifted foot to foot while he waited for Mother Magdalene to say something. When she finally did, he knew it wouldn't be in the same universe as pleasant.

He stood roughly at attention in the center of her office while the woman stalked around him, probably thinking up creative ways to disembowel him. Her golden robes flapped open and she kept clutching them shut as she paced.

This went on for so long, his legs got tired and his knees quivered.

Finally she stopped and stood in front of him. He shrank back as she shot her arms out and clasped both his shoulders in a powerful grip.

"How long have you been my assistant, Bernard?"

"A few years now, Mother."

"A week shy of four, but who's counting? And how many times have I punished you for failing me and your Lord?"

He took a while, parsing through four years' worth of incidents, trying to judge which she might deem as actual punishments versus the small cruelties she regularly—

"None is the answer you, you, *little man*. You have not once felt the wrath of a righteous God smiting you for such egregious failure as the one you have visited upon us today." She resumed her pacing. "The question God presents to me is this—what would He have me do about you?"

She stopped behind her desk and picked up that damn riding

crop. He licked his lips. He'd felt the damage she could do with that. She slapped it in her palm as she paced around her office, eyes closed, lips moving, silent.

"Mother, I—"

SShhh!

She pointed the crop at him. "Never interrupt when I am receiving His glorious message." She stalked some more, pausing to run fingers lightly over the shackles embedded in her whipping wall.

Bernard counted his blessings he wasn't tied up there. Yet.

Mother Magdalene stopped to stare out the picture window behind her desk. The view had begun as nothing special, an abandoned warehouse across the alley. But Mother had instructed a team of her acolytes to paint a mural on the building—something pleasant and festive to dress up the eyesore.

Her uplifting idea? Three crosses stabbing into the sky from the knoll at Golgotha. She wanted to capture the very moment the Roman Legionnaire jabbed his spear into Jesus's side and she made the artists return to the mural again and again to get the flow of blood right.

Bernard followed her gaze and stared with her for a full two minutes. His knees fairly wobbled by the time she turned around. But when she did turn to face him, the gleam in her eyes and her crocodile smile unnerved him more than any of her rants.

She tossed the riding crop on her desk and cinched the robes tight around her. Smoothing the front and adjusting the overlapping edges so they pulled taut around her breasts, she approached him with her hands clasped in prayer formation.

"Brother Bernard, for the little bit of information you have provided we are grateful. For the Mt. Ararat-sized void of information you have failed to provide, we are . . . vexed.

"And yet, I cannot blame you. You, a mere mortal, were in pursuit of a demon. I sent you upon a mission doomed from the start because I myself failed to appreciate the wiles of our enemy.

"So, it is I who must be punished." She stopped two feet in front of him, a serene look on her face . . . and that smile. "I will take your sins upon me. Just as Jesus did for us all from the cross."

She held his eyes as she undid the sash of her robe and let the silken material bunch at her feet. He tried mightily to hold her stare and not glance at the plump breasts and mare's nest of black hair below her navel.

"Come, Bernard. You shall be my Legionnaire."

She grabbed his hand and pulled him with her to the wall. Once there, she turned facing out and spread her arms so that each wrist reached a shackle bolted into the plaster. She closed the first shackle with a free hand then placed that hand in the other shackle.

"Do it," she nodded toward it. "Snap it closed. With the lock-pin in place."

Bernard stepped up and did as she asked. When he got close he smelled a concentration of lilac and frankincense emanating off her skin, the same scent that always permeated her office. This time another smell mixed with it, one he could only describe as woman musk; the earthy fecund aroma of a woman aroused.

"Do you like what you see, Bernard?"

"Mother?"

"Me, helpless before you? Naked, spread-eagled as our Savior on His day of atonement?"

"I don't understand, Mother."

"Get the whip off my desk and make me pay. Hurt me."

"But—"

"Mark me. Leave evidence of my atonement that He shall see and forgive. As you failed me, so I failed you *and* Him. I must suffer for my sins and you shall be my instrument. These," she rattled her shackled wrists, "shall be my cross."

In a daze, Bernard retrieved the whip from her desk, lust, glee and fear swirling in his mind.

"Good. Now, hit me."

He stood there, unsure really of what she wanted. Surely she did not mean for him to actually—

"Strike, coward. Whip me. Or, by the Christ who came before me, I will have you tied hand and foot and skinned while you beg your Mother for mercy."

And so he did. Warming to his task, strike after strike, he beat her until she bled. The slap of the leather crop against her skin and his labored breathing were the only sounds he heard.

She never whimpered. Never cried out.

Bright red stripes crisscrossed her torso and thighs. Blood dripped from the later strikes as he grew more confident and hit harder, embracing his role.

He only stopped when her head sagged forward and urine ran down one leg to puddle beneath her.

The acrid stink of pee shocked him into letting go of the leather whip. It dropped and he staggered backward. Only then did he have time to think and really look at the flayed, naked woman cuffed unconscious to the wall.

"Dear God what have I done? What have I done?"

41

Chapter Eight

A HOLE IN THE GLADES

The road stretched on ahead of them, a typical South Florida pastiche of fruit and vegetable stands, abandoned cars, parched scrub vegetation and the occasional lone palm.

B slowed as she approached a hand-stenciled sign nailed to a post on the side of the road. El had no trouble reading its message—Hazardous Beyond This Point. It also had a crude, radiation symbol painted below the words. Beatrix pulled her Camaro off the road and turned down the gravel road behind it.

"You saw the sign, right?" Eldridge said. "Hazardous Beyond—?"

"It's my sign."

"You're kidding."

"Been working for over three years. Radiation appears to be the ultimate asshole repellant."

"So, it's not really—?"

She looked at him and floored it. "We gotta get out of sight, El. Hang on—and don't breathe."

The car slewed on the chunky gravel road, stones pinging off the undercarriage and shooting to the sides as they darted for the shade of a copse of palm and hardwoods.

B slowed to a crawl once they were safely out of sight, nursing her beloved ride over massive humps and valleys in the mere suggestion of a road.

"For Christ's sake, El. Breathe. I'm kidding." She laughed and slapped him on the shoulder. "You *are* too gullible."

On several occasions she steered wide around black pools of standing water. Each time returning to her inexorable push deeper into the South Florida boonies.

The dim light of late afternoon cast a golden glow on the landscape as they topped a particularly steep rise to reveal a massive Airstream trailer squatting in a clearing below like an alien spaceship.

Beatrix pulled out of sight behind the trailer and parked. "We're home."

"This is yours?"

"Hope so. Or, one day someone'll show up and be righteously pissed."

Eldridge shaded his eyes against the falling sun peeking over the top of the trailer. "How the hell did you get that in here?"

"We have our ways, as you are beginning to learn. I must say, though. It took almost everything I had to schlep that baby through all that landscape back there."

She got out and retrieved a small overnight bag from her trunk. "Get your stuff out of the backseat. With any luck, we'll be here awhile."

Mindful of the brain-exploding headache he suffered before, Eldridge applied only enough mental leverage to lighten the fat duffel in the backseat. He had no wish to risk anything more. The swollen green canvas bag squeezed out between the seats and he set it on the ground at his feet.

"No one will find us here." El took in the tangled landscape of scrub and palm pressing in on all sides. "Only ones who know about this place are probably God and whatever snaky, crawly things live in it."

"Us and God—and whomever The Council sends to get me," B said. "My gator, python and cougar neighbors will be nothing compared to that."

"Cougars?"

"Relax. They're rare. And by the way, welcome to my humble home."

"When are you going to explain all this Council stuff to me?" El slung his slightly less heavy bag over one shoulder and followed her as she unlocked her door and stepped inside. "I think I need to know that at least."

"You need to know a lot of things." She pointed down the center hallway to the left. "Drop your stuff in there. I'll get the A/C going and hustle us up something to eat."

An hour later, after the final plate and glass had been rinsed and put in the drying rack, Beatrix and El sat across from each other on soft leather chairs in the front part of the coach.

"I haven't had fish sticks since the fourth grade," he said.

"I'm sure your Mommy fixed you everything her little boy liked to eat."

"I'm not dissing it. I liked your fish sticks. And that rice . . . stuff you made."

"Next time, you cook."

"B—"

"Someone will be by in a couple days with supplies. In the meantime, we make do."

"So, other people know about this place?"

"Only one. And Nicole Charbonneau isn't other people. She's a local, best fishing guide in South Florida and a friend. She helped me find this place." B tucked her feet underneath her. "Can't wait'll she gets a load of you." She chuckled. "One of me is bad enough. But two of us? Poor woman will think we're an alien conspiracy."

"Let's start there," El said. "What are we exactly?" He tapped his head. "Besides freaks."

Beatrix clasped hands in front of her and narrowed her eyes. "Get this through your big, beautiful head Eldridge Montcalm. We're a lot of things. We'll find out more about you in good time. But *freak* is not one of them."

"So, your childhood sucked, too."

"Big time."

"I don't like the word either. But—"

"Then don't use it. Ever. Christ on a Ritz." She sat forward and crooked a finger at the drying rack on the galley counter. Her plate and then El's rose from their slots. She twirled her finger clockwise and one plate began spinning faster and faster. She reversed direction and the other plate spun the opposite way. Both spinning bits of crockery spun into round blurs hovering side-by-side in mid-air.

"Shit. You're good, B."

"You idiot," she said.

She clapped her hands and the spinning plates smashed together, showering them and the interior of the trailer with tiny bits of crockery.

El closed his eyes and ducked. When he opened them again, B sat glaring at him.

"What did I do?" he said.

"We're not circus acts, El and no, that was NOT GOOD. We're not here to spin plates or bounce basketballs."

"Then why are we here?"

"It's my place to teach you that. And I've done a piss poor job of it up to now. But that is going to change mister, starting today. If they give me time."

"There you go again. Who are this *they* you always talk about? The Council?"

"That's as good a place as any to start." She shook her head and fluffed fingers through her hair. "You can ask questions, if you have to. But try to hold off until I'm done. Otherwise we'll be here all night."

El made a point to look out their windows at the evening blackness.

"You know what I mean," she said. "Try not to be an asshole. Before we get to The Council, I'll start earlier, try to explain how we're special, why we look the way we do and put things into a little more perspective."

Chapter Nine

JOHN SMITH PURSUIT

John Smith closed off his mental link to Council, settled back in his redwood hot tub and reexamined what the hell just happened.

That ass-wipe Speaker boxed him into a damn precarious position is what happened. True enough. But no one else volunteered to go clean up the Speaker's mess. No one else had the balls to question The Speaker's choice of Beatrix Goode as a Seeker. John Smith had no problem speaking truth to power. Never had, never will.

He pressed back into water jets aimed at his kidneys and let the pounding of the water massage his guts. He closed his eyes and barely made out the sound of crashing waves over the gurgling waters of the spa.

Having the Pacific Ocean for a backyard was only one of the perks of a secluded home in a private cove on the Monterrey Peninsula. He'd had two intermediaries purchase this house for him so he could stay anonymous. The price had been right. The rock star idiot who owned it previously put too much up his nose to hold onto it.

John sipped a chilled vegetable and ginger tonic of his own devising and stretched his legs, admiring their muscle tone in the warm bubbles. Not bad for a guy pushing 73 years old give or take a few months. The Speaker topped him by a decade or more. No big deal. Far as he knew, the two of them were the eldest on The Council. And if it's true that with age comes wisdom he, John Smith, had plenty smarts to spare.

OVERCOOKED

He put his head back and gargled a healthy mouthful of his drink. Earthy, grassy, with a spicy bite of ginger. An acquired taste, for sure. No one he'd ever offered it to could stand to choke down a swallow—which made it all the more delicious to him. He poured the rest of his green concoction into the swirling froth and rinsed his glass.

Taking care of that botched Seek by Speaker's prized pet B would not be easy. He knew she had skills. Shit, the Speaker trained her himself. No sir. It would not do to underestimate the task at hand. So be it. He shifted to aim the water jet at his ass crack. The Speaker's smug little bitch had a comeuppance in her future and he was just the man for the job.

John hoped everyone on Council would remember The Speaker had taken great care to lay the success or failure of the thing at his feet. He did not intend to fail.

He blew his nose in his fingers and rinsed them in the tub. He could see the prick now, holed up in the forest like a Keebler elf, sipping his beloved Scotch, and congratulating himself for his canny handling of the only real threat to his power on The Council.

John Smith stepped out of his hot tub and admired himself in the reflection of his sliding door. Naked and beautifully muscled, except for the freakish oversized baldhead, he could've graced the cover of any one of the muscle mags out there. He squeegeed off with a strigil like a Spartan warrior might have a millennia ago and laid the curved scraper on the edge of the hot tub. He stepped into a soft pair of slippers, being extra careful to wipe his feet. Only problem with living at the beach was the goddam sand and he'd had the house cleaned yesterday. Sandy floors drove him frigging insane.

He walked past the sliding doors, admiring his physique from the side, and headed for a seating area and a chaise of interwoven Japanese bamboo. Still naked, he gave no thought to being seen. He owned acreage on both sides of his property and people persistent enough to brave the rocks and tangled overgrowth along both sides were rare. Besides, if they wanted to look, let 'em.

He relaxed into the bamboo weave and embraced his situation; let his finely tuned sense of self-preservation begin working on a plan.

The Speaker may have crammed his over-large head with book smarts and cross-cultural nonsense he gleaned from a century of traveling the world. Piss on him.

Nothing compared to growing up in the barrios of East L.A. Living through the good early times when the people were mostly white. Then, all the bad. Surviving, hell *thriving* through the riots, bulbous head and all.

He felt the ridge of a knife scar along his ribcage and grinned at the memory. He could have made the scar go away, of course, but he kept it.

He liked the images the upraised edge of ropey skin dredged up.

#

The puffed up Chicano in his wife beater and black chinos sidled forward, slick black hair in a hair net, his posse of *vatos* ringed behind him. They thought they'd cornered him in the alley and were confident, joking back and forth in Spanish.

"Hey, *ese*. What you think, coming down here with that fucked up head, eh?" the leader said. His band of buddies laughed.

The street tough put a hand in his pocket and pulled out a butterfly knife. The silver glinted in the light of an overhead streetlamp.

"My *homies* and me, we got to live here, you know?"

He flipped the knife open with a practiced flourish.

Click-clack.

"You are too ugly to walk our streets, *mano*. Scare our women and shit."

The band of thugs hooted and crowded forward, eager to see what their leader had in mind.

Tossing the knife hand to hand, smiling wide, gold tooth in front, the young Chicano lunged.

John didn't have the control he'd develop later in life and so the near miss he'd planned—he had in mind a matador and bull thing—came a tad too close. The knife blade scraped his left side and sliced through shirt and skin.

The *vato* jumped back and looked at his arm and knife blade. "Hey! What the fuck?" Something unseen had shoved his arm aside at the last instant.

John pressed a hand to his ribs and came away with bloody fingers.

Silence reigned for half a beat. The predators smelled blood and surged ahead, restless, eager to jump but awaiting their signal. They didn't wait long.

"Get him, *homies*," the *vato* hissed through clenched teeth.

John would never allow another knife to get that close again. Granted, in the heat of battle that followed he may have overcorrected a bit to be safe. He proceeded to teach the tough guys a little respect. Arms snapped, knees distended, eyes gouged, with the worst—or, best depending on perspective—reserved for the leader.

John stepped from the center of a circle of fallen, screaming thugs cradling their injuries in various stages of agony to force push the head *vato* up against a brick wall.

To be sure, he raised the man a foot off the ground, arms and legs spread-eagled to the side and shoved hard against the bricks. All without getting close enough to touch the guy.

Eyes wide and head jerking left and right, the leader struggled and snarled to no avail, caught in the grip of a pressure he clearly felt but could not see.

John walked calmly forward and bent the man's arm that still held its bloody knife so the blade pointed at the hood's crotch.

He stepped close. "This is my neighborhood, too, *homes*. I don't think I want any more of your little *vatos* dirtying up the place. *Comprende?*"

He would get his wish. When the knife work ended and the man's screams died to rhythmic moans, he let him slide to the ground.

He leaned over and whispered, "*Lo siento, hombre.* I'm sorry. But you really pissed me off." Then spat on him and walked away.

Reminiscing over, John Smith padded through the open sliding doors of his home and into the master suite at the far end of the house. He pulled down a leather valise and shoved enough clothes into it for a week. They fit easily; he wasn't a clothes fanatic like The Speaker.

Before he zipped the bag shut, he walked over to the nightstand and extracted an object from the drawer.

The silver butterfly knife flipped open and closed in his hand several times—God he loved to do that—before he tossed it on top of his clothes.

You never know, right? You never know when a little lethal razzle-dazzle might come in handy.

Chapter Ten

WHAT ARE WE?

This ought to be good. Eldridge leaned back into the cushions of the leather camper chair ready for answers. Beatrix stood and walked to the far end of the trailer, crunching on bits of shattered dinner plates. She returned with a broom and dustpan in hand.

"Lift your feet."

She reached with the broom and swept, forehead knotted with concentration. *Because she wanted to get every last shard or something else?*

"Both, you moron." She straightened and tapped her head. "Remember? We read minds? HandiVac is in the cabinet to your left. You can suck up the bits and pieces on the table and in our chairs."

She stayed silent as they worked. Gathering her thoughts? Generally pissed? He tried peeking but *her* mind stayed shuttered tight. *I need to learn that.*

When they were finished to her satisfaction, she returned the broom and pan to their closet in the back. She used the opportunity to straighten curtains and check the closure on cabinet doors as she passed by. She never looked at what she did. Like a blind person, she focused her eyes on some distant point while she gnawed her upper lip.

"Okay, housekeeping's over." She sat back down on the edge of the chair across from him. "I'm thirsty. You thirsty?"

"No, B. Come on. Spill. How hard can it be?"

She jumped up to fill a glass of water at the sink. "It's not hard.

It's—complicated." She downed half the glass and sat again.

"I've never seen you nervous like this."

"This is important, El. I want to get it right and share what I can, without giving you a bigger head than you already have. That may have been a joke."

"Funny. How about you start at the beginning? Seems a logical place."

"We'll start at your beginning," she said. "How's that? Something I should have done a while ago. Your parents ever tell you anything about your early years? Your mom's extra long pregnancy? Little family stories? Anecdotes about their amazing little boy?"

He shrugged. "I never really thought about it. Mom always said she liked being pregnant so much she didn't want to let me out. The rest will sound like bragging. All parents brag about their kids."

Her face clouded for a beat. "Not all. Go on. Hit me with something."

"They say I never cried as a baby in my crib. Mom or Dad would come check on me, worried and I'd be sitting up waiting, watching for them." He cleared his throat. "If I needed changing, I lifted my legs to help. Kind of creeped my dad out. That's what they said."

Beatrix smiled. "What else?"

"What baby does that?"

"Apparently, you. Continue."

"You know all those happy moms pushing their kids in strollers? Propping their beautiful little treasures in shopping carts, walking slow down every aisle so people could exclaim over their precious babies?"

B closed her eyes.

"Not me. My parents stopped taking me out into the world after the first few rude comments and surprised gasps at the way I looked. Mom says the world wasn't ready for me."

"I like your mom, El. You are so lucky to have her."

"All the little stuff I did; like announcing visitors before the doorbell rang or telling them the person on the phone before they answered it. Mom just smiled and called me her little genius. Dad grumbled and never said much at all."

"Anything else—*bigger?*" B inched forward. "Things ever just break around you for no reason? Mirrors especially? Anything reflective?"

"How did you know?"

"Have any um, *incidents* with pets? Dog or cat?"

"Animals don't like me much. Cats yowl and dogs won't stop barking at me. We couldn't keep pets. How did you know?"

"I have a head like yours, El. Remember? We've all traded stories. Talked about our similarities."

"There's that *we* again."

"A lot of us, when we're younger, learn to hate what we look like. We pick up on cues from people around us. So, we learn to dislike surfaces that reflect our image. Mirrors mysteriously shatter. Windows crack. We don't even know we're doing it."

"And the pets?"

"Best explanation is that, in technical terms, we weird them out. If a dog is going to bark at a stranger—what do you think he's going to do around a *strange* stranger? They don't know what to make of us and react."

"I always wanted a dog."

"Didn't we all? Tell me about school."

"My salvation."

"Meaning?"

"I loved the work. I excelled. Skipped grades. For the first time in my life I made my parents proud. Mom, of course, ate it up. Couldn't wait for parent/teacher conferences. Even Dad softened toward me. Probably relieved his kid might have a future after all."

"I know you were smart, El. We're all that way. Way off the top of whatever chart they measure us with. I want to know about you socially. How'd the kids and teachers treat you?"

El stopped talking.

B waited a few seconds. "That good, huh?"

"Enough with the twenty questions."

"One more and I swear it's your turn. Yes? You can ask me anything you want and I'll answer best I can."

"Go ahead."

"You ever heal anybody before? Not even a person. An animal maybe? A squirrel?"

"You can't be serious."

"Maybe you didn't know it at the time. Anything odd like that? Maybe you were around someone sick or hurt and nobody could explain it but they mysteriously got better?"

"B, if I didn't know it at the time, how can I know it now? No, nothing like that. The cop the other night freaked me out. I think I'd remember if I did that before. How many folks have *you* healed Mother Theresa?"

Beatrix sat back in her seat and shook her head.

"Zip?"

"Listen to me very carefully, El. In the last couple weeks, the world became a very dangerous place for you and I."

"Because I saved that policeman?"

"It's not your fault. Not the cop's fault. Blame it on iPhone video and YouTube if anything. I tried to bring you along slowly. Fate apparently has a different agenda."

Eldridge reached for B's glass of water and downed a healthy gulp. "You said *dangerous*. Why? Anyone would have done what I did—if they could."

"But they can't, El. That's the whole deal. What you did the other night rocked some people. Hard. Now the whole world's seen it in all its video glory."

"Most will think it's all a trick."

"Many will want to *believe* that. Faith healers have been healing cripples for years. Right? People claiming medical miracles have been archived in medical journals for decades. But there's no *video* of them. Certainly nothing as real and raw as yours."

El sat thinking, trying to get his grubby mitts around the thing but it kept growing and changing shape the more she talked.

"Imagine, El," B continued, "Say you're a mother whose child is dying of brain cancer. Or, you're on a transplant list with a week to live. Or—"

He held up his hands. "I get it, I get it."

"No, honey. You don't. I don't either, really. But it won't be long until this thing gets *us*. The world's going to come knocking. Sick people. Crazy people. Curious people. *Our* people. We need to be ready for them. Both of us."

BAM. BAM. BAM.

El sloshed half the water left in the glass on the table and Beatrix lifted inches off her seat. The pounding shook the camper. El felt the vibration in his stomach and wondered when his heart might start up again.

BAM. BAM.

"Hey, B. I know your skinny little ass is in there." The voice outside the door croaked like a nasally frog.

B exhaled in a whoosh and her face crinkled into a relieved grin. "Damn, woman," she called out. "We about shit our pants in here."

She patted El's hand, "No worries," and got up to open the door.

Beatrix flipped a switch for the awning lights outside and peered through the blinds on the door. She squealed and yanked open the door. El watched his oh-so-together mentor leap out into the waiting arms of a character part Crocodile Dundee and part Annie Oakley. He couldn't decide which part intimidated him more.

He rose from his seat and watched the two women embrace outside in the artificial light and twirl at the bottom of the steps. The stranger lifted B and swung her around a few more turns before depositing her on the ground.

"El," Beatrix caught her breath as she straightened the new woman's clothes and tried smoothing her shock of bottle-blond hair, "I want you to meet my best friend on earth—Nicole Charbonneau."

The woman playfully slapped Beatrix's hands aside and strode forward with an outstretched palm. El leaned out to shake her hand and felt his knuckles crack in her grip.

"Pleased to meet you, um, Nicole." He so wanted to massage his hand but resisted the urge. "B said you might be dropping by—*tomorrow.*"

Nicole Charbonneau towered over B by a foot. Dressed in a faded Miami Dolphins t-shirt torn short to expose a muscled midriff, yellow cargo shorts and calf-high laced boots; her crystal blue eyes stared under narrowed brows. El felt like a specimen pinned to a dissecting tray.

"Been *tomorrow* a few hours already. 'Sides, I uz in the area," Nicole shrugged. "Figured them old fish sticks in your freezer might taste like driftwood." She lifted her chin in his direction. "I ain't no rocket scientist, but I'm bettin' he's either your brother or shares a big fat root off your family tree."

"Something like that," Beatrix said. "You bring my usual?"

Nicole smiled wide and a gold incisor glinted in the awning lights.

"Don't I always? Parcels in the boat."

"Boat?" El stepped down and out into the dark night, away from the awning. A swamp song of frogs and crickets greeted him. He looked around in the blackness. *Where's a boat? Where's the* water?

"Quick, ain't he?" Nicole snorted. "Guess he didn't inherit any of your smarts."

"There's a canal beyond the overgrowth behind us," B said. "Nicole and her canoe know more about the waterways out there than AAA knows maps."

She put an arm around Nicole's neck and the two women struck off around the trailer. "Come on Eldridge. Supplies aren't gonna carry themselves."

"Now? In the dark?"

Shit.

He hurried to catch up. Snatches of conversation wafted back to him....

OVERCOOKED

Tell me y'all ain't related . . . Later, Nikki. How you been? . . .
Same shit. No men around to speak of . . . So, all quiet in town? . . . You
been reading my mail, girl? We gotta talk."

His eyes adjusted to the low light, helped considerably by the silver shine from a carpet of stars and a half moon low on the horizon. A distant animal scream came from off to his right. He shivered. Neither woman paid it any mind.

El splashed in water over his shoes before he saw the canal. Sawgrass and reeds covered its surface. Damn thing could have fooled an alligator. The two women skirted the edge of it. But not before Nicole looked back at him splashing and chuckled. She elbowed B in the ribs, whispered something.

The canoe, skinned in a camo print, nestled prow-deep in a thick growth of cattails. A bright blue tarp tied down with yellow nylon ropes covered a payload that sat square in the middle.

"Don't get yer feet wet, Swamp Fox," Nicole called over her shoulder. "We'll toss packages over to you."

Beatrix held the boat as Nicole stepped in. Despite her grip, it rocked as the woman bent to her tasks, untying ropes and sweeping back the cover. Nicole never wavered or shifted her feet for balance. The woman clearly spent a lot of time in canoes.

Underneath the tarp, a pyramid of boxes, most open, some taped shut, contained obvious provisions. A pair of Styrofoam coolers at the bottom of the pile strained even Nicole's impressive musculature until B reached over and provided a little mental leverage. *Canned food, pasta, rice, cereal*—he inventoried the contents as the women passed him boxes.

Pretty standard stuff—until B handed him a thin aluminum briefcase.

"You be careful with that, El," she said. "Drop a food box if you have to. Not that."

"What is it?"

She ignored the question and turned to Nicole. "Thanks for retrieving my life. I hoped you hadn't forgotten."

"I got yer back, girl. Come on."

"No problems?"

"Folks who stash stuff in bus station lockers tend to mind their own business. I might have got a few strange looks." Nicole sniffed. "Nothing I don't get on a daily basis."

It took two trips for them to get all the boxes back to the trailer. They stacked the load by the door.

"I can help you put all that away if you like. I know where

everything goes."

"Tempting, Nicole. But we got this. El and I will want something to do to stay busy."

"I get it. Say no more." Nicole waggled a finger. "But you and I should talk before I go."

"How about now?"

"I'm not sure about yer boy, there."

"He's cool," B said. "I have a feeling whatever you're going to tell me, he needs to hear anyway."

"It's your funer—"

"Don't say it. Come inside. Enjoy some A/C and tell us both."

Chapter Eleven

DREAM CAR

John Smith looked down the aisle from his seat in the last row. The Southwest jet bounced hard on touchdown. An overhead bin flopped open and several passengers yelped. A few clamped down hard on their armrests and he smiled. Grips tightened to white knuckles as the reverse thrusters roared and the pilots hit the brakes. He let the extreme vibration and overwhelming noise cocoon him inside with his thoughts.

He jerked side-to-side in his seat—the tail magnified every move the airplane made—while he checked and re-checked his plans. No flaws so far, but he had too much riding on this. Beatrix Goode would present a formidable task. Not the least because of her Speaker's pet status. The girl also had skills. Yeah well, he had talents no one on The Council, even Speaker Calvin, knew about.

First though, he needed to wade through the herd of cattle clogging the aisle in front of him and get to the rental car counter before the premium rides got snapped up. He had no illusions that his reservation made only yesterday guaranteed anything. The drones at the counter would look past his request for a big SUV and give him whatever car had gas in it.

He shouldered past the families and businessmen on the gangway and blew by the Southwest agent greeting people as they deplaned. Humid Miami heat seeped in around the gangway seal and he hurried forward into the A/C chill of Miami International Airport.

He'd expected the redeye flight to give him a less-crowded airport. Apparently, there were a lot more cheap people in the world than he thought, willing to trade the early morning hours for a few dollars saved.

Fine.

He set his one bag down on the linoleum in front of the Hertz counter and made a conscious effort to smile. At least he stood first in line.

"Good evening, sir. I hope you had a comfortable flight."

"We all survived. Name's John Smith." He pulled a computer printout from his back pocket. "I have a reservation."

"Thank you for that." The Hertz agent took his paper and unfolded it. "Why, look at you. One of my first customers to try our new Quick Res Online System." The agent looked up from the paper and beamed. "I get excited over the smallest things."

"I get excited when the SUV I reserved shows up on your screen."

"One moment, please." The agent clacked a hundred or so keys. Frowned. Tap-tapped a hundred more. "Oh, dear."

"No, no, no."

"John *Smith*, you say?"

"Yes. It's a common name. Perhaps you've heard it?"

"Of course, um, according to your printout you reserved with us yesterday evening."

"I did."

"Unfortunately, that did not give us time enough to shift inventory to cover your request."

"What are you saying?"

"I have a brand new full-size with less than twenty miles on it. With GPS and Sirius which, of course, I'll include at no charge."

"A full-size."

"The Chevy Impala is a gorgeous automobile." The agent smiled. "I'm a little jealous, actually."

"I'm a little pissed, actually." Smith propped his elbows on the counter and cracked his knuckles. "A Chevy. *Impala*."

The agent recoiled and returned to his computer screen. He tip-tapped through another round of pursed lips and head shakes.

Finally, he turned back. "The best I have in inventory at the time is from our Dream Car category. It's all I have besides full-size. And I only have one."

"I'll take it—for the same price."

The agent gulped. "Of course, sir. I'll simply print out your papers and we'll get you on your way in no time."

Fifteen eternal minutes later John Smith opened the door of a silver Porsche Boxster. It took some squirming to fit his frame into the leather bucket seat and a few seconds lost searching for the ignition—it's on the left in Porsches. But when he turned the key and the German engine purred to life, his annoyance melted away.

Now this is more like it.

He had a couple of fleeting thoughts about the scene back at the rental counter. Low key and under the radar he definitely wasn't. Screw it. Not everyone has The Speaker's appetite for eating shit.

John Smith pulled out of the rental car lot and used the GPS system to guide him north. Somewhere between here and the frigging middle of this inferno of a state, Beatrix and her Wonder Boy had gone to ground.

She had been clever enough to cloak herself from his telepathic feelers. The girl may be as good as The Speaker seemed to think. He'd get nowhere with that approach. So, why waste another brain cell on her?

Nope, he had a different plan, one that, if her latest failures were any indication, she would be powerless to thwart.

Her Wonder Boy—the Amazing Frigging El—had no developed skills whatsoever. But if the kid proved to be everything she seemed to think he might be, the kid had a pulse. More importantly, a significant mind presence neither he—nor The Speaker's precious little pet—would be able to hide.

He only needed to get close. Once he felt the kid, he'd home in on him like a damn cruise missile. With similar, predictable results.

Chapter Twelve

SHE'S ALIVE!

T he figure under the sheet rocked gently in concert with the footsteps of the men and women who bore it aloft on its litter. Hundreds of fat candles on ledges and in niches in the roughhewn limestone walls added their individual light to the room.

Rows of tall white candles on the floor threw their wavering yellow glow halfway up the walls. Patterns of tapers placed in lines divided the floor, grouping acolytes by their levels of piety and service to Mother. The most pious in front. New souls to the back. All dressed in identical brown hooded robes.

Flickering orange light licked at the faces of the faithful. Instead of banishing the dark, the warm wavering candlelight gave it texture and presence. All the while, the crush of hushed people stood as they were supposed to and watched silently as the procession moved from outside in the corridor into the prayer hall to pass amongst them.

The hall echoed with the faint slaps of bare feet on polished stone. An occasional spitting, guttering candle added the only other sound.

Ranks of robed figures opened to allow passage and closed back up as the chosen ones who bore the litter cut through them, bearing their precious cargo.

The procession arrived at the exact center of the hall where an altar had been prepared. White silk sheets cascaded down a raised platform placed at the foot of a giant crucifix. The pallet bearers gently placed the object of their adoration on top of the sheets and melted back into the encircling crowd.

Mother's face, white as marble and easily as cold, had never looked more beautiful than in this moment. Rich purple robes clothed her from the neck down. Her arms lay folded upon her breast. Her feet, wrapped in gold slippers, looked incongruously dainty for all the opulence they accompanied.

A low chant began amongst the brethren. Lips moved silently at first, but in unison and soon the words of prayer whispered aloud echoed in the enclosed space.

The overwhelming communal power of the mass of the faithful caused several in the crowd to weep silent tears as they continued to pray.

Voices grew in strength and volume as each person drew strength from their numbers until the level rose to that of a crowd in full throat.

Suddenly, the swell of sound throttled to an abrupt, expectant silence.

The left foot of the one on the altar moved.

Murmuring began as the chest of the figure heaved upward and a hundred people gasped audibly as the Mother inhaled and began breathing rapidly. Up and down her chest pumped. Arms and legs twitched, as if getting used to the new life now coursing through them.

Sounds of weeping and crying sprang up in the crowd and grew more pervasive as the passion of the moment caught people in its grip.

Figures in the crowd swayed in religious fervor. Arms stretched heavenward from the open sleeves of coarse robes. Loudly they proclaimed their love for Mother and their undying devotion.

A tremor rippled through Mother and grew more pronounced as she bent a leg and propped up one knee. She rocked side to side as if taking the measure of her platform.

Wailing began amongst the more overcome in the crowd as Mother braced an elbow on the altar and tried to lift herself to a seated position. Two of the chosen, a man and woman, who'd borne her in came rushing forward to help.

She coughed a few times and the pair fussed over her. Leaving only when she shoved their hands away and croaked in a rasp like a file on steel, "Thank you, Father, for this gift you have given me."

Several in the crowd swooned and fainted. Others staggered into the arms of their neighbors.

The woman breathed deeper and exhaled loudly. She looked out over her flock, eyes glittering gold in the flickering light. "Thank God for what you have witnessed here. Thank God for what you have done."

She slid from her pallet to stand and wavered a moment, shooing back those who once again came rushing to her aid.

"My beloved, I have suffered to feel your pain. I bear the scars of that suffering for you. And for Him!"

She untied the sash and opened the purple silk robe, holding it wide to reveal her nakedness. Bernard had done his job well. Scabbed over welts and a landscape of black and blue bruises covered her, disguising any resemblance to a woman's body. A woman near the front screamed and covered her eyes.

Mother shuffled forward unsure on her feet and held her arms out to the woman.

"Come child. Come and stand with me as I want you all to stand with me."

The sobbing woman slipped from the crowd and ran to take Mother's outstretched hand. Mother pulled her close and hugged her. Then pulled away and wiped the woman's tears with a thumb. She grabbed both the young acolyte's hands and ran them down her torso, lingering over the welts and scabs.

"Feel my pain as I have felt yours. Touch the insults on my skin as I have touched the emptiness in your hearts."

Mother embraced the young woman once again and kissed her on the mouth before guiding her back to her place in the crowd. Stronger now, as if sucking sustenance from the young woman, she turned to address her crowd of believers.

"Soon, very soon, we will go forth to confront an evil spreading its vile message amongst the weak and the conflicted. It takes the shape of a healer when we know there is only One who heals. It takes the shape of a believer when its only goal is to deceive."

She stopped for a second and swayed back on her heels before continuing.

"The Devil spawn will soon feel the righteous wrath of the soldiers in my—*our*—holy army. It is they who shall deliver the blows that will fell him. They who shall spill his blood as surely as Brother Bernard cut my flesh to spill mine.

"I love you all. I will speak with every one of you. But first, I must gain strength for the battle ahead. I ask our Lord's guidance as I seek to do His will. God bless you. And God bless our living, breathing Lord and Savior who suffered and died for all of us."

Spent with the effort, Mother staggered forward and would have fallen but for the quick arms of her nearest acolytes. This time, she accepted their ministrations without objection.

Chapter Thirteen

BEATRIX SPILLS

The Airstream's A/C raised goose bumps on his arms. Or, it could be that raw-boned friend of B's with the shocking blond hair and pointed gold canine. The woman shot a low current of electricity into the air wherever she went. Not in a good way. More in a, *get any closer and I'll stun you* sort of way.

"You guys want anything?" Beatrix said. "Wine? Tea?"

"I'm good," Nicole said. She'd jumped up the Airstream steps first and commandeered the far side of the dinette. "Water, maybe. Ain't staying long." She sprawled back in her seat; arms splayed wide, taking up space. Grinning at him.

El and B did a do-si-do in the middle of the trailer.

"'Scuse you, El. Go sit with Nicole. I got this."

"That's okay." He quickly started opening cabinets. "You guys need to catch up." He opened three before he found Nicole a water glass. "I've been sitting all night." He lightly pushed B toward Nicole. "Go. Take a load off. I need to stand, keep the blood flowing."

She looked at him with amusement crinkling the corners of her eyes.

"Really. I'm right here. I can chime in when I want to. Go talk with your friend."

Nicole patted the seat next to her. "C'mon girl."

He thought how fucking awkward that had been.

B looked at him and nodded in agreement.

Shit.

He forgot about the mind-reading thing.

"Only got a couple things and I'll get out of y'all's hair. Three's company and all that."

"Nikki, stay as long as you like." B squeezed her friend's shoulder. "We don't see each other enough and you know that's true."

The woman smiled and remarkably, El saw edges soften in her as she relaxed. "Another time, hon. I didn't plan on coming out here early." She turned her eyes on him. "Believe me. I know I prob'ly startled you a bit."

El sat a glass of water in front of her and she actually smiled at him.

"Thank you. A couple things happened today that changed my mind I thought you should know about."

"Tell me," B said.

"There's something ain't right. Somethin's coming and I'm pretty sure it ain't good."

He leaned against the counter and tried to sound nonchalant. "What do you mean?"

"Well, it started off this morning. I'm having my egg like always. One egg. Fresh from Gerta. She's layin' again praise the saints. Cracked it in the skillet, it had a double yolk with a blood spot. You know what that means."

"Go on," B said.

"Don't eat it?" El had no frigging idea what that meant.

Beatrix shushed him with an outstretched palm.

"My antenna tweaked, of course. So later, I'm paddlin' my canoe, headin' to market for the last of your vittles, I couldn't miss him. Passed within three feet of him."

"Who?" El's stomach began to knot. "Who'd you see?"

"Worse than a who," Nicole said. "A what. I lifted my paddle and glided right past an albino gator and one of them damned constrictor snakes locked in a death struggle."

"I see," B said.

El didn't see at all, but he had a sick feeling he should worry.

"Thrashing, rollin' in the water. An *albino* gator, B. First I've seen in all my years."

"I'm sorry, I don't get it," he said. "I know I should. You two got this thing where you understand one another. But—an albino gator? So?"

"He is dense, ain't he?" Nicole said. "An albino gator, rare as a dinosaur, fightin' for its life? Jimminy." She grabbed B's arm and rolled back the sleeve. Laid her tanned, muscled arm next to Beatrix's translucent white skin. "Sign's clear as spring water."

"How long, you think?" Beatrix said.

"Don't know, baby. Signs ain't speakin' that to me. Not yet."

"Crap." B stood up and guided him to the seat across from Nicole and pushed him down into it. "I need room to think." She paced up and back in the confined space. The Airstream shook with every step. "If you can see it that clear Charbonneau, time's shorter than I'd hoped."

"My thought exactly," Nicole nodded solemnly.

"So, you're some kind of soothsayer? Tea leaves? Tarot?" He felt a twinge of disappointment that someone without a light bulb head and without his intellect might manifest special powers.

Nicole shrugged. His question and his attitude were apparently nothing new to her.

"Nicole shares a gift with her grandmother," B said. "One I've come to rely on."

"World speaks to me an' Gram like it don't to other people. Gift or curse, sometimes I wonder. It skipped my momma. But Gram and me, when the world has something to say, we listen. We see omens for what they are."

Beatrix slid into the seat next to her friend, hugged Nicole around the neck and kissed her forehead. "Thanks for doing this."

Nicole cradled B's face between her palms. "You need to be careful, girl. I'm here for you. Whatever you need."

"I need for you to go now," B said. "I can't let you get mixed up in our problems. You've done enough."

"I ain't done nothin' but bark like a dog to get your attention."

"Mission accomplished. Don't worry, Nikki. We'll be fine." Beatrix stood up and offered her friend a hand. "Come on. Leave us. We have lots of work and not much time."

"I'll know if you need me," Nicole said. "You won't be able to keep me away."

Beatrix grinned and tapped her head. "We have our ways, girl. Never doubt that."

Nicole lurched forward and wrapped B in a bear hug. She looked at me over B's shoulder. "If you're good for anything, you'll watch out for my girl, here. She's pretty special, I guess you know."

"She is. And I will."

"By the looks of you, I'm hoping you're kind of special, too. We never got into that. Maybe some other time."

Nicole's eyes were wet when she turned and left the trailer.

"You believed her. All that omen stuff," he said.

"More than you know. Now come in and sit down."

She picked up the silver briefcase that had been stashed behind a couch cushion.

"We have a ton of ground to cover."

She placed the case on the table and spun it to face her. Each clasp had a combination lock and she twirled the dials with her thumbs.

Two crisp snaps and the case squeaked open. A faint smell of roses and musty decay reached him as B poked at the contents, tongue embedded her cheek.

She looking for something? Taking inventory?

"What you got in there?" he said.

"Only our survival, yours and mine. Or, the survival of the entire human race. Take your pick."

She slid the open case to the end of the table so they could both see into it and pulled an object wrapped in faded lace from atop a pile of papers. A pistol gleamed dully at the back of the case, the one grip he could see looked like yellowed ivory. A raw divot marred the grip's otherwise smooth surface.

Beatrix placed the lace-wrapped bundle on the table between them and began unwrapping its layers. When she finished, in the center of the cream-colored fabric lay a baby's teething ring. The ring looked to be mother of pearl with a sterling silver bell attached to it.

"Is that—?"

"A teething ring, yes," B said. "Here." She plucked it from the lace wrap and handed it to him. "Knock yourself out."

The mother-of-pearl ring gleamed shiny and smooth, the silver bell dented with teeth marks. He shook it and the bell tinkled.

"Looks old," he said.

"Hundred twenty, hundred thirty, something like that," she said. "It was my mom's. Only thing I have of hers."

"Your *mom*? A hundred years old? B you really suck at math."

"A hundred thirty I said. And my math is quite excellent."

He let that slide for the moment. "Then, I'd say you look remarkably young for your age."

"You have no idea." Beatrix rummaged through the briefcase while she let her first bombshell of the night sink in. Eldridge would need proof. She knew that because she'd needed it, too. A lifetime ago, when The Speaker plucked her out of that Children's Home beside the stockyards in Chicago....

#

She watched trench coat make his way up the cracked sidewalk, avoiding piles of dog crap and up-thrust broken concrete with uncanny accuracy. He never looked down once, his eyes fixed on her.

People staring didn't faze her. When you looked like she did, staring became the least of your worries. The babushka she tied over her head like the other Russian women in her neighborhood did little to hide its shape.

She tried ignoring the man. Got busy pulling on her rubber boots and tying the rubber apron she'd need for her job later. She mucked out the animal waste and entrails on the killing floor of Building Six. Pushing on a wooden muck rake. It had a handle like a push broom, attached to a board at the bottom. Not a real rake *per se*. More like a functional way to shove steaming piles of gore toward the drain hole at the floor center.

A crap job but she felt lucky to have it. The Home took half her pay—fifty cents a day. The rest she squirreled away in a Prince Albert tobacco can under a loose floorboard beneath her bunk.

"Hello."

Well, ignoring the guy didn't work. She looked up and took in the camelhair coat, hat pulled low, and leather gloves standing at the white picket gate. He stood tall, six-and-a-half feet at least, and looked like a gangster. Or a union boss. Bad news either way.

"Yeah?" *Stay noncommittal. Give him nothing.*

"What might your name be little lady?"

"I'm called a lot of things. *Retard. Lame-o. Freak* is popular. Take your pick."

"I see." He removed his gloves and slapped them together in one hand. He shoved them in a coat pocket as he stepped through the gate. "I am looking for Miss Betty Charnoff. She around?"

How did he know her name? Not a good sign. Not good at all. What did Mr. Bad News want with a nobody like her?

"You're not *nobody*, Betty. Quite the opposite as a matter of fact."

Oh, my god.

"And may I assure you I am the *best news* you'll have heard in a long, long time."

"How did you do that?" She clapped her hands over her ears to keep him out of her head.

"I'm here to take you away from all this."

Hah, she knew it. These guys came by every other day, enticing the young immigrant girls with promises of a better life. They all ended up dead or in brothels.

"I'm doing fine on my own."

He put his hands on his hips and made a big show of looking her up and down. "I can see that."

"I need to go. My shift starts in thirty minutes."

The man didn't budge. Instead, he carefully lifted the fedora off his head and—

Sweet Jesus. He's got a head like hers!

"It's not like that, Betty. As you can see, you and I share certain—interests. We have a lot to talk about." He put his hat back on and settled it carefully in place.

"What is this? Who are you?"

"Someone like you, Betty. With big plans and big dreams."

"You don't know a thing about me."

"On the contrary. I know your parents put you here. Girls are poor wage earners and they had to choose between feeding you or your brothers. I know you are very, very smart. Too smart for your circumstances."

"They couldn't help what they did."

"I know you are an incredibly special young lady with talents and potential you have never imagined. I will open up the world for you, Betty. And I will never lay a hand upon you—or allow anyone else to do the same. I swear it on your dead sister's grave."

"How did you know about—?"

"If you believe me, which I hope you do. I suggest you retrieve your tobacco can from underneath your bunk. And come with me."

#

Beatrix dug around in the briefcase and pulled a dilapidated card from the bottom.

"Here."

She handed it to El.

"What's this?"

"Read it."

He peered at it intently. Held it up to the light. Turned it over. "This some kind of trick?"

She remained silent.

"Looks like a union card or something. *Meatpackers Local 436. Betty Charnoff. 1955.*"

"Yep."

"Picture looks like your sister or mother, maybe? There is a resemblance."

"You think so?"

"It's in the eyes."

"Think again." She leaned across the table and stared at him. Eyes wide. "Look close," she said.

He leaned back. "Crap, B. Quit it. You're freaking me out."

"I guess there's a frigging resemblance. The eyes are mine,

doofus. They're my eyes. And that," she lifted the card from his hand, "is me. From another life. A long time ago."

"Bullshit."

"When you get a minute, Google a children's home called Wayward Angels on Foster Street in Chicago. Located across from the stockyards." She stuck out a bottom lip. "The firetrap burned down one afternoon. Tragic. No one got hurt. But all the records and some shockingly horrible flowered wallpaper went up in smoke."

"You're telling me that you're—I don't believe it."

"How old do I look?"

"I don't know. Twenty-seven? Thirty?"

"Christ, El. You're hard on a girl's ego."

"How old are you then?"

"Best I can figure, I'm sixty-six. Or sixty-seven. The Russian village my parents emigrated from didn't keep great records."

She got up and pirouetted in place. Slapped a bicep. Pinched her midsection. "Not bad for a senior citizen, hey?"

"Let's say I believe you. You get older but you don't age. How is that even possible?"

"Believe me, because you're doing it, too. Only you don't know it. We of the egg heads and mind-boggling intellect tend to age slow."

"I'm twenty-two and I look twenty-two."

"You'll look like you're in your twenties for twenty more years. Now's about the time our Methuselah thing kicks in. And that *is* one of our perks."

She reached into the case and pulled out a revolver.

"Here's another. Which you have some experience with." She closed one eye and aimed at a point across the way. The hammer arched back as she squeezed the trigger.

"Hey, now, B—"

The hammer fell with a loud click on an empty chamber. "Relax, El." Beatrix broke open the gun to show a chamber with a single shell in it.

"That could have gone off! Hurt someone. Like me."

"Oh, this?" She plucked the cartridge from the cylinder and held it up. "Already did."

She held the spent cartridge under her nose and sniffed. "Still a trace, after all these years." She tossed him the cartridge.

He examined it; gave it his own smell test before handing it back. "I know there's a story there. What's with the gun?"

"Gun is so non-specific. This, my friend, is a Colt .45 Model 1873 that used to belong to none other than the King of Chicago."

"Didn't know Chicago had a king."

"Nothin' but a high-level pimp with an inflated idea of his place in society. Named himself King. Ran poor, immigrant girls in that city for over a decade."

"I see."

"This'll help you see better." B pulled a yellowed copy of the Chicago Tribune from the case. Its front page featured a sensational picture of a black man sprawled on the trunk of an old Cadillac with his neck cocked at a funny angle. She tapped the photo. "Meet Maurice Delacroix, aka The King."

She scanned the lead story, smiling and shaking her head. "Front page news in 1971. Made the local TV and everything. Maurice was a sociopath with a thing for young European girls, drugs and money. Not necessarily in that order. His sort of evil always crops up where humanity hangs on by its fingernails."

She inserted the spent cartridge, snapped the revolver back together and spun the cylinder. "This is the gun he shot me with. That shell held the piece of lead that tore through my stomach." She held the paper up. "That's what The Speaker did to him afterwards." She shuddered. "I can still hear the bastard's neck crack."

"Jesus, B."

"The Speaker and I had been together for a while. Him training me and me rebelling, pushing his buttons." She waggled the paper. "By now, I 'thought a lot of myself and what I could do." She raised her eyebrows at him. "Like someone else I could mention. We knew about The King and his dirty business. I decided to do something about it.

"Not my smartest move. King's goons saw me coming a mile away. I waltzed into their compound chill as an ice cube. Took care of every asshole who had a gun and one swinging a Louisville Slugger. No problem. But the King heard the commotion and came running. Big problem."

She kneaded her midsection and made a face like *what are you gonna-do?* "The gun went off to my right. Knocked me to the ground. My whole body blazed red-hot. You know the little trick earlier with the spinning plates?"

El nodded.

"Imagine that being done to a man." She chuckled without a trace of mirth. "Jesus, did he scream. Speaker had him four feet off the ground in mid-air, flinging him back and forth like a Raggedy Ann doll. After he dented The King's Cadillac with his body and twisted the head backwards, he tended to me. I need a drink. You want some wine? Nicole brought us a few decent bottles of red."

Without waiting for an answer she extracted two glasses from a cabinet and uncorked the bottle—without an opener.

"Nice," El said.

"Another parlor trick. I got a million of them. Anyway, where was I?"

"The Speaker, whoever that is, came and—?"

"Right. I figured I'm done. My guts are on fire, the street slick with my blood. I can still smell the tar in the asphalt. The Speaker knelt over me and did what you did for the cop; put his hand on my wound. Pressed hard. I passed out from the pain, figuring I'm headed to hell. I woke up on the couch in The Speaker's apartment."

"I like it," El said. "Resurrection. A perk we can all use."

"Except, we all can't." Beatrix poured a slug of cabernet and handed him a glass. "Speaker's the only one we know with that power, and it almost did him in."

"I remember how it felt." El shivered. "Headaches like I had rats digging out of my skull."

"Headaches? When I awoke in the man's apartment he lay unconscious on the floor. Pale, cold, breathing shallow. I had no idea how to do what *he'd* done for *me*. I stretched out beside him and held him in my arms. And prayed. To whatever god made us the way we were.

"I hugged him, rocked him, begging the Lord to step up and do the right thing. Speaker came around twelve hours later weak as a pup, blind in one eye—*and* he had a headache. My first real lesson in consequences. You'll hear a lot more of that word as we go.

"Compared to him, you got off without a scratch. And no one else—since what The Speaker did for me and you for that cop—has done anything like it since. None of the rest of us has that kind of power. And you're a baby.

She cocked her head. "Something about you is definitely different, El."

"Tell me something I don't know."

"I mean more than normal overcooked different. Have to tell you, it scares me a little. I can only imagine how you must feel."

Chapter Fourteen

GOD'S WORK

Mother worked the controls on the motorized recliner until she struck the perfect balance of forward tilt and extended legs. She'd commanded that the La-Z-Boy be brought in and her office rearranged to allow the chair center-stage focus. She'd intended for her healing *resurrection* to be a lesson for all of her followers. To illustrate God's forgiveness and the gifts He grants to those who follow His teachings. She wondered if she'd gone too far. *Nah.*

"Pillows," she snapped her fingers and an acolyte waiting by her side placed feather pillows behind and beside her. Mother groaned at the contact between flesh and fabric but bit it short when her helper recoiled in horror.

"That's okay, Alice. You're doing fine." Mother shifted, trying to find a position that kept the throbbing fire on her thighs and torso at bay. "Would you be a dear and bring my coverlet? The purple silk?"

The woman dashed off and returned with a shiny swath of material black as eggplant.

"Bless you my child." Mother waved her away with a shooing motion. "Go, tell Bernard I am ready for him now. He'll be right outside the door."

Mother arranged the silk cover from her chin, down, for maximum regal impact. She must project an image of strength and not let the debilitating effects of her injuries be evident. If Jesus could rise from the grave and show himself and his wounds to doubting disciples, she could certainly manage her paltry pains.

The door to her newly christened Healing Room opened and Bernard stuck his head in.

"Ma'am? With your permission?"

Mother smiled inwardly, pleased by the man's obvious discomfort. "Yes, yes, Brother Bernard. Please come in. Shut the door behind you."

Bernard did as she said and limped forward to stand at the foot of her recliner. She noted his black eye, swollen face and the awkward set to his right arm. They told her that a few of her believers, upon seeing what Bernard had done beat him senseless. The thought made her happy.

She had plans of her own for Bernard, but not until he'd served his purpose.

"Did you bring it?"

He bowed slightly and winced. "As you ordered." He reached into his shirt and pulled out the riding crop.

"You didn't clean it?" she said sharply. She held her hand out and he placed it on her palm.

"Nothing has touched this. Not water. No cleaner. Nothing."

"Excellent." She closed her fist around it and brought it close. Much of the lower half showed darker stains than the top. She detected dried clots of black crusted in the furrows and creases of the braided leather. *Her* blood. Shed for *her* Lord.

She grabbed a nearby tray table and slid it across her lap. The leather crop suspended above it, she held the leather at both ends and twisted. Flakes of matter fell to the table in a dark dusting.

Mother kept at it until she'd extracted all she could of the precious material.

"Bernard, fetch a blank offering envelope please—and a pen. They'll be in the left drawer of the desk in the corner. Also, empty the contents of the silver box you'll find in the same drawer into the trash and bring everything to me. "

When he retrieved them she used the edge of the envelope to push the remnants of her supreme suffering into a pile. The flap made a perfect scoop and she tapped the holy dust into the envelope and sealed it. On the outside she wrote *Blood for blood, consecrated on this 26th day of June 2020.* She placed the sealed envelope in the box and closed the lid.

"Brother Bernard, may I prevail upon you once again to help me with a most important task?"

"Of course, Mother. I am your willing servant."

"As we are *all* His willing servants, praise His name. Now, after we are done here, I want you to take this flesh and blood offering that you and I have fashioned."

"Mother, please."

She shushed him with an upraised hand. "Do you know the mural of our Lord's suffering I commissioned for the central hallway?"

"A magnificent work."

"And the alcove beside it framed by the centurion spears?"

He nodded.

"Excellent. Our pitiful efforts in service to the Almighty Father cry out for atonement." She handed him the box. "This will complete my part. Place it in the alcove so that my blood, shed in His service, might become a symbol for our followers just as His blood did for all mankind."

He bowed and prepared to scurry out with the box.

"Not now, after we are through here. Are the others waiting as I instructed?"

"All six of them. They're out in the hallway. Eager to serve their Lord," he said.

"Show them in."

Bernard limped to the door and opened it wide. He used the box gripped in his good hand to gesture to an unseen group.

Five men and one woman filed silently into the Healing Room and stood at attention in front of Mother's chair, eyes fixed at a distant point above and behind her. Only the young woman had the temerity to hold her gaze.

Interesting. I may need to watch that one.

Mother cleared her throat and all but the woman jumped.

"Look at me," Mother said. "You are my apostles, soon to embark upon the holiest of holy missions." She glared into each pair of eyes, sending willful fire to strengthen their resolve. "A crusade no less important than when our brethren tried to wrest the Holy Land from the filthy Saracens."

She waited a few seconds until, as she suspected, the young woman spoke first.

"How may we serve you, Mother?" The girl fixed her with a stare flat enough to communicate insolence, obedience, or nothing at all. "We are ready."

Mother snapped her fingers and Bernard scurried back to her desk. He sat Mother's silver box down and picked up the laptop waiting there. He opened it to a selection of several of the videos detailing the night of the policeman's resurrection, walking up and down the line to be sure each apostle got a good look at the screen. He froze the last frame and zoomed in on the exhausted man leaning against the wall, handcuffs dangling from one wrist.

"That, my children, is an abomination in the eyes of the Lord. Bernard, how many times have these videos been viewed by unsuspecting godless gawkers?"

Bernard turned the laptop and squinted at the screen. "Three million, four hundred and ninety six…seven…eight…"

Mother slapped a thigh and winced. "Over three million souls who have opened themselves up to evil and corruption. I—*we*—cannot allow this, this *demon* to continue his unholy work." She drew herself up in her chair and pointed a finger to the heavens. "Only God giveth. And only GOD TAKETH AWAY."

"What will you have us do, Mother?" said the young woman.

Mother spread her hands and pressed them on the tray in her lap. In a voice smooth as cream she said, "Find him. Bring him to me. But work together. Do not make the mistake of Brother Bernard who tried to take the wily one alone. That *thing*—" she pointed a shaky finger at the laptop in Bernard's hands "—is a demon of the highest order and you will respect its power."

She clapped her hands. "Now, go my children and do God's work. Bernard has information that will give you a starting point. I trust in you and our Lord that your efforts will bear fruit. The very soul of civilization hangs in the balance."

She shooed them off, but not before telling Bernard, "When you are through with them, and the box, return. We have another matter to discuss, you and I." His slight grimace, quickly squelched, warmed her inside.

Chapter Fifteen

KILLING TORTOISES

J ohn Smith silenced the damn GPS. The robotic woman's voice had all the charm of an enema administered by a stuck-up schoolteacher. Besides, he didn't need high tech satellite guidance to keep reminding him: *Stay straight on US Highway 41.*

The Tamiami Trail clocked three hundred miles, give or take, of excruciating boredom. Even with the top down and the Porsche roadster's tuned exhaust screaming behind him, Smith caught himself daydreaming and losing focus.

Trouble was, the telepathic feelers he blasted out into the void, trying to get a blip on Beatrix's charge, drained his energy. The distance he needed, the sheer force he required to scour the ether gave him a pounding headache and soured his mood.

His only respite came from stupid tortoises crossing the road, *trying to reach the other side*. At 90 mph he came upon them quick and it soon became a game. Spot the quarry. Judge the timing. Jerk the wheel at the last second and feel a satisfying pop as the sports car's fat tires crushed another shell.

The Boxster responded to the faintest input with immediate German precision. The sports contoured seat held him firmly as the little car flung side-to-side. The backend fishtailed a few times, quickening his pulse. It felt exhilarating. Shit, at least it gave him a reason to grin.

Pale pink tortoise guts spinning to the side of the road in his rearview mirror. If they were colorful enough, he rated them one to five.

Five reflecting the highest artistic merit in the new fine art of terrapin ballet.

What the hell? It passed the time.

He watched the clock in the instrument cluster and every twenty minutes, pinged B's Eldridge to see if he could locate him.

Nothing for the first few hours. But when the highway jogged a hard left and switched from north/south to east/west, he felt a tingle.

The deep-throated exhaust note receded and the grassy landscape of the north border of the Everglades faded as he focused every sense on the tiny buzz raising hairs behind his neck.

Son of a bitch. *Got him.*

Smith pulled to the side of the road to concentrate. He shut the engine off and sat. In the quiet, only the cracks of the cooling engine behind him and the whine of mosquitos broke through. Neither mattered.

The bounce-back on his mental sonar felt distant, but it was there. Strong enough to be reliable and it would only get stronger as he homed in on the signal.

Why, hello there. Pleased to meet you, Eldridge my man.

Smith rubbed his palms and twisted the key in the ignition.

Chapter Sixteen

BUSTED!

El watched Beatrix yank open closet and cabinet doors, piling sheets, blankets and pillows in her arms.

"Get up," she said. "You're sitting on your bed." She shoved the stack of linens at him, collapsed the dining table, and spread the seat cushions to form a double bed. "I'm not your mom. You'll have to make this up yourself."

He took a few moments to examine his new sleeping arrangements, aware for the first time of B's bedroom a scant twenty feet down at the Airstream's far end.

"Might as well be a mile," she said.

When he startled she tapped her temple. "Remember? Now, bottom sheet's the one with the elastic."

"I know how to make a bed," he said.

"See, I knew it. Genius." She clicked off lights as she made her way to the other bed and shut a privacy curtain. "Turn off the light on the wall when you're ready. We're running on batteries out here. Try to get in a few hours. Big day tomorrow."

He couldn't help himself. He watched her shadow on the curtain as she undressed for bed.

"Goodnight, El."

Her voice had a wry twist to it as she switched off her bedroom light.

Frigging telepathy.

A few minutes later he lay on top of a haphazard spread of sheets and blanket. He kept his clothes on to save time. No sense digging into his monster duffel bag now.

The dark inside the Airstream had a soft glow to it, courtesy of the moon and starlight seeping in around the blinds in the windows.

After awhile, his eyes adjusted and he lay back, enjoying the chance to take in the details of his new home away from home.

The Airstream trailer designers were masters of efficiency. Cabinets and countertops, accessories and appliances fit like puzzle pieces in the confined space. He focused on those wonderments because the alternative would leave him thinking about the bombshells B dropped on him earlier...Her previous life. Their shared . . . what? Ancestry? Could that even be true? Her age. His slowly unfolding skill set.

Nope. Not ready for all that yet.

He lay back and closed his eyes, trying to still the chatter in his head.

And that's when he felt it.

Deep in the center of his brain, the faintest tickle, like a tiny fingernail pick-pick-picking at a scab.

"Hey!" He sat up in bed and pressed palms to his temples. "B! Something's happening." He shook his head, trying to make the tickle go away but the tickle grew more insistent.

PICK. PICK. PICK.

"Beatrix. Something's wrong with me."

She hurried to him, bare feet slapping on the floor. "Tell me."

"I think I got a worm or something. Maybe an aneurysm. Like a wriggling in my head. Ahhh—" he grabbed his head again and pressed harder.

"Stop it, El. Be still. STOP IT." B laid her hand on top of his head for a few seconds then snatched it away. "Goddammit." She paced up and back, wringing her hands. "Shit, shit—SHIT."

"What? I'm the one with the aneurysm."

"You don't have an aneurysm and you're not sick. But you are— we are—in trouble."

"I don't get it."

"You're being probed, El. Crap, I am such an IDIOT."

"Explain," he said.

"They're tracking us, El. Council's freaked out over your stunt with the cop. Like I knew they would be. Someone's on our tail." She tapped her head. "They can't sense me because I cloaked them off. But you—" She hurried back to her bedroom and began shucking pajamas in favor of jeans and a t-shirt.

He tried not to look.

"Really, El? That's all you can think about? At a time like this?"

"Sorry."

"My fault. I forgot about you," she called over her shoulder. "You don't know how to close off and whoever's coming knows that."

"But if it's your Council—"

"It's your Council too, El."

"They're like us, right? So, they'll be on our side."

"Not exactly." She hurried back to her end of the trailer, picked up a brush and yanked it through her hair. "Get dressed—oh." She eyed his clothes. "Good. I sent out a call to Nicole."

"Jungle telegraph? I didn't hear anything—"

"I told you before. She's...sensitive. We're connected." She opened the fridge and slopped some orange juice in glass. "She'll be here. Want some?"

He took the glass from her and she got another one.

"What do we do?"

"Wait," she said. "For Nicole. Whomever they sent is still a ways off. But he's coming and he won't give up." She drained her glass. "Bet your balls it's that asshole, Smith."

"Who's that?"

"John Smith."

"Standout name."

"We're all named like that. Plain Jane names to cruise under the radar. Lucy Brown, John Smith, Calvin Jones—that's The Speaker's real name."

"Beatrix?" he said.

"Shut up. It used to be popular. So, John Smith. He's one of us. But there's something about him. He's old as The Speaker and...I guess *ambitious* would be the word. He's wanted The Speaker's job forever. He'll do whatever it takes to get it."

"Like—?"

"Like punish me for failing my mission."

"What mission?"

"You, numbskull. You're my mission. He'll take over your training. See what your potential really is. Not a good thing. The man is brutal."

Eldridge sat forward. "I don't like the sound of that."

"Me neither. He'll try his damnedest to marginalize you."

"That sounds worse."

"I will be punished for my overreach. You will be dissected until they know everything about you."

He wrapped his arms across his torso. "Oh, my god."

"Not like that." She sniffed. "But you won't like it." She sat beside him on the folded down bed and put her face in her hands. "I might have over-sold you to The Council."

"What the hell does that mean?"

She raised her head and he saw tears shine in her eyes. And that scared him more than anything that had happened so far.

"I saw something in you, El. I felt it. Remember that day on the street?"

"Like I'd forget?"

"I'd been watching you for weeks before that. Making notes, evaluating. When we started working together, I knew. From how fast you learned, how strong you were. You were special, unlike any of us."

He sat straighter and grinned. "Ask my mom."

"That may or may not be a good thing, you nut."

"You can do stuff I haven't even thought of," he said. "How special can I be?"

"You're young, El. I've got a couple decades on you. I'm good, yes. The Speaker trained me well and I'm a hell of a pupil. But I don't have your natural abilities. None of us has, that I know of."

"Here's the question of the hour," he said. "So what? What does it matter? And whose business is it?"

B took his hand in hers.

He enjoyed the feeling. Screw her if she glommed onto that telepathically.

She chuckled. "You're a mess Eldridge Montcalm." Then she got serious. "There are hundreds of us, El. Like you and me; big heads, pasty skin, genius intellects. All over the world. But, we're still incredibly rare. Drops in the bucket when it comes to overall world population.

"The Council watches over us *overcooked* souls and keeps an eye out, looking for the rarest one of us all. Our teachings refer to him or her as only that—The One."

"You think I might be—?"

She shrugged. "I don't know. Maybe. After all I saw, before the cop and after the cop, you're certainly a contender."

"What if I am?"

"The One has a destiny to fulfill. That's all we rank and file really know. We have a saying, like a creed:

The world must never hear us, never see us, never know us. Until The One brings us to the Given Goal. For the good of all mankind.

The Council knows more. The Given Goal, for example. Don't even ask me. I don't know what that is."

He massaged his temples. "This shit is hard, B."

"It's a lot all of a sudden. I know, sorry. But we don't have much time. By the way, that tickle in your head. Is it growing worse?"

He nodded.

"Try this. You ever watch TV so late that a station goes off air and leaves nothing but snow and white noise?"

"Yes," he said.

"Fill your head with the snow. Think about the screen. Hear the *sssshhhh* of it. Amplify that sound in your head."

"Okay, guru."

"Try it, smart guy. Please. Then tell me what happens."

So he did. Closed his eyes and replayed the TV scene from *Poltergeist* with the little girl. Saw her point to the screen and heard *They're here!* Zoomed in on the flickering snow and amped the noise level.

The insistent tickle in the center of his brain blinked a few times. And then winked out like a faulty light bulb.

The grin on his face must have given it away.

"Good. Hold that thought." B slapped him on the leg. "Nicole will be here soon and I've got shit to do before we can leave."

He opened his eyes.

"Sit tight. Think snowy thoughts and jam John Smith's radar. I got this."

Chapter Seventeen

NICOLE WAITS ON JOHN

John Smith almost wrecked the car when he lost it. Agonized tires squealed in protest when he stomped the brakes and pulled the car down from 90+ mph to zero. A white cloud of burnt rubber settled around the car while he cast his mind about frantically, pushing harder, shoving further.

But the beacon he'd been homing in on flickered a few times and disappeared. No matter what he did, stopped dead in the middle of the Everglades and S.R. 41, he couldn't raise it again. Even with his powerful mind.

He dented the dash with his fist and yanked the little sports car off the road in time for an 18-wheeler to blast by, klaxon horns blaring. He rocked in the semi's backwash and barely felt it.

His mind stayed focused elsewhere.

After ten minutes on the side of the road and still nothing, he needed a new plan, before his quarry got smarter and their trail grew colder.

Smith wasn't worried so much as pissed.

Only a matter of time now and The Speaker's pet and her protégé would be toast. Might as well settle in and enjoy the contest for what it signified—his time to shine and The Speaker's time to start packing bags for retirement.

He clicked through a few screens on his GPS to get the lay of the land. Closest town, marked by the tiniest dot on the screen, called itself Glade. Probably big enough for a gas station, a church, a couple of traffic lights and a bus depot. Asking for a McDonalds's would be asking too much.

Wrong again.

He realized it thirty minutes later when he pulled off the highway and coasted through the thriving metropolis of Glade. The town had one stoplight, not a couple. It blinked red at the town's one intersection, tired as the buildings along the dusty streets it guarded.

What a shithole.

A slow cruise down the town's main street, cleverly called Glade Avenue, ended fifteen seconds after it began when the eclectic parade of stores—pharmacy, Ronnette's Boutique, Fred's Brew-Ha-Ha, True Value, Trailways Bus Station, and Nicole's Diner to hit the high points— ran out.

Smith spun the Porsche into a tight U-turn and pulled into a diagonal space in front of the diner. He left the top down and strolled into Glade's one restaurant expecting nothing much. The smell of coffee, hamburgers sizzling on a griddle and the fresh cinnamon tang of homemade apple pie made his stomach gurgle. He realized he hadn't eaten all day and hunting fugitives made for hungry work.

He headed for the counter, picked the red vinyl stool with the fewest cracks and slid on.

Woman behind the counter clumped by with a coffee pot in one hand and a menu in the other. She slid a menu in front of him without looking and proceeded to the far end of the counter to refill a couple of mugs. He leaned forward to watch her retreating back and took in the laced boots, shorts and Dan Marino jersey under the woman's apron.

A typed sheet of paper sandwiched inside a plastic sleeve served as the menu. Apparently the selections in this elite establishment changed fairly regularly.

Smith chose a cheeseburger, onion rings and coffee. He'd focused on selecting a dessert—either homemade apple or cherry pie, pudding and fresh churned ice cream—when she returned, coffee pot in hand.

He looked up and she stopped short, sloshing coffee over the rim of the pot. Startled, eyes wide, she covered well by swiping at the brown coffee stain now spreading down her apron.

He'd gotten over the effect he had on people decades ago. If they couldn't handle a pasty-faced dude with an odd-shaped head, too bad for them.

"So," he leaned close, made a show of reading the name sewn in blue on her apron, "Nicole—hey, you must be the owner of this fine restaurant."

"I am." She nodded, lips set in a line.

"What's good?"

"Everything." The woman recovered well, meeting his gaze with a cool one of her own. "Been here going on fifteen years without a single complaint." She crossed her arms and rose slightly on her toes. "Everything on the menu's cooked fresh, made to order. If you don't see it, ask. We try to accommodate our *customers*."

The odd emphasis on the word did not escape him. *What the hell's her problem?*

"I'll go out on a limb and try a cheeseburger—well, onion rings crispy, and a cup of that coffee you're wearing. Looks good." He smiled to put the woman at ease. "If I have room after all that, your apple pie is calling my name."

She scribbled his order on a pad and tucked a pencil up into an impressive hedge of white blond hair standing at attention on her scalp.

"Speaking of names," she said, "You know mine." She extended a hand. "What might yours be?"

"Smith. John Smith." He took her hand and felt a cool, surprisingly hard grip.

"Welcome to our quiet little town Mr. Smith John Smith."

He tried to read her as she pulled her hand free. Out of habit and to get a peek at her out-of-sorts reaction to him. He got nothing. Even with the flesh on flesh connection, the woman's mind stayed closed to him.

Sometimes people sloughed off psychic probing due to some weird-ass defect in their wiring. They were rare but out there. In those cases, when he cared, he merely bore down and focused harder, made his probing more pointed.

Nicole stood with her back to him, hands planted on the counter, his order newly clipped to the short order turnstile.

He shoved with a needle-sharp mental probe and saw her shoulders stiffen and hands splay out. Knuckles whitened as her fingers curled into claws.

Still, he got nothing. Occasional glimpses, like flashes on a flickering screen, of a swamp landscape and a waterway, maybe. He couldn't tell. What he did receive sounded like rhythmic chanting, a mantra or a prayer vigil.

When he concentrated, really tried to make out the words, he was rewarded with a streaming phrase that grew stronger as his pressure increased. Finally, he deciphered it.

Fuckyoufuckyoufuckyoufuckyou.

Nicole turned around and treated him to an enormous smile. A bit red in the face, with a sheen of sweat sparkling on her brow, nevertheless she approached him and put her hands on the counter in front of him.

"Your order will be right up, Mr. Smith," she said. "Let me know when you want that apple pie. I'll make sure you get everything you asked for."

Chapter Eighteen

B MAKES A POINT

B eatrix pulled a suitcase from under her bed and flopped it open. She mumbled to herself as she yanked open drawers, closet doors and cabinets. El watched an arc of clothes and toiletry items sail through the air to land with amazing precision, divided between the two suitcase halves. If he hadn't been sitting atop his duffle bag in Beatrix's trailer and witnessed it for himself, he would never have believed it. The more he spent time with this woman, the more off center his world became.

"Can I do anything, or—?"

"I won't be long," B said. "You're lucky you hadn't unpacked yet. We'll be out of here as soon as I have contact with—"

BAMBAMBAM.

El jumped and Beatrix smiled.

"—With our guardian angel." She nodded toward the door and El rose to open it.

The thing flew open a shade before he got to it and an out-of-breath and disheveled Nicole hopped up the entry steps. She had on a coffee-stained diner apron with *Nicole* stitched on the left breast and reeked of grilled ground beef.

"Girl," Nicole began, "something happened a bit ago." She forked trembling fingers through her blond mane. "You need to know about."

"He's here, isn't he?" Beatrix didn't let her finish. "You saw him? Sort of like one of us, but—"

"Definitely one of you, but a whole lot darker on the inside. I thought you were the good guys?"

"Most of us," B said.

"So, you know about him? Bad news broadcast from that dude like a terminal case of B.O."

"El sensed his coming an hour or so ago." B massaged her temples. "We've been trying to jam him ever since."

Nicole came over and hugged B. "I don't mind sayin', that man scared me a little bit. An' I don't scare easy."

"Did he hurt you?" B pushed Nicole away and held her at arm's length. "That is strictly against our rules."

Nicole patted B's cheeks with both hands. "Nah. If he had I woulda crushed him. Did try that mind thing you showed me. *Whew.*" She wiped her forehead with a forearm. "He pushed hard, too. Not nice like you did to me. More like he wouldn't take no for an answer. Angry even."

Now B patted Nicole's cheek. "That's okay, hon, we'll take it from here."

"He didn't get nuthin'. I closed him out, like you taught me. I did leave him a message, though. I couldn't help it. Arrogant asshole made me mad."

"Did he tell you his name?" Beatrix raised her eyebrows, hoping against hope—.

"Smith. John Smith is what he told me."

B's shoulders drooped. "Of course. It would have to be him."

"But if he's one of us," Eldridge couldn't stay silent any longer, "surely you can talk to him. Reason with him."

"First," B held up a finger, "he's not one of us. John Smith is, different. A community of one. Second," she now had a peace sign going, "the man has no more reason in him than an attack dog. He'll see me as a rival and this as an excellent chance to get rid of me. Third," she hesitated a moment as if choosing what she would say next very carefully, "if you are what I've hinted that I thought you might be, he cannot allow you to exist."

"What'd I ever do to him?" El said.

"You're my discovery, mine. I found you and Smith won't like that. I'm sorry, but this is no time for happy thoughts and rainbows."

Nicole cut her eyes at him with a bit more respect than her usual.

"I still don't understand why all the fuss."

"I wish I had more time," B said. "But Mr. Smith gives me no choice. Sorry about this, Nicole." She opened a drawer next to the sink and removed a long knife. "If I'm wrong about everything, swear to me you'll get El out of here and on the road back home."

"What are you doing, B?" He took a step forward, but Nicole beat him to it. She grabbed Beatrix's wrist and pinned it.

"Beatrix, baby. What are you doing now?"

B leaned forward and kissed Nicole on the nose and with improbable speed, shifted the knife to her other hand and buried it to the hilt in her own stomach.

Beatrix straightened, pain drawn across her pretty face like cracks in a mirror, and tried to wink at him. At least he though it might be a wink. But she closed her eyes quickly after that and sank to her knees with a groan.

"Jesus Christ, B! What have you done?" He crouched beside her while blood from the wound in her stomach pumped out around the embedded knife blade.

"God, god, god." Nicole knelt behind her and cradled B to the floor, her friend's head in her lap. "Must've cut an artery." She narrowed her eyes and glared at him. "What did she mean *if I'm wrong*? Huh? *Wrong?*" Nicole held B and rocked, her voice rising with every word. "Wrong about you? What the hell's so special about you?"

"I don't know. I don't know." He barely heard his own words through the jumble of panic in his head. "C'mon, B. Please don't do this. Please don't—"

"SHUT UP." Nicole's voice crashed through his paralysis like a freight train through hay bales. "She needs help and 911 doesn't reach out here."

"Ahhh." *He knew what she expected of him, what B's cosmic plan must be. Save her like he saved the cop. Problem is he didn't know* how *he saved the cop.*

"El. Do something." Nicole pounded fists on her thighs. "EL."

"Let's turn her flat on her back," he said. *That ought to give him a few seconds to relive his cop episode, maybe pick up some clues. Trouble is, this was no random accident of destiny. This was intended; a big fat I dare you flung in the face of whatever had possessed him before. Because that's exactly how he remembered it. He'd been possessed. No thinking. No planning.*

Some weird-ass instinct took over that night and worked its magic without him knowing anything. B's little stunt? Not the same thing at all.

Nicole clapped her hands. "HEY, I suggest you get your ass moving Mr. Special. Because my girl is bleeding out on the floor while you sit wringing your hands and whining like a baby." Nicole bent over Beatrix's head and whispered. "Don't you leave me. What were you thinking? Hold on baby girl. I got you. I got you."

El squeezed his eyes for a second to shush the clamor in head.

"Ready?" The thought came quietly, from somewhere unbidden.

He had no idea what to do except move by feel. If it felt right, do it. Trust that B knew more than he. Put faith in what she saw in him. *Concentrate. Concentrate. CONCENTRATE.*

The knife pinned the front of her shirt to her stomach and it took a surprising amount of force to extract it.

It pulled free finally and blood gushed from the dark, two-inch slit like water spurting from a dike.

"Oh, god, baby girl…." Nicole rocked her friend, sobbing.

Eldridge slapped a hand over B's wound and pressed. Her warm stomach gave under his pressure and for a split second he felt a pang of guilt for the intimate violation.

He pressed harder. Blood oozed past his fingers and left red tracks dripping down both sides of her abdomen.

"It's not working," Nicole sobbed. "It's not stopping."

Chapter Nineteen

CLEVER GIRL

John Smith ate half his burger before he realized the kitchen had swallowed up his waitress. One minute she leaves to get him a piece of pie. *"That ol' thing's been settin' there all morning. I'll fetch ya a fresh piece from the back."* The next, she's nowhere to be found.

A local sitting at the far end of the counter, tapping his coffee mug with a spoon and looking pissed, sealed the deal.

Smith held the remaining half of burger in his mouth while he fished his wallet out of a back pocket. He threw a ten on the counter. No sense walking out on the bill and causing a disturbance in the pea-brained crowd of this fine establishment.

He gobbled the burger down in chunks as he slid into the seat of his sports car and turned the key in the ignition. His irritation at being duped amplified by the interruption to his meal. Damn hamburger tasted better than most he'd had in a very long while. Apple pie would have probably been amazing.

He shoved the gearshift into reverse and squealed tires pulling away from the curb. Clearly, waitress Nicole with the closed mind and smart mouth had something to hide. He had a pretty good idea what—or who—that might be.

The girl had skills, he had to hand her that. But no civilian had natural-born immunity that could hold out against his mental onslaught. Nope, waitress Nicole had been taught *to close her mind to probing. It's the only explanation that made sense. But the slippery little twit couldn't hide herself forever. Whatever secrets she held onto in her head were of little consequence now.*

Draw a line from Point A the waitress, to Point B Beatrix Goode and the damn thing tracked straight as the part in his hair. Follow the waitress and she'd lead him to Beatrix and she to her wonder boy, a fait accompli.

Clever Nicole may be able to close her mind, but she couldn't make it invisible.

He whistled *Bad Moon Risin'* as he powered through the gears, following the blip on his mental radar that pointed him toward the waitress.

He barely saw the road as he drove. No need. He let his instincts take over while he entertained himself by imagining the end of his quest and how it would go down.

The end loomed so close he felt it in his crotch. *The Speaker's Pet on her knees, sniveling like a spoiled brat, pleading her case. He'd let her talk; let her think she got to him with her stupid logic.*

Wonder Boy—no, what did she call him—The Amazing El? Yeah, well, he'd amaze Mr. Amazing. Maybe suspend him upside down in mid-air. Maybe open the earth underneath him and bury the little pretender up to his neck. God, the last act would be so righteously good—shit.

He stomped brakes and clutch to the floor and skidded sideways to a stop. A cloud of dust and burnt rubber swept over him and carried out over an expanse of muddy water that came out of nowhere.

Goddammit that was close. Submerging his Boxster in a canal at the edge of the Everglades would have put a serious dent in his schedule.

Those flickering images he'd wrested from waitress Nicole's shifty brain came back to him. Swamp. Waterway. Of course, the bitch hopped onto a boat and sailed off into her sunset, thinking she'd pulled a fast one.

Maybe, she had no idea he'd latched onto her? Right. Maybe the White Sox would sweep the Series this year.

The refrain she'd closed herself off with returned to tease him. *FuckyouFuckyouFuckyouFuckyou....*

In all his fantasizing about the end of his mission, he'd completely ignored Nicole the Waitress. Can't have that now, can we?

Equal pain is the name of this game. She would pay for meddling in affairs that were not hers to meddle in. Pay for standing in his way and worse, actually thinking she could get away with it.

They weren't supposed to mess with civilians *unless it couldn't be helped.* The better to cruise unnoticed under the radar of the common folk. In his considered opinion, exacting a bit of sweet revenge on waitress Nicole belonged in the *Couldn't Be Helped* column.

He smiled to himself and cast outward, anticipating, searching for the meddlesome waitress. *There.* His internal radar put her smack in the middle of the expanse extending out ahead of him. She floated out there somewhere, pulling away with every minute that passed.

No big deal.

He'd find another way to get at her. Surely even this godforsaken country had roads that led somewhere close.

Beatrix had proved a skilled adversary. He brooked no illusions about that. But even the Speaker's Pet couldn't fly. Much less add a carryon to her flight in the form of a certain less than amazing young man.

He'd get them.

This minor setback ate up a little time and convenience. So, this thing wouldn't end as early as he'd imagined. No doubt though, it would end. And he meant to enjoy it.

Except now he'd take longer enjoying it than he might have if things had gone smoother.

Good for him. Too damn bad for Beatrix Goode, Foul-mouthed Nicole the Waitress, and the not so Amazing El.

He meant to squeeze every drop of joy from his end game. He deserved it. And he would have it.

Chapter Twenty

BELIEVE ME NOW?

Eldridge shut Nicole's voice out and closed his eyes, focusing. He saw B's wound in his head, felt the gushing hot blood slow to a trickle, the slits of the wound begin to close. Like before, heat tingled in his palm and fingers.

The warm blush traveled up his arm, growing so hot that he felt sure his arm must be glowing. He risked a peek. Nothing. It looked depressingly normal.

"She's not breathing, El," Nicole whispered. "I think she's getting colder."

Eldridge never broke focus. Never stopped believing. He added his other hand and pressed harder, raising the temperature of the heat in both to blistering levels.

"Oh, Jesus," Nicole said. "Something's happening."

El barely heard her.

Heat traveled up his arms and met at his shoulders and his neck. This time he felt like he knew the process and what to expect and he dialed it up higher.

He felt the flush in his neck rise to his face and homed in on the feeling until he felt like the top of his head might explode.

Then, he felt something else: hands grabbing his and a voice screaming in his ear.

He opened his eyes to see Nicole's desperate hands yanking at his. Her screaming voice snapped him to.

"Stop it, El. It's over. You're hurting her. Quit now."

Focus slid into place like throwing open a dirty window and he looked into B's exhausted face. Her color had gone whiter than white, but those green eyes glistened wet with tears and that wonderful mouth of hers kept trying to smile.

He pulled his hands away and saw the clear imprint of his fingers outlined in a red wash of blood. In the center, where his palm had pressed hardest, the faint outline of a slit grew to a slight filament etched in her skin. It grew fainter as he watched, until it disappeared altogether.

"Thank god I was right about you El," B said. "Now do you believe me?" Her voice sounded reedy and whispery thin. "There's Tylenol in the cabinet. I'm afraid you're going to have another doozy of a headache."

'

Chapter Twenty-One

BAD CONNECTION

John Smith enjoyed the howl of the Boxster's tuned exhaust as he blasted down the highway, warm Everglades wind in his hair, and quarry within striking distance.

After fiddling with the dashboard GPS and overlaying distances his internal radar reported back to him he mapped out a route on the few spider web lines the display offered him. Roads in this part of the country had more to do with accidents of geography and animal trails than people planning.

None of which mattered in the slightest. The end game loomed ever closer. He tapped the dash display and blew a kiss at the red cursor—him—tracking along the faint yellow line on the map.

Somewhere in the map's scrolling expanse of green, dotted with ponds and waterways, his prey—the waitress—puttered along in her boat, heading for a meet-up with Beatrix and her hapless charge, oblivious to the doom zooming toward them in a kickass silver Porsche.

My god, it feels great to be me!

He sent out a tiny feeler, nothing intense, enough to keep tabs on his prize, for reassurance more than anything else. The waitress was a cinch to follow. Her rough energy shone like a headlamp in a coal mine. Last few times he checked, she hadn't moved from the same general area. *Could mean boat trouble, which he doubted. Or, she's reached her destination and tied up somewhere.*

He much preferred that scenario and laughed out loud as he imagined the scene—panicked waitress, wringing her hands, trying to explain *him* to a disbelieving Beatrix and the kid. Then, the mad scramble as they rushed about, getting ready to scurry off like rats.

He widened his scope, centered it on the waitress, and upped the pressure. *Might as well confirm the three musketeers in a tidy little bunch.*

Let's see—ah, yes. Bingo. The whole fam-damly clustered there, blissfully unaware of the judgment speeding their way.

Smith downshifted to pick up speed then shoved the stick back up into fifth gear. *Ooh, baby. I might have to get me one of these....*

He focused his radar because he had nothing better to do, zeroing in on each of the three. *Waitress first? Nah. Too easy.* He moved off her and onto the kid. *No real challenge, either. Beatrix should have spent more time schooling the boy in their ways, at least give the guy a fighting chance.*

He spit into the wind rushing above his head and steeled himself. He saved Beatrix for last on purpose. She would require a bit of finesse, considering her talents.

He probed all around her, using his senses like scalpels, slicing and trimming her protective aura, paring down to expose the soft center of the woman.

BAMMM!

Out of nowhere, the impulse exploded in his head like a psychic tsunami and snapped his neck back. If the headrest hadn't been molded into the seat, the violent wrenching might have cracked a vertebra.

His senses, hijacked by the energy surge, tried to reset themselves. Vision came back slow—black faded gradually up to thinning gray. Deafening white noise lowered its volume but the *SSSHHH* stubbornly held on. Numbness that turned his hands to wood and his legs to stumps subsided to stabbing tingles as feeling gradually returned.

Along with them came awareness. He must have jammed on the brakes when the attack hit and spun the little car to the side of the road. When smell returned, the stink of burnt rubber pierced his consciousness, confirming that he'd stopped beside the highway.

His head felt cleaved down the center and he pressed both palms to his temples and pressed to relieve the pressure. The head felt bad, no doubt. But the agony in his belly quickly gained top billing as stabbing heat flared behind his belt buckle. It felt exactly like someone had sliced his stomach open and poured hot coals inside.

GAAAHHHH!

Smith clenched against the pain and when he had the presence of mind to realize what happened, summoned his wits and switched off his internal radar.

The circuit he'd been maintaining to monitor his quarry out in the ether closed down in an instant and the energy spiked agony disappeared with it.

He sat back in his seat, breathing deeply and consciously slowing his heartbeat. One hand snaked through the front of his shirt to check his abdomen for telltale signs of a wound. The other grabbed the rearview mirror to show him his reflection.

Pale, sweating, hair blown to hell and back. *You've looked better, John boy.*

After several tries the stalled engine finally coughed to life and Smith swerved back onto the highway, pointed in his original direction of travel.

Fists clenched around the wheel in a death grip, Smith snarled out loud into the onrushing wind: *"Don't know what the hell you sent my way, Beatrix. But I promise you, bitch. You want a war? I'm the man to bring it to you."*

Chapter Twenty-Two

THREE AMIGOS

Nicole walked up and back along the Airstream's length, yanking cabinet doors open and slamming them shut. She stepped over Beatrix and Eldridge, both of whom remained slumped on the floor.

"Where's your Tylenol? I'm not finding any."

"That's okay Nicole." El said. "I'm fine."

"My girl says you need Tylenol, you need—"

"Please," he said. "I can't think with all your banging around." He looked at his hands, red blood already darkening in his knuckle creases and under his fingernails. "I'm a little freaked out right now."

"I'm sorry, El," B whispered, pushing herself up to a more comfortable sitting position. "You had to know. Actions speak louder, right? We didn't have time for me to convince you so," she shrugged, "I had to show you."

"You could have died," he said.

"I had faith you wouldn't let me."

"I CAN'T FIND THE TYLENOL." Nicole stood wringing her hands. "Hate to interrupt your chitchat, guys. But I've looked everywhere." She sniffed and wiped her eyes. "You said he'd need it and I'm trying to get it for him but I can't find it."

"Oh, honey," Beatrix said. "Come here." She patted the floor beside her. "Come on, please? Sit." Nicole hesitated a beat before planting herself beside her. Beatrix put her arms around Nicole and the two women hugged. Nicole sobbed while B whispered in her hair.

"There, there, crap, I am so sorry Nikki."

"You. Scared. Me." Nicole huffed the words out between gasps.

"I know. I'm an idiot." Beatrix stroked her hair. "Please forgive me? Can you?"

"You *are* an idiot," Nicole said, her reply muffled in Beatrix's shoulder. "What were you thinking?"

"I wasn't. I do stupid things sometimes and I am so sorry." She cupped Nicole's face in her palms and wiped the other woman's tears with her thumbs. "Forgive me?"

"I don't know yet." Nicole sniffed. "I also don't know what the heck happened. Want to tell me? Anyone? 'Cause from where I'm sitting," she bumped butts with Beatrix, "as God is my witness, your friend there performed a flat out miracle."

Eldridge cleared his throat but Nicole held up her hand.

"You shut up Mr. Amazing. I'm not finished with you. I already got me one Jesus in my life. I don't need another. He and I aren't on speakin' terms, granted. But I been known to spend a Sunday morning at First Congregational in town and I know a miracle when I see one."

"It wasn't a miracle," El said, staring at Beatrix. "Was it?"

"If you both don't mind," Beatrix shifted, "I don't heal as fast on my own without—help. El? Grab my hand for a second?"

He scooted closer and reached out a tentative palm. "Sorry it's kind of gooped up—"

"It's my blood. Let me worry about it." B gripped his hand and leaned her head back, eyes shut.

"Oh, my god." Nicole leapt to her feet.

"It's okay, guys." Beatrix muttered, "I'll move slow for a few hours, that's all. No biggie. El's getting me where I need to be. My body'll do the rest. Relax."

"No biggie?" Nicole snorted. "You two are, I don't know what. Different? I've known you three years girl? Four? Him I've known a couple days and now seeing you together, I'm thinking the two of you are aliens? Angels? Mistakes of nature?"

"I vote for that last one," El said.

"Calm down, Nikki." B shuddered and opened her eyes. "Help me up."

When Nicole didn't make a move she said, "Nicole, it's me. I'm all right. Now, give me your hand."

Beatrix stood and opened the drawer by the sink. She removed a Tylenol bottle and shook it before tossing it down to El. "Humor me," she said.

"Hey—" Nicole said.

"Sorry, Nikki. I said cabinet. I meant drawer." She pulled a bottle of Clorox and paper towels from a narrow closet at the far end and handed them to Nicole. "Could I ask you one last thing? We made a pretty good mess on the floor there."

"Give me those," Nicole said. "Now sit down and heal or whatever it is you have to do." She poured a liberal splash of bleach on the congealing puddle of blood and began mopping it while El flopped his legs side to side to stay out of her way.

"Thanks," B said. "And to answer your other questions Nikki, we're none of those. Least I don't think we are." She leaned against the counter and braced back on her hands.

"El and I are different, yes. We look different. We can do some things. But we're not angels or aliens. We're 100% human, only a tad more *evolved*, let's say. Our mothers carried us much longer than normal and this is how we came out."

"Longer?" Nicole said. "How much long—"

"Twelve months," Beatrix said, "instead of nine. Give or take a couple weeks."

Nicole stopped scrubbing long enough to whistle. "Your poor mothers."

B shrugged. "Things happened to us in those few extra months. Evolution threw a few switches, DNA swapped around. I'm no geneticist, okay? Short story is we took an evolutionary jump ahead. But, we're very rare. Most die of complications. Those that don't, come out like this."

El stood to wash his hands in the sink. "So, *accidents of nature* nails it after all." When he passed near Nicole she made a point of scooting away from him.

"Nicole, we're nothing to be afraid of." Beatrix said. "You're my girl, you know that. And El here, he may be terrifying to look at—"

"Hey, now—" Eldridge tested water at the sink for heat.

Nicole huffed.

"But he's harmless," B rubbed her stomach thoughtfully, "in a very special way."

"What he did," Nicole made one last swipe and wadded up the paper towels and stood, "you can't?"

B shook her head. "That's why we're hiding out here. 'Cause of what he can do that no one else can."

"Seems to me," Nicole placed the sopping pink towels in B's outstretched hand, "a gift like that ain't somethin' you hide. I've only known your boyfriend for a little while—"

"He's not my boyfriend."

"I'm not her…she's not my…"

"Shut up," Nicole held up a hand, "not the point. I'm saying people need what he has, in all kinds of ways. Not only those magic healing hands. But what he represents. He's hope, B, in a world that doesn't have much. I'm not very smart, okay? Or religious. But I know folks in every religion on earth been lookin' for a sign of better things comin'. Jesus or the Rapture or whatever they want to call it. Well, I seen the *sign* with my own eyes."

"Honey," Beatrix tossed the towels in the sink, "it's not that simple."

"Like I said, y'all are the geniuses here. I'm a simple country girl. What do I know? Sermon's over."

"She's right," El said.

Both women stopped and looked at him. Nicole smiled. Beatrix started shaking her head.

"Eldridge, you don't know enough yet."

"I know I healed a stab wound in your stomach with my *hands*. If they weren't attached to my own arms I wouldn't believe it." He waggled his fingers. "But I did it, with *these*. I told myself the cop might have been a fluke thing. Nope."

"There's more to it than that," Beatrix said. "You don't know the half of it."

"I know enough of it. Nicole's right. Hiding away from people isn't the answer. Taking it to them, is."

"But—"

"I get it'll have to be managed. Don't worry, I'm not still on my Amazing El thing."

"Amazing El?" Nicole said.

"Don't ask," Beatrix grimaced.

"You said it yourself, B. I'm different. I'm special. Okay, fine. Let's see how special I am. I got you to help me."

"I'm in, if you'll have me," Nicole raised her hand like a schoolgirl. "Just keep those mitts of yours off me."

"And there, we got Nicole," El clapped his hands. "Who can stop us? *Ahhh!*" El grabbed his head.

"Headache? I told you—"

"No headache. It's like from before. A tickle in my brain."

"Who can stop us? Funny you should ask," B said. "I got a feeling we rang John Smith's doorbell big time earlier. I'm guessing he's royally pissed about now and heading our way."

Chapter Twenty-Three

POOR BROTHER BERNARD

When Bernard returned, Mother deliberately pulled the edge of the purple coverlet down below her breasts and widened the gap in her robe. She wanted Bernard to see the evidence with his own eyes. To witness the scarlet stripes and bruises, the welts and black crusting blood he had inflicted upon her—at her urging, of course. A fine point she chose to ignore.

"Come closer, Bernard."

"Yes, Mother." He shuffled forward with his head down.

"Look at me."

Bernard stayed unmoving. Did he have his eyes shut? If she had a better angle she could be sure.

"I said, look to the heavens with me, Bernard. Cast your eyes up so the Lord may see your obedient countenance. Let us both share our love of the Lord."

The trick worked. Bernard raised his head and opened his eyes to look skyward. She raised her own head, of course, but kept her eyes fixed upon Bernard. She needed to see a true reaction from him when confronted with his handiwork.

She harbored a secret belief that he'd actually enjoyed flogging her with the riding crop, that the extent of her wounds came as much from his own pleasure as hers.

That she could not allow.

"My child," she whispered. "I wish to thank you for your devotion."

That did it. Bernard lowered his eyes and she drank in every shift in them, every twitch of his mouth, every nuance of the way he held his body. Battered and broken as it may be, and thus an unreliable indicator of how a healthy Bernard might react, his body should still mirror his inner self.

She prided herself on reading people and she focused her immense gifts on reading Bernard.

Nothing.

She shifted and let slip the slightest groan. Even swiped a finger at an imaginary tear.

Bernard held her eyes with the unflinching gaze of a life-sized doll.

Still nothing. After she suffered so grievously? Not even the faintest hint of remorse?

This squirmy little worm of a man had blood on his hands he would never be able to wash off. He may as well have dashed his arms up to the elbows in a bucket of her blood.

God help him should those narrow lips of his reveal the tiniest upturn at their corners. She narrowed her eyes and focused intently, praying as only a Mother can, to sense the bare quivering hint a smile.

Again, nothing. Whatever emotions he possessed, beyond the usual fear and greed that drove all men, he gripped them tight. The man was wood inside and she respected that.

She still intended to make him pay, of course, and the price would be dear. But the little coward's stoic act robbed her of exacting any real pleasure from what she planned on his behalf.

"I am worried, Bernard." She let that sink in a beat. "For you."

The man finally reacted. He shifted his bandaged arm in its sling and flinched slightly. "How so, Mother?"

"I am worried that you did not go far enough with the task I appointed." She opened her robe and pulled the silk coverlet all the way to her knees. "I still see flesh unadorned with your punishment." She lightly traced a finger from neck to knees. "You missed some spots."

"Mother, I despair at the damage I inflicted upon you. I truly do." His voice slid from his throat in an inflection-less rasp. "My soul is sick at what—" he licked his lips, "at what you made me do."

"Not I, Bernard, the Lord. At what the *Lord* made you do. I cannot believe my ears, Bernard. Will you really stand before me, His holy instrument, and question His motives? His actions?"

The man chose not to answer. Probably realizing no adequate answer existed. He shook his head and remained silent, but his shifty eyes shot glances right and left like a cornered rat. *Perhaps he thinks he might still escape my trap?*

Mother smiled at this small weakness. At least she had that. She could always rely upon fear as her most reliable lever with Bernard.

"I have been asking the Lord's guidance about you, Bernard. About what He suggests I do with you." She heaved a deep sigh to show how much it pained her.

"But, Mother, I acted solely at your direction. You don't know how it hurt me. How I ache for you now."

"You think I don't know about pain?" Her voice climbed from a hissing whisper to a shout. "You dare stand there and look at me and say that? I DON'T KNOW PAIN? I DON'T KNOW ACHE?"

She saw a faint quiver run through the man's body, but only a faint one. The old Bernard would have been reduced to trembling custard. This one standing before her shut down his emotions and turned to a statue worthy of Lot and his wife.

Fine, then. She would get no more pleasure from Bernard. Either put him out of his misery or hers. Neither choice made the slightest difference.

Mother crawled sideways in the bed sheets and extended her hand to the side table. She grasped the brass bell sitting there and shook vigorously. She gritted her teeth against the bright *CLANGCLANG* so close to her aching head and shook the bell all the harder until her door opened and a meek acolyte stepped inside. Mother had no prayer of recalling the young woman's name.

"You."

"Yes, Mother?"

"Get this man from my sight."

"Yes, Mother. Right away."

"Write him a check from my personal account for one thousand dollars. Not a penny less. Then show him the door."

"But, Mother." Blood drained from Bernard's face and made the bruises on his head and neck stand out stark against his pasty skin.

Mother held up a finger. "No, no, Bernard. Don't thank me. It's the least I can do for your service."

She turned her attention back to the young woman. "Escort him from the premises. Ask for help if you need to. He is to be banished from our Order."

"Mother, please, I beg you," Bernard shifted his feet.

Finally, a reaction.

"And when you do, let it be known amongst our faithful that this man attacked me. That already weakened as I am by his hand, he wanted more and tried to finish what he started."

"God, no, Mother." Bernard gripped his hands in fists and croaked his protest. "That is not true."

"That even now, with you and I as witnesses dear young lady, this vile creature has invoked the Lord's name in vain," she pointed at Bernard with a trembling finger, "and threatens me with balled up fists."

"I have always been faithful to you, Mother. Always."

"Come to think of it, young one. Go get help right now. Bernard and I will wait. And don't worry about me, the Lord will protect me."

The young lady scampered out the door and Mother smiled as she heard the woman shouting for assistance down the hallway.

"How could you do this to me, Mother? Why?"

"So that your part of our atonement might be as complete as mine. Thank you, Brother Bernard. May He protect you in His mercy and His love."

The door banged open and two muscular young men with the young woman trailing behind, rushed into the room and clamped hands on Bernard's arms. The arm in the sling got no deferential treatment and Mother smiled as his howls of agony echoed out of the bedroom and down the hall to be quickly silenced by the immensity of the complex.

She had built an amazing tribute to the Lord and she knew in her heart the thick walls and marble floors of *In His Name* were necessary for moments such as this. She knew they pleased Him and her pleasure, though great, was only a reflection of His.

Chapter Twenty-Four

TROUBLE AHEAD

Beatrix's little Camaro barely fit Nicole in front and El in the back, with the bags and boxes of supplies hastily crammed in amongst them. Every time El shifted in back, like every five minutes, B heard bags rustle and crunch.

"Jeez, El. You have the whole backseat to yourself. Which you asked for I might add." She adjusted her rearview mirror to see El staring out the side window. "Please don't squash the merchandise."

Eldridge remained silent. Not like him at all and that worried her. Granted, bringing back someone from the brink—twice—could mess with your mind. She looked over at Nicole in the passenger seat and her friend raised her eyebrows.

B tried again. "I want to apologize again, El, for putting you through that. Spur of the moment, you know? I had to make you see yourself for what you are. Or, have the potential to become."

She gripped the wheel and concentrated on navigating the last of the rough off-road terrain. Blacktop approached over the rise ahead and they would soon put real highway under their wheels.

El bumped and swayed with the antics of the car, silent and staring.

She readjusted her mirror. "Fine. We'll talk when you're ready."

The wheels spun as Beatrix slid up onto the road and put pedal to metal. She scanned the road behind them for cars. Any vehicle approaching fast might be Smith and she had no wish to be overtaken by him.

The needle climbed past 80.

"Girl?" Nicole made a point of clicking her seatbelt. "You know they do occasionally patrol this get-me-anywhere-but-here piece of Florida highway."

The needle nudged past 90 and settled on 95. Beatrix looked over at her friend and grinned. The big engine roared and the wind and tires whistled and hummed.

"Okay, okay. I tried. Don't want us to push our luck, is all."

"Nicole, I need to get him somewhere safe," she inclined her head toward the backseat, "and I know John Smith, whom you had the distinct displeasure to meet, is on our ass. I need to put distance between us, wherever we go. Trust me. That man will ruin our day."

"I want to go home." The voice from behind her spoke low, not a whisper, but quiet. "That's where I am being called."

"What's that?" B said.

"Home. I need to go home." El straightened and pulled himself forward. "It's where I belong."

"Absolutely not, El. Bad idea. Epic bad idea."

"I need to be grounded, Beatrix."

It's Beatrix now?

"I need people around me I can trust. Who love me. People with no hidden agendas."

B twisted around to look at him and Nicole placed a steadying hand on the steering wheel.

"My only agenda is you, El, that's it. End of story."

Eldridge gritted his teeth and visibly struggled to compose himself. "How many people have you brought back from dead, B?" he asked quietly. "Huh? Tell me."

"You know the answer to that."

"You know those consequences you keep bringing up? What's supposed to happen to me for using my so-called gifts?"

"El—"

"Guess what, B? I felt nothing this time. No real headache. No disorientation. No negative effects at all."

Beatrix turned her eyes back to the road to process that little gem.

"Nothing? Not a twinge?" She angled her mirror to see El staring back at her, shaking his head slowly.

Definitely getting stronger.

"I'm not sure what that means, El," she said.

"I am." He shoved back into the seat and crossed his arms. "It's pointing the way; showing me what I *have* to do."

"Don't read too much into this."

He smiled to himself and resumed staring out the window.

"Eldridge Montcalm. I mean it." Beatrix raised her voice. "We can't afford to be divided on this."

El propped a foot on his knee and picked at his shoe, engrossed.

"I'm serious, El. Home is the last place you need to be. Don't you think it's being watched? I know our people have it on their radar. Think again, Mr. Amazing."

He looked up suddenly and frowned. "You think people have forgotten about me? What I did? Saving that cop?"

She glanced in the mirror. "Most, not all of them. News outlets probably still keep tabs on where you lived. You were big news, once."

"Yeah, past tense. What if they have forgotten me and moved on?"

"We can only hope."

"I can't have that."

Nicole cleared her throat. "Um, girl? You might want to slow down."

"You can't have what, El? You don't know what you're—"

"B. SLOW DOWN." Nicole pounded on the dash and pointed.

Shit.

B stomped the brakes and brought her thundering car to a screeching, sliding halt. She fishtailed a little but held her lane. She and Nicole strained forward against their seatbelts. El thrust forward between the front seats, clawing at the vinyl to stop his momentum. The tang of burnt rubber filled the car.

At least a couple dozen cars stopped ahead of them, brake lights shining red. No traffic moved on either side of the highway. Farther down the road, red and blue flashing lights clustered beneath a wispy plume of black smoke. A bright lick of flame tinged the base of the smoke orange.

"Oh, my good Lord." Nicole leaned forward, squinting. "What's happened?"

"There's been a wreck," B said. "Looks like a bad one." She pounded the wheel and scanned the highway behind them for fast-approaching cars. "How the hell does somebody wreck on a perfectly straight road with practically no traffic? Tell me that."

"You know it's a bad one, B," Nicole said. "The speeds cars go out here." She shuddered and glanced back at El. "Please God watch over those folks up there. Touch them with your mercy and your grace." She crossed herself.

The strident blare of a car horn sounded behind them and a TV news van rushed up, straddling the road and the shoulder. It swooshed by them, the driver leaning on and off his horn.

"Where the hell did those vultures come from?" Beatrix said.

"Must have been a while since the wreck," Nicole said. "Time enough for them to get their heads outa their scanners."

"Well, that's great. The only road for miles, no turn-offs, we can't go forward. We're damn sure not going back. Only thing worse would be for John Smith to drive up our ass while we sit here."

She scanned the road behind them. All clear, thank god.

"Ladies," El said as he rummaged through the bags and boxes on the seat beside him. "If you'll excuse me." He cleared a space to the door and scooted over. "Nicole, I believe God has answered your prayer."

He opened the door and a rush of heat sucked all the A/C out of the car. "There's no place *safe*, B, for me or anyone. Ask those people in the cars up there."

"El, what the shit do you think you're doing? Close that door."

"Sorry, Beatrix." He stepped out and bent to look in before slamming it shut. "I have to do this. I'm called to do this."

He looked at her with a sad, scared look that broke her heart. "Damn it, El," B said under her breath as she yanked her door handle. "Stay here, Nikki. You won't want to see this."

"Not likely," Nicole said. "I go where you go. What if our boy needs our help?"

The two women exited the Camaro and scurried after Eldridge, already jogging along the line of cars toward whatever nightmare waited up ahead in the flame and smoke.

Chapter Twenty-Five

GOTCHA!

Smith drove fifteen or twenty minutes with his internal radar gone dark. Pain didn't frighten him. He kind of liked it in fact, in the correct doses. But that fire that sliced open his gut a while ago he'd rather not ever feel again. Obviously, Beatrix Goode and her little band got into some shit and he paid the price.

He kneaded the memory behind his belt. Having no internal radar compromised his search big time. But, from what he remembered of their previous position, they probably lay somewhere east and north of his current position.

Fine, John boy. Go with your gut on this one, abused as it is.

He smiled at his clever turn of phrase.

Gut it is.

He raised the internal shades on his search radar and found his fugitives immediately. No pain in the gut. No hazy location in the middle of the frigging swamp. The sheer speed of their retreat meant they had to be on a highway. And there weren't that many damn highways in this shitty part of the state.

He probed once again to confirm his results. The kid, like before, completely unshielded. Beatrix may or may not be there. She showed up as a hazy presence at best. *But hey now, what's this?* He pushed a little to be sure.

No shit! That waitress from the diner with the decent firewall in her head—she wasn't on high alert this time so he penetrated easily— she's along for the ride? What the hell is that about?

111

No big deal. He grinned and stomped the accelerator. In fifth gear, the little Porsche's exhaust note fairly sang.

Let's party, folks. And Beatrix, Speaker's little pet or not, you and I are going to have us one helluva dance.

He set cruise control on 95—he had to make up ground on his quarry. Beatrix obviously didn't give a crap about attracting attention rocking along at her speed. Why should he?

Thirty minutes passed, sixty. The itch in his head grew more squirmy-delicious the closer he got to his prey. It felt good to let the sensation wash through him and he became reckless with his probing.

No pain, not even a whisper of pain, in the last hour convinced him none waited to pounce on the horizon. So be it.

Reveling in thoughts of ending the chase and fantasizing about what he might do to Beatrix Goode and her little companions—anything that wouldn't leave an outward mark counted as fair game.

Smith prided himself on his creative flair when it came to exacting revenge. He liked to think his particular skills marked him as uniquely gifted.

He could boil bone marrow with a look. Cramp every major muscle group. Fracture a femur with cracks so tiny only a microscope would detect them. Yet, the pain he'd inflict. Sweet Jesus, it would be so exquisite.

Thoughts like these almost ran him into the rear of a jacked-up pickup at the end of a long line of traffic stopped dead on the road ahead. Only his unearthly reflexes and German engineering saved the little car and him from an abrupt and very untidy consequence.

When the tire smoke cleared and his wits yanked him back into the present, he took stock of the situation. Traffic stretched at least a mile in front of him. People milling about outside their cars told him no one had moved in quite a while.

If his luck held, Beatrix and her crew were caught in the same tie-up. Maybe she and her friends were the cause of it. How sweet would that be?

Far, far ahead he saw black smoke rising into a cloudless, azure sky. He loosened his tie and rolled up his shirtsleeves. *Why not?*

In the convertible, the sun felt warm on his skin. The air tasted fresh, if a tad humid. All in all, a perfect day for a car wreck. He got out of his car like the rest of the traffic victims and strolled down the line of stopped cars. He intended to go only so far. Maybe push the edge on a quick return in case traffic began to move suddenly.

It became depressingly apparent that a quick return to highway speed would be a ways off. The sound of an approaching helicopter, news or Life Flight it made no difference, seconded that thought.

Whatever stopped traffic this long and required a helicopter's presence had to be significant.

The sound of rotors thump-thumping overhead deafened him as a white helicopter with a red cross on its side, blasted down the line of cars, skimming the air barely thirty feet above them.

He debated going back to his car to relax and kick back in the seat. Satellite radio gave him a ton of choices. Maybe he'd find a good comedy channel or better, a sex addicts call-in program.

Then the car halfway down the long line with open doors on both sides caught his eye. A yellow Camaro, exactly the sort of forbidden flash Beatrix Goode cultivated. It called to him.

He broke into a jog—quick return to his own car be damned— and reached the Camaro in minutes. The interior looked like thieves had tossed it. An array of supplies—bags and boxes— crammed into all corners. Someone had beaten a hasty retreat in this thing.

He bent down and laid a hand on the steering wheel.

The sharp presence of Beatrix Goode cramped all the way up his arm. *Oww.* He yanked his hand back and rubbed it on his jeans.

YeeHAW. Good times ahead!

He hurried toward the front of the line. *Beatrix and her boy had to be there.*

He almost let loose a lightning bolt of presence to signal his approach but resisted at the last second. Their shock at his appearance built anticipation in him so exquisite he felt it in his penis.

The closer he got to the action, the more he focused on the sights and sounds surrounding him. Radio chatter from walkie-talkies, people screaming and yelling, the crackle of fires blazing out of control, the background roar of engines from ambulances and the helicopter filled him with fierce delight.

He stopped a moment and closed his eyes to savor the full effect.

My god, nothing compared to the deadly chaos of a disaster going full bore only footsteps away.

A sudden burst of people shouting and cheering, whistles and handclaps snapped him from his pleasurable reverie.

What the hell? Not something you expect to hear at a tragedy.

He edged forward to get a closer look.

Chapter Twenty-Six

THE AMAZING EL

Eldridge pushed to the front of a crowd forming a rough perimeter around a nightmare. The ebb and flow of people moved steadily front to back as those closest to the horror lost the stomach for it and had to retreat.

He wormed his way around the last couple of holdouts standing in his way only to be blocked by an ashen-faced trooper with his arms stretched wide, trying to keep people from pressing closer.

"Back up. Back the hell up. You don't want to see this."

Two of his uniformed counterparts broadcast the same message at other spots around the circling crowd, their efforts helped considerably by thc gruesome carnage itself.

Fire blazed in three vehicles, two others were covered in blankets of white foam. A charred pickup squatted on four melted tires. A motorhome lay on its side on the shoulder, the skin along its length peeled back like a tin of sardines. A collapsed mangle of twisted metal and glass, recognizable as an automobile only by one turned-under wheel, occupied prime position in the center of the nightmare.

Everywhere, officials in uniform—firemen, EMTs and state troopers—raced between vehicles. El counted at least ten in the multi-vehicle disaster. Cars and SUVs in various positions, slewed sideways, overturned. Bits and pieces of car parts, bumpers and mirrors and a set of car seats sitting unaccountably upright smeared with blood littered the highway. Shattered glass sparkled everywhere on the ground, gruesome jewels reflecting light from a million tiny prisms.

The stink in the air came thick and fast and touched a gag reflex in the back of El's throat—scorched meat and metal, burnt rubber and gasoline, chemical from the sprayed foam and vomit from weak stomachs overcome by it all.

What didn't fit the scene was the quiet. Sure, shouts came from first responders going about their jobs, cops on radios and traffic control, the whoosh of fire hoses and the crackle of flames.

But no one in the gathering crowd spoke much above a whisper. Out of horror, respect, numbness, El couldn't guess.

Blue tarps dotted the tragic landscape. Draped over pieces of cars and shapeless forms on the ground. Beneath the blue, bulges and soft protrusions and sharp points invited speculation as to what grimness they hid. Certainly nothing anyone in the crowd would admit, in their heart of hearts, to really wanting to see.

Eldridge surveyed the scene, silent as those crowded around him, when a compulsion from deep inside seized him. He mirrored the trooper in front of him, spreading his arms wide, palms turned *toward* the scene. He threw back his head, closed his eyes, and let this new sense absorb the energies crisscrossing in front of him.

He felt and saw what normal eyes could never discern. Thick currents of life bending and twisting together, like eddies in a pond. Brighter, stronger flows came from the workers at the scene. The energies moved with their hosts, streaking purposeful auras in their wake.

He didn't reflect on this newfound sense. Something told him he had no time for it.

He concentrated on the auras, focusing especially on the faint, flickering pulses that hovered around the victims. He knew, from the strength of the impulses, which of the victims clung most precariously to life and which had more time.

The dimmest glow came from off to his left. Masked by the intense life flows given off by two EMTs, he almost missed it. The fading life force hid behind the strong pulses from the frantic pair working to forestall the inevitable.

"Clamp it. Clamp the artery, Jesus."

"Pulse is thready. We're losing her."

"Come on, honey. We're right here. Hold on."

"Shit. Starting compressions. One - two - three...."

"Charging!"

Eldridge mapped the scene in his head, using the faint auras as touch points, starting with the young woman being worked on to his left. He started forward when a hand grabbed his shoulder.

#

Beatrix and Nicole reached the back edges of the crowd and pushed through, following in Eldridge's wake. B took the lead with Nicole glued to her rear.

Beatrix sidestepped pale-faced gawkers shuffling to the rear, hurrying to leave whatever they'd been so eager to see minutes earlier.

The two women made good time through the crowd. B saw Eldridge at the very front, standing with his arms wide and head back.

Oh, no.

She felt him pushing outward, reading the scene. Something he'd never done before and she had certainly never taught him.

Crap.

"EL," she tried yelling to get his attention. "Stop it. NO." But he remained transfixed, motionless.

Dammit.

She caught up to him as people started edging away. Several scooted by her, glancing back fearfully at the crazy man gripped in a trance.

"El," she clapped a hand on his shoulder, "what do you think you're doing?" She shook him. "Stop it."

He snapped to and turned to look at her. She saw tears glistening in his eyes and overwhelming sadness.

"I know what I have to do, B." He shrugged out of her grip and dodged to the left, scooting past the harried trooper and across the debris-filled ground.

She had no choice but to follow.

He headed straight for two EMTs working frantically over a young girl. One performed CPR while the other tended a monitor, checking for a pulse. Beatrix had enough time to take in the Disney mermaid t-shirt ripped up the middle and shiny shank of metal protruding from the girl's chest.

El reached them a few seconds ahead of her and crouched beside them.

CPR guy snarled at him. "Hey, you. Get the fuck out of here."

"MOVE." El shoved the EMT aside.

The man toppled sideways and scrambled back to his knees, fury wrinkling his face, as Beatrix arrived.

She knelt in front of the man and grabbed his shirtfront. "Please," she said. "Let him work."

The wailing alarm on the monitor interrupted them and they turned to see the second EMT shake her head and stand up. "She's gone," she said.

Beatrix shifted all her attention to El in time to see him ease the piece of metal from the little girl's body and fling it aside. It clanked as the woman EMT kicked it and said to her partner, "Leave them. We have others who need us."

The pair grabbed their bags and equipment and scurried off while El stroked hair from the little girl's face and arranged her arms and legs into more natural positions.

He pressed both hands on the wound in her chest and closed his eyes. B knew what he was attempting and she and Nicole shielded him as best they could from prying eyes and any first responders that may want to intervene.

A full minute passed, then more. It felt like an hour, when a tiny voice called out, "Mommy?" The quaver turned to a shriek. "MOMMY."

"You'll be okay, now, honey." El left a bloody streak on her forehead as he tried once again to push that stubborn lock of hair aside. He looked up at his two friends. "Nicole, take care of her. B, follow me." He jumped to his feet and hesitated a moment before running across to a different EMT team.

Beatrix left Nicole to comfort the little girl and chased after El.

"Leave me. Save my wife. Leave me be." A man crumpled on the ground, leaning against the tire of a smashed in sports car, pounded a fist on the car door. He slapped the hands away of the EMTs trying to render aid and repeated his pleas. "My wife. Save my wife."

"Sir, she didn't make it. We need to get you stabilized."

"No. Her, save her."

"Tranq him or we'll lose him, too."

Beatrix followed Eldridge around the mangled vehicle to the passenger side and the point of impact. The man's wife, pinned in crumpled metal, had open, staring eyes. Jagged tears in the sheet metal and doorframe showed where firemen had applied pry bars to get to her before giving up and moving on.

El leaned in close and touched his forehead to the woman's before straightening. He grabbed the side of the doorframe with both hands.

"No, El. It's too much. You can't."

"Grab me around the waist."

"Please, El."

"I need your energy. Together, we can do this." He set his feet and pulled.

B had no other option. She did as he asked. She circled her arms around him and almost let go. The surge of power coursing through him shocked her and forced her to renew her grip and hold tighter.

She heard it before anything else—the squeal and groan of metal being forced to take a different shape. A loud crack split the air and she fell backward. She landed on her butt and saw El sitting on the ground in front of her with a piece of door in his lap. He turned and flashed a goofy grin that lasted all of a second before he scrambled to his feet and hurried to the woman in the car.

A pushed-in dash crushed her against the seat back. El shoved it off her as if the splintered vinyl and plastic connected to nothing but air. He cradled the still form of the woman in his arms, lifted her free of the wreck and laid her on the ground.

Like with the little girl, he arranged her limbs comfortably beside her. "I'm going to need your help again, B."

"She's gone, El." B took in the woman's caved-in chest and glassy eyes. "You can't save this one."

He paid her no mind as he traced his hands lightly up and down her torso. "Sit here, beside me. Don't be afraid."

"This woman is gone, El."

He scanned the air above the car. "She's not gone far. Trust me, B." He spread his hands wide and placed them on the woman's chest. "Put your hands below mine, but touching. We have to be touching." He glanced quickly upwards. "Hurry."

She did as he asked, laid her spread-fingered hands below his. Their four hands spanned up and down the length of the woman's torso. She felt El's little finger reach for hers and she linked with it.

"Don't press hard on this one," he said. "This one's different."

She felt instant heat emanate from their linked fingers, like electricity glowing in the coils of a space heater. The warmth transferred to the woman's body under her hands and they stayed that way, she and El, hands pressed to the poor dead woman's body as heat built up between them.

An eternity passed before she felt the first movement. Beneath her right palm, something shifted under the woman's skin. She glanced at El but his eyes were closed, sweat beading on his forehead. Another, sharper jolt came as movement traveled up and down the woman's form.

She knew what was happening, in her head. Could even rationalize it. She, of all people, knew El's capabilities. Still, in her heart, astonishment gave way to awe.

The woman's chest expanded beneath their hands. Ribs knit back together, spine popped and straightened. She felt the first clench of the woman's heart and the swell of her lungs as the dead woman took in air for the first time.

"Barry," the woman coughed weakly. "Honey, where are you?"

"Baby?" the voice called from the far side of the car. "That's my wife. I told you. I TOLD YOU."

El fell backwards and took Beatrix with him. His face glistened with sweat and tears flowed from cherry red eyes. "Thank you," he said. "Without you," he wiped his face on a short sleeve, "I couldn't…she wouldn't…" He didn't finish the rest, collapsing instead into a wrenching bout of sobs.

The EMTs working on the husband hurried around the car and quickly surveyed the scene. They looked from the woman to the two of them and back to the woman before kneeling and getting to work.

Beatrix hugged El and let him cry. She rocked him for a few moments, feeling his sobs, until he stiffened and pushed away. "El?"

"I'm good. Thanks."

He tried to stand, but wobbled and fell back to his knees.

"What the hell do you think you're doing? You sit there."

He reached out a hand. "Help me up."

"You're in no shape to—"

"IT'S NOT FINISHED." His shout halted activity happening around them for a brief second before the actors in the tragedy resumed their duties. "Fine, I'll do it myself."

He made it to one knee before she relented and came to his aid. She pulled and he stood, wavering. She ducked under one arm as Nicole ran up and slipped under his other.

"There," he indicated with his head. "Those two."

She looked over at what had to be parents, pacing behind a pair of EMTs. They were the same two EMTs that worked over the first young girl.

"NOOO," the mother wailed as the first responders quit their ministrations and sat back. The woman EMT rose to comfort the woman, who shook her off. "Get away from me. Save my baby. MY BABY."

El and Beatrix shuffled up as the EMTs began packing equipment.

"You again?" the male EMT stood, hands clenching and unclenching. "Get the hell away from here, buddy, before something bad happens to you."

"Let 'im be, Sal," the female said quietly. "Haven't you been watching?" She stood beside her partner and grabbed his arm. She looked at B, El and now Nicole and said, "Can you really do this?"

Beatrix had no words and El didn't have the energy to waste. She walked him toward the still form of a young boy lying on the ground. About twelve, maybe thirteen, he wore a Little League uniform. The *Yankees* emblazoned across his chest looked huge for the little boy wearing it.

Unlike the other victims, this one had no visible signs of trauma, other than the support collar the EMTs strapped around his neck.

El turned to her and licked his lips. "I might need your help. I'm a little weak—"

"I know, El. Shut up. I'm here."

He knelt beside the still body and, like earlier, scanned the space above him. He nodded and leaned forward, laying his head on the young boy's chest.

He stayed that way for a moment and then groped behind him with a free hand. Beatrix stepped up and grabbed it with both of hers. "I'm here, El. I'm here." He pulled her close and she knelt beside him while he remained bent over, head on the young victim's chest.

Like previously, she felt the heat pulsing from El to her. They stayed locked in that position while, this time, as far as she could tell, nothing was happening. Absolutely nothing.

Chapter Twenty-Seven

GRAB HANDS

Smith knew something happened from the people in the crowd around him. The mood actually shifted as he walked amongst them, pushing his way through. He felt it and heard it when excitement and curiosity supplanted stunned horror. Energized gawkers spread whispers through the crowd.

"It's a miracle."

"I saw him do it, no lie."

"I'm tellin' you, he pulled the door right off in his bare hands. No bullshit."

A young man spoke wide-eyed to anyone around who'd listen. It stopped Smith in his tracks.

"She came back to life I tell you. One minute, dead meat. The next, crying for her mommy. It was epic, man."

Smith grabbed the man by his shirtfront. "What did you see? Tell me. Exactly."

"Hey, fella. Cool your jets."

Smith let go reluctantly and tried his best to actually smile. "Sorry … It's only … I think I have family involved in that."

"You're right, man. You do," the young man said.

"How's that?"

"Two of them. Your family has some crazy screwed up DNA I'll tell you."

"My family?"

"Dude that looks like you and a woman, big heads and all, doing some wacko shit."

Smith shoved the young man aside—*"Hey, not cool dude."*—And pushed forward.

The people barrier in front of him gave way begrudgingly. The closer to the front, the harder it got. Men and women pressed forward eagerly to get a glimpse of what the whispers were saying.

He finally made it through to the edge of the cordoned off area. A few overworked cops stalked the front lines behind hastily strung yellow tape, desperate to keep back a crowd growing increasingly disgruntled and eager to SEE SOMETHING.

Smith took in the scene before him with relish. The chaos, the carnage, the multi-layered stink of burnt *everything*. *My GOD this is exhilarating.* Strung tight as tripwire, he inhaled the thick swirl of emotions and let them sink into his skin.

Smith focused on the people, singles and groups, unwilling actors in a tragedy none chose and many would not survive. Victims, who could, wandered aimlessly with stunned looks until corralled by a uniform and taken for treatment. Those who couldn't move sat moaning or crying in pain.

Law enforcement scurried from body to body, calling for medical aid when appropriate or waving it off with a shaking head and unfurling tarp.

A flurry of activity beside a smashed-in blue minivan caught Smith's eye and he squinted through wafting black smoke and a meandering screen of bodies.

A pair of EMTs and two adults, parents he surmised, stood arguing beside the still form of a youngster prostrate on the asphalt. He couldn't make out their words but he didn't need to. The two first responders argued about something. The two parents ignored them and focused their anguish on the activity surrounding their child.

Crouched over the tiny form, at the epicenter of that activity, his quarry worked. Beatrix he recognized immediately. The other one, had to be the imposter she called "El," knelt with his head pressed to the injured one's chest. Smith had never laid eyes on the kid, but the head shape and pale skin he knew intimately. No wonder the punk in the crowd thought he saw a family resemblance.

Apart from the pair, the bitch waitress from the diner stood with eyes closed and her hands plastered together. Her lips moved like she was praying.

Well, time for daddy to serve up a little tough love to his family. Smith would have preferred a less conspicuous place for their takedown. But he craved food, his back ached, he'd come a long frigging way to end B's little charade and with the end in his grasp, the prospect of attaining the goal he'd boldly announced to The Council proved irresistible.

He ducked under the yellow tape when the cop had his back turned and picked his way to the scene beside the crumpled van.

Smoke stung his eyes and he held his breath passing through a particularly thick smoke cloud. He felt himself grinning as his pulse quickened and he closed the distance between them.

He got there in time to hear Beatrix pleading with her star pupil.

"El, he's gone," she said. "It's over. You've done too much and you're too weak."

"No. He's still here."

The one she called El raised his head off the chest of a little boy in a baseball uniform. He looked up at nothing Smith could see.

"There's still a chance. We can do this." El quickly laid his head back down on the little chest and tugged B closer. "Please, help me."

Smith saw the boy's mother look over at him and her eyes widen as she took in his *family resemblance.*

"Help them," she shrieked. "Why are you standing there?" She rushed over and tugged at his arm. "Save my boy. SAVE HIM."

Smith watched Beatrix turn at the mother's pleas. She saw him standing behind them yet, what should have been a triumph for him, seeing her surprise and despair, gave him nothing. *What the hell? She had to know he won and she lost.*

If anything, Beatrix looked relieved, almost happy. "Hold on, El," she said. Then, she thrust her hand behind her. "Grab it," she said.

What was this?

"Come on, Smith." She snapped her fingers. "We need your help. Grab hands."

Fine. If that's how she wants to play it.

He grabbed her hand, intending to yank the bitch to her feet, but the moment they linked fingers, all thoughts of that vanished.

A muscle spasm closed his hand in hers and a low level buzz tickled up his arm. Like those Test Your Grip Meter carnival games the tingling grew unbearable, followed immediately by heat that jumped from her hand to his and coursed through his body. It felt like his insides glowed and the light pushed itself into every dark crevice in his muscles and joints.

What the shit?

He tested their connection, tried opening his fist and pulling away but nothing doing. His body either failed or chose not to respond to his brain. Not knowing which would bother the crap out of him later.

Right now he had no choice but hold on and see where this thing might take him.

"Yes," El whispered, his head glued to the boy's chest. "PLEASE."

"We're with you, El," B said. "Bring him back."

"Praise Jesus. Praise Jesus. Praise Jesus." The chant came in a loud whisper from diner woman standing nearby.

"Come on, Kenny. Come on, Kenny." El's voice grew stronger and more insistent.

"He knows his name," the mother exclaimed. "He knows my baby's name."

Suddenly, the small body on the ground inhaled, the boy's chest expanded under El's head. Once, twice, three times. El's head rode each inhalation until they became less sudden and gasps subsided into deep breaths.

Movement stopped all around them as men and women in the crowd and in uniform, witnessed the miracle. Shouts and cheers erupted from everyone, uniformed and civilian. People clapped and high-fived one another.

El sat up. "Hey, doc," he croaked to a standing EMT. "I think he's going to be okay, now. But you better check him." He sat back on his butt and smiled at Beatrix. "You did good," he said.

"Sweet mother of God, he did it," said one of the EMTs. He fumbled at an oxygen mask. "Get the paddles," he snapped to his partner. "In case we need them."

"You won't," El said. He looked up at Smith and nodded tiredly. Sweat and tears coursed down his cheeks. "Thanks for your help. Glad you came when you did. We couldn't have done it without you."

The link between his hand and Beatrix parted and Smith wrung his arm like shaking out a cramp.

He had no words for what happened and said nothing. He tried formulating a Plan B but Plan A had been so soundly trashed that his damn brain refused to work, still buzzing with the events of the last few minutes.

Then, suddenly, it felt as if the clouds parted and the sun closed half the distance to the earth. It took a few seconds for him to register that the *sun* issued from halogen lamps raised high on ring stands all around them.

A newswoman, followed closely by a cameraman and sound guy dangling his boom mike, scooted close and began shouting questions.

"Who are you people? … What's your name? … How do you explain the miracles we've witnessed?"

El closed his eyes and fell against Beatrix in a dead faint.

Chapter Twenty-Eight

FREEWAY MIRACLE

T he young acolyte closed her laptop and grinned. Finally, the abomination Mother sent her out to battle had risen from the depths and surfaced on a lonely highway in the middle of Bumfuck, Florida no less.

She tossed the computer into the front seat and climbed over the center console. Living in a car had its advantages. Low overhead being one, if you could find an out-of-the-way place to park where the cops wouldn't roust you. The other and most important takeaway from today's lesson?

Fast getaways.

Sister Evelyn cranked the ignition and woke up half the bums sharing her underpass.

Wake up you Godforsaken heathens. God's Work coming through.

Evelyn nosed her ancient Honda Accord around some still-sleeping clumps of rags and kissed the side of an oil drum used for fires on cold nights. It clanged over on its side and rolled down the embankment spewing coals and charred trash. She didn't care one bit.

Last night would be her final one spent at the underpass motel. Mother Magdalene would reward her handsomely for her initiative. She did it for all of humanity and God, of course, but even better, for access to Mother's Inner Circle.

She set a general course for I-95 in Florida and pulled up onto the highway leading to Atlanta's Downtown Connector and all points south.

#

Bernard turned up the volume on his piece of crap TV. This particular Red Roof Inn apparently invested in their *in-room entertainment systems* shortly after the remote control was invented.

The talking head on screen breathlessly recounted what she called the Freeway Miracle. Directors back at her station headquarters obliged her by endlessly looping scenes of what looked like a young boy coming to in the middle of a horrific traffic accident.

Uniformed personnel and onlookers had tears in their eyes. Dramatic footage enhanced by a shaky camera showed the boy being strapped to a stretcher and hurried into an ambulance. What had to be the parents ran beside all the way and jumped into the Rescue Unit with him.

The reporter managed to wrangle a few onlookers before the police shut her down. Like most people, they were only too anxious to recount their stories when faced with the prospect of making it on the evening news:

"He was dead and came back to life. One second, nothing. Then like, boom, he's back."

"If it walks like a miracle, talks like a miracle, what would you call it? God is among us and working His saving grace."

"Them freaky folks with the big heads, they did it. Get them on camera. I'd like to see 'em up close anyway. God's Messengers or aliens, I'd say."

"Remember that dude from the internet? Saved that cop shot a while back in Atlanta? Well, that's him. I know it is. Big head and all."

Bernard took the sling off his arm and chicken-flapped as far as he could, testing his range of motion. *Shoulder height at best and it still hurt like a bitch.* He tossed the sling on the bed. Damn thing got in the way more than it helped.

He set the A/C to stun before closing the door behind him and hanging *Do Not Disturb* on the knob. He paid for the room three nights at a time and this was the last night. Screw global warming. Doing his part to hasten the End of The World made him smile as he limped for his car.

He blamed that religious wacko he used to serve for his present circumstances, no question. She spawned the wide-eyed crazies who'd beat him for beating her. But he blamed that freak of nature on the tube even more.

If he'd done his job and delivered the egghead to Mother as she requested, God would have blessed him. At least, He wouldn't have cursed him. Not that he, Bernard, could ever hope to predict God's ways.

Bernard crossed himself and vowed never to question or ascribe motive to Him again. He was certainly not worthy.

Mother Magdalene may have a screw or three loose. Bernard had no doubt. But the woman had some divine ties somewhere. He'd seen enough of her in action to fear what powers she did possess.

The crazy bitch may get the details wrong. But he believed she got most of the big things right, this abomination she'd latched onto being a prime example.

What the creature might be, Bernard didn't know. Sent from hell? Spawn of the devil? Possibly. A perversion of nature? One look tells you that. Alien? Who the hell knows?

What he did know, from what he saw on Channel Nine News, the creatures were multiplying. Mother Magdalene may very well lose her mind. She'd need all hands on deck for this and he, Bernard, may be able to twist this Satanic Invasion—she'd see it as exactly that, no question—to his own devices.

He needed a way back in and the Big Heads would be his ticket.

#

Mother hurled the water pitcher at the TV and paced up and back, wringing her hands. She dodged the two young girls who scurried about her, cleaning up the shattered crockery and mopping up the water.

"Dear Lord, protect us. Dear Lord, protect us." The incensed woman pointed a shaky finger at the TV which, by the divine GRACE of THE ALMIGHTY, the water pitcher missed. "Do you see? Do you see?"

She grabbed fistfuls of her hair and muttered as she stalked back and forth. "The Abomination of it. The sheer evil of IT."

She scooped everything off her desk and flung it to the floor. Papers flew, pictures shattered, the phone bounced and clanged and a cup full of pens and pencils shot across the room.

"Freeway Miracle? MIRACLE?" The last word came from deep inside and exploded in a guttural growl. "God works miracles. The Devil plays tricks. Is that God down in Florida? Do you believe that is GOD?"

Neither of the two young women dared to answer. They'd learned long ago that Mother rarely expected answers from them, indeed, preferred they hold their tongue.

Not this time. Mother's tirade had suspended for the moment and they risked a glance. She stood with fists on her hips, glaring at them expectantly.

"No, Mother," said the first girl. "It is not God."

"It is the Devil," said the other, braver of the two.

Mother Magdalene pursed her lips and fixed the brave one with a stare. "And what do you know of the Devil, young lady?"

The young girl wet her lips with her tongue. "I know that he is a master of tricks and temptation." She got no response from Mother and added, "and we must always be on our guard lest we be led astray."

Mother nodded. "How are we doing so far?"

The girl looked troubled. "I don't understand."

"Come, come. You're a smart girl, an inquisitive child. The question is simple." Mother beseeched the heavens as if for strength. "Who's winning? In the contest between good and evil, who would you say IS WINNING?" Her voice rose to a screech.

Both young girls paled.

The brave one stood straighter and cleared her throat. "It is not for us mere mortals to say, Mother. God is all-powerful. He can never be bested by the Devil. By definition."

"Ah," Mother clasped hands in prayerful pose as she paced back and forth. "You think you are so clever."

"No, Mother."

"Then, why worry?"

"I'm sorry?"

"Why do we worry? If, by DEFINITION, God can't be bested," she pointed at the TV, "who are we to worry?"

The young girl hung her head and remained silent.

"Shall I tell you?"

Both girls looked at the floor and nodded.

"Because we are His instruments. He works through US. God informs us. God gives us strength and wisdom. The Devil will never win because it is UP TO US not to let him."

Mother crouched and snatched the TV remote off the floor. She stabbed it at the TV, raising the volume until the breathless TV announcer's voice vibrated the cabinet.

People are hailing the events on the Florida highway as nothing short of miraculous. According to reports, victims of a tragic multi-car pileup previously judged to be dead, were—and there is no other way to say this—brought back to life. By this person or persons. We will have the full story on this, complete with commentary by clergy and medical personnel, in the next hour....

The picture on the TV held on the still image of three individuals as he ended his dramatic announcement.

A young woman and slightly older man froze in the glare of TV lights. The older man cradled the unconscious form of another in his arms. The man's fierce expression looked demonic. The two standing ducked their heads and tried to turn from the cameras.

All three bore an eerie resemblance to one another. Over-sized heads with a slight swelling at the crown, and pasty skin flaring ghost-white in the harsh glare of the TV cameras.

"Do you see that?" Mother screamed above the TV volume. "One hell-spawn has become three." The woman stalked back and forth, no longer aware of the young girls. Fixated instead on the offending image on the television.

"THREE. We were too slow to act, to do His bidding. The Devil is assembling his army and this is our warning. God is showing me— *us*—what must be done.

"The evil is spreading, already bending weak minds, seeding its trickery. And the Devil is laughing, make no mistake. He is daring me to stop him."

She fell to her knees; hands clasped at her breast, and began to chant:

"I shall be His instrument. Seek the Devil and vanquish him *In His Name.*

"I shall be His instrument. Seek the Devil and vanquish him *In His Name.*"

The two young girls gathered what mess they could carry and slipped from the room, pulling the door softly closed behind them. Mother's voice, strident over the TV, followed them out.

"I shall be His instrument. Seek the Devil and vanquish him *In His Name.*"

Chapter Twenty-Nine

IF YOU CAN'T BEAT 'EM

John Smith had not thought of anyone's wellbeing besides his own for at least a half-century. The experience took him by such surprise that he spent precious minutes examining the feeling. He sat semi-stunned, on his ass, still in the spot he landed when the three of them broke their connection.

Across from him, Beatrix Goode sat on the asphalt, shielding her young charge from prying eyes and cameras. The young man she called "El" collapsed across her lap, unconscious. She covered him with her upper body as she rocked, head bent low over him, eyes closed and lips moving. She appeared to be talking to the young man.

The bitch waitress from the diner—her apron had *Nicole* stitched on it back then if he remembered right—stalked around the pair like a momma lioness, daring anyone to even try and get close.

Nicole kept up a running harangue, shoving people away who ventured too near. She ripped the mike from a female reporter and tossed it aside. The woman's cameraman almost lost his precious Sony Digital News Cam to the same fate. He managed to wrestle it free at the last minute, cursing Nicole and threatening to sue.

Smith widened his focus beyond his tiny trio to take in the whole scene.

The events of the last few minutes apparently proved too much for the crowd to resist. They pressed in, despite the efforts of the outnumbered cops, to get a look. Twisted faces and open mouths indicated they must have been yelling, probably shouting questions, demanding attention. Smith heard nothing but a low level rumble like stamping feet in stadium bleachers.

Bewildered EMTs and harried law enforcement did their best to continue working in the deteriorating conditions. Brown uniforms and firemen blue crisscrossed in front of him. Smith gave the responders five, ten minutes max before the situation got too out of hand.

That would be five minutes too many.

He jumped to his feet and those in the crowd nearest him backed up a few steps. He glared, mentally commanding them like dogs to STAY, and walked over to Beatrix on shaky feet. Diner Nicole interposed herself between them, or tried. But he shook his head briefly and that stopped her.

John Smith crouched close beside Beatrix and El and he heard her voice cut through the background white noise of the crowd. *You're all right . . . You're all right . . . You're all right . . .*

"Beatrix," he placed a hand on her shoulder, "we need to go."

She continued rocking and clutching El without comment.

"Beatrix Goode," he shoved the thought into her brain, right behind her eyes, "let's get you and El out of here. NOW."

She flinched as if zapped by a cattle prod and rounded on him, teeth bared in a snarl.

Smith held his ground and leaned in. "Stupid woman, I'm trying to help you."

He bounced to his feet without waiting for any acknowledgement and scooped El's slack form from underneath her.

Beatrix squealed, "Stop it. Leave him alone!" But she hadn't the strength to resist him.

"Follow me," Smith said.

Nicole stood by confused, wringing her hands.

"You too, waitress." Nicole could be useful to them and leaving her behind to be questioned by law enforcement or the press was not an option.

John Smith forged a path through the crowd, cradling El's still form in his arms like carrying a child to bed. Those in front of him foolish enough to attempt an intercept took one look at Smith's face and jumped aside. Several knocked people down to get out of his way.

"We'll take your car and stay close," he yelled over his shoulder. "Beatrix, get your keys ready."

He carried El as if the young man weighed nothing at all. Several eyewitness accounts in the newspapers would in fact, describe it later as if El's unconscious form floated weightless in Smith's arms.

When they got to the yellow Camaro, still with its doors wide open, he parked El in mid-air while he ducked into the backseat and hauled its contents out onto the road. Damn car looked like homeless people lived in it. He didn't have time to worry about the effect a levitating El might have with onlookers.

"Oh, God in heaven look at that. The boy's floating."

"Is he dead? He looks dead."

"Those are some scary people, Harry. Mark my words it's the apocalypse. We're all doomed."

El hung in mid-air and Nicole stood open-mouthed at the spectacle. Beatrix busied herself retrieving articles Smith pitched to the side of the road.

They got into a tug of war over some stupid old briefcase until Beatrix blasted him with a message that told him THIS was coming with HER.

He chose to let that go rather than waste any more time.

"Fine," he pointed Nicole to the passenger seat. "You take shotgun. Beatrix Goode, you sit with El in the back. I'll drive." He held out his hand for the keys. "Come on," he snapped his fingers.

"This is my car," Beatrix said.

"Fine," he grinned. He knew from past experience the effect his smile had on people, "That's also *your boy*. You want me in the backseat with him? Good. I look forward to getting to know him better."

The two locked eyes, Beatrix scowling, Smith grinning.

"Come on, B," Nicole looked at the crowd of people forming around their car. "Let the man drive. For El."

Beatrix spit to the side and tossed Smith the keys. "You wreck my car you'll buy me another."

He said nothing as Beatrix maneuvered El into the back and scurried around the other side to climb in with him.

Smith and Nicole slammed their doors about the same time. He looked over at the waitress and winked. "Thanks for breaking the stalemate back here."

"Didn't do it for you," Nicole said.

"Suit yourself." Smith fired up the Camaro's grumbling V-8 and whirled out of the traffic line. People dove out of the way as he spun tires and toggled the wheel side to side, rocketing them forward.

They straddled the edge of the highway, slipping two wheels on and off the grassy road shoulder. Smith fought for speed to keep them pointed north and swerved back and forth to avoid entanglements with errant bits of wreckage from the accident.

In the rearview mirror, Beatrix would not meet his eyes. She stared stone-faced out the window, her arm wrapped tight around El's still unconscious form.

The highway ahead had zero traffic, thanks to the wreck at their backs. A few disgusted drivers caught in the backup on the far side crossed the median to go back the way they came.

Clear road ahead and not much else gave Smith time to think about all that had happened. More importantly, it gave him enough breathing room to examine what it meant.

Incredible as it may be, could this kid really be all Beatrix Goode had claimed to The Council? That damn resurrection act of his had surely been caught on camera; probably be front-page news tomorrow.

Where did that leave him? After his bold talk about bringing the Speaker's Pet to heel, and tidying up her mess, he'd jumped into the center of it. Thanks to the news crews and cameras, he owned Beatrix Goode's mess himself now, not at all what he'd signed up for.

Still, when nut-cutting time came around and he had it out with Beatrix Goode, he felt confident he could handle her. The waitress on the other hand? She had seen way too much and knew too much—God knows what Beatrix spilled to her. She would have to be dealt with.

And that left El.

What the hell would he do with him? Was the kid really The One? Beatrix Goode had bet her life on it.

He would not make that same rookie mistake.

If El *were* The One, he, John Smith, would require a lot more proof than a few people brought back from death's door.

"What kind of proof do you need, John?"

The voice snuck quietly into the middle of his brain and made him jump. He practically ran them off the road.

"The first step is always believing, isn't it?"

Smith shot a glance into the rearview. El and Beatrix hadn't moved; El slumped in her arms while she stared out the side window.

"I think one wreck is enough for the day. Don't you? We don't want to end up like those poor souls behind us."

Smith wrestled the car back under control and glanced into his mirror again. El's eyes were open this time and staring at him.

Chapter Thirty

WE NEED AN ARMY

Mother spent most of the last two hours crunching numbers in the accounting program she'd paid an ungodly sum for. Custom designed for *In His Name*, the software went far beyond the normal checks and balances of the typical QuickBooks program. The genius of her design came from the predictive models built into it.

It used psychographic data, demographic clustering, past performance and future trending to paint a picture of what tomorrow might look like for her church.

She called her program The Tablets and much like the stone versions Moses brought down off the mountain, it contained wisdom and commanded action. The only difference: Mother's modern-day Tablets etched its commandments in digital code.

She pushed the compile button at the bottom of the page. Her designers shaped the button like a stone tablet and named it The Word. Their little joke. But she liked it and decided to keep it.

She'd developed a regular ritual right away. In the early days it had been fun. The church grew, bursting at the pews with eager minds and open wallets. Money filled *In His Name* coffers to over-flowing and she plowed every dollar back into the church. Bought more land, imported marble and the latest technologies with equal abandon.

She built her church as a fitting monument to Him. St. Peter and St. Paul had their cathedrals. Could she not do the same?

Apparently—and she received the identical answer every time—

The Word software came back a simple and resounding *NO*.

She stabbed a finger on the icon again. Re-worked the numbers, fudged the attendance at her sermons and seminars, even generously padded the roles of the faithful servants signed up for Special Acolyte Training.

The numbers wouldn't even let her lie to herself. The Word came through as clear as *thou shalt not kill.*

She pressed the tablet icon a final time and read the result at the bottom of the page. *The Word is—you are failing Him. It is not enough. You must do more.*

Mother clicked out of the program and dropped her head to her hands.

Had she not been His most faithful and trusted disciple? Sharing His goodness and mercy? Converting the godless and guiding His lambs? Had she not shed her own blood in His name? What more did He expect of her?

She cast her eyes to heaven and spoke her plea aloud, "Dear Lord, show me the path and I will follow it. I beseech Your Son and Spirit, as a lowly servant unfit to utter His Holy Name, tell me what to say and I will say it. Counsel me where to go and I will go there. In the name of the holy Triune, I pray. Amen."

The angels replied with harp strings.

The heavenly music filled her with righteous joy and she closed her eyes to let the sound flow over her. Harp music. The gentle glissando of gently plucked runs. Oh, the rapture of it.

Harp strings.

The sheer soul stirring—

Harp strings.

The angelic voices—

Harp strings.

She opened one eye to look at her computer screen.

The sound came from her computer speakers. *Oh, yeah.* The audio alert she'd chosen for her RSS feed to let her know another live web episode had commenced. She clicked on the link.

A live panel discussion in full swing featured a round table of religious *scholars*. It checked all the boxes: Catholic, Baptist, Jewish, Muslim, the token god-cursed atheist, and not a woman in the bunch. Each man more anxious than the next to share his views about the *Freeway Miracle.*

Mother heard the moderator's first question: "Would you define what we all saw on that shocking video from Florida as a miracle? Yes or no?"

She didn't wait to hear their answers.

IDIOTS. Clearly, the Devil controlled them. These *scholars* could not see that? Did they not see the evil slouching toward them from the freeways down in Florida?

And then the light dawned and she heard Him.

So blinded by her self-pity and her hubris that she almost missed Him.

That, right there, His answer opened a path made manifest before her. True joy buzzed electric in her bones and loins and SOUL. He spoke and she heard Him.

She stabbed the intercom button on her phone.

The receptionist replied, "Yes, Mother Magdalene? How may I bless you today?"

Even the stupid telecom answer script spoke to her. Could this be a more blessed day?

"What is your name, child?"

"Rebecca, Mother."

"Rebecca, you will bless us *all* if you can connect me with our Audio/Video Department. I forget the manager's name there…."

"That would be Pat, Mother."

"Of course, please connect me with her."

"Um, *him*, Mother?"

"Yes, yes. Him. I wish to speak with Pat. Immediately."

#

"I want to make a video. Surely, you can do this?"

Pat stood before her in her office and cracked his knuckles. "Of course, Mother. We have one of the finest audio/visual studios in the area."

"*One* of? After all the money I've sunk into that high tech black hole of yours?"

"Well, I mean—" The department head gulped and yanked at his fingers in earnest.

"Relax, I'm kidding." Mother Magdalene came from around her desk and motioned them to the sitting area arranged against the wall with the manacle rings, the wall where Bernard had whipped her. "I think we'll be more comfortable here."

They sat. Pat perched on the very edge of the chair cushion and cleared his throat. "What sort of video did you have in mind?"

He gulped again and this time Mother noticed the tiny cross, tattooed on the man's Adams' Apple. He would do.

Mother clasped her hands in reverence. "Pat, I want to move hearts and minds and *souls* in His name."

The nervous little man nodded. "Of course."

"It will not be easy."

He nodded, "Of course," then shook his head, "not."

She leaned forward, conscious of the way her purple robe parted in the front. "Have you seen the news?"

"Um, what?"

"The news, TV, it's all over. The heathens call it the Freeway Miracle."

"Oh, yes. I would say everyone has seen that by now. It's already been almost a day."

"Which means *everyone* has been exposed. The Devil and his spawn—these swellheaded abominations to the Lord—have made inroads. They are after souls, Pat. Make no mistake. The Devil is recruiting his army."

"His army."

"Yes, God help us. Most are not equipped like you and I to see the Trickster at work. Many of the weak-minded will see those hellish videos and actually believe they have witnessed a miracle."

Pat stayed mute.

"Our brothers and sisters here at *In His Name* know the difference. But we are few in number Pat, compared to the army the Devil is recruiting. I watched a video earlier with several of them acting like authorities. Talking as if they knew. Giving credence to the Devil's lies."

"Yes, Mother."

"We are at war, Pat. The ancient war. Good versus evil. Devil versus God. And we are His instruments."

"Praise His name?" Pat said, tentatively.

"Preach, brother. They have fired the first salvo, but the Devil has tipped his hand. I know what he intends. And you and I will be ready."

"Yes, we will. But, how exactly?"

"Our army here at *In His Name* is small. We do not have enough warriors for the fight ahead. We need more. Our army must grow until it too, is legion. Until our numbers match the Devil's."

"You want to produce a recruitment video?"

"In simple terms you might call it that. In un-simple terms, we are recruiting souls. That won't be simple."

Pat nodded. He seemed relieved to be on solid ground, talking about something he knew well. "We can do that. I used to produce the recruitment ads for the US Army."

"I am not talking ads," Mother grimaced. "I'm talking about a message of faith and the holy Word of God. Of carrying a warning to His children of the coming threat. Of saving souls from the fires."

Pat shut up once again, but continued to nod in agreement.

"I am talking a video that goes—what is your word for it? Viable."

"Viral?"

"That's it. I will deliver the Word of God to the world. To recruit an army to save the world." She smiled. "How is that for a *recruitment* video?"

She noticed Pat stopped nodding. He seemed paler than usual.

"Mother, even if we produce the greatest video ever—"

"Which we—with your help—will."

"There is no guarantee it will go viral. Viral simply happens. In fact, if you try to plan viral, it rarely does."

"So, you are saying that the pure Word of God delivered through me, his humble vessel, might," she placed a hand over her heart, inside her robe, "fail in its mission?"

Pat's eyes widened. "No, no, I mean…"

"Do not be afraid, my child. He cannot fail." She stood and opened the flaps of her robe wide. "Do you see the commitment and sacrifice I am willing to endure?"

"Yes, Mother."

She reached down and pulled him to his feet to face her. She grabbed a hand and placed it on her abdomen, right above her mound where a few deep welts crisscrossed. "Do you feel my commitment?"

"Yes, Mother."

"I will not fail. You will not fail." She crossed herself and looked heavenward. "He will not fail. Now," she pushed him toward the door, "go make ready. We are about to recruit our army."

Chapter Thirty-One

ASSEMBLY!

C alvin Jones paused the video on his computer screen and shoved away from his desk. Time to assume The Speaker role—before that crew in Florida spins so far out of control that he and The Council won't be able to cram the inflated genie back in the bottle.

He'd already been fending off insistent pleas from others on The Council. Tanya Patel in Mumbai had been especially persistent: *"What are we doing Speaker, that we should allow ourselves to be put in such jeopardy? Why are we not taking action?"*

Michelle in Paris, sweet Michelle who rarely spoke up and held herself above anything that could remotely be construed as petty squabbling, even she sent feelers his way: *"Mon ami, monsieur Speaker. I am becoming much concerned."*

Her mental push contained no trace of an accent, of course. He liked to add it for flavor.

May as well quit fighting it. The time for the conclave he'd half-hoped would never be necessary had come. The Hail Mary he threw by allowing John Smith free rein to try his hand hadn't worked. Though the man possessed a dogged persistence, overshadowed only by an inflated sense of self-worth, contrary to his braggadocio earlier Smith had failed in his self-appointed mission.

The Speaker replayed the moment when he'd closed the trap on Smith and committed the man to a course with a fifty percent chance of success, at best. Smith had said, quite boldly:

"I shall take over her duties. I will remove Beatrix and begin an immediate evaluation of this Eldridge person myself. If he is The One—which I doubt—I will know it quickly. I will not fail."

Well, John Smith had failed. The Speaker had yet to decide how he really felt about that.

In the meantime, he looked at the frozen image on his screen—the young man being scooped up in John Smith's arms in the midst of a crowd on a lonely highway in south Florida. By any measure, Smith had failed miserably. A few on The Council used the word *catastrophic*.

It would be easy to agree with them.

Calvin paced to help organize his thoughts. It usually worked. His sanctuary, carved into the mammoth trunk of a downed sequoia, overlaid a skein of peace and calm to every moment he spent inside it. Not today. Today he walked a kite string without a net.

A crystal decanter on the far wall beckoned and he hesitated a second before answering. He plucked a Baccarat old-fashioned glass from the tray beside it.

Did Smith fail, really? Could he ever have succeeded? Perhaps they all should have taken Beatrix Goode's assessment of her discovery more seriously. Had the time finally come? Was that young man in Florida the reason they were all here? To finally realize their ultimate Given Goal?

The Speaker steeled himself and prepared to summon The Council. He debated inviting Beatrix and Smith to join their mental conference. After all, they were, along with their out-of-control young agitator, the problem.

In the end, he decided to exclude them. The mental shouting match from all corners of the globe would be unproductive at best. No sense setting them up to be pilloried. His decision would either prove to be a major error or, a brilliant move that would herald the beginning of their end.

He poured a glass of his favorite Macallan Scotch and drank half of it down in a single gulp. Might as well get this over with. He knew what had to be done. His job would be to get them all in agreement.

Calvin sat back in The Speaker chair and pushed out his call worldwide, damn the time zones. Damn the inconvenience. Time to bring the entire Council, excluding Smith, up to speed. Beatrix was not a full-fledged Council member and her out-of-control young man had no rights whatsoever. They would find out their fate when he and The Council settled on it.

Responses came through loud and immediate. Everyone chimed in, even Lars in Sydney, and he took his Council duties as casually as his beach attire.

"'Bout time you stepped up mate."

"Mes amis."

"Thees ees a momentous day, tovarisch."

"What took you Speaker?"

"Please, everyone, I understand your concerns. I have them as well. We want to hear from every one of you. For now, let us not forget protocol."

They quieted, but he sensed the mental equivalent of grumbling from most of them.

"Who wants to start us off?"

Michelle in Paris, bless her, stepped up. She started with the pledge they used to begin every meeting and the rest joined in:

The world must never hear us, never see us, never know us. Until The One brings us to the Given Goal. For the good of all mankind.

"Thank you, Michelle. Now, before you all start in again, indulge me. I'll sum up the situation as I see it and invite you all to comment after I am through. It will save us all a good bit of time. And bring us to the real reason I have waited so long to make this call."

"Which is?" Karla said. Always direct, entirely without dissembling. Calvin appreciated her Ukrainian manner most times. Today was not one of them. Her question started another avalanche of comments:

"It is He isn't it? Beatrix got it right."

"Impossible. Why now after so many generations?"

"Do not believe everything you see on the Internet, my friends."

"I am in hiding in my own village. I cannot leave my home."

"The world certainly hears and sees us now I'll tell you."

"SILENCE."

The Speaker pressed the heels of his palms to his temples and tried again.

"May I begin? Please? Can you control yourselves for that long?"

More mental grumbling, but he had their attention.

"Thank you, everyone. This is the situation we are faced with as I see it. In this world of the Internet and cell phones and connectivity that reaches all corners of our globe—even into your village outside Mumbai, Tanya, if I heard you right—what in earlier days may have been dismissed as a hoax, hysterical gossip or witchcraft, is not so easily explained away today.

The Speaker continued. *"You have all seen the videos, the newscasts, the hand-wringing commentaries and the breathless debate on the talk shows. I, of course, am referring to what some idiot journalist dubbed the Freeway Miracle. I despise the name, naturally, but it stuck.*

"We all know that miracles are simply events for which there appears no rational or scientific explanation. Go back in time a few hundred years with a butane lighter and you'd probably end up tied to a stake. The bravest of the crowd might even torch the kindling at your feet with your miracle."

"Get to the point, Speaker, hey? With all due respect mate. You're hopping all around the problem like a lovesick roo."

"Thank you for the encouragement, Lars."

"I'm just sayin'—"

"And I am just saying—I believe the video footage we have all seen, dissected more times than the Zapruder film from 1963," he waited a beat. "I am convinced it is real."

He sat back and let the firestorm wash through him.

"Impossible."

"Hey, now—"

"So you think it IS a miracle like they say?"

"What do we do now?"

"What does this mean?"

"Think it's bad now, wait until—"

"My friends please. PLEASE. IF what the video shows us truly happened, we have no choice but to take it seriously. Which means, I'm sorry but I have no choice. I am moving for Assembly."

Silence.

"You are serious, Speaker?"

"Yes, Karla. And to answer your previous question, that is the real reason I have waited so long to convene. I move for Assembly. Do I hear a second? This is important, my friends."

"I second."

"Thank you, Michelle. Now, I ask that we vote. I know it will take time. Most of you are days from the eastern seaboard of the United States. I would not call for this and put you through it if I did not feel in my bones that it is warranted. Concentrate. Do not make this decision lightly. Take your time and send me Yes or No within the next few hours and—"

He needn't have bothered. The response blasted him back in his seat and he sloshed Macallan's down his robe front. Their votes came flooding in before he finished pushing.

"Thank you, people. I will send information on where and when by the end of day tomorrow. Should any of you experience difficulty making the journey contact me and we will work it out. This is historic,

everyone. To meet you all, face to face, finally. I am honored you have chosen me as your Speaker."

He shut down communication and downed the rest of his Scotch. God help us, and God help them he thought, as he reached for his decanter.

Beatrix Goode, I am entrusting you with our very existence. I pray you were right and we were all wrong.

Chapter Thirty-Two

FREE BREAKFAST

John Smith focused his eyes on the road ahead and shielded his thoughts with an extra-protective layer. Images of rebar-reinforced concrete walls always did the trick around The Speaker. Far as he knew, that fool in his stupid tree house in Big Sur had never broken through.

The kid in the backseat posed no real challenge. Smith only threw up his mental barrier as a precaution. No way that youngster had the mental chops to take him on. El's irresponsible flouting of his gifts earlier merely underscored his impetuous nature.

Still, no sense tipping his hand, and Smith liked making sense.

"That makes no sense at all, if you ask me." The voice exploded inside Smith's head.

Smith shot a quick glance in the rearview and saw El smiling at him, eyes half-lidded and sleepy. Like he couldn't be bothered. Like this whole botched escapade was a lark.

"Botched is a little harsh, don't you think, dude? And what's with that tree house in Big Sur? Sounds cool."

"You read my thoughts?" Smith pushed hard; the mental equivalent of a shove.

"Can't everyone?"

"No one has that ability."

"Interesting." El straightened in his seat and worked a crick from his neck. *"I take it you think what we did back there might be a mistake?"*

"We fly under the radar, kid. That is how we are most effective. We do not call attention to ourselves. We do not perform parlor tricks. We do not make life difficult for the others like us around the world."

"Translation: you do not DO anything. Real effective."

"Our members work quietly for the greater good—the Given Goal we call it."

"How's that?"

"Like everyone, we possess skills and talents that vary. With a few gifts in common. We are all smart. We're all telepaths of different levels. Most have the ability to apply extreme focus to any problem."

"And, bonus, we all get to look like bulb-headed, white-skinned freaks in the bargain. Sweet." El crossed his arms and looked out at the passing landscape.

"Would you rather be one of the herd?" Smith offered. *"The undeveloped? We are the future of humanity. Evolution's next step."*

"You certainly drank the Kool-Aid, Mr. Smith," El pushed back. *"I'll give you that."*

Smith abandoned building his mental wall. It pained him to his dick to admit it, but the kid's raw power and talents made his shielding efforts a waste of brain cells.

"Whereas you, young man, with all your well-considered actions of late," Smith stared into the rearview until El met his eyes. *"Your highly developed skill-set honed over what,* months *of diligent practice? You plan to set fire to the rules and protocols that have kept us all safe for generations and flush all our preparations down the crapper?"*

"Eloquently put, Mr. Smith. Colorful. My highly developed skill set *gets that you're pissed. But you got one thing right. I do have a plan. It's time we came out of your little self-imposed closets. Hiding is for people with something to hide. We, on the other hand, have something to share."*

Smith was distracted from his telepathic repartee by a passing billboard announcing a Marriott Courtyard south of Jacksonville. He liked Courtyard, mostly for the free breakfast.

"We'll be stopping at the Marriott up ahead," Smith announced out loud to the car. "Give us a chance to get off the highway, regroup, get cleaned up," he said. "And me to impress upon you all the gravity of our situation." He fixed eyes on El as he said it.

El smiled and went back to staring out the window.

"You boys have a nice talk back there?" Beatrix said.

Nicole looked at her funny. Of course, her friend had no idea what B was talking about. Smith and El hadn't said a word out loud.

Beatrix pointed from her own head to El's and Smith's.

Nicole nodded. "Yeah, yeah, your mind-reader act. I don't want to know, so don't tell me."

El turned from the window, to look at B with eyebrows raised. "*You* didn't hear?"

"I heard your half fine," Beatrix said. "Mr. Smith is a tougher read."

Smith felt a small glow of satisfaction at her admission. At least something worked.

"But, I got the gist. Your side of the conversation told me all I need." She leaned forward and clapped Smith on the shoulder. "How's it feel?"

"Meaning?"

"Dealing with the younger generation, Smith. Welcome to my world. Now you know what I've been facing the past few weeks." She sat back, grinning widely at Smith in the mirror. "I do like me some Courtyard," she said. "Free breakfast."

El punched her in the shoulder and she punched him back.

"I feel like I'm not in on the joke," Nicole said.

"It's all right," Smith said. "It wasn't funny."

They pulled in at the motel entrance and sent Nicole inside to book their rooms. Smith parked away from the entrance to minimize being noticed. Three big heads in a car would be tough for anyone to ignore.

He drummed a ragged tattoo on the steering wheel with his thumbs until Nicole came out of the lobby waving two keys.

"Thank God," Beatrix said. "Give those thumbs a rest. Jesus."

"One for you boys," Nicole handed a key card to Smith. "And one for us girls." She leaned in the back window and handed a key to Beatrix. "Rooms are around the corner, second floor, quarter way down. I'll meet you guys there. I wanna stretch my legs."

Smith pulled the car around the building and spotted their room, 246, on the top floor not too far down. He kept driving and parked in a spot at the far end.

"One more layer of security," he said. "All right folks, let's make it quick. We get out, go in, pull the curtains in both rooms and keep them pulled. Questions?"

Beatrix had her door open and jumped out before he stopped speaking. El followed, dragging a couple of bags with him. "Supplies," he said.

Nicole leaned against the door to the girls' adjoining room, hands in her cut-offs, watching with a bemused grin as they walked up.

"Smooth move, James Bond," she nodded to the car parked at the far end of the row. "Way to plan for a quick getaway."

Smith debated whether to school her right then and there, point out her tragic lack of intellect, or let it slide.

"Let it slide, dude," El murmured as he pushed by her into the motel room.

Chapter Thirty-Three

LIGHTS. CAMERA. MOTHER.

Mother couldn't decide which video monitor to look at. Her frozen image looked damn good on all three. "Tell me why we need three monitors again? Seems a sinful waste of money when one is perfectly adequate."

Pat quit typing on the edit console and turned to her. His composed expression told her how hard he'd worked on his answer.

"The one on the left is calibrated for color and we update its settings weekly. It is the more expensive of the screens. But, in the interest of saving money, we purchased the other two lesser models; one, for active edit and the other for backup and to keep TV safe grids up for cropping."

She nodded as if she understood his gibberish.

"We could certainly do everything on one monitor, Mother. But, the risk of interrupting workflow should we have an equipment failure, added to the time waste shifting between work functions on the one screen," he shrugged, "I didn't think you would appreciate that."

"You are correct. I would not." She waved off his explanation as if it were a pesky fly. "More importantly, how do I look? In your professional opinion, of course."

He cleared his throat. "You look, um—*imposing* is the word I would choose," Pat said. "And commanding. Imposing and commanding."

"Like I'd been called?"

"To deliver a divine message by the God of Hosts himself."

"Which is true."

"Exactly."

"Can I see me—it—one more time before we go live?"

"Of course."

She smiled. That would make an even dozen times she'd watched it. She could watch a dozen more, but that would delay the whole reason for the thing. Her opening salvo in the war against the Dark One must be allowed to begin its holy work.

The Devil tipped his hand in Florida. It would be *her* hand, her church—*In His Name*—that would rise with divine guidance to chop it off.

Mother had every confidence in her message and her delivery. She leaned forward to study her image. The purple silk cinched with enough open in front to show off her healing scars below her throat. Not too much. Adults and kids from all over the world would see this. No sense distracting them.

What did her tech say? She looked *commanding*? *Godly* is more like it. The glow she had him add to her image, subtle but *there*, made her look damn well angelic.

She shivered in anticipation. The masses had no idea what would soon be visited upon them.

"Play it, please," she said and sat back to take in the glory of it one last time.

"My lambs, my children, my family. I have watched for too long. I have agonized and I have prayed. Seeking a sign from the divine Father, asking for His guidance.

"My beloved and all who thirst for God's Word, my soul rejoices to be able to tell you He has spoken to me and asked that I share this with you. To break my silence where, like a coward, I hid, surrounded by the safety of my—our—church In His Name in Atlanta."

Mother smiled as www.InHisName.com appeared onscreen below her image. It was her favorite part of the video.

"While the Devil has seduced the weak-minded and secular among you with his evil trickery. I, and my church, offer you a salvation that rips away the blindfolds the Devil has put upon you. I am speaking of course, about the so-called Freeway Miracle in Florida."

In the video she paused for effect, crossed herself and looked heavenward as if beseeching help from the angels. She thought it a powerful piece of moviemaking.

"I have seen the videos, God help me. I saw those, those swellheaded abominations of God's image perform their tricks. For that is what they were. Make no mistake. God works miracles, children.

Freaks—and the Devil—perform tricks."

On screen, she sipped from a communion chalice to break up the action. Here at the edit desk, she remembered how the vodka burned her throat like holy fire and spurred her to continue.

"It is up to all of us to resist the evil thrust upon us from every quarter. From the news channels and the YouTube. It is you and it is I who will expose the Liar for what he is. You and I will stamp out his unholy influence. You and I will send him back to Hell with his demons.

"I pray you join me, join God's Army of Right, and hound these spawn of the Devil until they flush from their darkness into the light. Find them. Follow them. But keep a safe distance. My own, chosen acolytes have failed twice to corral the youngest demon. He is powerful and he is wily."

Mother set her hands in prayer pose.

"Let me be clear."

She leaned in close to the screen to watch this part. Saw how she shifted in her seat and pointed at the camera for emphasis. *Imposing* indeed.

"Your job is to find the Devil. It will be my job to send him and his minions back into the fire. This," she held up a photo blowup of a bright yellow Camaro, *"is the vehicle they were seen driving away in. God's blessing on the person in the crowd who snapped this picture.*

"Look for the yellow car. Look for the big heads. If you spot them, send an email to the website on the screen or text the number beside it. God's faithful are standing by to take down your information.

"And God's army here at In His Name *stands ready to send the Devil in our midst, straight back to hell.*

Thank you and God Bless."

The video ended with a slow zoom in to the front entrance of *In His Name.* The white marble looked heavenly against clear, blue Georgia sky. The web address pulsed as if with holy light. The effect made her wet.

"You did a marvelous job, Pat, marvelous." She flapped her robe to cool herself. "The Lord thanks you. Push the button, or whatever. Make it go vital. I will check back with you in an hour to see how it is doing."

Mother watched for a minute as Pat clicked the mouse, typed a few words, clicked some more. He remained stone-faced as he called up Safari and connected to their channel on YouTube. She saw the YouTube logo come up and had a vague thought about the spelling.

Not important.

She left him to his machines and swept out into the hallway, purple silk robe billowing behind her. The slight breeze from walking felt deliciously cool between her legs and she felt exhilarated.

Summoning an army. Calling the Devil to task. Going to war. Could anything be more exciting?

She resisted the temptation to skip on the way back to her office.

Chapter Thirty-Four

SHE'S A HANDFUL

The deep grumble of a diesel engine thrummed through the motel walls and Beatrix went to the front curtains to look out. A jacked up Ford pickup pulled into a space halfway down the row of rooms and sat idling. The engine revved and black smoke puffed from twin stacks behind the cab before it silenced.

Sun glare on the windshield made it difficult to see inside the truck from her vantage point. The driver took his own sweet time getting out and when he did, he had a cellphone pressed to his ear.

Violent head nods and sweeping arm gestures indicated he was in deep conversation with someone.

"Hey, Nicole? Take a look." B opened the crack in the curtain a bit wider. "What do you make of this?"

Nicole peered over Beatrix's shoulder and watched the show. "Hm. Lynyrd Skynyrd Tour t-shirt. Cowboy boots. Red Man pouch in the back jeans pocket. I'd say we're lookin' at a prime specimen of *gooberus americanus*."

"I got all that, thank you. But what do you think he's doing—oh, shit."

Still on the phone, the truck driver walked down to the yellow Camaro and peered into the driver's window.

"That's not good," said Nicole.

"Go bang on our connecting door and get Smith, would you?"

She watched the man walk all around the car and cup his hands to stare into each window. He stood a long while at the car's rear, gawking at the back of it and emphatically repeating a phrase. She couldn't hear what he said but his body language announced itself several times before he took the phone from his ear and shoved it into his back pocket.

He went to his pickup, stepped up on a running board and rummaged about in his truck bed. A second later he came up with a can of Budweiser, popped the top and gulped it dry before crushing the can in his fist and tossing it in back of the truck.

"What do we have here?" Smith's voice by her left ear made Beatrix jump.

"Dammit, Smith. Wear a bell or something. That's what we're trying to figure out."

"Lynyrd Skynyrd," El said. "I've heard of them."

"Jesus," B said. "Why don't we pull the curtains wide so we can all stand at the window with our faces hanging out?"

"What's he doing standing there?" El took his own side of the curtains and peered intently.

"Trying to decide his next move, probably," Smith said. "Downing liquid courage before he comes knocking. I told you things were going to get sticky for us. We should have kept moving."

"Running, you mean," El said. "Like all you guys do. Running. Hiding. Well, I've got nothing to hide."

El stepped away from the window and headed for the front door.

Nicole's murmured words stopped him. "Oh, crap. He's got company."

El returned to his peek-a-boo spot and they all watched silently as a beat-up silver Toyota took a hard left into the parking lot and screeched to a tire smoking halt next to the pickup. The old car clattered and rocked on its springs. Blue smoke belched from the tail pipe.

"Bringing his buddies, I'll bet," Nicole said. "A little extra muscle to—son of a bitch. That's not it at all."

They watched without comment as a woman exited the driver's seat and ran to the back door on her side. She leaned in the car and appeared to be wrestling with something.

She backed out in frustration and yelled something to the truck driver.

He hurried over and gently pushed her aside, leaned in and backed out with a pile of rags in his arms.

The rags moved and he struggled. An arm shot out to the side, then a couple of legs flailed free and kicked.

The man appeared not to care, like he'd done this many times before. He simply held on tighter and bent over the bundle, speaking something to it they could not hear.

Soon the struggles stopped and he and what had to be his wife marched to the center of the parking lot. They turned to face the back row of Marriott Courtyard rooms straight on . . . and stood there.

Silent. Staring.

They didn't say anything. They didn't move from their spot. They simply stood.

After a minute, the wife hooked a finger in one of the man's belt loops and stepped closer, but otherwise the couple remained motionless.

"Kind of creepy," said Nicole.

Beatrix couldn't agree with her friend more.

They stayed that way what, a minute? An hour? Beatrix leaned more toward the hour. But she never got a chance to explore her time sense any further.

The front door to their room opened and El stepped outside.

"What the—? Eldridge Montcalm get your ass back in—oh, hell."

B felt the bounce from the outside walkway as El made his way toward the center stairs.

"Showtime, people," Beatrix said, and followed El's lead.

The couple in the parking lot made their way toward the stairs as soon as they saw El.

He waved on his way toward them and they waved back.

B could only think of the way magnets drew together, without hesitation, the bond strengthening as distance between them closed.

El and the couple met in the parking lot, a couple car lengths from the bottom of the stairs. Beatrix descended the stairs a dozen steps behind El.

The woman, a perfect female match for the truck driver, only somewhat prettier, wiped her face and sniffled.

"O, Lord praise His holy name, it is you."

"Tol' you Annie. I recognized that sweet ride of theirs. From the Facebook."

"Can you help us, mister?" the woman said. "Please?" She shoved the truck driver forward and he held out the bundle in his arms.

El stepped up and peeled back a flap of damp blanket. Beatrix saw a face come into view, covered neck to nose with an angry red strawberry birthmark. The mouth hung open, slack and drooling. A pink tongue lolled to the side and brilliant blue eyes darted back and forth without fixing on anything.

"Can you help our baby, mister? We don't got no more options. I saw you on the TV and the Google and I know God sent you to us. I prayed it and here you are. We didn't know what else to do and when Petey called me, I told him I said *Petey, you stay right there and do not let them leave—*"

Her breathless tirade ceased when El took her hand.

"What's your name?" he said.

"My name, oh my goodness, it's…it's—"

"Annie," her husband said. "Name's Annie. Collect yourself, girl."

"Annie Wynona Wilcox," the woman said. "From Live Oak."

"Annie Wynona Wilcox, my name's El. And this is my, er, *colleague*, Beatrix."

"Colleague!"

Nicole came up behind in time to hear that and chuckled. Smith followed close on her heels.

"What seems to be the problem here, folks?" Smith said.

"These are the rest of my um, crew," El said. "The pretty one's Nicole and the ugly dude is Smith."

The couple nodded. "Pleased to meet y'all," the truck driver said. "I'm Pete. Annie's my wife. And this here's our daughter. She got the palsy."

"Hmm. I can see that," El said. "May I?"

"Oh, mister, I wouldn't do that—"

"El. Please, call me El." He ignored the truck driver's warnings and took the young girl in his arms.

She let out a shrill squeal like a trapped rabbit and writhed and wriggled in El's arms.

"Tol' ya, El," the trucker rubbed the back of his neck. "She's a handful that one."

El laid his cheek atop the child's flushed, damp head and closed his eyes. The girl quit struggling and B watched her legs shoot out straight and her arms tuck back into the blankets.

El unwrapped the little girl completely, peeling away the blanket and dropping it to the pavement. A soiled Hello Kitty t-shirt and matching pink shorts, unbuttoned, hid a little girl's body at least thirty pounds underweight.

Stick legs and stick arms looked like they came from a five-year-old. Her rib cage fluttered up and down.

"Kinda in a pickle, aren't we Presley? Hm?" El's voice came out in a soothing monotone, unlike anything B ever heard from him. "Your mom and dad are pretty worried about you, you know?"

El shifted her in his arms until she dangled, feet down, and he hugged her tiny frame close. His hand cradled the back of her head like it would a baby's. Her arms hung loose and he carefully pressed her cheek to his.

"What do you say we make their day a bit brighter?" he whispered in her ear. "Want to do that, Presley? Want to help me out here?" El's voice continued its soft, hypnotic cadence.

"How'd you know her name was Presley?" Pete said. "I didn't tell you—"

"Shut up, Petey," Annie said. "This is God's work."

El kept on as if he hadn't heard. "I know, right?" he said. "I can tell. They do look like great parents. Ah, now quit that. You got nothing to be sorry for. They want you better is all."

Husband Pete began pacing and running fingers through his hair. His wife closed her eyes and lifted her face to the heavens. B felt a mixture of everything they were feeling mixed with a disturbing certainty El had crossed another line.

She'd yet to hear a peep from the little girl.

"Come on now, Presley," El said. "I need your help with this if we're going to—ah, I know it's hard, I do."

Then, little Presley's arms twitched and tentatively lurched, scraping up El's sides to cling around the back of his neck.

"Oh, sweet Jesus," the father said.

Presley's eyes flew open and squinted up at the bright sky.

"Praise Him, oh praise HIM." The trucker clapped his hands and danced an impromptu jig.

Presley gasped a couple of times and curled her legs around El's torso. Her head straightened and fell back against his, as if exhausted.

When she began sobbing, her mother and father joined her and all four—mother, father, little Presley and El—group-hugged in the parking lot.

"Hey, now. Hey, now, let the little girl breathe, folks," Smith said. He stepped forward, hands outstretched, as if to pry the clutch-fest apart but Nicole stepped in front of him and slapped his hands away.

She walked over and rubbed the mother's back and whispered in her ear. She did the same to the father. He broke away first, followed by the mother, until only El and little Presley remained.

El turned to face B and Smith, grinning widely. He tossed the little girl up in the air like an enthusiastic uncle. She squealed and giggled and when he set her on the ground she stood, on her own, blinking and swaying in the sun like a newborn colt.

No trace of the birthmark remained and B noticed the once stick-thin limbs already looked stronger and more filled out.

"Momma?" The little girl reached out her hands and clenched

and unclenched her fingers. "Momma?"

"Oh, oh, blessed be. BLESSED BE." Annie rushed forward and snatched her daughter in her arms, huffing sobs like an idling locomotive.

"Thank God," the father said. He ran to El, grabbed his hand and pumped it vigorously. "And you, thank you Mister El. Thank you. You done us a miracle. A God-blessed miracle."

He ran to his two crying females, encircled them with his arms and joined in.

"El, what have you done?" Beatrix said.

"Isn't it evident?" he said. "They needed help and I could so I—did. Something you people don't seem to get—"

"Not that, you idiot," B said. "*That*."

She pointed to the motel entrance as another car came screaming into the parking lot. A shiny blue pickup bounced into the lot hot on its tail.

Mother Annie jumped up and down, shrieking at the cars.

"Marcie. MARCIE. HE DID IT. I TOLD YOU." The mother wrenched little Presley from her father's grasp and ran toward the approaching cars.

The car driver locked up the brakes and the vehicle slid sideways. The pickup behind it slowed deliberately and stopped.

Annie never broke stride.

"PRESLEY'S HEALED. HE HEALED HER," she screamed.

The car door popped open and a plumper version of Annie leveraged herself out as Annie arrived with Presley. The new woman looked at Presley then at Annie and back to Presley with her mouth open.

Annie held her forward for the new woman to see. But the woman backed away, now looking from healthy Presley to El and B and the rest of them.

The woman made the sign of the cross and shook her head.

"Guys," Smith whispered. "Leave your shit in the rooms. We're out of here."

"Can't do it," B said. "Gotta get my stuff. Go start the car."

"We're not going anywhere," El said. "These people need our help and—"

"GET HER AWAY FROM ME!" the voice from the new arrival shrieked across the pavement. "DEVIL. *DEVIL!*" The new woman stumbled backward, away from Presley and her mother until a meaty flank fetched up against her car's fender.

Arms thrust forward, eyes wild. The woman began hyperventilating. "HENRY," she gasped. "HELP ME. HENRY."

The door to the pickup flew open and a wiry little man exited with a shotgun in his hands. "I GOT 'EM MARCIE," he hollered. "I GOT 'EM." His ball cap flew off as he raised his weapon.

Beatrix got a fistful of El's shirt and yanked him aside as the gun went off. Smith and Nicole dove to the opposite side.

"I'll get your things," Nicole yelled. "You guys get to the car."

Nicole ran for the stairs. Smith, Beatrix and El ran for the Camaro.

B fought with El, shoving him forward every step until the gun went off again.

She heard pellets whistle by but felt nothing. She looked back to see the man with the double barrel gun open and cradled over one arm. He slapped his pockets, searching for more shells.

El cooperated then and they made it to the car. She pushed El into the back, turned and collided with Smith going for the driver's seat.

"I got this," he said.

No time to go all alpha now. B let him by and slipped into the back seat with El.

The engine roared and Smith spun tires. The bright yellow muscle car spun its wheels and Smith steered straight for the man with the gun.

"What are you doing?" Beatrix yelled.

Smith gritted his teeth and mashed the accelerator. The car lurched forward and he jogged the wheel right at the last minute, catching the shooter with the side-view mirror.

The gun went flying. The man bounced off to the side.

Smith slid to a screeching halt at the bottom of the stairs as Nicole jumped down the last couple of steps.

She snatched the door open, threw their bundles into the backseat and jumped in. The door slammed shut of its own accord as Smith stomped the accelerator and headed for the exit.

"That was fun," Nicole said as she settled back in her seat.

Beatrix leaned forward in time to see her friend glance down at her shirtfront.

"Huh," Nicole said and pulled the neck of her t-shirt down. She peered in and thrust a hand inside.

It came out dripping blood.

"Nicole, you're hit? How did you get hit?"

"B girl, you point the thing and pull the doohickey and boom. It's not that hard."

159

Chapter Thirty-Five

ATLANTA BOUND

C alvin Jones intended to enjoy the break from his role as The Speaker and a First Class seat at 32,000 feet provided the ideal distance. Events promised to spiral at a frantic pace in the coming days and he needed every faculty at its peak. He slid his fedora down over his eyes and settled back for the four-hour flight to Atlanta. Not easy wearing a hat in a high-back airplane seat. Most people would have stowed the thing in the overhead. But then, most people didn't walk around sporting an overlarge, odd-shaped head.

Thanks to El in his sensational new role as miracle worker, the world had awakened to their existence. Heads turned his way at the airport in California. People whispered, pointed fingers. No one had been so bold as to speak to him outright. He planned to keep it that way for as long as he could.

The world was not ready for them.

More to the point, they—especially Eldridge Montcalm who'd only begun waking up to his remarkable abilities—were not ready for the world.

A violent lurch and the roar of the L-1011's engines at reverse thrust stirred him from a fitful sleep. Welcome to Atlanta-Hartsfield International Airport. He checked his watch. A habit from the old days. He never needed to; his sense of time never failed him. But habits are comfort and he took comforts whenever he could.

Speaking of—he plucked the hot towel the steward held for him in a pair of wooden tongs and wiped sleep from his face and eyes. He rubbed the terry towel behind his neck and finished with his hands. The steamy towel smelled like lemon and eucalyptus, a perfect combination.

And that was that; his real world respite, the five-hour trip, felt like ten minutes. Sleep will do that. He must have dreamed. Everyone dreams. It's a biological process the brain needs for repair and processing. It had been decades since Calvin remembered a single one of his.

He yawned and settled the hat firmly over his brow. Row A in First Class came with many perks. Isolation from most of the plane's passengers, permission to act eccentric and withdrawn, but being first off the plane ranked highest on the list.

He almost willed the plane to increase speed on its way to the gate and smiled to himself. *Even if he could do it, and, who knows, maybe he could? Why deplete his strength on something so insignificant?*

Welcome to Atlanta, the disembodied female voice squawked from the speakers inside the airport tram. She tried to sound welcoming and sincerely glad he'd made the trip. Few in his car seemed to notice, fascinated as they apparently were, by him.

He fought the urge to whip off his hat and give them all a real good look at what they clearly all suspected lay hidden beneath its Savile Row-fashioned felt.

The only one to venture within six feet of him turned out to be a four-year-old boy who escaped the grasp of a mother overwhelmed by a slightly older set of twins playing tag around a grab pole. The young boy, decked out in a Mickey Mouse t-shirt and tiny red Nike sneakers, toddled toward him, head tilted upward, gaping at Calvin's head.

"BRETT." The mother, realizing one of her brood had wandered off, shrieked in panic. "GET BACK HERE THIS INSTANT."

Brett, apparently unimpressed with the urgency of *this instant* chose instead to stop a foot from Calvin's polished wingtips and stare upward with an open mouth. The little boy removed the finger he'd been sucking and pointed at Calvin's head.

"Brett McMasters, you move your fanny, now," the mother tried a different tack.

Brett's fanny remained where it was, though the boy it belonged to turned around to see if his mother saw what he saw.

"Momma," the boy squealed. He turned around to be sure Calvin hadn't disappeared and leveled his finger once again. "Momma, look."

Next Stop Baggage. Next Stop Baggage.

What the hell? Might as well give the young boy a reward for his boldness. At least he had the honesty to act on what every other person in the airport tram merely thought.

Calvin squatted in front of the boy to give him a better look and removed the fedora. After wearing the damn thing all this time, all the way from the West Coast, it felt good to take it off.

The boy stamped his feet and clapped his hands, laughing with delight. "Mommy," he turned to his mother. "Hat, Mommy. Hat."

Calvin chuckled and handed the kid his hat to hold. The boy's eyes grew round as dimes as he held the object of his fascination. No oversized, pale-skinned light bulb head could compare to a $1,500 Brooks Brothers fedora.

"Momma. Hat." The little boy held out the hat for his mother to marvel at.

"Give the nice man his hat, Brett. Go on." She looked at Calvin with an expression that couldn't decide between fear and mortification. "I am so sorry, sir."

"Oh, he's a good boy, ma'am." Calvin ruffled the tyke's hair. "I can tell he's being raised right. And we were all children once, weren't we?"

She looked relieved and mouthed a *thank you* as she focused stern eyes on her son. "And what do we say to the nice gentleman, Brett? What do polite boys say?"

The boy handed Calvin the treasured fedora and screwed up his face, thinking hard. "Nice hat," he said.

Several in the crowd watching the interchange chuckled, a couple laughed out loud and like that, the tension in the tram evaporated.

The tram drew to a stop, people leaning against the inertia.

Baggage Claim. Baggage Claim.

The doors whooshed open and the crowd, intent upon securing prize positions at their respective baggage carousels, surged forward. The little boy, the hat, and the man with the funny-shaped head all but forgotten.

#

Calvin slid his keycard in the electronic lock at the door and walked into the Presidential Suite of the Peachtree Plaza Hotel. He tossed his carryon onto the king-sized bed and stood at the floor-to-ceiling windows looking out over the city. A slight haze obscured the far horizon and created the feeling that he floated among clouds. Rooftops of all shapes and heights spread out below. A beautiful panoramic of Centennial Park gave welcome space to the building density. But, the trees made the view truly spectacular. Clusters of treetops sprouted everywhere, thick and dark green, proving Atlanta's 'City In A Forest' nickname an apt fit.

He yawned and checked the time on the Herman Miller wall clock. He'd traveled the world and stayed in all the finest establishments. The Plaza in downtown Atlanta certainly held its own. But he would have preferred the Ritz-Carlton.

Architecture decided his hotel choice for him. The Plaza's distinctive glass cylinder soared 70+ stories in the sky. It couldn't be missed or mistaken by anyone unfamiliar with the South's premier city—and he had folks flying in from all over the globe.

May as well make the best of it.

He unzipped his bag and removed a new bottle of Macallan 1824 and placed it center-stage on the bar. Crystal glasses on the mirror-backed bar shelving were a Presidential Suite perk he planned to make good use of.

No time like the present.

The Speaker poured a generous glass and sat at the dining table placed strategically against a wall of glass. He sipped, looked out over the view and saw none of it. He'd arrived in Atlanta a couple days early, but would soon be joined by the rest of The Council. He expected them to arrive on time and had booked them all into the Plaza in rooms carefully spaced throughout the floors of the facility.

They'd create a big enough stir as it is. All these strange-looking folks with the pasty skin and big heads. No sense inviting attention by clumping themselves all together.

However, after the scene at the airport with the crowd and the little boy, he suspected his careful plans to avoid detection would be for naught.

C'est la vie. Couldn't be helped now.

He'd enjoyed his time off from being The Speaker. Relaxed, re-charged, he felt sixty years younger. But the welcome timeout expired the second he got off the plane.

Actually, Assembly began the instant all Council members voted for it. *Might as well push forward.* He had certain duties to perform and details to arrange before everyone arrived.

The Speaker drained his glass and got up to pour another. Their time of living in the shadows, pushing, controlling, shaping events and making preparations for someday had ended.

Someday had become today.

#

The knock on the door came softly, tentatively, but they all heard it. All eyes followed Calvin as he opened the door. A svelte woman in a stylish white linen suit removed her large, floppy-brim hat and oversized Gucci sunglasses.

"Michelle," he said. "You are as beautiful as I imagined."

"Speaker," she batted her eyes and smiled. "It is a pleasure to finally meet you in person."

"Please. Come in. Everyone is here," he stepped back and opened the door wider.

Michelle entered, removing lavender calfskin gloves. "Forgive me, please. An incident at De Gaulle grounded every plane for a day. *Merde!* I do apologize for my tardiness."

Everyone stood and crowded around, meeting this person they had all linked to, but never met in person. The Speaker watched and smiled inwardly. They had all come without a second thought. Most over great distances and immediately. It spoke to how seriously they viewed their positions on Council. More important, it showed they all understood the gravity of the current situation.

"Everyone, please take a seat," he said. "You'll find plenty to choose from. I gathered us all here in the Presidential Suite for that very purpose. It has ample room for our needs."

"And a superbly stocked bar." Ramon's Spanish accent caressed the words. He held up a tumbler of clear liquid and ice. "Not bad for an American hotel."

"Vie should haf a toast zen," Karla strode to the bar against the wall opposite the floor to ceiling windows and ducked behind it. Bottles clanked as she rummaged around, finally coming up with a bottle of Stolichnaya vodka. "You spoke too fast, Ramon." She shook her head. "Even in Ukraine we have better. Our farmers drink better than this yak piss."

Ramon shrugged and sipped his tequila.

"Karla, cherie," Michelle settled back into a leather barrel chair and crossed her long legs, swiveling back and forth on the spike heel of a white leather boot. "Would you be a dear and pour me some red wine? Any will do. I am not so picky."

Karla raised her eyebrows and opened her mouth to reply.

Calvin guessed it would not be spoken in the spirit of camaraderie he was trying to foster, given Karla's penchant for bluntness.

He patted Michelle on the shoulder as he hurried to the wine rack against the wall beside Karla. "I'll find one I think you'll like, Michelle.

"Karla?" he forced Karla's attention off Michelle and onto him, "I think a toast is an excellent idea. Everyone. Looks like Karla has volunteered to be bartender. If you have nothing to toast with, I'm sure she'll be happy to fill a glass for you." He held Karla's gaze. "Yes?"

Karla smiled tightly and finished unscrewing her bottle of vodka.

"Da," she said. "It would be my *honor* to serve our—how do you say it in America—our little freak show? Welcome, Council, to Assembly!" She downed her first shot of Stoli and immediately poured another.

"Mr. Speaker?" Patel from Mumbai had been gazing out over Atlanta's skyline and treetops. He spoke without turning around. "Perhaps you could share your plans with us?" His melodious Indian inflection, colored by a slight British hue, rounded every word. "I am assuming, of course you are possessed of one?"

"Does everyone have something to drink?" Calvin ignored Patel's question. "Patel? Someone get Patel a—"

Ramon handed the man a glass of Don Julio. "Here, my friend. Broaden your horizons."

"Thank you, Ramon." Calvin raised his glass. "I want to thank all of you for responding to this, our first and only call for Assembly. Most, me included, probably thought it would not happen in our lifetimes. But it has and you have stepped up to the task like I knew you would. It is my honor to be your Speaker, especially today." He cleared his throat. "To the Given Goal!"

"To the Given Goal." His Council spoke in unison and sipped their drinks. No one spoke for several seconds. The silence lent their gathering a momentary, solemn respect he appreciated. Considering his next request, he would need it.

"All right, everyone. Let us not waste any more time away from the real reason we are here. I believe a small demonstration is in order. Everyone? If you would all would clasp hands and face the window?"

"Now?" Michelle sounded worried. "Mr. Speaker, are you sure? Perhaps we should discuss this—"

"We need to flex our muscles a bit, Michelle. See, for our own peace of mind, if we will be up to the challenge ahead of us. Please?" he held out his hand to her, "there is no other way."

Glasses clinked and clanked as they were set down. He took end position, followed by Michelle and the rest of his Council as they linked hands and faced out the window.

"There is a radio tower off in the distance, with a blinking red light on top. Everyone see it?"

He took their various grumbled assents as a communal *Yes*.

"Good. The sun is now reflecting off its west side. I want us to concentrate and collapse the tower on that side."

"What—"

"Hold on a second, Speaker—"

"What if there are people—"

"I have checked the area and marked the distance from here.

Nine miles if anyone cares. The land around that radio tower is deserted and the tower is old. One of the first ever erected in the Atlanta metro area. Verizon may disagree loudly, but most others will simply surmise that girders on that side rusted through and collapsed under their own weight.

"Now, I have been patient. We laugh and joke. You have come a long way and a little latitude is to be allowed. But you all know why we are here so please, do as I ask—as your Speaker commands.

"I will say this only once, so hear me. I want us to be clear on this because it is important. I am The Speaker, selected by process and my authority is absolute. I know what I am doing. For the good of us all as well as for those whom we are chosen to serve. From this point forward never, EVER, question one of my commands again."

He made eye contact with each of them to drive home the point, held a bit longer on Karla. He felt them all get in line behind him. Even Karla.

"Thank you. Lecture over. Now, concentrate on the middle of its western face and let's bring down that tower."

To an outsider watching from behind, they may have looked like a group of friends admiring the spectacular view. A closer examination might have thought it odd how they all held hands and how the linked hands grew white, as if squeezing with enormous strength.

An especially observant watcher may have even picked up a flock of blackbirds spook from trees below and the brilliant orange flare far out in the carpet of green treetops that seemed to come from the direction of that tower way off in the distance with the red light on top.

Even a casual observer, however, would not miss the slow red arc of that same light as it fell slowly to the side. The tower's metal girders splintered and bent in the grip of something far more powerful than old age and gravity. Doubtless, the old tower's death came about with the violent shriek of metal on metal and explosive pops as rivets failed and shot free or sheared through from unaccustomed stress.

At this distance however, and encased in the sumptuous confines of the Peachtree Plaza Presidential Suite, the members of The Council heard nothing until Karla sniffed wetly.

Calvin looked over in time to see her break her grip and swipe at a bloody nose with her fingers.

She came away with them dripping red. "Shit," she said.

Chapter Thirty-Six

GOING HOME

El sat back in his seat and closed his eyes to think. The little girl, healed in that parking lot. The grateful parents. Their friends driving up frightened. Frightened of what? HIM?

He knew if he'd had time to explain he could have made them see. Helped them understand. Then again, he wasn't all that sure he understood himself.

What the heck's going on with him? What kind of freak-a-zoid had he morphed into?

Be calm, dude.

Behind his eyelids he detached from the frantic goings-on in the car around him.

He felt the commotion, sure. Braced his hands down into the seat to steady himself against the violent side-to-side swaying as Smith scooped Nicole into the passenger seat and powered them the hell out of Dodge.

He heard B's cry and Nicole's calm response. Felt B's Camaro porpoise over the dips in the pavement at the parking lot entrance. He flopped up and down with it. Banged against the doorframe. He couldn't worry about mundane stuff like physics with the thoughts he had spooling in his head—even after Smith squealed the tires hanging a tight left turn and B slid into him.

Nope. Too much real important stuff going on.

"Home," he said.

No one reacted. Probably couldn't hear him over Smith's loud cursing and liberal use of the Chevrolet's impressive dual horns.

He tried again. Louder. "HOME. I WANT TO GO HOME."

Smith's only answer came in a quick glance to the rearview.

Beatrix didn't hold back. "No friggin' way," she said. "I told you before. The whole world is going to be camped out at your door. Not happening."

"I'm counting on it. And I'm going, with you guys or alone. I'm going home."

To the only place he'd ever really felt safe. To the comfort and peace he'd need to FIGURE THIS STUFF OUT.

"I'm going home." He repeated it, with his eyes closed. Speaking the words out loud again took some of the pressure off and he smiled.

B and Smith and Nicole could come if they wanted. Smith he wasn't so sure about. His mom would probably enjoy a houseful of guests to torture with new casseroles. His dad might grumble a bit. But grumbling is what his dad did best.

It'll be good to see them again. Maybe they could shed some light on where he'd come from and how he turned out the way he did.

Six exhausting hours later, after several aborted attempts by Beatrix and Smith to dissuade him, he and his misfit crew squealed to a halt at the curb in front of his Atlanta home. He opened the door and prepared to exit when Beatrix whirled and fixed him with her patented, God-you're-such-a-screw-up glare.

"Where do you think you're going?"

He met her gaze with calm. "We've been over this. You all are welcome to come—though I apologize in advance for my mom. She means well."

Smith angled the rearview to look at him. "This is a very bad idea, El. I can't guarantee your safety in a place I've not checked out."

"Thanks, but I don't need your guarantee, Smith. This is safe. It's my home for God's sake. What could happen?"

"I've already thought of about a hundred things," B said. "None of them good."

"B, I need to do this. I feel like it's the right thing for me now. I can't explain it any better than that."

"Nicole, you get me, right? You understand—hey, what's wrong with Nicole?" He noticed Nicole leaned back in her seat. Pale. Sweat beading her forehead.

"I'm fine," she said.

"You're not fine." Beatrix pounded the top of the seat in

frustration. "She's not fine."

"What happened?"

"Seriously? Where have you been, El?" B grabbed twin fistfuls of her hair and pulled. "GOD. I really don't get you sometimes. She's hurt. Those wonderful folks you helped back there? They shot her. Remember? You were sitting like, I dunno, eighteen inches away? The squealing tires? Smith torturing my car? Our getaway?" She leaned forward and rapped on his head. "Ring a bell in there?"

"I'm sorry. I was busy thinking."

"How lucky for us."

"Nicole," El scooted to the edge of the backseat. "Show me."

"What?" Nicole's eyes flew open. "No."

Beatrix pulled up Nicole's blood-soaked shirt gently, murmuring to her friend all the while. "Sorry, Nicole girl. Let him see where you're hit. You know what he can do."

"I'm not in the habit of pulling up my shirt for strange men," she said.

"Nicole. Come on," El said. "I'm not strange. We're friends."

"Uh huh. Ooh, ow." Nicole grimaced and closed her eyes.

"Sorry, sorry," Beatrix said.

"El," Nicole opened one eye for a brief second, "I love you but you are the definition of strange."

"I accept that," El said. "Not like it's a surprise or anything." He leaned forward to examine Nicole's side. Dark red blood welled from two black holes about the size of BBs. "Let me—hold still, okay?" He pressed his palm against her side and closed his eyes too.

The two of them stayed locked together in that weird embrace for several minutes until El opened his eyes and pulled his hand back. In the center of his bloody palm two black pellets swam in crimson. "That should do it," he said.

Beatrix and Smith looked at the evidence in El's hand before trading glances.

Smith cleared his throat. "They were probably right under the skin. No big deal."

"You okay Nikki?" Beatrix said. "He didn't hurt you?"

Nicole opened her eyes and probed her wound, pushing and prodding where an imprint of El's fingers could be seen in the blood on her skin. She pushed hard.

"Easy, girl," B said.

"No, no. I'm good. He did it."

"No pain?"

"Not a whisper," Nicole said. "Add me to his list of miracles."

"It's not a miracle," El said. He opened the back door and pushed himself out of the opening. He leaned down and grinned at them. "I can't explain it. It's what I do." He dried his hand on the front of his jeans. "I'm going in to see my folks. If you don't want to join me, I'll understand. There's an okay Holiday Inn an exit up on I-285."

B grimaced, "Like we're going to split up now? Let's go people." She opened her door. "Let's all say *Hi* to the folks."

His mother yanked the door open before the doorbell chimes subsided. "Eldridge, why are you ringing the bell to your own home?" She stepped out and scanned the street both ways before ducking back inside. "Come in, come in. We were hoping you'd—there's so much I want to know—are you all right?"

"Mom," he laughed, "slow down. I'm fine. I have friends with me so I thought I'd better—"

"We saw your friends on TV, Eldridge. And the computer. Please, get inside the house. All of you." She stepped back so they could enter the foyer. "Hurry." When they were inside she locked the door and twisted the deadbolt.

"Mom? Is everything okay?"

"Little late to be asking that, isn't it?" His dad, who rarely looked up from his newspaper crossword, uncharacteristically came over to stand behind his wife.

"Mom, Dad. I don't know what you've seen or heard. That's one reason I'm here. I need you to know what's going on."

"That's a start," his dad nodded.

"I'll not stand here grilling my child, Kevin. No matter what he's done."

"Mom, we haven't done anything," he said.

"Tell that to the reporters," his dad snorted. "And the police, the FBI, the TV reporters, the religious whack-a-dos, the gawkers—"

"What'd I tell you, El?" B punched his arm. "We're not safe here. More to the point, you're not safe. We need to go."

He closed his eyes and sent a resounding *NO* to her and Smith with all the force he'd learned to focus.

"Oww!" Beatrix grabbed her head. "Quit it."

Smith twitched once, shook it off and glared at him.

Nicole felt nothing, of course. But she looked at the other two and fixed him with raised eyebrows.

Squeak. Squeak.

The foyer hanging light swayed a few times and his Mom and Dad stared at it with open mouths.

"Let's start over," El said. "Mom, Dad, these are my really good friends. B—Beatrix—you met before Mom. This is Nicole—she's not like—she's normal."

"How nice of you to say, El." Nicole said wryly. "I never thought of myself as normal."

"This is John—"

"Smith," John Smith stepped forward and offered his hand. "I must apologize for barging in on you like we have. We tried to talk him out of it, but your son can be very—"

"Mule-headed," B said.

"I was going to say, persuasive," Smith finished.

His mom took Smith's hand tentatively.

His father didn't hesitate a second. "I see you do know my son, Mr. Smith." He stepped up and shook Smith's hand, smiling for the first time. "We've been expecting you, someone like you, I mean, for years now."

"Please, let's all sit down." His mom led the way into the dining room. "Can I get you all something to eat? Drink? I'm sure you must be tired from your um, adventures?"

"Got any of your iced tea?" El said. "I've been missing that."

His dad took a seat at the head of the table and the others picked their spots while his mom scurried off for the kitchen wringing her hands.

"Mr. Montcalm," Smith began, "I want to assure you that we have no intention of causing harm to come to you or your wife."

"How many of you are there?"

"Dad."

Smith silenced him with a headshake. "That's okay, El. It's a good question," he said. "I've wondered that myself, sometimes. The honest answer is, I don't really know. Hundreds. Maybe thousands. Between those who are aware like Beatrix Goode, your son, and myself. And those who were like El here a short time ago." He looked at El and smiled. "Clueless."

"*What* are you?"

"DAD. Jesus."

"Another excellent question, sir. I will tell you what I can." Smith folded his hands on the table in front of him. "We are human, exactly like you, in absolutely every way."

"But—?" his father looked from Smith to B.

"But," Smith continued, "We have certain, let's say, characteristics, you already know about that are shared by many of us."

"How we look for instance." Never one to stay silent for long, B took over. "Like many segments in the population who share certain traits—Asians, albinos, gabby Irishmen," she inclined her head toward Smith, "ours are entirely human and remarkably consistent." She rolled up a sleeve. "We're pigmentally challenged. None of us will ever get a tan unless we spray it on. Head shape is another obvious trait. We don't know why—"

Smith cleared his throat.

"Smith likes to say our big bald heads are shaped the way they are to fit our overdeveloped brains. That's Smith. We have not determined the real answer."

His mother reappeared with a pitcher of tea, glasses, and a plate mounded with oatmeal cookies. "But you all can do things," she said. "Things we cannot—I hope you like these, I made them last night."

"Mrs. Montcalm, you shouldn't have—but I'm glad you did." B reached for a cookie. "Yes. We can do things. You probably noticed that Eldridge, as he grew up, had certain abilities. He tested off-the-charts smart, anticipated people on the phone or at the door, things like that." She chuckled, "I hear he broke a few mirrors."

His mom's eyes widened. "Why, yes! His father always thought he was clumsy."

"Oh, El's clumsy," B chuckled, "but not in the way you mean. Your son has a very strong telekinetic ability—that means he can affect objects with his mind. Many of us can but his ability is pretty special. My guess is he simply didn't like looking at himself in mirrors."

"Oh, we know he's special." His mom stood behind his chair and kissed him on top of his head.

"Mom," he squirmed aside, "this is serious."

"So am I," she said primly and set about pouring glasses full of tea.

"Sir," Smith broke in, "you mentioned all the *visitors* you've been having? Reporters, police, and the like. I noticed you have shiny new locks on your front door."

His father cleared his throat. "Yes."

"May I ask how long it has been since someone last contacted you?"

"Not long," he said. "What honey, a few days?"

His mother sat down with her own glass. "I'd say. That poor homeless woman, you mean?" She tapped fingernails on her glass. "Referred to my baby as Satan? Imagine."

"That's the one," he said. "I'd say half the people knocking on our door are gawkers and fanatics."

"Or sick," his mom said. "After that video thing of yours, people seem to think you can heal them or someone they know."

"So," B speared El with narrowed eyes. "Get a lot of those?"

"More all the time," his mother said. "They don't worry me. I feel sorry for them, but—"

"Don't," B said. "They are what we must fear most."

"But they're hurting. We have nothing to fear from them." His mother shook her head. "Surely, they—"

"Mrs. Montcalm," B said, "They? It's their numbers that scare me. I could fill a stadium with the government folks and the wackos interested in your son. The number of sick and dying people in the world would fill up the map."

"Shit," his dad said. "They're back."

"Kevin, language."

"Who's back Dad?" El said.

His dad pointed to the ceiling. "Listen."

They all stopped for a moment and sure enough, El heard the approaching rotors of a helicopter.

"Oh, dear," his mother rung her hands. "I'd hoped they gave up on us."

His dad waved a hand. "They'll fly around a few minutes and be gone. Nothing to worry about."

They sat and listened to the pilot get closer.

"Huh, that's different," his dad said.

"Why's that Mr. Montcalm?" B looked worried.

"He's lower than before. And he's not going away."

B rubbed her face in her hands. "You didn't have a bright yellow Camaro parked in front of your house before."

They all got up and ran to the front living room curtains. A chopper with no discernible markings hovered over their street, way below legal height. Outside its open door, a man balanced on a skid and trained a video camera down at them.

Everyone, distracted by the commotion outside, missed El slipping away for the front door—until the clack of the door latch gave him away.

"What the hell are you doing, El?" B shouted.

"Get back in here, son." His dad tried a more measured tone.

"FREEZE." Smith tried the more direct approach.

They really don't have a clue about what we're doing here. Guess it's time they found out.

El pulled the door shut behind him and stepped out onto the front porch.

The rotor wash kicked grit up from the ground and he shielded his eyes as the particles stung his cheeks and forehead. He waved his other arm, beckoning, encouraging the pilot to set down.

The pitch of the chopper's motors changed as the man at the controls feathered his throttle and teased the craft to settle in the middle of the street. The rotors *chuff-chuffed* the air as they slowed and finally ceased turning.

Behind him, El heard the front door crash open. He whirled and let his mind slam it fast before any of his group could exit.

Two people climbed down the helo's steps. The first, a stylish black woman in a tailored blue suit. The second, a cameraman in a Hawaiian shirt and jeans.

"Did you get that?" yelled the woman. She clutched a microphone in her armpit. "Tell me you got that." Her videographer nodded and stayed focused El.

The woman straightened her blue suit and patted her hair, smiling that reporter smile; the one that does more for the camera than the folks she's interviewing.

He watched bemused while the cameraman and his reporter hurried up the walk.

"Don't worry," he said. "You look fine."

"I'm sorry, what?" the reporter said.

"Your new haircut. I don't know what you looked like before, but it does make you look young."

She paled and turned wide eyes back at her guy. El heard the man chuckle under his breath.

"Well, thank you Mr. Montcalm. That's kind of you to—*notice*." The woman cleared her throat as if trying to right herself. She waited a beat before shifting the mike to her left hand and thrusting her other hand forward. "I am honored to finally meet you."

He shook her proffered hand. "Is that thing connected?"

"To—?"

"Live. Are we live?"

She turned raised eyebrows on her cameraman and he gave them a thumbs up. "Yes, Mr. Mont—"

"Call me El. Please. No need for formalities. Mr. Montcalm's my dad." He let go of her hand and smiled his best smile to put her at ease. "Sareena, like the tennis player. I like it. Spelled different though."

The woman stood open-mouthed.

"Sorry. I don't mean to frighten." He leaned forward and whispered, "Close your mouth."

"Oh. Oh, my gosh—"

"Don't laugh, Carlos. I can read you, too."

The videographer dropped the camera and crossed himself.

"Come on, dude," El said. "Camera up, camera up. We're all professionals here." He placed his hand on the reporter's shoulder to ease her aside. He noticed her shrink away from his touch. *She thinks I'm going to bite her or what? Crazy.*

He walked by her and toward Carlos and his camera, staring all the while into the camera lens.

"Stay with me, Carlos," he said.

"I got you, El."

"Thank you." El composed himself for a few seconds. "I know that many of you out there have questions about me and my...friends." He leaned forward and adopted a serious face and tone. "You've seen things. Heard things. You're wondering what's true, what's going on. Are we some kind of—I don't know what. I can assure you. We're not anything bad, anything to be afraid of.

"Fact is, I am pretty new to all this like you guys. I'm still trying to work things out. New stuff surprises me every day. Really.

"What I do want you to know is this, I am not here to hurt anyone. Quite the opposite. If you or a loved one are in pain, if you've given up hope because doctors can't help you. I can. And I want to.

"Come see me and I will try to help. Not here. Not at my home. I will not see you here. A lot of you have tried and you've scared the sh— crud out of my Mom and Dad. Not good." He wagged his finger at the lens.

"We will see you at the baseball stadium, where the Braves play, SunTrust Park, in three days. That should give the authorities enough time to figure things out."

He turned his back on the camera and pushed past the reporter who stood speechless, and waved his hand at his front door. Bolts threw and the door crashed open, spilling B and Smith and Nicole out onto the porch.

El winked at B and turned back around. "Carlos," he called.

"Yeah, man?"

"Thanks for your help. You did good. I don't know about Pulitzer good." He shrugged. "But—see you in three days." He stepped onto his porch. "Come on guys. We've got stuff to talk about." He walked by his friends like he had the poor reporter. His mom and dad stayed silent as he returned to his seat at the dining room table and waited with folded hands, for everyone to rejoin him.

The reporter finally found her voice as the front door shut behind his friends. "Pulitzer? Really Carlos?" Her voice raised two octaves. "For pointing the camera while he made us look like idiots? Are you insa—?"

The closing door cut her off and El shoved the woman from his mind. He had bigger worries now, in the shape of a certain pissed off big dude with no sense of humor and a feisty young woman who stomped up and back, red-faced, cracking her knuckles. The loud pops and snaps sounded like popcorn.

Beatrix came up to the dining room table and leaned both palms flat on it. He noticed the shine of tears in her eyes and that scared him. More than anything they'd faced in the last few days. For the first time he felt a tiny niggle of doubt pluck at the hairs on the back of his neck.

"What?" he said.

"Jesus, El," B said. "You have no idea what you've done."

Chapter Thirty-Seven

NEWS AT ELEVEN

The Director in the booth counted her down in her earpiece. The Assistant Director on the news set flashed his fingers under Camera One lens. Three, two, one—
All crew activity ceased and the red light blinked on soundlessly.

The air-brushed, blow-dried, poster woman for capped teeth looked straight into the camera with carefully rehearsed excitement and breathlessly announced a Channel Nine News exclusive interview with the 'man at the center of the Freeway Miracle in Florida!'

"Who is Eldridge Montcalm? In case you were wondering, yes, that is indeed his real name. How did the Amazing El—that is the name he uses to describe himself—come to be? Is this man a charlatan? A god? Is he a man at all? We get to the bottom of these questions and more, with answers from the 'amazing' man himself. Our exclusive interview airs promptly at 6 this evening. Only on Channel Nine. And only with yours truly, Sareena Kirkpatrick."

We're off! Great job Sareena!

She tapped her earpiece and nodded to the crew in the booth. "Thanks, Harvey," she said. "That ought to boost our ratings by a few points." She stood and stripped off her microphone and laid her earpiece on the news desk. "See you all a couple minutes before six."

Early that evening, Sareena sat while the makeup girl daubed on last minute adjustments and fixed her hair. The Director spoke in her ear.

"We cued up your tape and it's ready to roll. Management came down to review it before airtime. Everyone's pretty excited about this.

And the way you spliced the footage together—like a network pro."

"You're a prince Harvey. I'm only doing my job. Trying to make us all look good."

"I hope the world is ready to hear what we have to say."

"You mean what he has to say. People want to know about this man. And I'm—*we*—are going to bring them the good news, as they say."

Three. Two. One.

#

Outside Atlanta in the inner sanctum of the *In His Name* compound, Mother Magdalene fumed. One of her acolytes brought the news promo to her attention earlier in the day and the big screen in the media center had been tuned to Channel Nine ever since.

Mother stalked back and forth in front of the TV screen, alternately muttering and shaking fists at the sky. Every station tease raised her blood pressure by a few notches. Every sly hint at the 'amazing revelations' to come pushed her closer to the edge and her staff farther away. Every breathless station break announcing the 'broadcast event of the century' sent the woman to new levels of froth.

No one at *In His Name* had the courage to wait out the broadcast with their leader, seizing upon any excuse to tend to important business elsewhere. Only the most foolhardy or unlucky planned to be anywhere nearby when the actual newscast finally aired.

The only exception being her hapless audio/video director, Pat. He had no choice. And God help him if any technical glitch interrupted the newscast only minutes away.

"PAT."

"Yes, Mother?"

"How long now?"

He eyed the wall clock mounted right above the TV screen. "Soon, Mother." She had to see the clock herself every time she scowled at the screen. "Two minutes."

"The Devil counts down the minutes and we wait like lambs for the knife to open our throats. This is not right," she pounded a fist into her palm. "This is not right."

At fifteen seconds to the top of the hour, Pat dimmed the lights in the media room and turned up the volume. For the first time since the installation of their state-of-the-art media center, he worried that he'd been too exacting with the video and audio equipment. Thanks to him, their equipment would catch every nuance, every whispered breath and project every bright pixel on the screen in Ultra Hi-Def detail.

The images and sounds Mother would soon be subjected to

would leave no room for equivocation, no hiding behind shadows of doubt.

The woman paced, wringing her hands. "The Devil has come to our sanctuary this day and, God help me, I am the one inviting him in."

"Good evening faithful viewers...." The image on the screen showed every pore on Sareena Kirkpatrick's glistening cheeks.

"Faithful?" Mother screeched. "You Satan's slut. You have no faith. You have no soul."

"I know you are anxious to begin, as am I. So let's not wait any longer, shall we?"

#

In downtown Atlanta, in the Presidential Suite of the Peachtree Plaza hotel, a group hung on the words of the newscast talking head for a completely different set of reasons, but with markedly similar emotions.

"Turn it up," the Speaker said.

Tanya grabbed the remote and thumbed the volume.

"The images you are about to see have not been doctored in any way. I made a few edits in the interest of brevity and for clarity but I assure you, no important communication from Eldridge Montcalm—the Amazing El—has been compromised whatsoever.

"And so, without further ado, I give you what you have all been waiting for. Here is the man himself, in his own words and without any prompting."

The image on screen pulled in and out of focus as the camera swung wildly side-to-side as the cameraman and reporter descended the helicopter steps. The sound of the copter's slowing rotors overhead overwhelmed the audio. The scene settled on the front of a house and a white-skinned man with the by-now familiar odd-shaped head walking forward, smiling.

The man turned to say something to the open front door behind him. The camera focused on it in time to show the door slamming shut, apparently of its own accord.

"Did you get that? Tell me you got that." Sareena's voice cut through the sound of the rotors with piercing clarity. The camera wobbled as it followed Sareena up the walk toward the approaching man. It caught Sareena patting her hair, trying to undo the effects of the rotors mere feet above them.

The cameraman did a decent job scurrying ahead of his newswoman, angling the shot to catch both her and the man smiling and walking toward them.

A clear edit point came as the scene jumped. Sareena appeared more composed and less breathless. Eldridge Montcalm had stopped in front of her, smiling expectantly. She extended her hand. *"I am honored to finally meet you."*

In the hotel room the murmuring started:

"What is he doing?"

"Zis is not good, you guys."

"Shut up, Karla. We need to hear this."

The interview progressed beyond introductions to the point where El shouldered past the reporter to speak directly into the camera. His face filled the screen. The Speaker winced at every other sentence:

"You're wondering what's true, what's going on. Are we some kind of—I don't know what? I can assure you, we're not....

"If you or a loved one are in pain, if you've given up hope because the doctors can't help you. I can...."

"Mon dieu, thees is bad for us, no?" Michelle said. "Oui? Ver bad."

Ramon spoke eloquently by refusing to speak at all and swigging straight from his tequila bottle.

"Pipe down, people," The Speaker said. "Please."

Then, it got worse.

"We will see you at the baseball stadium, where the Braves play, SunTrust Park, in three days. That should give the authorities enough time to figure things out."

To emphasize the point, the TV station froze the image of El, his face smiling triumphantly with not a lick of guile. And unfortunately for everyone in the Presidential Suite, without a hint of a clue.

The smiling face of Sareena came on. Eyebrows knitted solemnly, hands clasped in front of her.

"I hope you got that, ladies and gentlemen. In case you weren't ready to make any notes, we're putting the information on the screen for you. Notice that Eldridge Montcalm said, *we will see you.* Not I or me, but WE. What does that mean? Are there more of his kind?" She chuckled. "Are we being invaded?"

#

North of town at *In His Name* Mother Magdalene turned over two chairs and pitched a potted plant at the screen. Thank the lord, Pat thought, she missed.

"Write that down," she hissed. "Write it down. Three days. SunTrust Park. Got that?"

"Yes, Mother." He circled the words on his paper with a flourish.

The old woman resumed stalking back and forth, wringing her hands and talking to herself. "Turn it down. TURN IT DOWN." She pressed palms to her ears. "I can't think over that Devil's minion blathering away."

Pat left the image of the newscaster with the date and time frozen onscreen. The white type glowed in an unearthly way.

"That's it. That's it." Mother turned to Pat beaming wildly. He thought it might be one of the most frightening things he'd ever witnessed. He wisely chose not to ask what *that* might be and waited for Mother to tell him.

He didn't have long to wait.

"The Devil has announced his plans, Pat. That is your name? Pat?"

He grimaced and nodded.

Mother carried on without noticing. "The Evil One has chosen his battleground. We shall choose the time. And we shall choose our weapons. Send facetext or what you call it to all of our brothers and sisters. Tell them the war is upon us—are you writing this down?"

He hastily scratched pen across paper. "Yes, Mother. Of course, Mother."

"Tell them all to gather here at seven no, six that morning. Bring their holy texts. And tell those who wish to strike a blow for our Lord— this is important—to fill their pockets with stones. We shall cast stones as in Jesus' day and our aim shall be true, guided by His holy hand."

"But, Mother. If we show up with pockets full of rocks—"

She stilled him with an upraised hand. "Their dogs and their metal detectors will not trifle with the odd bits of granite. Trust your Mother. I have thought this through."

She stopped talking and raised her arms to the heavens.

"End our message with this: 'Brothers and Sisters, we have been trained to do God's work and He has called us this day to prove our faith. We shall not falter. We shall not waver in our mission. The Devil has stirred up a nest of righteous hornets and our sting shall drive the vile creature back to Hell where he belongs. *In His Name.* Amen!'"

\#

El's dad clicked off the TV and the group sat in silence.

"I hope you're satisfied," Beatrix finally said. "You have made such a mess of things. We may never dig out from under it."

"I have given people hope and a chance at a better life. That is all I have done."

"No, my man," Smith said. "You've put a target on all of us; those sitting here with you now and others around the globe who look like us."

"What do you think, Nicole?" El asked. "Might as well add your two cents to the Inquisition."

"I believe you have gifts and you want to share them with the world. I understand that."

El nodded. "Thank you."

"But I have to agree with my girl—and him." She jerked a thumb in Smith's direction. "We have more immediate problems. I bet City Hall and Atlanta PD are scrambling right now trying to figure out what to do about your stunt—er, proposal."

Smith looked at Nicole with raised brows. "Look at you. All that and brains, too."

"Shut up."

Smith continued, "The waitress is right. No way they're going to let your little coming out party *come out* El. Too many liabilities. Fact, I wouldn't be surprised if they come—"

BRRINGGG.

A jangling telephone cut him off.

"Speak of the devil," Smith chuckled. "Bet that's the mayor right now. Or another reporter asking for comment."

"Don't answer that Mom," El said. "The world already has my comment."

BRRINGGG. BRRINGGG. BRRINGGG. BRRINGGG.

"What do *you* guys want to do?"

"I don't know genius," B said. "Didn't think that through, did you? Didn't think about the hordes that'll descend on your mom and dad—despite your oh-so-cute plea to the contrary."

El squirmed in his seat.

"Didn't think about having every cop in every Metro-Atlanta squad car on your—check that, *our*—butt? Didn't think about how we'll get near that stadium, much less deal with the hundreds probably on their way there right now. See the common thread here?"

"Didn't think?" El's mom said.

"Thank you, Mrs. Montcalm," B said. "I mean, Christ El. Who do you think you are? And let me disabuse you of something right now. Despite what the press and the TV are saying—you are no damn miracle worker. And you are most especially not a GOD."

El clasped his hands between his knees and looked down. "Never said I was."

"What then?"

"I'm still working that out."

"No matter who gets hurt in the process?"

No answer.

"Consequences, El. Remember? You want to work things out? Go find yourself? Go pull a John the Baptist and wander around in the wilderness a few years. Preach to the squirrels."

Nicole crossed herself.

"Oh, come on Nikki. Really?"

"I've seen what El can do," Nicole said. "I was there. Every time. And I think he's—he's Biblical is the right word. How do we know he's not heaven sent?"

"For goodness sakes you—you—*people*." El's mom jumped to her feet. "Eldridge may be a genius."

"Humph." His dad crossed his arms.

"You hush, Kevin. He is smart. He is different. Lord knows no one had a better front row seat to all that than us. So, he can do some things. He's not a freak. He's certainly no god. He's my son."

"Mom—"

"Quiet, honey. You had your turn. Now it's mine." Mrs. Montcalm paced up and back. "He's my son and I am frightened to death for him. The authorities, the cuckoo-birds, the people. They're all going to come looking for Eldridge. And now, thanks to that stupid thing—" she pointed at the TV—"the whole darn world knows exactly where he is."

His mom scanned the room, daring anyone to say different.

"No, no," said Beatrix. "You're doing fine, Mrs. Montcalm."

His mother walked over to him and held out her hands. He stood and she hugged him tight and kissed him until he turned bright red.

"I can't believe I am saying this and I never thought I ever would. But Eldridge baby? You need to leave."

His dad chimed in, "Like an hour ago."

"And you people," his mom fixed every one of his friends with a glare, "you take care of my baby. He's the only one I've got."

She walked over to Smith. "I'm talking to you, especially Mr. Smith. Something about you, I think you may be a man to have around in a crisis. If someone messes with my El—"

"I understand," Smith said. "And I will."

"Now go, go." His mother looked out the front drapes before opening the door. "Coast is clear. Go do what you have to do. Follow your heart, like we raised you. And don't worry about getting in touch with us. They can track you. I know. I saw it on *Sixty Minutes*."

Beatrix went over and hugged Mrs. Montcalm. "I think you're a big part of why El is so special," she said. "I swear to you, we'll do our best. Despite him."

The two women chuckled and his mom wiped a tear from her eye.

"We're out of here," Smith said. "Harder to hit a moving target.

Let's go."

The gang said more brief good-byes and headed for the door.

Once they were all in the car and belted in, at Nicole's insistence, Smith started the engine. "Any idea where we're headed?"

"I know exactly the place," El said. "B reminded me of it back there. No one will find us and no one, almost no one, will see us."

Chapter Thirty-Eight

CAMPING OUT.

Tires crunched on gravel then shushed as rocks turned to pine needles and dirt. The car full of refugees nosed its way through stands of trees and around sharp outcroppings of granite.

"Up ahead you'll see a burnt tree sticking up with a craggy top." El sat forward from the back seat into the space between the Camaro's two, bucket seats. "Slow down when we get there. Don't want to run over anyone."

"Run over anyone?" Smith said. "What do you mean—?"

"THERE," Nicole screamed. "WATCH OUT."

A white face all wide eyes and open mouth flashed by in the headlights.

Smith jerked the wheel and slammed on the brakes. The car slewed sideways and bumped none too gently up against a dead pine blackened the full way up its trunk. In the descending dusk, it loomed blacker than the trees that surrounded them.

"We're here," El said. "You can turn off the engine. Good job not killing the neighbors. Leave the parking lights on. We'll need them."

The Camaro driver's side door rested against the tree. All the other doors worked fine and they wasted no time bailing from them.

"Coney," El called. "That you? Are you okay?"

"Who the heck is Coney, El?" Beatrix said. "More important, where are we?"

"Home. For the next few days anyway. And Coney *lives* here."

"But where *are*—?"

"That your friend over there?" Nicole pointed to a camouflage tarp sagging between two trees. A bearded man covered in pine needles and debris mumbled and fussed at the lengths of yellow ski rope holding it up. A lopsided tinfoil hat sat crooked on his head.

"Coney?" El called. "You all right?" He walked slowly in the man's direction but stopped when the odd figure stiffened. "We're not here to hurt you, buddy." He spread his hands. "You remember me don't you? Eldridge? I used to bring you and the other guys Doritos?"

Coney scratched his head and peered hard at El.

"Super sorry for that mess back there," El continued. "Our driver really sucks sometimes. We're looking for a new one."

Smith finally climbed out the passenger door in time to hear El and then Coney's reply.

"Coulda killed somebody, Eldridge. Driving all crazy. Oughta be locked up. Throw away the key is what Coney says."

"Maybe if you'd watched where you were—." Smith stopped when B grabbed his arm and shook her head.

"Locked up is too good for him, ask me. Throw away the key, Eldridge."

El made it to the far side of the sagging tarp and pulled on the rope opposite from Coney. Coney relaxed and adjusted his piece of rope as well. Two old friends, lashing down shelter for the night.

El looked over at the man, concern knitting his eyebrows. "You're not hurt are you buddy?"

"Only my stupid old head. Like always. Coney Stupid Head."

"Can I see?" El yanked his knot tight to the tree and approached the man slowly. "Do you mind? I won't hurt you. Please?"

The man dropped his hands from the yellow rope and they trembled as he stood swaying in place. "Coney is okay. A-OK. No problemo." He backed away when El drew near.

In the yellow glare of the parking lights, El's friend could have passed for forty or eighty or anywhere in between. The full beard, a healthy layer of grime and the lopsided tinfoil hat obscured his features.

"That's Pop-Top's shirt isn't it?" El stopped walking.

"I didn't steal it. Pop-Top gave it to me. I didn't steal it." Coney grabbed two flaps of a blue denim shirt three sizes too big for him and held on tight.

"How many shirts you wearing tonight?" El said.

"Gotta bundle up. Gonna be a cold one. Coney says."

"El," Nicole whispered, "May I?" She'd slipped closer as they talked.

He looked at her with raised eyebrows.

"I have an older brother back home. Like—your friend." She walked toward Coney, speaking softly without looking directly at him. "Hi, there, Coney. My name's Nicole."

Coney shifted his eyes sideways at her then off of her. At her. Off her.

She kept walking and talking without looking at him, and the man stopped swaying and looked at the ground. This time he stayed rooted in place and didn't retreat. Even when Nicole got close enough to touch him.

"You sure have a nice place, here in the woods. I really like the woods. Don't you?"

He shrugged but said nothing.

"Eldridge told us all about your place here. We're Eldridge's friends. Like you."

Coney knit his brows. "Okay then. Sounds good. Okay then."

"Coney," El said, "we need to stay here with you for a while. Is that okay?"

"We're all friends here. No problemo."

"I bet I can fix your hat for you," El said. "It got a little bent up when we got here."

Coney's eyes widened, as he felt all around the crush of tinfoil askew on his head.

"It'll only be off for a minute, I promise. And it'll work good as new. No laser beams. No voices. Okay?"

Coney nodded and squeezed his eyes shut. He flinched when El removed his hat but otherwise stayed still.

El fiddled with the hat until Nicole snatched it from him.

"Let me, El. Criminy, you're all thumbs." She pushed and shaped the crinkled foil, making little headway until B handed her a brand new roll of foil.

"Where'd you get this?" Nicole whispered.

"Remembered I still had stuff in my trunk from my trailer. Go ahead," she smiled. "Work your magic."

"Mmm. Mmm." Coney began touching his scalp and rocking. "Oh no. Oh no."

"Almost done, Coney," El said. "Hang on."

A few minutes later, Nicole held up her handiwork for all to see. A fair representation of a derby, complete with brim, shown gold in the yellow glare of the Camaro's parking lights.

"Damn," Smith said. "That actually looks like a hat. How'd you do that?"

"Balloon animals," Nicole shrugged. "I have nieces."

She walked over to Coney. "Tinfoil. Balloons. No big diff—here Coney. All fixed."

The man opened his eyes and immediately teared up. "Oh my. Oh my."

He bent forward for Nicole to place it on his head.

"Oh," she said. "I'd be honored."

Hat now in place, Coney felt around it with trembling fingers and sighed. "Thank you, um—" he furrowed his brow.

"Nicole, Coney. My name's Nicole."

"You are a good friend, Nicole. Cross my heart."

Nicole crossed her heart. "Me, too. You are a good friend to us all."

Coney nodded and retreated to his tarp. He sat underneath, cross-legged and grinned out at them all; the picture of bearded, grimy contentment.

"What else you have stashed in that car Beatrix?" Smith asked. "How about a little inventory?"

"What's mine is yours," B walked to the rear of the car to the opened trunk, "mostly."

An hour later they'd removed assorted tools, a flashlight, coiled rope, a smashed box of power bars—and a tarp.

"Oh, my God. I can't believe you have a tarp," El said. "How big is—?"

"Perfect size for me and Nikki," she said. "You boy's will have to pick a tree and lean. And before you ask, the health bars are not what I'd call fresh."

"No biggie," El said. "Me and Smith will take the car. You get the mosquitos."

"El. Have I taught you nothing?" B tapped her head. "They won't get near us."

Chapter Thirty-Nine

PERFECT STORM

T he Speaker switched off the TV and waited for the inevitable. It took about .25 seconds by his calculations.

"But if I may interject," Patel started them off. "All those people streaming in? We will never get near them at that soccer stadium."

"They call them ballparks in America," Ramon said. "But I agree. This Eldridge person *es muy loco, Señor Speaker.*"

Karla, as always, preferred the blunt approach. "He is a danger. To himself. To us. He must be dealt with."

"Michelle?" Calvin asked. "What do you think?"

"Monsieur Speaker," the attractive Parisienne leaned back and crossed long legs. "It is clear that we are, shall I say, disappointed as a group? I may even be, how is it said? Nervous as a *chat*? But I am more interested to hear what you have to say. *Oui*? If you would be so kind?"

The Speaker took his time and a long sip of Macallan's before answering. He swallowed and felt the silky Scotch heat in his cheeks.

"Thank you, Michelle." He bowed toward her. "Thoughtful as always. I'll start with a question—why are we here?"

"Because, señor, you invoked Assembly." Ramon pointed at Calvin with his glass. "We are here because we have no choice."

"Too easy, Ramon. I meant, why do you *think* we are here? Why go so far as to call an Assembly when such an option has never been called within the span of any of our shared histories?"

"You think it is the time," Karla said. "You think this, this *child*

189

who has put us all in danger is truly The One? You are as insane as your little pet Beatrix Goode."

"What I think does not matter."

"Explain, *s'il te plait.*"

"Because, Michelle. Eldridge Montcalm has given us no choice. Like it or not—and I do not—he has dragged us from the shadows and exposed us to scrutiny.

"Those stares you got in the airports and on the streets as you traveled here? They are courtesy of Eldridge Montcalm. Those whispers behind your backs? From the streets of your little village, Ramon, to the alleys in Calcutta, Patel? Thank your friend The Amazing El."

"This is so much bullshit." Karla turned her back on the room and stared out at the magnificent Atlanta skyline.

"And whether he meant to or not—I am betting not—B's little discovery could not have picked a more perfect time or place for us. We should thank him."

"Speaker, all due respect," Ramon said, " what you say makes no sense to me."

"I am tired of living in the shadows," Calvin said. "Aren't you? I'm tired of wearing my hat every where I go and being careful to hide my abilities."

"Speaker," Karla turned back around, "are you saying what I think you are saying?"

The Speaker counted off the points on his fingers:

"All eyes are tuned to the funny-looking people with strange-shaped heads. SunTrust Park will have hundreds, maybe thousands, cramming and jamming in. Some in need. Some merely curious. The media will be out in force. And lastly, Eldridge Montcalm, Beatrix Goode and Mr. John Smith, if I know the man's ambitions, will all be front and center.

"It is the perfect storm ladies and gentlemen. A storm we have waited decades for." He pointed out the window. "We tested our power earlier. We know what we can do. The rest of the world does not. If Eldridge Montcalm is indeed The One, we will be that much stronger and all will proceed that much faster." He took a sip. "Then we can really let the world know that times have changed. That the world they once knew is no more."

No one spoke. He looked around the room at a bunch of open mouths and wide eyes. "You want to know what I think, Michelle? I think it is about damn time."

Karla strode over to the bar and grabbed a bottle of vodka. She swigged from it and wiped her mouth on her arm. "I did not vote for you,

Mr. Speaker."

Calvin nodded. "I know that."

"Because, up until this very moment, I have to say I never thought you would have the balls. I am wrong. And I want to change my vote."

Everyone laughed and began high fiving and pouring more drinks. Discussions took up between pairs and groups. Alcohol flowed copiously long into the night. No one got drunk, of course. They never did.

The Speaker hopped from conversation to conversation, struck by the undercurrent of excitement and buoyed by an overwhelming sense of relief. *What comes next might just damn work.*

#

Mother stalked the hallways of *In His Name* in bare feet and flowing silk robes. Silent, she padded over the marble floors like an angry phantom. Heard or unheard, seen or not seen, she made sure every acolyte and disciple and assembled warrior for God knew her heart—and her spleen.

Few in history were chosen as she had been chosen. St. Joan of Arc, certainly. St. James the Moor Slayer, Constantine—and now Mother Magdalene! To be honored thus swelled her bosom with righteous pride. So much so that she prayed immediately to be forgiven for her weakness.

It is work that must be done and that is all. To be handpicked by God. To assemble His own heavenly hosts to smite the Devil and send the Foul One back to Hell where he belonged. This is what she had been born to do. This is where her life had been leading. This moment. This time.

And. She. Would. Not. FAIL.

"Our kitchens fill their pots and load their trays with sustenance for us this night. For tomorrow is the holy day of days. We will be strong. We will be ready!"

In room after room, from meeting place to assembly hall to office, she flew between them spreading the word: *Eat. Rest. Pray. For tomorrow we fight.*

Eat. Rest. Pray. For tomorrow we fight.

Excitement thrummed through *In His Name* and buzzed up through the balls of her feet. She felt it. Saw it spread to the assembled brethren and cover them with its holy heat.

My God. MY GOD!

Mother ran with fists upraised and mouth wide thanking Him for this task. Thanking Him for His faith in her.

Past midnight now, the night before the day that Devil spawn had chosen, and preparations raced to meet the dawn. Ever the field general, Mother pressed her troops onward for the glory.

At six a.m. Mother had breakfast brought into the great congregation hall; orange juice, coffee, cold water, cereal, huge platters heaped tall with mountains of scrambled eggs and warm loaves of fresh-baked breads.

She waited patiently while all assembled, newly energized from a night of prayers and strategies, mini-alliances and solemn oaths to support one another, fed. Men and women stirred from their torpor and took in sustenance from the food and from the woman who'd been at them all night, urging them onward toward their holy mission.

Mother strode up and down the long tables, patting her people on their backs and kissing the tops of their heads, blessing them for their commitment to faith and to God.

When most had eaten and the furor died down, Mother ascended the steps of the chancel area at the front, plucked a microphone headpiece off the lectern and put it on.

"You are my heart. My arms. My raised and mighty fist." She gestured to the crowd. "It is IN HIS NAME that we are assembled here. And IN HIS NAME that we dedicate ourselves this day.

"Morning is coming. As He has provided for us before, He will again. But today is a different day for today we do battle for Him against—" she waited a beat, screwing her face into a fearful wrath, "against the DEVIL."

She snapped her fingers, a cue for the video crew in the balcony and a verse from Ephesians 6: 10-13 scrolled on the giant screen behind her.

"Read it with me, my children. Read it aloud and draw strength—for that is the intent of this Holy Scripture."

She recited the verse as the congregation read out loud with her:

10 Finally, be strong in the Lord, and in the strength of His might. 11 Put on the full armor of God, that you may be able to stand firm against the schemes of the devil. 12 For our struggle is not against flesh and blood, but against the rulers, against the powers, against the world forces of this darkness, against the spiritual forces of wickedness in the heavenly places. 13 Therefore, take up the full armor of God, that you may be able to resist in the evil day, and having done everything, to stand firm.

"The Apostle Paul knew that war had come. He knew two thousand years ago what we would be facing today. And I like to think he left this message expressly for us. To fortify us in the face of evil. So we would be successful in this most holy fight.

"Gather in your groups. Fill your pockets with stones. Take as many as you can but disguise your weapons. Do not draw attention to them or yourselves because the Devil has his protectors and they will be many.

"Some in the crowd will be desperate and misguided, seeking relief. Some will be sympathizers. Some merely curious. But the ones to watch out for will be those sworn to *protect and serve*." She air-quoted this last and got a smattering of chuckles.

"They know not what they do—but we do, don't we my children? We know what is at stake here. And it is nothing less than the soul of humanity. Dear God. Dear God."

She wrung her hands.

"We are humbled by your choice, by the faith you hold for us. And we swear on the blood of your only Son that we will not disappoint you.

"Go forth, my children. Make ready and make your way to the Suntrust Park. I am sure crowds have long been assembling. Join them. Become them.

"And when the time is right—watch for me, I will strike the first blow for us all—be swift and be unswerving in your aim.

"Go. And may God give us all the strength to do what must be done."

Chapter Forty

CONSEQUENCES

B awoke to the sound of sobs. She rose up on one elbow and saw they came from Coney's tarp where El squatted back on his heels trying to comfort his friend. Coney sat cross-legged, face in his hands, wracked by shuddering cries. Every time El reached out to touch him, the man shrank away.

"Coney, I'm sorry. Really, buddy. It'll be all right."

No answer from Coney. Only louder sobbing.

Nicole awoke then and sat up. "Oh, no." She rose and hurried over to the two and B followed.

"What happened?" Nicole asked.

El shrugged.

Tears in his eyes added urgency to Nicole's voice. "Tell me, El. What did you do?"

Eldridge swiped an arm across his nose and sniffed. "I, I fixed him."

"Sure about that?" Smith said.

All up by now, they formed a semi-circle focused on El and Coney.

"I couldn't leave him like, like he was. Not knowing what I can do now. After all I've done." El looked at the group, tears running free now. "Could I?"

"Oh, El," B said. "What you can do is pretty amazing—to borrow your favorite word. But you can't fix everything. Or, everyone."

"But I did. He is." El knee-walked to his friend who promptly scooted away from him. "I know it." El threw his hands up. "I've been getting stronger every day. Every hour. I feel this *thing* growing in me."

"For God's sake, El," B put hands on her hips. "You still don't have a clue about you. Us. Why this is happening. None of it."

El stuck his chin out. "I know what I can do. That's good enough for me."

"Not good enough for Coney," Nicole walked over carefully and squatted beside the man. She slid one arm across his shoulders and pulled him to her. He came willingly and buried his face in her chest. His cries escalated and the two of them shook, wrapped in an awkward embrace.

"Shh, shh, there. I'm here, Coney. I'm here." She looked over at El and speared him with her eyes. "We're not leaving until we—you— make this right."

"But I did—"

"You didn't. Shush now." She hugged Coney hard and rocked him like a baby. "SunTrust Park can wait. He can't."

"What am I supposed to do?" El said. "I fixed him. I felt the broken places heal. The spaces fill in. I know it. Coney's fine."

"I'm getting a bad feeling about today."

"Shut up, Smith," B said. "Tell me exactly what you did."

"Like always," El wrung his hands. "I laid hands on his shoulders. Took awhile but he finally let me. I saw inside him. Clear as that rock and that tree. Then, I fixed him."

"How did he respond?"

"Nothing at first. He got real still. Then he looked at me like he didn't know me, and grabbed Nicole's tinfoil hat off his head. Crumpled it in his fist." El pointed to a shiny ball of foil beside the tarp. "Then, this. Been non-stop since before you guys woke up."

Coney pushed away from Nicole about then and used his shirt to dry his eyes. Face red, streaked with tears and dirt, he shook his head and cast eyes to the sky.

He closed them for a few seconds before turning to Nicole.

He smiled and put his hand over his heart.

She smiled and did the same.

Coney cleared his throat and spat to one side. "Oops, sorry Nicole," he said.

She shook her head.

"Eldridge," Coney said. He repeated the word two more times. *Eldridge. Eldridge.* Like savoring the flavor of something delicious.

"I'm sorry. I'm not used to being so—" he pounded a fist against his forehead.

Nicole grabbed his arm and he patted her hand and grinned.

"So *aware.* Everything is so different. Sounds different. Feels different. The feel of words in my mouth is different. I think what Eldridge did for me, it piled up on me, and I couldn't—I didn't know what to do."

"How do you feel, Coney?" B asked.

"Beatrix, right?"

She nodded.

"Sad. I feel sad. Look at this." He gestured around at his encampment. "Look at me. How I've been living. How I am—or was. Another animal in the woods. Nothing more. Not a man."

"That's not true, Coney," Nicole said. "You helped us. Been a good friend to us when we needed you."

"Nice try, Nicole. You have a good heart. I can say that out loud now. But I'm a waste. My life is a waste. Litter on the roadside—like that tinfoil over there. Nothing more."

"You're wrong, Coney," Eldridge tried. "You're—"

"*You* named me Coney, Eldridge. Remember? You and your friends found us here in the woods; me, Pop-Top, Franko. Remember? You all made fun of my hat. That's where Coney came from."

"I didn't mean it." El looked down. "I didn't think you'd—"

"Know?" Coney said. "That you were making fun of me?" He stood up to face them all. "Guess I didn't care then. Now, I do." He brushed leaves and pine needles off as best he could.

"I'm sorry, Coney. I am."

"I know you are, Eldridge. No problemo." He winked. "But it's time for you to go. Do whatever big thing you have planned and don't come back here. Won't be anything left here but trash and a bare place on the ground where the old Coney used to sleep."

"Are you going to be okay?" Nicole stood next to him and brushed leaves off his shirt he didn't see.

"Who knows? I surely don't. But at least I'll be me finally, for once. I'll see where that takes me."

He hugged Nicole hard and she returned his hug with one of her own. She swiped at an eye when they let go.

"Before you go, Nicole, I want you to know something."

"Okay?"

"It's Ben," he said. "My real name. It's Ben Johnson."

Nicole stuck her hand out. "I am honored to meet you Ben Johnson."

"Likewise," Ben said. "Give 'em hell, you guys. Or, whatever it is you have planned. Coney, out." He headed off through the woods, toward the road then stopped.

"Oops. Where are my manners?" He turned and crooked a smile at El. "I do want to thank you, Eldridge really, for opening my eyes. You did *fix* me, I guess. I only wish, before you did, you'd asked me. Maybe ask before you fix the next one? For your old pal, Coney?"

Chapter Forty-One

POLICE ESCORT

Metal clanged in the cool evening air at SunTrust Park and the banter of men hard at work ebbed and flowed. The squeaks of bolts turning and the diesel chug of cranes and Bobcats lifting scaffolding in place reverberated off empty banks of seats. Stadium lights turned the night into day.

The outfield fence formed a backdrop for concert acts in Atlanta's new sports stadium, with raised platforms tricked out in whatever drama the stage crews had in mind for its artists. This "act" would be treated similarly, if in a bare bones way. No fancy colors, graphics, light show or stage effects. Nothing but columns of interlaced iron girders supporting a half-circle platform of medium-weight fiberglass and gray wood.

Stadium management, bowing to the inevitable, decided at the last minute to embrace the coming event thrust upon them by providing the stage and taking payments at the turnstiles. A hasty PR push on local media claimed the nominal $10.00 fee would all go to charity—after expenses.

Clarence Eason worked on the stadium crew at the old Turner Field and came over to the new facility, adding his name to the list of hundreds such a facility required to function. He'd done games, concerts, political rallies, monster trucks and motocross. Tomorrow would be a first.

"I seen this guy on TV." He yanked hard on a carriage bolt nut, his ratchet click-click-clicking. "You think this Amazing El dude is for real?"

Possum, named for his sleep habits on breaks and one of Clarence's best work-friends, held the piece of platform in place while Clarence pulled on the ratchet. He spit once off to the side, "C-man, you believe in Santa Claus and the Easter Bunny?"

"Huh." Clarence snugged the nut tight and moved to the next one across. "My wife is outa her mind waiting for tomorrow. All the shows and shit we done over the years? Never gave a rat's behind about any of 'em. This one? You'd think Jesus Christ hisself sent her a personal invite."

"What is it about women, man? They gullible about all this crap. My lady been cracking the Bible and reading me passages out loud for the last two days. Tell you C-man, I fear for my sanity. Big time."

"All those clips they running on TV got my attention," Clarence said. "I'm wondering, funny lookin' dude raisin' the dead and shit? What if he can do that?"

"Can't believe what you see on TV, man." Possum shook his head. "Some folks sayin' he's the Devil. My cousin goes to this church east of town? *In His Name*? You should hear what they sayin' over that way."

"Believe in one, you gotta believe in the other."

"I believe in neither," Possum said.

"I heard that."

"So you comin' tomorrow?" Possum slapped the platform piece as they finished.

"Old lady'd hang my balls on a hook if we didn't." Clarence grabbed his crotch and stuck out his tongue. "And I'm kind attached to 'em."

"Sounds like your wife been talkin' to mine. Keep by the East Entrance and we'll look y'all up. *If* we can find ya. Got no idea how many'll show for this doin'."

"TV says," Clarence held up a hand, "I know, I know. TV lies. But, they say could be thousands." He chuckled, "Maybe I'll see if this dude can make me a genius while we're here."

"I was you? I'd see what he might could do for that ugly mug of yours."

"Look who's talkin'. Still can't believe you landed that wife of yours. She had her eyes checked lately?"

"Shut up and hand me some more of them bolts," Possum said. "I'm out. You and me ain't going to be the last crew leaving here tonight 'cause you kept yappin'."

#

Hidden off the road in a wooded area well north of Atlanta, a yellow Camaro sat with engine idling and all lights off. The moon and stars overhead painted a silver sheen on the landscape. The mood inside added extra chill to the night air.

"Your move, Boss." Smith angled the rear-view mirror to focus on El in the backseat. "Where to?"

Eldridge remained silent, eyes fixed on a thumbnail he'd been picking at for the last fifteen minutes.

"Well?"

"Leave him alone, Smith," Beatrix said. "El?" She shifted in her seat and nudged him with her butt. "What's going on in that funny-shaped head of yours?"

She tapped his temple and he slapped her hand away.

"Coney was my friend," he said. "Before, when I was—like I was—I didn't know you. I didn't know anything. A couple guys and me would come out here at night and mess with the bums. That's what we called them. Nothing real bad. I was a kid."

"You're still a kid, El," B said. "In your head. That's the problem. Kids do wacked out stuff all the time. Never think of the consequences."

"Coney knew. All that time we had our stupid fun and I thought he didn't know what we were saying and doing. He knew and let it go." He shifted attention to the other thumb, picking and peeling at the nail. "Coney. Messed up wiring and scared of the world. Hiding in the woods so people would leave him alone. What did I do to him?"

"Then? Or now?" Smith grunted.

"Shut up, Smith," Nicole said. "You didn't mean your friend any harm, Eldridge. Back then. Or today. You were oh, I dunno, a clueless asshole."

El raised his eyes and the glint of moisture in them reflected the night's ambient light. "I'm still an asshole," he mumbled.

"Finally, we agree on something," Smith slapped the dashboard, hard.

"Don't break my car, dickweed." Beatrix punched Smith in the shoulder.

"Dickweed?" Smith laughed out loud. "Christ, I haven't heard that since 1982."

"Bet it was aimed at you then, like now," Nicole chimed in. "Dickweed. Guess what? Nothing's changed. It still fits you. *Dickweed.* I do like saying it. Has a certain ring to it."

"He is a dickweed, isn't he?" B laughed. "I know things." She solemnly tapped her own funny-shaped head. "Genius, you know."

"Dickweed," El said.

The others in the car stifled their laughter, looked at him expectantly.

"Smith is a BIG dickweed. Doesn't take a genius to know that, B," El said.

That started them all laughing again.

"If you like, I can try to fix that for you," he said.

That got every one of them guffawing. Even Smith chuckled a little bit.

"No," Smith said. "This dickweed's fine the way he is. All he wants to know is where the hell are we going?"

Thirty seconds later, the laughs tailed off. B and Nicole dried their eyes.

"I don't know anymore," El said. "After what happened with Coney...."

"I'm glad," Beatrix said. "Finally you're getting it."

"Consequences, right?" El sniffed. "I don't want to do anything dumb. Not ever again."

"Good. I vote for the west coast," B said. "California, Oregon. As far away from here as we can get. We lay low, stay out of trouble. Let things blow over and give people time to forget."

"I hear Mexico is nice this time of year." Smith leaned his seat back and closed his eyes. "Let me know when you decide."

Nicole turned around in her seat and addressed the back seat. "I can't believe you people. I may not be a big-head genius like y'all, so forgive me. But there's no running away from this. Not now. I've seen what you can do, El. With B in the trailer and those poor souls on the highway."

Smith opened his eyes. *What B in the trailer?*

"Shut up, Smith," Nicole said.

"You don't understand, Nikki," El mumbled. "I don't want to do any harm trying to do good."

Nicole ran a hand through her hair. "You already did the harm. Don't you get it?"

"No."

"You've been on national TV, granted, not always by choice. And you did something amazing; more *amazing* than your stupid name."

El raised his eyebrows. "Don't hold back, Nicole. Jeez. I know what I did."

"Not the healing stuff. Not bringing folks back from the dead."

"What then?"

"What you did *was* a miracle, sure as gators eat their babies. All caught on tape." Nicole screwed up her face, looking for the words. "But you did more than that. People are hurting in this world, El. Lotta horrible stuff going on out there. And you gave them hope. Hope that maybe there's an answer for whatever is wrong in their lives."

El wrung his hands. "I didn't start out to do that."

"You ended up doing it." Nicole reached over and grabbed Eldridge's hand. "Hope is a powerful thing, El. You can't desert them now."

Beatrix crossed her arms. "Nikki, I love you girl, you know that. But, you don't understand what is really going on here. What we are. What he is. You have a big heart, but leave this decision to us—"

"She's right," El sat up straighter.

"What?" B swiveled to look at him. "No."

"Yes." El patted Nicole's hand. "She's right. You're right, B. Seems everybody's right but me. I don't know what all this is about. I don't get why I am the way I am. But I have a destiny *somewhere*. Maybe this is what I need to get me there."

"Oh, my God," B said, exasperated. "Thanks, Nikki. It's not all those poor souls I'm worried about. Not exactly. It's the others. Like him. And me." She flicked Smith in the head.

"Hey."

"Where do you think he came from? Where I came from?"

"The mythical Council I keep hearing about?"

"You have no idea, El," B said.

"That's why I got *you* guys. Let 'em come," El said. "It's time we met." He slapped the back of Smith's seat. "The stadium," El said. "We head to the stadium."

"Now?" Smith rubbed the back of his head where B thumped him. "It's 5:00 in the morning."

"We don't know what we're going to find when we get there," El said. "We didn't ask permission, you know."

"No *you* didn't," Beatrix said.

"They may try to keep us out," he continued. "Who knows how many people will show? Could be hundreds."

"I think you underestimate the effect you have on folks, Eldridge," Nicole said.

B nodded beside him. "El, we could be looking at ten times your number."

"All the more reason for us to get going then," he said. "Put it in gear, dickweed. Let's go find us a parking place."

#

Cobb County Police Officer Christina Jenkins pulled her cruiser to the side on Cobb Parkway and watched the traffic build. Six in the morning on a Saturday and the newly widened thoroughfare bulged with cars, trucks and pissed off drivers.

Like rush hour before a Braves game.

She flipped on her light bar. The reds and blues generally had a calming effect on drivers. *Like smoking a beehive.*

She settled back in her seat and prayed for an easy day. That pileup on I-285 yesterday had been a nasty one. Two fatalities. One, an infant.

"Where were you yesterday, Mr. Amazing?" She spoke it aloud in her silent car. Silent, until the radio squawked:

Attention all units: Be advised. A yellow Camaro with possible suspects spotted near Akers Mill Road. If sighted, stop vehicle and ascertain occupants' identities. Call for backup if confirmed.

"Shit." She angled her rearview for an easier scan of approaching cars. "There goes easy." Akers Mill was only one mile down the road.

At least the idiots had the good graces to pick a car that'll stand out in this parking lot.

After three taxis, a yellow pickup, a Dodge Charger she almost hit her siren for and two sun yellow Miatas, her fingers beat a tattoo on the steering wheel, the double espresso shot in her chai kicking in.

"Who the hell buys a car colored like a lemon?" She got no answer from the empty backseat. "Apparently," she squinted at the traffic, "a ton of people with exquisitely bad taste."

A yellow flash behind a Roadway semi caught her eye in the rearview. Still too far away for positive ID, but the car's low profile and erratic behavior looked promising.

"Come on, come on. Show yourself asshole."

Finally, the car squeezed into the next lane over and showed itself in full when it crossed the white dotted line.

"Bingo."

Sure as shit. A bright yellow Camaro.

Horns blared as the driver tried to squeeze back into the hiding place it'd vacated behind the eighteen-wheeler.

Ah, what's the matter folks? My flashing lights spook ya?

Officer Jenkins waited for the car to get closer. At eight car lengths she hit the siren and began nosing out into traffic. It took several cars passing before a Good Samaritan got the hint and stopped to allow her in.

The yellow Camaro stopped dead in the center lane two car lengths back.

Horns blared. Middle fingers drew creative diagrams in the air as drivers tried weaving around the roadblock.

Christina inserted her cruiser into the center lane and stopped like the Camaro did. She keyed her mike:

"Dispatch, this is car 119 on Cobb Parkway. Yellow Camaro acting erratically. Looks like it could be our guys. Over."

The car got close enough now that she could identify four passengers. The rising sun's glare on the windshield made seeing anything more impossible.

"Can you make a positive ID Unit 119?"

"Give me two minutes. Unit 119, out."

Traffic around her all but stopped, posed no immediate hazard. She eased her car door open slowly all the same and took care stepping out of her vehicle.

She clamped a whistle in her teeth and directed traffic with both hands, sprinting across three lanes for the cars behind her to get the message and stop.

Traffic finally halted completely when she unsnapped the Glock in her holster and pulled it free.

That's at least one report I'll be writing later.

She spit out the whistle and yelled, "STOP RIGHT THERE!"

All lanes stopped now, from her car back, she focused all her attention on the yellow car.

She kept her pistol pointing down in a two-hand grip as she made her way toward the Camaro. Occupants in the one car trapped between her cruiser and the Camaro stared with wide eyes and open mouths.

"It's all right folks," she spoke loudly as she passed their car. "No problem here."

Her words didn't close a single mouth as she walked by.

"HANDS UP!" She stood off at a diagonal from the driver. "EVERYONE! HANDS!"

One look at the four passengers in the vehicle and she keyed her shoulder mike: "Dispatch. I have stopped southbound traffic on Cobb Parkway about a mile north of Akers Mill. ID is positive. I repeat. ID is a positive. Please send backup. Over."

"KEEP HANDS WHERE I CAN SEE THEM AND STAY IN THE CAR!"

She relaxed only slightly when she heard the siren and saw lights approaching fast along the outside shoulder.

Her backup slid to a stop in a cloud of red Georgia dust and parked on the shoulder, even with her cruiser.

She exhaled and grinned as her Sergeant stepped out of the car to join her.

"Christ, Jenkins," he said. "See what a mess you've made of my highway? Traffic's backed up clear to Kennesaw."

"Sorry, Sarge."

"Bet you are. Watch them." He walked close to the Camaro and bent once to get a good look inside before straightening. "What do you say we clear this mess of yours and let the rest of these fine people go on about their day?"

"Ten four on that."

"Pull your cruiser ahead enough to let this car out then back tight to the Camaro. We'll escort them to the side of the road, tucked in safe between us. And be careful, Jenkins. Don't give them room to bolt."

"Copy. I'm on it."

The sergeant motioned for the driver to roll down his window. "We're going to get y'all out of here presently. I want you to follow Officer Jenkins here to the side of the road. Follow close on her tail, but not so's you put a dent in her cruiser. She's kinda partial to it. Stay in your vehicle after we park. We'll tell you what to do after that."

#

The three cars made their way to the side of the road slowly and parked in a line, the two Cobb County Police officers bracketing the Camaro front and back. As traffic resumed, Christine and her sergeant got out of their vehicles and approached the Camaro, sergeant on the driver side, Officer Jenkins on the passenger.

The sergeant removed his hat and wiped his brow. He bent low to look in and spoke first. "Which one of you folks is Mr. Incredible?"

"Amazing," Christine called.

"What's that?"

"He's Amazing."

"Whatever...So?"

"My name's Eldridge Montcalm, officer," El spoke from the backseat. "These are my friends John Smith, Beatrix Goode and Nicole Charbonneau."

"Uh, huh. Not pleased to meet you," the sergeant said. "Officer Jenkins and I have the immense bad fortune to be your escorts to the stadium."

"Escorts?" John Smith said.

"Boy howdy. Like TV only better. We have instructions to deliver you through this god-awful mess you've created for us *un-*Amazing folks straight through to the VIP gates of SunTrust Stadium."

"What then?" B chimed in.

"Chatty bunch, aren't you?" the policeman said. "Below my pay grade. Though rumor has it you're to meet someone from the mayor's office." He fixed El with a glare. "Y'all have already caused enough trouble. We don't want any more. So sit tight. Do as you're told. Once you're off our hands you can go save the world on your own time."

Chapter Forty-Two

STANDING ROOM ONLY

T he Cobb County police cars, yellow Camaro still sandwiched between them, used their lights, siren whoops, and loud speakers to part the throngs of people milling across the streets and parking lots leading up to SunTrust Park.

Inside the Camaro, Smith drove grim-faced and stared straight ahead. Nicole waved and smiled at people from the passenger seat. Beatrix sat in stony silence and El watched the crush of people, sweat popping on his forehead in the air-conditioned car.

"Look at them all," he said. "So many, I didn't think…."

"Sure didn't," B said.

"I thought they'd be sicker. Or, I dunno, limping or—"

"This isn't the movies El. What's cancer look like?" Nicole said. "Or leukemia? Depression? Lymphoma? Heart failure?"

"I guess you're right," El said.

"You're not seeing disease, El," B said. "You're not seeing sick people who need help. You're seeing curiosity, pure and simple. These folks are here for the freak show, nothing more."

As if to underscore her point, a strange figure hurried alongside the car dressed in a flowing purple robe. Eyes wild, and stringy red hair more mane than hairdo, she screamed an unintelligible froth, stopping periodically to cross herself.

El smiled and waved to placate the woman. But it only seemed to incense her more, as she redoubled her efforts to keep up. He turned and watched her disappear in the throng as the cars hit a patch of open space and sped quickly forward.

At the very last she raised a fist and shook it at them. For a second he thought he saw a rock gripped tight inside it.

Nah. Probably not.

He turned back around. "Guess we'll see, won't we?" he said. "That TV reporter must have done a real good job getting my word out."

"I don't believe you," B said. "You think this is *good*?"

"Of course. We'll be able to help way more people than I thought."

"El, you numbskull. You're not going to be able to help a fraction—"

"We're here," Smith said. He hit the brakes hard enough to squeal the tires. "That must be our welcoming party."

They pulled up onto a circular, smooth concrete area that looked tailored for limousines. Beyond a series of fat, chunky pillars set in cement—a familiar site in this post-911 era—a trio of people waited. A man wearing a Polo shirt under a sport coat cradled a bouquet of red roses. A trim blonde in a tailored navy-blue suit held a manila envelope. The third person, an attractive black woman, carried a microphone.

After a tense, awkward few moments when no one stepped forward to open their doors, they exited the car. Smith's door opened with a screech after its earlier brush with a tree trunk. It had been a long and intense morning and every one of them stretched and twisted to relieve the kinks.

Everyone but El.

He marched right up to the black woman with the microphone. "Nice to see you again, Sareena," El said.

"I wasn't sure you'd remember me, Mr. Montcalm," she patted her hair and looked curiously relieved.

"Of course I remember you." He gestured to the crowd of people surging and yelling at them from behind the roped off area. "I see you got the word out about us."

"I only reported what you said, sir. In your own words."

"Don't worry, it'll be all right." He strode up to the woman with the envelope. "Hi there. I'm—"

She backed away a half step before regaining composure. "Eldridge Montcalm. Yes, I know. And you are Beatrix Goode. John Smith. Nicole Char—Char—"

"Charbonneau," Nicole said.

"Yes, of course, forgive me." The woman fanned herself with the envelope and cleared her throat. "I am here to welcome you to SunTrust Park on behalf of management and the Atlanta Braves."

"The Braves are here?" El craned his neck, trying to see through the reflections on the glass windows and revolving doors behind her. "That is so awesome. I'd love to meet—"

"No. Wait, I didn't mean to imply—They're in Florida. Spring training." She shrugged. "Sorry. No Braves. You're stuck with us. And this." She thrust the manila envelope at him. "In there will explain what arrangements have been made. What security we have provided. Where you will be able to go once inside. How to access the facilities, your staging area, the sound system and the stage we have put in place."

"You put up a stage?" Smith said.

"Carlson, here," she continued, "is your SunTrust liaison."

The man with the roses nodded at them. "Hey, guys."

"Any questions you have, any arrangements you may require that we did not think of, food, drink, anything at all, he's your man. SunTrust welcomes you and is pleased you have chosen us for this most auspicious event."

She finished the last in a rush as if it had been hastily memorized and she couldn't wait to finish.

"Oh, my gosh." The woman raised a hand to her mouth. "I totally forgot to introduce myself. I'm—"

"Temperance Baxter—Baxy—to your friends. Say hi to your husband Fred for us." El grabbed her hand and shook it. "Don't worry. We won't tell anyone."

The woman shrieked and yanked her hand back.

"Relax, Ms. Baxter. I am not the Devil, last time I checked."

"You—I—I'm sorry. I can't do this anymore."

With that she turned and fled through the doors Carlson would presumably soon lead them through.

"Had to do that, didn't you?" B said.

"What?"

"*Say hi to your husband Fred?* Way to go Carnac. You had to show off and scare the poor woman."

"Maybe, a little," El said. "Sorry."

"How's that *growing up* coming along? Hm?" B chucked him on the arm. "Might want to work on that."

Smith stepped forward. "Hey, there Carlson. Any way you might be able to scare up a few cold beers when we go inside?"

"Domestic or imported, sir?"

"Imported, of course," Smith said. "You know what El? I changed my mind. I think our coming here's your best idea yet. Lead on Carlson. We're with you."

"Right this way, folks." Carlson pointed to the doors ahead.

"We'll be going through there and hanging a left up the immediate stairs."

As the entourage moved forward, Sareena the reporter scooted along beside them. She waved to the crowd of people held back by security guards and a circle of stanchioned blue velvet ropes. A cameraman with an oversized video camera ducked underneath the ropes to follow, waving a Press Badge at security.

"Ho, hey, wait a second," B stepped in front of Sareena. "Where you think you're going?"

"With you. I'm sure Mr. Montcalm will want his time here shared faithfully and truthfully with the people and I assumed—"

"You assumed wrong." B turned to El and pointed a finger at him. "And you don't say a thing."

He backed off and grinned, zipping his lips shut.

"Good," B said. "Smartest thing you'll say all day. You," she turned to Sareena, "wait out here with your microphones and cameras and fake newscaster smiles. I think you've *shared* quite enough already."

By then Smith and Nicole had followed Carlson through the glass front entrance and Beatrix and El hurried to catch them.

El stopped for one last look at the press of people, yelling and calling out his name.

"I got to tell you B," he said. "This is pretty cool. Now I know how John Lennon must have felt."

B yanked his arm to get his attention. "John Lennon? Idiot. They killed John Lennon."

#

The Speaker and the rest of The Council, well-disguised with hoodies, hats and whatever devices they employed in their home countries, mingled with the SunTrust crowd.

Per plan, after paying at the entrance turnstiles, each struck off in a different direction. Communication would not be a problem, of course. Telepathy kept them all in touch like they still sat together in the Speaker's Plaza suite.

Calvin walled off his thoughts for a bit of privacy as he shouldered his way through the swarm of people and down onto the field. It wouldn't do for the rest of The Council to know the doubts polluting his feelings about their upcoming agenda. He, however, couldn't shake them:

Is now really the time for all this? Were they truly ready to come from the shadows? Is mankind capable of accepting a more evolved version of itself?

News reports from across the globe, written in smoke and blood,

209

argued no. Territorial disputes, old religious hatreds, economic pushing and shoving.

Maybe they'd waited too long.

Perhaps the Given Goal had become unattainable.

No. Beatrix Goode's boy wonder had only surfaced a bare few months ago. He played a key role in the Given Goal and fate had delivered him.

Calvin squared his hat on his head and pushed his way through the throng, still loosely gathering in and about the stage area set up in the outfield. As time shortened and especially when Eldridge Montcalm decided to show, The Council's ability to gain front and center views without drawing undue attention would disappear.

May as well claim his spot now.

He scanned the crowd clustered around him; curious to see what Eldridge's message to the masses had brought to the stadium.

His senses revealed all without anyone being the wiser. That of course, was the problem. Humanity harbored a full gamut of problems and he saw them *all*. Incurable diseases comprised only a small subset of today's visitors.

Greed, hatred, jealousy, envy, moral weakness and on and on pressed in on him from every side. Several in the crowd embraced one or more of those flaws elevated to psychopathic heights.

At least half of the people, no matter what their true affliction, were here solely out of curiosity. Either they were unaware of their problems or didn't believe Eldridge Montcalm held the answer for them.

Typical of people in the U.S. especially, many in the crowd gathered here simply to be a part of the EVENT.

An interesting category of people on the field gave off distinctly hostile vibes. He spent a little more time probing those people. Many fed their hostility with mind-numbing loops of what sounded like prayer. Though from what books or liturgies Calvin could not say.

He knew most religious tracts intimately and what these people kept repeating to themselves had roots in the Bible and Christianity. But the roots had grown into grossly perverted versions of their original selves.

Several of the twisted ones had the capacity to be overtly dangerous. In more then a few he sensed a willingness to embrace violence *In His Name*. The phrase echoed back to him many times from many minds.

Yeah, yeah. With all the whackos in the world and with what he and The Council had planned, let them rant and rave. They'd soon have more pressing items worry about.

The Speaker opened his mind back up to his Council and silently checked in on them.

Several in this crowd are pursuing violent itineraries. Are any of you picking up on that?

He heard from Patel first. *It is most disturbing Speaker, yes. They appear to be spaced out in the crowd.*

A few imbeciles. Not many. From Miguel.

I am not listening to their thoughts. Too noisy. Too whiny, said Karla.

All of you start listening to those around you right now. You too, Karla. If this is a coordinated effort, and it has that appearance, we need to be ready. I do not intend for us to be surprised by anything that may happen here today. Especially by something we failed to apprehend. Agreed?

He sent the message out with enough force to show the level of importance he ascribed to it. He sensed his nearest Council members physically wince and it made him smile.

#

The gang of four, with Carlson hovering at the back, stood at the wall of glass windows in their skybox suite and stared down at the crowd swarming on the field below.

"Holy crap," El said. "Look at all those people."

B, standing beside him, sniffed. "Way to go, genius. Not even *The Amazing El* has enough juice to work his Amazing Magic on a fraction of them."

El looked at her with raised eyebrows. "How do you know?"

"Give me that." She snatched the manila envelope from Eldridge's hand and dumped its contents along the bar top in front of the window wall. "Maybe we can figure out how to beat a fast exit from this darn place."

Nicole stepped up and massaged Beatrix's neck. "We had a police escort getting in here, B-girl. That was hard enough and thirty minutes ago. We'd never make it out now, by ourselves."

Smith, feet up in a recliner in the corner of the suite, drained his third Dos Equis and belched. "I say we stay here and let the whole mess wither and die. We got all the comforts, no stress, no hassle—ow! Shit."

He and Beatrix winced at the same moment.

Eldridge merely scratched his head and looked curious. "Hey, now. What was that?"

"Perfect." Beatrix rubbed her temples and ducked away from Nicole. She stood straighter and scanned the crowd below. "How many of The Council you ever met in person, Smith?"

He collapsed the recliner footrest and jumped up to join B at the window. "More than I ever wanted to. A few good ones. Most are The Speaker's obedient little foot soldiers."

"You wanted to meet The Speaker one day El?" B said. "Guess what."

"He's here?" El said. "Awesome."

"He *and* The Council, doofus. And no. It's not awes—what are you doing?"

El closed his eyes and smiled. Head cocked, he appeared deep in thought.

"Eldridge Montcalm." She punched him in the arm.

He remained un-phased, nodding periodically.

Beatrix and Smith looked at one another.

"Shit," Smith said. "They're talking and Speaker has cut us out of it."

A minute later, El rubbed his chin and opened his yes. "Wow. The Speaker seems nice."

"Nice?" B paced wringing her hands. "NICE? What did you talk about?"

El shrugged. "I introduced myself. Welcomed him to Georgia. Invited him up to join us."

"WHAT?" B and Smith chose the same word at the same time.

"He said he's good where he's at."

"That's it?" B said.

"One curious thing."

"Yes?"

El scratched his head and looked perplexed. "Last thing he said was for me to be careful out there. Like I said, a nice guy."

Chapter Forty-Three

CATTLE HAVE HORNS

C arlson led them to a freight elevator down the hallway from the entrance to their skybox suite. He slid a keycard along the keypad and the doors shushed open. Fluorescents winked on and cast stark white light on dark blue quilts hanging on the walls.

The car could easily accommodate a pair of dueling pianos and a family of elephants for accompaniment.

"Wow," El said.

"I know," Carlson slid his key card once again and the doors shut. "Everybody says that. Believe it or not, some of the acts make this seem small. We have a much larger elevator further down. But this will get us to field level where it'll be easier for you guys to walk out onto the stage platform."

"About that," Beatrix said. "I read in the papers you gave us that the stage has ramps on both sides descending from stage height to the field."

"We didn't know what sorts of folks may be visiting with us today, their states of health, if you know what I mean. We wanted it to be as easy on them possible. And, we had no idea what you guys may be considering, how you were going to approach this whole thing."

"Join the club," B said.

"Billy Graham Jr. held a crusade here a couple months ago. We sort of borrowed from what we learned on his setup."

"I'm sure it'll be perfect," El said. "I also heard there's a sound system?"

"You will be issued mike headsets, we have those for you in the immediate staging room. Some people call it the green room. Though ours is blue, actually. I had the same snacks and beverages set up in there for you as well."

"Could you arrange to have chairs brought to the stage?" El asked. "A dozen or so ought to do it. Set them up in a line facing the crowd?"

"No problem." Carlson keyed his walkie. "Jackson. You on stage prep today?"

No answer but static.

"It's the elevator," Carlson said. "We'll get that for you, sir. No worries."

"Call me El, Carlson. Jeez. *Sir* creeps me out. And one more thing, green M&Ms. Only the green ones. Could you round some of those up for us?"

"Um—"

"I'm *kidding*, Carlson. Lighten up," El said. "All we'll need is about an hour or so to prepare. And we'll be ready to go."

"You got it, boss." Carlson swiped his key card after the elevator halted. "Staging room's this way."

#

Beatrix shut the door behind Carlson and waited for his footsteps to recede. She leaned her back on the door and crossed her arms. "Want to let us all in on your plans, El? Or, you going to keep bullshitting your way along until the world lands on your odd-shaped head?"

"I think I might need a little help here, guys," El said.

"You don't have a plan, do you?"

"Not exactly."

"The chairs?" Nicole said.

"I needed to come up with something."

"Brilliant," said Smith. "Love it." He pulled another beer from one of several iced buckets with assorted beverages and smoothed the ice from it with a finger. "Never been this close to a meltdown before."

"Shut up, Smith," B said. She walked over to El and cupped his face in her hands. "Talk to me, Mr. Amazing."

"I want to help people, that's all. 'Cause I can. We can. I know that now. After all that's happened. What we did. Something's growing in me, B. Way stronger than before. Only—"

"What?" B prompted.

"I'm not sure how to pull it out of me. And all those people. Did you see them all?"

Smith unleashed a long wet burp.

"You don't owe those people out there a damn thing," B said.

El looked at her. "Oh, B. That's where you're wrong."

"What you can do and what, to a lesser extent we can do—yes, Smith I'm including you in that—is not magic. It's not parlor tricks. I told you that in the very beginning with your stupid spinning basketball. Remember?"

"Consequences, you said. I remember."

"Look what happened with your friend, Coney. There were consequences. You didn't foresee them. You didn't think it through. That dumb heart of yours got in front of your head. Multiply Coney times a thousand." She jerked her thumb toward the hallway. "Through this door you have consequences you can't imagine."

"What do you suggest we do?" El said. "You have a plan?"

"Retreat," B said. "Simple. I studied the material they gave us. I'm pretty sure I can get us out of here. Let this all blow over. Folks will forget. Eventually. News cycles come and go. We'll be fine."

"No," Nicole elbowed Beatrix aside. "You can't. Sorry, girl, but El is right. He has a gift."

"Do not encourage him, Nicole. Please."

"I'm sorry. I believe God touched him with something special, holy. I know he did. You need a plan? I say, use God's plan. Let Him be your guide in this."

"I need to think," El said. "For a minute. You guys eat or whatever while I get my dumb brain to work with my dumb heart. If Nicole's right, maybe I'll get a sign or something."

"See what you did?" B rounded on Nicole. "I almost had him convinced. We need to leave. Before a horde of freaked out people rushes the stage and tramples us all to death."

"You're exaggerating," Nicole said.

"You don't know people like I do, Nikki. I'm sorry. For the most part they're not too bright, self-centered, easily spooked."

"Huh," Smith dropped an empty in the wastebasket. "People are cattle. You're describing a herd of cattle. And cattle have horns."

"Smith, Christ. Lay off the beer, would you?"

"Nothing like a good goring, hey El? Really give you something to heal—*shit*. El?"

The door clicked shut on El's retreating back. The doorknob twisted once, twice and fell back into the room.

"El?" Beatrix shouted. "What the hell are you doing?"

In her head, B felt his reply. *"You were right, B. I dragged you all in this without thinking it through. Without asking you even. I'm sorry. If a thundering herd tramples anyone, no reason it has to be you guys. Thanks for all your help. Love you all. Bye."*

#

Eldridge saw Carlson waiting down at the end of the hallway, backlit from the stadium lights already on in the late afternoon. The man stood off to the side, hidden from view behind a large column, sneaking peeks at the crowd building on the field.

"Hey, Carlson," El called. "How do you get this thing to work?" He twirled the headset he'd copped from the staging room when he made his escape.

Chapter Forty-Four

CAST THE FIRST STONE

El stepped out onto the stage and thought right away how small it seemed tucked against the wall at one end of SunTrust Stadium. He gazed upward and the sky stared back down on him through the monocle of the stadium's encircling walls.

Chairs had been arranged as he'd requested, lined up facing the crowd, spaced evenly along the stage center. But chairs were the furthest things from El's mind at the moment.

He paced up and back the full length of the stage, buying time, steeling himself for this encounter he'd orchestrated. He fiddled with his headset as he walked and realized he'd turned it up too high when the speakers blasted the sound of his footsteps. His nervous cough sounded like an avalanche.

"Sorry, sorry," he said. "Not used to this stuff. Please forgive me."

The words boomed through the stadium sound system speakers flanking both ends of the stage.

"I want to thank you all for coming here today. I didn't expect so many of you and I have to say I'm a little freaked out about that. But let's see where this all goes, shall we?"

He stopped pacing at the stage center front and faced the audience, really faced them, for the first time. He lifted his head and tried to make out individuals in the sea of bodies. No good. The faces resembled an impressionist painting in a fine art book, a blurred collection of expressions and emotions.

He couldn't pick faces out of the crowd so he did the next best thing and opened himself to the humanity spread before him. Closed his eyes and stood there, arms opened wide, listening, feeling.

Every raw emotion in the human spectrum beat at him from the surge of bodies pressing forward. Random thoughts emerged in swarms of clarity: *Help me, please . . . It's my heart . . . Do something cool, man . . . Faker. Magicians are so lame . . . Devil. DEVIL.*

"Wow." He shook himself. "Thanks, I needed that," boomed from the speakers and he took up pacing again.

"I asked you all here to do a couple things. First, to introduce myself and show you I'm nothing like the news says. I'm a guy. Not an alien. Not a monster. I'm a dude with a funny-shaped head is all. Here, take a good look."

El swept his beloved wig from his head. "Check it. Not easy growing up with this let me tell you. Lassiter High School in Marietta was not my friend."

"Lassiter sucks!" came a shout from somewhere in the crowd.

"Must be from Walton," El said. He laughed and some in the crowd joined him. "Or East Cobb, Wheeler, Pope." He pointed to his head. "Trust me, none of those probably could've handled this thing any better. And that's okay." He flung the wig out into the crowd and a hole opened as people stepped back to let it fall. "Guys, it won't bite."

Finally someone bent down and retrieved it, twirling it round and round like a trophy scalp. "You don't know how that hurts," El chuckled. "That thing cost me a ton of money. It's expensive trying to cover a dome like this."

"See, I wanted so bad to be normal, like everybody else. But I'm not normal, any more than you or you or you are normal." He pointed into the crowd at random. "There's no such thing as normal. And who wants to be normal anyway?"

El sensed the crowd getting restless as people shouted:

"C'mon, man. Do something."

"Quit talking and do that thing you do."

"Yeah, Mr. Amazing. Heal somebody."

"I knew you were fake. FAKE!"

It became a chant as the crowd pressed in.

Fake . . . Fake . . . Fake . . . Fake . . . .

The chant died when he stopped talking and stood still with his arms crossed, scanning the crowd.

Silence met silence.

"Which brings me to the second reason I asked you all here.

Would Terence Richardson, Amanda Hightower, Akeem Grayjoy, Flo Farmer and Bobbie Lee Franks join me up on stage please?"

The crowd murmur swelled as one by one, the folks named made their way forward. Two of them had people helping them walk.

"Security, could you help those folks?" El said. "Make way everyone, please?"

El met each person as they ascended one of the ramps on either side of the stage and made their way with him in the middle. He shook their hands and escorted them to the line of chairs, helping each find a seat.

The last one, Flo Farmer, gasped from the effort it took to mount the stage and clutched her chest. The large woman, dressed in a pink, go-to-church dress, fanned herself with a hand. "I'm sorry, Mr. El, I . . . It's my heart and I can't . . . I'm afraid—"

El rubbed his hands up and down her arms and felt the familiar tingle start in his bones. "That's all right. Don't be sorry, Flo. I've got you."

"Whoowee, I declare I am such a mess Mr. El."

"That makes two of us. I need a hug, can I have a hug?"

A stadium camera zoomed in from somewhere to catch the embrace and flash it to the giant screens mounted on the scoreboard. It caught the woman's red, sweaty face with eyes squeezed shut as the two stood rocking.

Another camera zoomed in on El's face from a different direction. Serene, smiling, also with eyes closed, El held the woman and while he did, the crowd hushed to respectful silence.

Minutes passed.

A few in the mass of people got bored and the whistles and catcalls began. But they stopped and breathless silence reigned once again the moment El released the woman.

"Are you all right, Flo?" El held her at arm's length. "Your heart had a few problems. But you should feel—"

"Oh, my god." Flo pulled away from El and clapped her hands like a schoolgirl. "My god. My god." She bounced up and down, fairly jumping. "My heart. My heart."

He felt the tremors through the stage flooring and wondered vaguely how well the whole apparatus had been constructed.

"Thank you, thank you," Flo wrapped El in a bear hug and lifted him off his feet. "Oh, my. Oh, I'm sorry." She released him and stepped back, eyes wide and mouth open.

"No problem, Flo," El smiled and the Jumbotron showed a split screen of Flo and him. "Your husband Charlie's waiting for you," he pointed to a man jumping up and down forty yards back. "Why don't you go tell him the good news?"

"Charlie, CHARLIE." Flo's screech got picked up in El's mike and echoed around the banks of empty seats.

The woman who barely made it up the ramp fairly sprinted down it, clomping along in ever-confident strides.

She reached the ground and the crowd parted to make way for the charging woman. Two different cameras followed the husband and wife until they met and Flo did the same thing to her husband she did to El, lifting him and spinning him around. The crowd erupted in cheers and applause.

Many, intent on the emotional drama on the giant screens, missed El's progress as he knelt in front of Terence Richardson. He'd mastered the gain adjust on the mike and turned it way low.

"Hey, there, Terry. Don't be frightened," El said.

"So, this ain't no joke?" Terence rocked slightly and pulled a clear oxygen mask from inside his jacket. He twisted the knob on a small green tank without looking and whooshed through a couple quick breaths. "You're for real?"

"Tell me in a minute," El said. "When you take your next few breaths."

"They say I got chronic lung something or other."

"I know," El said. "Shh." He leaned forward and placed his hands squarely on the man's chest. "I need to push a bit. Tell me if it hurts."

By now, the crowd had turned its attention to the stage once again. Quieter, it surged forward, straining to make out the conversation on stage through El's newly adjusted mike.

A full minute passed until Terence jerked and out came a loud, "Oh."

El leaned back on his heels. "Did I hurt you?"

"Not a bit," Terence said. "Felt funny is all. Kind of crackled in my chest." He coughed once, twice, bent over and hacked some more, hard. Then he stood up and hurried to the back of the stage where he spit out a long, beautiful plume of white.

When he came back to El he grinned ear to ear. "Been wanting to do that for five years. Finally got it all out. And I swear, my knee feels better." He flexed his left leg. "Did you—?"

"A little," El said. "Gotta keep up with those grandkids, am I right?"

Terence guffawed and slapped El on the arm hard enough to rock him. "I guess you are what they say you are. That's for certain." He winked. "Mr. Amazing."

The cameras got all that and the crowd ate it up, cheering and clapping.

El progressed through the next two people. Then, knelt in front of Akeem Grayjoy. Unlike the previous folks, Akeem seemed in the peak of health. A black man of impressive stature in a purple tracksuit, two hundred pounds plus, he sat weeping, his face covered by two plate-sized hands.

"Akeem, listen to me. It's going to be all right." El stood and walked behind the distraught man to place his hands on two massive, shaking shoulders.

"Don't know why I'm here. You can't help me. I know that." He choked the words out. "Nobody can."

"How about if I try? You're right. This is a big one. What do you say, you up for it?"

"Don't be foolin' with me, El. God ain't gonna be wastin' no miracles on me." He grabbed his pants above the right knee and pulled. The cuff rose on that leg to expose an aluminum prosthesis disappearing into a red and white Air Jordan. "Can't fix what ain't there to fix. I know that."

The crowd went silent.

The cameras zoomed in and the aluminum prosthetic leg shined in reflected light.

"This is going to be a little weird," El said. "But I need to get to it, okay?"

"Knock yourself out," Akeem said.

El sat on the stage in front of Akeem with his back to the crowd and Akeem's Air Jordan sandwiched between his legs. He leaned forward and hugged Akeem's leg to him. Before he laid his head against Akeem's knee he turned up the volume on his Mike.

"Folks, this one will be a tough one and it will take longer than the others. Please. Give me a chance to do my best for this man and be patient." He looked up at Akeem. "You ready?"

The man nodded.

El scooted in closer and settled in, laying his head on Akeem's knee and closing his eyes.

Three, four minutes passed.

The crowd stood patient, quiet for all of it.

Until a loud shriek pierced the calm and a fist-sized rock came flying from somewhere near the middle front.

The rock struck El in the back of the head. His mike picked up the faint clunk and the louder clatter when it and El landed on the wooden floor of the stage.

Chapter Forty-Five

LET THE HEALING BEGIN

Beatrix still chafed at being locked up in the staging room. Nicole, ever the resourceful one, had simply stuck a finger in the hole where the doorknob had been and pulled the latch free. Even Nicole's casual, *"Boy's watched too many movies,"* couldn't cheer B up.

They'd chased after El but didn't catch him before Carlson shoved him out on stage. By then, the wheels on El's plan, whatever it might be, had begun to turn.

Beatrix didn't know what else to do but stand and watch the boy make a complete ass of himself.

She, Smith and Nicole clustered to the side with Carlson and watched El gather his wits and start his dialogue with the crowd.

"I think he's doing great," Nicole said at one point.

"You would," B said.

Smith stood with his arms folded and stayed silent.

B watched El go through his spiel, trying to bond with the sea of humanity out there. She had to admit he seemed to be doing okay. Which did not help her humor one bit.

He healed the big woman, the old man with the oxygen tank, a young woman with an uncontrollable head twitch and an older woman with two canes, the kind that clamp over the arms.

It finally struck B why the whole scene bothered her so. Not that El seemed to be doing what he set out to do. Not at all. It's that all he needed to complete this side show production was a damn revival tent.

For all her preaching at him that what they did and what *he* could do especially hadn't been given to them to play parlor tricks with, it looked exactly like that.

May as well give the boy a sexy woman in glitter tights and a dwarf with a bullhorn. Jesus. His gifts were being mocked and the dang fool didn't even know it.

She'd halfway determined to rush onstage, yank him off it and slap him around a few times, with Smith's help, when she saw a fist clenching a rock rise above the horizon of heads in the crowd.

She followed the arc of the rock in slow motion, thinking all the way what were the odds? No way the thing might actually hit its mark, right?

Her feet propelled her forward before the rock connected. "EL!"

She slid on her knees and caught him as he slumped to the side. She felt Smith beside her and Nicole soon after.

Beatrix glared out at the crowd as a hailstorm of rocks rose above it and arced toward them.

She barely had time to yell to Smith, "Help me shield him," and crouch over El to protect him from the missiles.

She closed her eyes and waited for the impacts.

They never came.

She risked a glance behind her and saw a curtain of stones suspended in mid-air.

"What the—?"

"Here they come," said Smith.

He wasn't referring to the stones, but a group of people pushing through the crowd untouched, as if people couldn't or wouldn't get in their way.

"The Council," Smith said. "Every blessed one of them by the looks of it. Stones have got to be the Speaker's trick. Only he and El could stop them in mid-air like that."

The Speaker, with Patel, Karla, Michelle, Ramon, Lucy and several more that Beatrix did not recognize, lined the front of the stage.

Each calmly removed whatever head covering they may have worn in, scarves, hats, wigs, and stood facing the crowd.

The effect of the sudden appearance of all those big, white eggheads stunned the crowd into frozen silence.

The Speaker, dressed in a white linen suit, turned from his place in line and walked over to Eldridge's slumped-over form and removed his headphone mike.

He adjusted the volume as he walked slowly back to resume his place in the center of his Council lineup.

"Ladies and gentlemen, may I please ask for the courtesy of a little bit of silence? I'll not mince words or try to put a delicate face on today's events. I, *we*, are here to let you all in on a little secret. Your world, our world, as of five minutes ago, has changed forever."

The Speaker waved both arms at the crowd as if trying to get someone's attention and the shower of rocks suspended in mid-air fell straight to the ground.

Chapter Forty-Six

REAL POWER

Smith made his way to the Speaker and nodded to show a deference he didn't feel. He'd have much preferred a butt exam.

The Speaker nodded back and smiled. "Butt exam. Picturesque, I'll give you that. I have always appreciated your flair for the dramatic, John Smith."

Smith closed off his thoughts and inside that safe space cursed himself for forgetting. He was not among friends and needed to be careful with what he said *and* thought.

"If I remember our deal," Speaker said "You were to track down Beatrix Goode and her wayward charge and get them under control." He smiled with all the warmth of a grouper on a bed of crushed ice. "I believe your words were: *I will remove Beatrix and begin an immediate evaluation of this Eldridge person myself. If he is The One—which I doubt—I will know it quickly.* The Speaker widened his grin. "Then you ended with something I find most amusing, given our present circumstances. You said, and I'll never forget it: *I will not fail."*

"Speaker, I know I have not kept you in the loop with all this and I apologize—"

The Speaker clapped Smith on the shoulder. "Would you say, looking out over the sea of these misbegotten people crammed into this stadium, and given the enormity of the trouble this El character and B have caused all of *us*, that you have *succeeded?*"

"It's not that easy." Smith cracked his knuckles. "This kid is not what I thought. He's not what any of us thought."

"That boy there? Felled by a simple rock? Flung by some malcontent in this crowd of broken and damaged people?"

Hey, you up there. You freaks missed the train. Circus left town a month ago.

The heckling came from over to the right. And the crowd parted as those near the heckler tried to distance themselves from him.

The Speaker narrowed his eyes and swung around.

The man stood alone in the crowd on a circle of outfield turf. Hands on hips, chin forward.

The Speaker extended an arm and clenched a fist.

The front of the loudmouth's Georgia Bulldogs T-shirt gathered tight around his throat and he gasped and clawed at the material.

The Speaker lifted his arm and the man rose off the ground, kicking and choking.

"Perhaps I did not make myself clear, earlier." The Speaker's words thundered from the sound system. "I asked for simple courtesy and quiet. Not too much to ask, considering."

The dangling man's face changed from bright scarlet to dark purple and his struggles slowed to a few feeble jerks.

"Anyone else feel the need to display another shocking lack of manners? Please. I am all ears."

"Put him down. Now, asshole."

John Smith watched Nicole hurry to The Speaker's side and punch him in the shoulder. He tried to warn her. "Nicole, I wouldn't do that—"

The Speaker turned to stare at Nicole, eyebrows raised. "And who might you be?"

"I said drop him." Nicole shifted her worried gaze between The Speaker and the levitating heckler.

The Speaker shrugged. "As you wish." He opened his fist and the man fell to the ground taking in ragged lungfuls of air. "Now, I don't believe I've had the pleasure." He held out his hand. "My given name is Calvin Jones. My people call me The Speaker."

"Nicole Charbonneau." She crossed her arms, pointedly not taking the proffered hand.

"I see." The Speaker winked at Smith and all vestiges of pretend humor and friendliness faded in an instant. "I have a tiny quirk Ms. Charbonneau." He held up his thumb and finger to show her how tiny. "I place a high value on civility and manners. They are what separate us from the animals and other less-enlightened beings." He made a sweeping gesture that took in the assembled crowd. "As I believe I may have demonstrated. In light of that, perhaps we can start again?"

Smith heard Nicole squeal one brief, little chirp as her face registered surprise that rapidly dissolved into horror as her right arm disentangled itself from across her chest and extended in jerks and stops toward The Speaker.

Smith watched the blood drain from Nicole's face and chords stand out in her neck as she fought to regain control of her arm, to no avail.

"Isn't that much better?" The Speaker said.

Nicole's arm stuck out rigidly and her fist unclenched finger by finger. Panting now with the exertion, her breath whistled wet through gritting teeth.

"Let's start again, shall we?" The Speaker grabbed Nicole's rictus hand and solemnly pumped it up and down. "I am called The Speaker. You may call me Mr.—"

"Calvin." Beatrix's strident voice cut through the crowd noise.

In all the Nicole drama, Smith had missed Beatrix rising and pulling El to his shaky feet. The boy leaned on her as she walked the two of them forward.

"Nicole is my friend," she said. "Please release her."

The Speaker slapped a palm to his forehead. "I should have known. Of course she is, B. She has your flair for insubordination." He sniffed and Nicole's arm snapped back, the abrupt end of the tug of wills staggering her. "Glad to see you, Beatrix Goode. Though I fear you have been too long without proper supervision. Something I had hoped John Smith might correct."

"Speaker—" Smith tried to defend himself.

"Why don't you go introduce yourself Mr. Smith?" The Speaker swept an arm wide, taking in The Council standing in a line across the front of the stage. "As you can see, I felt the need to call Assembly and our Council has responded as I knew they would. I daresay you know most of them. Not by sight of course. But there are several I know you have never met in Council or otherwise."

"But you should know that I never—"

"Not now Mr. Smith." The Speaker waved him off casually. "Take your place in line with the others. Link hands as many are already doing. I trust you can follow *that* simple order? I have more pressing matters that need tending to."

#

Nicole trembled like an aspen leaf and Beatrix felt the shivering the moment she placed a hand on the young woman's shoulder. Nicole stood transfixed, mouth agape, and Beatrix shook her hard to snap her out of it.

"Nikki," B said. "You're okay. I'm here." Nicole did not respond. "Nicole. Please."

"Who is that ... what did he do to me? ... I never felt so violated ..."

"El needs help, Nicole. Help me. Grab his other arm."

"Oh, my god. *El*."

The mention of their friend's name accomplished its purpose. Nicole came back to herself and scooted over to slip El's other arm around her neck.

B felt Nicole's arm curl over hers when she slid it around El's waist and the two of them squeezed one another.

The Speaker abruptly abandoned interest in them and strode over to his Council lineup. Beatrix saw Smith try to squeeze into place in the center of the line. The other Council members tightened their ranks and held fast, hands linked tight. He slunk to the far end and took his place, grabbing the hand of the person there, one B did not recognize.

Beatrix watched The Speaker lean in close to a stylish woman of slender build in a form-fitting sea foam green dress. He spoke into her ear and she nodded.

B concentrated, trying to tap into their conversation. Not easy tapping into The Speaker on a normal day. Today he'd apparently taken pains to shield his thoughts. She gave up.

Beatrix contented herself with keeping her ungainly trio slewed around to face The Speaker straight on. She wanted to be ready when the time came that he renewed his interest in them. And that time would come soon enough.

She took a moment to cast glances at the crowd of people milling about on the SunTrust field and wondered at the spectacle she and her two friends must present. El, the man they had all come to see for various reasons, who'd started off strong but got laid low by a fist-sized rock to the back of his head, now held up by the two women at his sides. The Council, standing like some sort of Odd Squad all in a row, their bulbous heads and white skin more pronounced when replicated by so many in one place.

The crowd hung together for the most part. Probably stunned by what they'd witnessed, certainly cowed by The Speaker's display of power. A few called out to the stage, demanding to know what was going on but not many. She had to hand it to The Speaker. His brand of crowd control had proven quite effective so far. In the far fringes of the mass of people, she noticed several breaking away to head for the exits. Some walked fast. Some sprinted. She envied them.

Beside her, El shook his head periodically as if trying to clear it.

"El, speak to me. How are you? Can you talk?"

El straightened and shook off the women's arms. "God, my head. What happened?" He staggered and they reached to steady him but he waved them off. "Give me a second, I'll be fine."

"Breathe through your nose," Nicole said. "Deep breaths, and exhale through your mouth. It will help."

He did as she suggested and they watched color come back to his cheeks and balance return. "Wow," he said. "That was pretty freaky."

B clapped her hands to her hips. "No. It was a rock some asshole hurled at you."

El dabbed lightly at the back of his head. "Good shot, heh? Braves ought to sign that boy up."

"Not funny, El," B said. "As you can see, we have visitors."

"Relatives of yours?" he said. "I mean, the resemblance is eerie, don't you think?"

"Shut up you idiot. This is serious. Way serious. Those folks are The Council."

"I thought as much."

Nicole elbowed El in the side and pointed at the Speaker. "And that self-important prick in the white plantation owner getup calls himself The Speaker."

"Nicole, please hush," B whispered. "You don't know who or what you're fooling with."

The Speaker turned to look at her with that odd smile of his and, after giving each of his Council members an encouraging pat on the shoulder, came over to join them.

B unconsciously took a step closer to El.

"Now, B, I would say your friend is beginning to learn *who* and *what* she's fooling with. Wouldn't you say? In the meantime, perhaps you could introduce me to your other friend here, the one we have to thank for all this."

El's left hand hung between them and Beatriz clasped it before answering. "El, I think it's time you met—"

"Calvin Jones," the Speaker said and extended his hand. "I also answer to The Speaker on occasion."

El turned to wink at Beatrix before taking The Speaker's hand. "I've been looking forward to this," he said. "Big time."

"As have I," The Speaker said. "We have heard so much about you. If everything turns out the way our Beatrix has indicated it might, we have big plans for you."

The two men shook and B felt the electric jolt course through El as soon as the men touched hands.

The Speaker did not break his grip, nor did El, for a full ten-second eternity. Not until B said, "That's enough, Calvin."

The Speaker raised his eyebrows and smiled broadly. Almost, B thought, as if a great weight had been lifted from him.

"Come, El. May I call you El? I have some very important people I would like you to meet." The Speaker placed an arm around El's shoulders and led him toward The Council lineup. "Thank you, Beatrix. Be a dear and take your place in line beside your new best friend, John Smith."

Chapter Forty-Seven

THE ONE

El sensed B's fear as acutely as if it were his. He'd come to his senses in time to catch a bit of Nicole's run-in with the man whose arm draped not-so-casually across his shoulders. He touched fingers to the back of his head to check on the progress there and came away with a bright spot of red on his middle finger.

Redder than ketchup.

The power he'd felt emanate from this man when they shook hands had stunned him. B and Smith he knew. Their abilities and strengths held no surprises for him anymore. Heck, they'd joined together to save people. The Speaker presented a new set of puzzles to unlock.

No problem. All in good time.

"…These oddly familiar-looking people," The Speaker had been talking as they walked, "are The Council. Introduce yourselves, people. You have all come a very long way to meet this man and I am quite pleased to tell you that in my humble opinion, your trips have not been in vain."

The Speaker nudged him forward and El stepped up to a lineup of people who looked so much like B, Smith and him that chills started at the back of his neck and tickled down his spine. *To be part of an odd-looking few is one thing. To take your place as one more member of what looks like a whole nother race is something else entirely.*

He had no more time to question his humanity before the first member in The Council broke into his thoughts. The rest introduced themselves the same way. He met every one on that stage with a weird-shaped head and white skin like his. He went down the line and shook hands with each of them.

As soon as he made a mental connection he picked up a name and received impressions of the person's home then moved onto the next in line. He saw images from around the world; India, Spain, Ukraine, England, France and tons more he'd never remember.

Each seemed eager to meet him for reasons he couldn't really define. Several times he heard *The One* come across their connection, whatever the hell that meant. After awhile they all ran together.

When he got to the end of The Council line, Smith and B stood clasping hands like all the others. Smith looked unhappy for some reason, but then, Smith always looked unhappy. B wouldn't meet his eyes.

"Hey, I know you guys," he said. He laughed, trying to lighten the mood, but neither of his friends returned the feeling. "B? Not to worry. Everything is okay. Bleeding's about stopped."

She met his eyes for a brief flash of a second and nodded before looking away at the crowd still crammed in below them.

What the heck's wrong with her?

The Speaker came up behind him and the communication blazing from the man felt like the difference between a polite tap on the shoulder and a punch on the face.

"We all good?" he broadcast.

The Council answered by standing straighter and stiffening in their spots.

"Excellent," The Speaker said. "El? Let's you and I stand together here in the middle."

Two of The Council, Italy and France, dropped their hands so he and The Speaker could squeeze in between them. The pretty one next to him, like France in a designer gown, grabbed his hand in hers and held tight. She smiled at him and in his head said, "*You are so sweet, El. It is a Dior.*" The Speaker held onto his other hand.

"Whoa, hey, wait a second," El dropped his hands. Not easy to do when the other person doesn't feel like cooperating. "What's going on? This is getting a little creepy."

The Speaker smiled tightly. "Not at all, El. You didn't think we'd let you try all this on your own, did you? Look at all those poor souls. How were you going to minister to each of them? You're only one person, El. We're here to help."

El let that sink in. Made sense, though he'd been on a roll there until the dang rock clocked him. "I had no idea how many would show up."

"Unforeseen circumstances," The Speaker pursed his lips. "They can derail the best intentions if we let them. You have some amazing gifts, El. Same gifts we all have in various degrees. Alone you can only do so much. But together," he spread his arms, "imagine what we can accomplish. Shall we?"

The Speaker lifted his hand and raised his eyebrows. El shrugged and re-clasped hands with The Speaker and the beautiful woman on his other side.

The Speaker raised his arms and the line of eggheads did the same, hands gripped tight and eyes forward. "Focus Council. As we rehearsed it. Far edges first and work backward toward us."

El closed his eyes and felt the power tingle in his bones like a tiny itch at first, tickling at his center and then increasing to a violent buzz. Similar to his experience with those folks on the freeway; when he'd been flagging and needed help, finally linking hands with B and Smith.

That was static electricity compared to this power line charge.

He exulted, drank in the force of it. All these people here. His new friends and him would be able to help every one of them and the thought of it filled him with such joy he felt he must have been glowing. Or was it the power coursing through him? He wouldn't be surprised if light actually burst from his skin like a beacon.

He tried to open his eyes and look to be sure but the spasm caused by the surge would not allow it. El gave himself over to the powerful delight that seized him and went with it.

"Now." The Speaker's voice scraped from his throat and El felt a violent shift in the force, sensed it gather on either side of him and concentrate itself in him until it became unbearable.

Boom!

"Again," The Speaker croaked.

Boom!

"Again."

Boom!

It happened several more times and every time, El felt the power coil tight inside his chest and when it seemed as if his ribcage must explode it discharged all at once. The tension/release from unbearable pressure to blessed relief cycled through him and coincided exactly with each explosion.

"Arms down," The Speaker rasped. "Excellent work."

El opened his eyes and gasped. Straight ahead and then fanning out on either side of the home plate area, the entire upper deck canopy that previously ringed the field with lights lay in a collapsed ruin on the bleachers below it.

Tangles of twisted metal girders and chunks of concrete smoked and sparked. Mini-avalanches of settling debris shot dust in the air as rows of seats gradually crushed under weights they were never meant to bear.

To the left, the whole top level teetered then fell onto the level below it. Even over-engineered as it undoubtedly was, the sudden weight from above proved too much. The collapse came with shrieks of protesting metal and more booms as pillar after pillar of concrete failed to hold. Clouds of dust billowed from the far stands as more levels followed suit.

El watched spellbound as images from 9/11 he'd watched on TV came rushing back, replayed on a slightly smaller scale here.

The people on the field responded the only way they could; fleeing the destruction at their backs and pressing forward toward the outfield stage and the line of strange beings standing across its front.

The screaming began like flipping on a switch. Or, perhaps it took that long for the sound to break through El's consciousness. The open mouths and panic-stricken faces on the people in front of him stabbed at his heart and turned the volume from a loud white noise to a crashing roar punctuated with raw shrieks and wordless yelling.

The images of people turning on those who shoved from behind to escape the carnage went from human to animal in seconds as fists and clawed hands grabbed and pounded flesh and bone.

El tried calling to them, begging them to stop, useless as swearing at the waves to cease their crashing. He knew that but he kept on, caught up in the same panic that gripped the poor people below him.

Triumph pulsed in unspoken waves from The Speaker and El sensed the others in The Council luxuriating in their leader's approval, sharing in his feelings.

"Like the herd of cattle they are."

The sheer venom and intense disdain in The Speaker's thoughts punched through to clench El's stomach in a vise and make it hard to take a breath.

"Time for the big finale." The man's face positively beamed as he grabbed El's hand again. This time he extended his arms forward, pointing above the heads of the crowd and the line of The Council did the same.

Those in the mob of people who noticed covered their heads and cowered. They might have fallen to the ground to escape whatever horror they imagined came next but were held upright by the crush of roiling bodies around them.

"*Cull the herd.*" The Speaker's focus shifted from far to close, to the crowd milling and fighting at their feet.

El pulled at the hands gripping his but to no avail. Try as he might he could not break the bonds that cinched him tight. He felt the same surge of power as before, starting small then cresting to impossible intensity.

He had enough perspective and presence to stand beside it and watch it happen inside him. He had no strength to fight it. But the sheer will it took to do even that much rippled the force emanating from either side of him and he felt the brief interruption in the currents.

It did no good. The crescendo reached its impossible height like before and exploded from him. His new awareness showed him with crushing clarity The Speaker's role in the terrible operation—and his.

The Speaker may be the one aiming the gun. But he, Eldridge Montcalm, the Amazing El according to the shirt his mother made for him, was the trigger.

And The Speaker pulled it.

Instantly, the crowd screaming and tussling and fighting in front of them silenced. They stilled in place as if engaged in a monstrous playground game of freeze tag.

Within seconds most of them crumpled to the ground, dead. The four or five hundred left standing didn't twitch a muscle.

The Speaker tapped the headset still curled around his head and sound burst forth, amplified by the remaining sound system.

"Welcome to the next step in the evolution of mankind." The Speaker's voice boomed and echoed. "We have spared you because, unlike those flawed and broken individuals at your feet, you have no real serious flaws and therefore possess redeemable promise. In a few days you will begin to notice that promise taking shape inside you. Now go home, kiss your loved ones. Hug your friends. Touch them. Make contact. Tell everyone you meet what happened here."

The Speaker clapped his hands and as if waking from a trance, the terrified individuals left standing sprinted for the stadium exits that remained accessible.

The Speaker raised his head and smiled and waved at the camera emplacements stationed around the stadium. They'd left those intact by design.

He turned his back on them and the retreating people and rubbed his palms, smiling at The Council like a proud father before concentrating solely on El.

"Quite a coming out party, wouldn't you say Mr. Montcalm?" The Speaker's focused thought smacked El behind the eyes. *"We couldn't have done it without you."*

Chapter Forty-Eight

MOTHER MAGDALENE II

Mother Magdalene let the sea of panicked retreaters swirl around her. She would not be hurried, nor would she succumb to fear. Her strength came from one whose power surpassed an entire stadium full of egg-headed devils. She gathered the flaps of her flowing purple robe in a fist and waded toward the nearest exit.

She took little solace that *her* rock smote the devil to his knees. They had accomplished nothing. Of the few who emerged unscathed from the demon's purging, only one other served as an acolyte from *In His Name*. She did not remember the lone woman's name. It wasn't important. The others who'd heeded their Mother's call were laid flat on the devil's killing ground.

Nevertheless, she exulted. The devil has shown his hand and revealed the nature of his minions. Now they knew what they were up against. More importantly, the whole world knew. One acolyte would be but a snowflake in the coming storm as the world clamored to cleave to their side and join in their holy fight.

She vowed to avenge the deaths of her faithful no matter what the cost. God would see her commitment and guide her hand. Her faith told her so.

Later that evening, Mother stood in the needle-sharp shower spray and let the tiny pinpricks of scalding water serve as her penance. She had underestimated their enemy so completely. She'd stood frozen in the grip of pure evil and watched as he snuffed out so many of her flock with the snap of a finger. Her hubris put them in harm's way and it got them killed.

She pounded her fists against the shower stall's cool marble and bowed her head beneath the hot spray. "Lord, I am your vessel. Fill me with your righteous anger. Grant me the wisdom to vanquish your enemies. And steel me with your strength to do what must be done."

Mother turned up her face to the shower's scald and opened her mouth to let the hot water flush all her openings, her eyes, nose, ears, to cleanse them and make them ready to receive his pure inspiration.

She toweled off in the steamy aftermath, the thick terrycloth one last indulgence she allowed herself. There would be no others. She bent over to dry her legs and feet and felt the pounding pulse of a headache announce itself behind her eyes.

She shook it off. *Small wonder, after all she'd been through.*

She padded naked to the huge walk-in closet stocked with brightly colored silks and satins on velvet hangers. The flowing robes she'd adopted as her signature had pleased her once. No more.

She turned her back on the colorful array and walked to a little used bank of drawers. She pulled open several before finding exactly what would serve her in the coming war.

White cotton pants, so simple and shapeless a monk might wear them. She slipped them on and the scratch of the material felt heavenly on her legs. A white tunic came next. Long enough to hang below her waist with sleeves that flared over her hands if she didn't push them back.

She walked back into her bedroom in her new outfit and surveyed the walls. Surely, in all the trappings and thick tapestries there would be one—ah! The ancient hanging she'd appropriated in her visit to the Holy Land. A Templar Knight astride his armored charger.

She hadn't paid it any mind for years. Today, the crimson Templar cross on the knight's chest fairly glowed. She imagined it beckoned her as a fellow warrior.

Get on with it. Time enough for self-congratulations.

She yanked the old tapestry down with little fanfare and cast it aside. The knotted hemp rope it hung from is really what she wanted. She untied both ends and slipped it from the iron rings that held it in place. The length of hemp wrapped twice around her waist and she cinched it in front with a square knot.

Shoes would be her final accouterment. And though sandals would be more in keeping with the humble tone and sensibility of this new Mother, she could only go so far. If she'd learned anything from yesterday's disaster, speed and maneuverability were two qualities that may become very necessary.

She retrieved a favorite pair of Nike's from her closet and laced them on nice and tight. Again, bending over to lace her shoes rewarded her with more pounding headache. She pressed fingers to her temples and squeezed. The pain felt welcome, additional penance would sanctify her cause all the more.

Mother swept from her inner sanctum and strode purposefully down the cold marble hall toward her office. The Nike's squeaked a bit on the polished floor and she smiled. Not as auspicious as a blast of heavenly trumpets, but it would do.

The halls of her compound were deserted and she wondered briefly if, after yesterday, anyone might have lingered. The shock of the spectacle at the stadium had to have frightened everyone who saw it. At the very least it would have filled them with questions they could not answer alone. Without God and without Mother.

She blew through the doors to her office and stabbed at the phone on her desk to call up the receptionist. A long two seconds ticked by before *Yes, Mother* came back on the line.

Thank you Lord.

"How many of our brethren remain on the premises child?"

"I am not sure. Many have stayed home."

"I see. Please contact all you can, call the homes of the others. Summon them to our auditorium for an assembly at noon. Can you do that?"

"Right away, Mother."

"Good. Is Brother Bernard still with us by chance?"

"He came in late this morning."

"Excellent. Send him to my office an hour before and do the same with my video expert Pat. If Pat is not here, find him. It's important."

"Yes, Mother."

#

Bernard sat on the edge of the chair facing Mother across her desk. He drummed his fingers on a knee and she let it go. Last week she might have said something about his lack of focus. Not today. Perhaps she'd changed after all.

"I see you did not join your brothers and sisters at the stadium yesterday. Makes me wonder about your commitment to our Lord."

"Mother, I tried to get there but the traffic—"

She waved a hand. "No matter, Bernard. Thank that *traffic* for saving your life or else you'd be dead like so many of our brethren."

Bernard stayed silent.

"You may have noticed some changes around here." Mother spread her arms to show off her new look.

His eyes stayed focused on hers.

Harrumph.

"Our war against the devil has shifted to another phase and I intend to be ready. To do that, I need a core of trusted—*advisors*—that will never be afraid to speak their mind. I trust you have not lost that ability?"

She watched Bernard run his fingers over the welted scars on his chest. No doubt reliving scenes from the beating others in the order gave him at Mother's behest.

"I have learned much at your hands, Mother."

"Not exactly an answer."

"I serve God and you, in that order." He swallowed and she watched the bob of his Adam's apple.

"Those of us who remain, and I am assured that we can still muster strong numbers from our brethren, have an assembly scheduled for noon today in the auditorium. I would like to present you among several others as my trusted inner circle. Will the Lord and I be able to count on your commitment?"

Mother resisted the urge to paw for a tissue from the dispenser in her desk. The massive sneeze crackling in her nasal passages grew more insistent with every heartbeat. It wanted release, but she could not break eye contact with Bernard. The man must see the importance of her reliance on him and must accede to her will in this.

"Yes, Mother." Bernard bowed his head.

Ah, the break she needed.

She snatched a tissue and blew a trumpet blast of a sneeze into it. She felt relief to her toes.

"Good. The Lord thanks you, as do I. We have much work to do and it begins at noon." She pushed back from her desk but not before grabbing a second tissue. Another sneezing fit took hold of her and she barely registered Bernard's departure.

#

Mother stalled as long as she could to give stragglers time to join them. Her new core of advisors sat in a line of chairs behind her; Bernard, Pat her video tech who cradled a remote gizmo thing in his lap, a feisty acolyte named Evelyn who Mother thought she ought to remember but didn't, and two larger male congregation members who would double quite nicely as bodyguards.

She strode to the lectern and tapped the mike. Half the auditorium sat empty but it could not be helped. Faith was faith and in a rare flash of forgiveness, she allowed as how the recent events may have been so soul shaking that many of her flock were simply too gripped by fear to think straight.

Perhaps, God will change their minds later.

"Brothers and sisters, my strongest and bravest faithful of *In His Name*, I am heartened and humbled by your presence here today. The Lord and I will remember the statement you make merely sitting there. But I must ask more from you than that. I pray, we all pray, that together we will be up to the task."

She turned to her video tech and nodded.

Pat thumbed a button and adjusted volume with a slider. The giant screen hanging at the back of the stage flickered to life and a compilation of footage Pat had gleaned from local and national news broadcasts rolled.

The scenes were almost identical, no matter the outlet. Spliced together footage from SunTrust Stadium camera feeds replayed the shocking events of the previous day.

Pat had done a masterful edit job, using software to enhance detail in the video, zooming in and out of key scenes.

Breathless news announcers commented over top of the footage. Some of them exclaiming loudly, giving themselves over to the excitement of the horror. One or two nationals intoned somberly, interjecting mostly inane questions for dramatic effect:

What are we witnessing here? ... Who are these strange-looking people and why are they here? ... Are we witnessing the end of an era and the start of a new one? ... Was this a deliberate attempt to amass a number of unfortunate souls and then slaughter them for no apparent reason?

Idiots.

Mother snorted and immediately reached for the box of tissues she now carried with her at all times. She let the footage roll. She'd seen Pat's treatment over and over until the damned stuff held no shock value for her anymore. But many in her congregation had not yet had the full effect.

It was important they did.

The sham miracles came first. The fatheaded demon's supposed cures of the afflicted, no doubt hand-picked for effect. Next and in well-timed slo-mo came the collapse of the stadium structures. Pat amplified the sound and edited for full effect. The screech of metal and shocking roar combined well with the billowing clouds of debris. Placed strategically in the footage for dramatic effect, close-ups of the group of demons lined up along the front of the stage left no doubt as to the perpetrators of the disaster.

The footage ended with the lineup of the devil's entourage trembling and vibrating in the collective grip of whatever evil powers they tapped into to commit their destruction. A slow zoom stopped on the face of the apparent leader and this still surprised her, the leader did not appear to be the media darling they called El. The new-revealed leader's smirk and stare back at the cameras he must have known were watching clutched at her insides.

She locked eyes with the thing onscreen and knew beyond any doubt that the devil dared her to come for him. She smiled back at the thing, knowing full well that responding to day-old video footage was an empty gesture. Nonetheless, it made her feel better and steeled her for the battles yet to come.

She blew a final blast into the last of the tissues in her box and grabbed the sides of the lectern in trembling hands. She cleared her throat. "War has come to our world brothers and sisters. The devil, with his sick and twisted demonic ego, has judged us no contest. He stood confidently before us, before the *world*, and announced his presence in no uncertain terms. Unafraid!"

Mother pounded the lectern to emphasize her next few words. Many in the audience flinched with each thunderous blow.

"That. Was. His. First. Mistake."

A ragged sneeze trumpeted forth at the end of her tirade and the unfortunate crescendo ruined the drama of her moment. She flung the now empty tissue box aside and scraped a forearm across her nose.

"I have asked you all here to enlist your help as soldiers in our righteous cause and I have something here for each of you that is at once a memento and a weapon for the war that will soon consume us."

She reached into the lectern and lifted out a basket. "I sent many of our brethren to that place, that devil's killing ground in downtown Atlanta, armed with a symbol." She pulled a rock from the basket and held it up. "I acted foolishly and ask your forgiveness. Seduced by pride I allowed love of my own perceived cleverness to cloud my judgment. We all saw what happened." She tossed the rock onto the wooden stage floor and the crack and clatter amplified by the microphones caused some in the audience to jump.

"We love you Mother," a voice called from the back of the auditorium.

"Use us as you see fit for the glory of God," shouted another.

Mother clasped her hands and raised her face to heaven. Even those in the back rows could see the tears coursing down her cheeks. "I will not fail you a second time my children. I swear it. Please come, ushers will guide you by rows, and receive the only weapon we will need to vanquish the evil that is upon us."

With this she reached into the basket a second time and extracted a crude wooden cross strung on a leather thong. She'd had the compound's crafts shop churning the six-inch artifacts out by the dozens for hours. She held it high for all to see, kissed it and placed it around her neck. "God's love and our love for him will see us through. Please come and receive the one symbol of our faith that has never broken in the face of evil."

One by one, the faithful filed up to the front where Mother met them and bestowed her gifts, kissing each cross before placing it around the next acolyte's neck. "Thank you for your commitment to him and to your brothers and sisters of *In His Name.*"

Later, reflecting in her study, she felt pretty good about how the afternoon had progressed. Her people seemed truly moved by the ceremony with the crosses and pleased to wear them. Looking out over her crowd the swaying symbols of God's righteousness at every breast filled her heart with joy.

Only thing that could have been better was God granting her a miracle and banishing the damn wheezing cold that gripped her all of a sudden. Thank the Lord someone had managed to locate another box of tissues for the sneezing fits that came more regularly lately.

Chapter Forty-Nine

GO WITH THE FLOW

Nicole crouched beside El's trembling form and tried once again to budge him. Only she and Beatrix remained on stage. The Council and the others had slipped out in the ensuing panic of the fleeing crowd. On the field, hundreds of bodies lay crumpled in place like so many colorful piles of laundry.

"What have I done? What have I done?" El kept repeating the phrase, hugging knees to his chest, wracked by sobs. "So many people. So many people."

Nicole tried again. "We have to get you out of here El. Now. We can't stay here."

Sirens echoed in the cavernous confines of the remains of SunTrust stadium. Help coming in a hurry announced itself from all directions. Helicopters whup-whup-whupped overhead.

Nicole and B strained to lift El to his feet, pulling at him, poking him, anything to shock him from his private grief. Nothing worked. He shrugged away from their touches. If anything, he gripped his knees tighter and sobbed louder.

"El!" Nicole, desperate to get him moving, knelt in front of him. "I'm sorry to have to do this but you leave me no choice."

Nicole reared back and slapped El across the face so hard it yanked his head sideways. A red handprint rose quickly into view on his left cheek. She prepared to do the same to El's other cheek when he looked at her as if recognizing a long lost friend in a crowd.

"Nicole?" he said.

"Thank god," Nicole said. "Are you back with us?"

"Oh, Jesus." He covered his face with his hands.

"No, no. Don't you go there." Nicole grabbed his wrists and pulled his hands down. "We'll cry later. B and me will sit beside you and have us a real good one. Right now we need to go."

At the mention of Beatrix, El raised his head.

"You. Don't touch me."

"Eldridge—" B tried to say something.

"You're a monster," El shrieked. "A monster. Get away from me."

Nicole framed his face with her palms and forced him to look at her. "The monsters have all gone, El—look at me—they're gone and we need to fix this."

El looked past her to the stadium grass littered with bodies and started to giggle.

"Didn't you see? My big moment? The Amazing El coming to save the world? What a show. They sold tickets. Did you know that? Tickets. *Why, hello sir. Here's your ticket. Hope you enjoy it. Gonna be a killer show.*"

"Shut up, El," Beatrix finally spoke. "If you don't quit this poor me pity party I swear I'm going to knock your ugly head off. Nicole's a gentle soul. I'm a monster, remember?"

Beatrix bent down and pinched his nose, hard, until he started to squirm.

"Ow. Led go ob be." He swatted her arm but she held on.

"You going to quit this crap and come with us?"

"Yes, yes. I'b cubbing. Quit it."

The young women pulled him erect and the trio stumbled their way toward the side of the stage where B had watched El greet his crowd of followers not so long ago.

As they walked, El supported between them, he stumbled and would have fallen if they hadn't been holding him. A large rock skittered sideways and Nicole bent quickly and snatched it up. She cocked her arm and prepared to heave it when El grabbed her elbow.

"Wait. Hold on. Is that the—?"

"The rock some asshole hit you with?" B said. "Yes."

"I want it," he said. "Give it here."

"Why?"

"I don't know why but I do. Hand it over Nicole."

She shrugged and slapped it into his palm. "One measly rock ain't gonna be much help against all the folks out there who want our heads."

"My head," El said. He nodded toward B. "And hers. Not you. Our weird-ass heads are targets now. Not yours. Leave us. You'll have a way better chance without us."

"Nice try, El," Nicole said. "I'm not goin' anywhere. B, you're the one who studied the map they gave us. Said you could get us out of here without anyone knowing."

B nodded.

"But I know how your mouth sometimes overloads your rear end—"

"I can get us out of here," B said. "Follow my lead. First, grab us a couple hats left behind by our fellow monsters. We'll need them. Next stop, we retrieve the stuff we left in the green room."

Several stadium levels, back hallways and too many stairwells for Nicole to count later, they emerged from a side door to the outside.

They had not encountered too many people on their circuitous journey. The ones they did never gave her or her friends' hastily donned disguises a second look. Probably too intent on escape.

The air wafted hot on their faces and carried the oily stink of idling diesel engines. Overhead, news choppers carved up the sky.

"Holy crap, look at all that," Nicole said.

The streets and most available spaces outside the stadium large enough for a vehicle were occupied. Atlanta Police, black SWAT vans, Fire and Rescue, ambulances from every Atlanta hospital, all crowded together. Latecomers inched forward in the confusing crush of people and cars as best they could, flashing lights and blasting sirens to no avail before giving up and claiming the spot they'd already achieved.

Doors opened and disgorged uniforms of various stripes and colors that grabbed equipment from their vehicles and headed for the stadium front. They fought like salmon wading through streams of panicked, milling people heading in every direction but there.

B's bright yellow Camaro, unaccountably, squatted right where they'd left it in front of the stadium entrance.

"Sure would like to hop in and get the hell out of here," B said. "It has my stuff in it, stuff I can't do without."

"Don't even think about it," Nicole said. "Besides, all roads in are blocked off. We wouldn't get three feet before someone recognized one of you two, hats and wigs and all."

"She's right," El said. "Crowd's our best bet. We keep our heads down and go with the flow. See how far it takes us. If we make it to one of the outer parking lots I can get us out of here."

B crossed her arms and looked ready to dispute El's logic. So, Nicole linked elbows with her and strolled away from the action at the entrance. One good tug and B followed more or less willingly. To do otherwise would draw too much attention.

The trio made the Windy Ridge Bridge over I-75, stopping for a brief second to watch the traffic. Red and blue lights still approached from north and south, mixed in with cars of commuters.

Nicole looked at the cars racing by underneath them and felt jealous of the occupants who had no idea what had happened back at the stadium. Blissfully unaware, they'd go home, join their families. Maybe stop at the store to pick up food for dinner. They'd find out soon enough. Word of the tragedy and the bigheaded freaks who'd caused it would spread like the plague and nowhere would be safe.

She knew in her bones that her two friends had not been willing participants back there. Beatrix she'd known for years and El, from the moment back at Beatrix's trailer when he'd lifted bloody hands away from B's self-inflicted knife wound, she knew he had something special to give the world.

What that might be Nicole had no idea and right now she couldn't think too hard on it. They needed to get to safety. Thank god El seemed to know where they were going.

By the time they reached the end of the walkover, signs for Braves East Parking came into view. The parking lots had numbers on them and directionals: Braves East 31, East 43.

"Pick a number," El said.

"Pick one yourself," she said and sneezed once, twice, three good ones. She wiped her nose with a sleeve and staggered. Pressure from the sneezes pounded in her head and pain flared behind her eyes like a new-lit blowtorch. "Dang it," she said and pressed fingers to her temples.

"Nikki? You okay?" B came to her and put an arm around her shoulders. "You don't look so hot."

"It has been kind of a day, hasn't it?" Nicole snapped. "I'm all right. Let's keep going."

They crossed a plot of grass into Braves East 43 parking lot and another sneezing fit took her. The pain in her head swelled until it felt like something very mad trapped inside her skull wanted to get out.

She groaned and doubled over against some family's parked van.

"Nikki! Oh, god El. Something's not right."

"Let's get her inside," he said.

"What?"

He placed a hand over the driver's side door lock and the locks on all doors released with a series of *thunks*.

"Get in the back with her," he said. "I'll drive."

"I'm fine," Nicole slid into the back passenger seat. She sneezed again and groaned. "Dang it. I could use a Kleenex if someone had one." Through her stuffiness she smelled hints of gasoline, wet dog and corn chips. The combination gagged her and her stomach cramped around a beginning retch.

B slid in on the other side of Nicole as El pushed the START button and the blue Dodge van fired up like he had a key on him. "We monsters do have certain skills," he said. He revved the engine and leaned over to pop the glove compartment. "Hey Nikki, this is your lucky day." He handed a new box of tissues back to Beatrix. "Slump down, don't look into any of the cars we pass. Don't catch anyone's eye. We'll get out of this yet."

Nicole felt the car lurch when El put it in gear and she bit back a yelp. The movement lit new fires in her brain and she gritted her teeth against the pain, pawing for a Kleenex.

B handed her one and Nicole tried to clear her nose, blowing softly so as not to shift the piles of rusty nails scratching behind her eyes.

Chapter Fifty

CDC

Thalia Etienne eyed the boxes lining the hallway of her apartment. She'd yet to unpack from her last posting to Burkina Faso. Tsetse flies had been particularly nasty this past rainy season and sleeping sickness had been ravaging villagers up and down the river regions. Before that, her dance card included cholera in the Congo and small flairs of hanta virus and Ebola in Guinea.

She refilled the Keurig reservoir in her kitchen and stabbed the brew button. The rich spice of Starbucks dark roast spread like a warm air comforter and she hugged herself. God, it felt great to be back home.

Two whole days of rest and pure vegging before she'd need to report to work at CDC headquarters in Atlanta. She kicked off her shoes and held the fresh cup of coffee to her lips and breathed deep of pure heaven.

Yes, she craved fieldwork. Her supervisor knew it and saved his most challenging postings for her. She enjoyed being one of his best epidemiologists and she nagged the crap out of him if the time between world crises stretched too long. Nothing she liked better than beating back the ugliest creatures the viral world threw at mankind.

But this, tucking her feet underneath a quilt on the couch and reaching for the TV remote, had its definite upsides.

Fifteen minutes into the Young and The Restless and the life and death dramas that weirdly hadn't changed all that much from the last time she'd watched over a year ago, her iPhone whined. The ringtone, an angry buzzing mosquito, never failed to make her grin.

She glanced at the screen. *Francis Fairhope.*

How the hell did her supervisor know she'd arrived home a day early? She debated letting the call roll to voicemail before finally answering.

"Hey, boss." She colored her voice with a soupçon of fatigue for effect.

"Unpacked yet?"

She glanced at the mess in her front hallway. "Only my toothbrush."

"Sorry to *bug* you so soon—"

She didn't rise to his lame pun. "I know, I know. I'm due into the office bright and early Monday morning."

"We have a sort of situation."

She sighed audibly. "Where am I going? I heard about the refugee virus in Germany. Alex in over his head?"

"He has that handled, I am glad to report. Nope. Somewhere a bit closer to home."

"Mexico City? Never should have built that thing on a lake."

"I need you at Northside Hospital as soon as you can get there."

"*Our* Northside Hospital? Ten minutes up I-75?"

"The same. You will need to speak with the resident there, a doctor Patel. Calm him down."

"What's going on?"

"Probably nothing. He's a little freaked out over some flu cases that came into emergency yesterday."

She sipped from her markedly cooler cup of coffee. "How often do we get calls from jumpy doctors about flu cases?"

"Too often, you're right. But I got a feeling about this one, Thalia."

She paused. His 'feelings' had achieved near legendary status among CDC field personnel. "I can be there in thirty minutes."

She heard him sigh.

"Thanks. I owe you one."

"You owe me more than one. But I owe you five times that. I'll call as soon I figure out our good doctor's cause for concern."

Twenty-nine minutes later a sweating Doctor Patel met her at the door to Northside Hospital. He handed her a facemask and clamped his own tight over his nose before leading her down the hospital corridor at a jog.

She barely kept up. Thank god her legs were longer than his. They rode the elevator in silence broken only by the soft tap-tap of Dr. Patel's blue Croc.

Thalia cleared her throat. "How many cases?"

Dr. Patel started, as if from a daydream. "So far, five."

"What stage are they?" she said.

"See for yourself."

The doors whooshed open and he directed them to a set of automatic doors posted with large red quarantine signs. A smaller, warning sign over a keycard mechanism cautioned that only authorized personnel were permitted entry.

Doctor Patel slid his card through and they pushed forward into what had previously been the hospital's ER. The curtained off bays were all empty but for five. "We've shut down our ER and are re-routing incoming patients to other area hospitals."

"I see." Thalia paused to pull a pair of gloves from a wall-mounted dispenser. "Let's begin with your most serious patient and move up from there."

"That would be Divine Buransky in this first bay." He slid open the curtain and stepped through.

A still form lay in the center of the bed. The electric monitors mounted on the wall shown dark. A sheet pulled up over the patient said it all.

Thalia paused a half-second before stepping up to the covered head. "How long?"

"She came to us yesterday complaining of headache, chills, respiratory problems. She passed an hour before I called you people."

Thalia pulled back the sheet and noted the crusting blood around the eyes and nose. She thumbed open the lids of both eyes, their whites now a darkening cherry red. "You have blood samples for me?"

The doctor nodded, his dark eyes expressionless above the mask. "For every one of them."

"Then let's see every one of them."

Thalia peeled off her gloves and donned new ones before entering the next bay. She repeated that process for each of the remaining patients. All four were on oxygen, breathing raggedly, their monitors showing varied degrees of oxygen uptake, heart rates slightly elevated. However, none presented with signs of hemorrhage. They seemed remarkably calm for all the drama they'd caused.

"Doctor?" Thalia inclined her head and Doctor Patel joined her outside the room. "It would appear that you had one case with, I'll admit, frightening symptoms—"

"Yes, but—"

She held up a finger to stop his protest.

"Which could be explained by any number of special

circumstances barring a complete workup and autopsy. The other four patients look to be, indeed, suffering from the flu. Their cases, though at first glance seem bad, even problematic, appear to be nothing more than bad cases of H1N1—and not avian flu, if that is what you were thinking."

Her phone vibrated in her pocket and she pulled it out. *Francis Fairhope. Again.* "Sir, this looks like nothing more than your garden variety—"

"Kennestone Hospital and Grady downtown called two minutes ago. They're reporting more cases similar to Doctor Patel's in Northside. I'll need you to check those out, too, Thalia."

"I'll let you know what I find." She hung up and thought for a few seconds, tapping one foot. "Doctor, which hospitals exactly would be the ones to take up the slack from Northside?"

"First would be Kennestone up north. If the emergency proved serious enough of course, Grady downtown is a world class Trauma One center."

"Thank you, you have done a wonderful job of containment here." She smiled. "Exactly what I might have done in your shoes. I would like those blood samples from all five of your patients packed in ice."

"So, you think these cases could be more serious—?"

"I think I don't know enough yet to even speculate."

"Your blood samples are already waiting for you. What do I do for my four patients in the meantime?"

"Exactly what you are doing. Maintain your quarantine. Monitor them. Keep their airways clear. I do not believe they are in deadly danger. If this flu, or whatever it is, could have compromised their immune systems to the extent it did the first patient, it would have done so already."

"But—"

"I am sorry, but I really need to be on my way. Apparently yours is not the only Atlanta hospital to suffer a flu scare. Those blood samples?"

"Are at the nurse's station on the way out."

Thalia jumped on I-75 and sped north as fast as traffic would allow. On the passenger seat beside her, the red and white biohazard cooler waited patiently strapped in, content to reveal its secrets when she could rush it into the lab back at headquarters.

An eternal fifteen minutes later, she screeched to a halt in Emergency at Kennestone and left the car at the entrance. A quick flash of her CDC credentials and a don't-try-me glare got her past security in record time and up to the ICU.

A harried young resident, *Virginia Peebles, MD* by her nametag, met her at the elevator. The woman exhaled when she saw Thalia like she'd been holding her breath for hours.

"Show me," Thalia said. "Have you instituted quarantine protocols?"

"Quarantine?"

"I'll take that as a no. How many cases?"

"Six, so far."

"How many deceased?"

"How did you know?"

"How many, doctor?"

"One, soon to be two I am afraid."

They pushed through the key-carded swinging doors of Kennestone's Fourth Floor ICU into a watchful stillness Thalia knew well. "Point to the rooms your flu patients currently occupy."

As Thalia feared, the flu cases had been placed at random among the ICU occupants. "Doctor," she said, "I need you to listen to me. Please don't overreact, scratch that, a little overreaction may be warranted." She rubbed a thumb on her opposing palm; a not so unconscious habit that helped her think. "First thing we do is quarantine this floor."

"But I don't have—"

Thalia placed a hand on the young doctor's arm. "Next, get me syringes for blood draws. I'll need separate vials for every patient and a biohazard carrier with ice."

Doctor Peebles ran a hand over her forehead.

Thalia had no time to be patient. "Put any other flu patients who come into your ER up here. Divert all other *non-flu* ICU patients to wards on separate floors."

"We are not equipped—"

"Post quarantine and contagion warnings outside every flu patient's room, gather your staff and alert them to the situation. I wish I could help you with the fallout from this but I do not have the time. Now, remind me which bays house your flu cases—"

The second flu fatality occurred as Thalia and the resident approached the room. *Code Blue Code Blue* came over the intercom with matter-of-fact calm. Thalia and Doctor Peebles gloved up and donned facemasks as they hurried into the room. The resident pushed aside an agitated nurse and bent over her patient while Thalia met the Code Blue team at the room's threshold.

"Ladies and gentlemen," she held up her hands to prevent them from entering, "CDC has initiated quarantine protocols for this and the other flu cases on this floor. Please take extra precautions, even during Code, to protect yourselves. At your earliest convenience, call your homes and tell your spouses and/or roommates that you may not be coming home for a while."

Thalia saw a nurse standing in the hall at the back of the pack with a fistful of syringes and vials, a red and white cooler in the other hand. She pointed to him. "Stay right there. I will come to you." She stepped aside. "The rest of you, tend to your patient now. Doctor Peebles will fill you in on our situation."

The Code Team hesitated a half second, no doubt at the mention of CDC. But then, like a well-trained unit, they rushed in to assist.

Thalia allowed herself a tiny smile. Nurses and med techs had always been among her favorite people for reasons like this. Equal parts compassion and earnest competence, they were as necessary to a well-run hospital as electricity.

She visited each of the other flu patients and drew blood. None protested or even questioned her. She took extra time with the last one. The eerie quiet and pulled up sheet said it all. She pulled back the sheet and noted the signs of severe hemorrhage and respiratory distress exactly like the earlier fatal at Northside.

What the hell is this thing?

She asked herself the same question again after making the long trip through downtown Atlanta to Grady Hospital. Three fatalities there and ten people holding their own, presenting with nothing more than variously bad cases of the flu.

#

The centrifuge spun down and Dr. Kasey Krueger ignored it. Busy with the stockpile of slides her friend Thalia had rush-prepared for her in the past thirty minutes, she adjusted focus on the electron microscope. The image projected onto a monitor two workstations over.

Thalia scooted forward and squinted at the images. "Shit."

"My sentiments exactly," Krueger said. "Where the hell did you dig these up and I mean that literally. Last Spanish Flu virus I had under my scope came from our dig in the frozen tundra up in Alaska. Entire Inuit village wiped out in 1918."

Thalia nodded. "I assisted on that dig."

"Spanish flu doesn't exist anywhere else. Except in a few Level Five labs around the world, us included."

"I dug these samples from the arms of flu patients at Grady, Kennestone and Northside two hours ago."

"Jesus wept."

"Ten percent of them succumbed to the virus. The rest appear to be fine, if you can call splitting headache, muscle cramps, nausea and shortness of breath *fine*."

The researcher nodded. "Makes sense. When the Spanish Flu killed its twenty to fifty million people back in the day, whatever number the historians are touting nowadays, no one had any antibodies for it." She pushed back from the microscope. "Now we do."

"Except for an unlucky ten percent."

"No. They probably have the antibodies, too. Been a lot of flu virus mutations since 1918. We'll need to autopsy our local fatalities to know exactly why they succumbed. I'm betting on some distinctive disease path similar to the cytokine storm that did its work a hundred years ago. And that's the good news."

"I think I already know."

"I'm sure you do. We may be better prepared to fight Spanish Flu today. All our computer models prove that out and no one has studied that little bugger more than the CDC. But—"

"Tell me."

"The damn virus is as contagious now as a hundred years ago. Over five hundred million people around the globe were infected back then. Now flash forward to today and a ten percent infection rate. Apply it to this way more connected world of ours."

Thalia dropped her head to her hands and paused a brief few seconds before standing up.

"We have to try, Kasey. Run our containment protocols as best we can. Alert the major pharma players. Tamiflu won't make a dent in this thing. Demand for vaccines will likely skyrocket to levels we have never seen. We'll take inactivated vaccines *and* recombinant, whatever they can produce most of in the shortest time."

"Want me with you for backup when you share this good news with your boss?"

"I appreciate it, but no. Fairhope has more experience with this sort of thing than either of us. If he wants to see your work, you can be sure he'll ask."

"Will do." Krueger paused before slipping another slide under her scope. "I'm sorry. Wish I had better news for you Thalia."

"No time for sorry, Kasey. I have to get my team assembled and back out there doing what they do. Need to figure out the links between all our flu cases and backtrack from there to find the source."

"What do you think?" the scientist said. "Terror attack? Botched lab experiment. Facility breach?"

Thalia shrugged.

"It wasn't us, Thalia. I swear to you—"

"I know." Thalia's tight little smile contained a smidgen of rueful apology. "First place I checked."

"So?"

"So where the hell has the Spanish Flu been sleeping for the past century and why did it choose now to wake itself up? And *who* set the goddamn alarm clock?"

Chapter Fifty-One

I'M THE MONSTER

The van bounced over ruts in the path leading back to their earlier camp in the woods. It rocked and swayed as El picked his way further in than before to put as much forest screen between them and the road. B's low-slung yellow Camaro had been a challenge. But this big blue van presented a much larger target for prying eyes.

"How's Nicole?" he called over his shoulder.

"Worse." B's one-word answer told him everything he needed to know.

By the time he maneuvered the van into cover, pointed outward for a quick getaway, Nicole's wheezing had worsened to a wet, spasmodic cough.

"It's okay, Nikki. We've got you." Beatrix mopped her friend's brow with a succession of tissues. Nicole lay groaning in the van's back, curled into a fetal position.

El threw the van into Park, jumped out and flung open the back doors. He saw B rocking on her heels beside Nicole, smoothing the woman's hair and murmuring. He hopped into the van beside them.

"We did this to her, El," Beatrix had tears in her eyes. "Only you can fix it."

"What do you mean *we*? I know what went on back at the stadium. Christ I was there, remember? When I became a one-man 9/11? But *this*? How did we do—?"

"It wasn't you, El." B extracted the last tissue from the box he'd found in the glove compartment. She dabbed at Nicole's mouth and the tissue came away spotted with red. "I mean, not *all* you."

"The Speaker said it to my face. *We couldn't have done it without you.*"

"We don't have time to get into this now, okay? I'll tell you all about it later. Right now, my best friend in the whole world is dying. I prayed she'd be one of the lucky ones. She's not."

Nicole convulsed into a fit of violent coughing and speckled the both of them with a fine bloody mist.

"You *know* what this is?" El said. "You *knew* what The Speaker had planned for back there?"

"I told you about the Given Goal, remember?"

"You mentioned something like that back at your trailer. Never explained it though. Trust me, I'd remember—"

Nicole interrupted their exchange by drawing in a ragged breath and letting it out in a long, drawn out shudder. He and B listened. When the poor woman's expected inhale failed to follow, the pregnant silence in the van galvanized B into action.

She screamed and shook her friend by the shoulder.

"Nicole. Breathe. Don't you give up on me! Breathe, damn it. Come on. *Nicole, breathe.*" She continued shaking her friend and got no response. The form curled on the van floor lolled about like a full-sized rag doll.

El leaned forward on his knees and put his hands on Nicole's shoulders, pressing the lifeless woman's form flat onto its back.

"Fix her, El, please. There's no one else. I know you can do it."

"Fix her? I'm the monster who kills people remember? How many died today because of me? One hundred? Three hundred? A thousand?"

Slap.

B's hand left a pink palm print on the left side of El's face.

"I told you I'd explain everything to you. *Later.*" The last word came out in a shriek. "But I swear to you over my friend's dying body Eldridge Montcalm, if you don't stop this poor me shit and save this woman, I'll leave you right here, right now and you'll never learn a thing about who you are. Or what."

El touched a hand to the sting on his cheek, looked across Nicole's still form at B's tear-streaked face and shook himself. *What the hell are you doing? This is* Nicole *for god's sake.*

He cupped his hands on either side of the prostrate woman's face and held them tight, feeling, searching. The sickness inside her bloomed like a swarm of black moths and threatened to blot out what faint light remained.

He prayed the stadium disaster hadn't drained him.

He pulled Nicole's legs straight and crossed her arms on her chest. Carefully, he positioned himself over top of her, propped on his hands and feet then lowered himself to cover her body with his.

The questing sense in him found the dying glimmer and he fanned it with the white brilliance that roiled inside him. His light pulsed, like breathing on an ember and Nicole's glow grew stronger with each flare.

He felt the transfer of life force as the black sickness shied from her light in ever-widening circles. His white light brightened and dimmed. Nicole's light followed his until they linked like sympathetic heartbeats. Hers growing, his ebbing. Growing. Ebbing.

Chapter Fifty-Two

CONTAGION

The bright lights hit Mother's senses like a physical punch in the face and she yelped, holding up a shaky hand to shield her eyes from the glare.

"I am so sorry, Mother." Tension and fear lent a quaver to Patrick's voice. "We need the lights for the broadcast."

Mother swallowed and it felt like gagging down a ball of feathers. "Water, please Jesus. Someone get me—"

"Here, Mother. Tiny sips. We don't want a repeat of last time." The young acolyte leaned close and extended a glass with a straw bent at an angle.

A month earlier that light caution might have earned the smart little thing a strict scolding on the benefits of knowing her place. Today, Mother had little energy left to do anything but sip meekly. The cool liquid doused the flames in her throat for the moment. She hoped it would be enough.

She tried to smile at her video tech to show him she bore him no ill feelings but, by the shade of white he turned, she figured her smile fell somewhat short.

Can't worry about him, now. Let the contagion in her body rage and do its worst. This trial God sent her confirmed what she'd long suspected and gave her comfort. She had become his instrument and he had plans for her. That it might mean death for her come sunrise filled her with a hesitant joy.

She welcomed the chance to meet Jesus, of course. The parallels between herself and God's son were clear as the image of him on the cross.

He suffered in the garden the night before his crucifixion. He knew his fate, yet followed his father's design and let Judas betray him to the soldiers.

Well, *she* certainly had the suffering down. She eyed the array of faithful crowded into the master bedroom of the apartment she kept at *In His Name*. The only two names she could recollect, Patrick of course, and Bernard, her most abused and loyal follower, were there. Patrick fiddling with his camera and lights. Bernard pressed against the far wall, standing with arms crossed and expressionless.

"Perhaps we should clean you up a bit first, Mother?" The young water bearer tugged at Mother's sodden sheets and the simple cotton shift she wore. Both were stained in varying degrees of scarlet. A particularly violent purging episode in the night brought up more blood than sputum.

"NO!" She slapped weakly at the young woman's hands. "They must see this. See what has happened. What evil has been wrought by those demons. The world must bear witness. This is my Gethsemane. Jesus's final hours come to us through dusty biblical texts. Mine will be in high definition video."

She coughed and sprayed the sheets with another fine, red mist. The people in the room recoiled slightly as she resisted the urge to dab at the corners of her mouth. She felt a tickling drool travel down one side and prayed it was blood. Good for ratings.

"Before we do this," Mother looked around at her assembled faithful, surprised frankly at how many had stayed, "let us pray for strength. We have little time and we have multitudes to save."

She bowed her head and the others followed her lead. She cocked one eye at Patrick. Something about his bent head infuriated her. "Patrick? Is the camera on?" Her harsh tone brought about another round of coughing and wheezing.

"Sorry, Mother." The tone in her voice galvanized the man. "Yes, Mother." He stabbed a finger at the camera. "We're rolling."

She let the coughing subside, testing her throat with several deep breaths before speaking. "Water please." The straw appeared before her and she realized she never saw the young woman move.

Not much time now. She focused on the camera.

"Brethren, my faithful followers and all who can hear my voice, believers and non-believers. Do not be upset at this spectacle I present. Do not turn away. For this horror is evidence of the plague visited upon us by the devil's minions a few short days ago.

"Do not weep for me. Do not chafe at what must surely be my impending death. I have resisted several entreaties by my church family to seek medical help. I—we—have chosen instead to rely on the power of prayer and the benevolence of God's will.

"Many in my assembly have fallen ill as, no doubt, have friends and loved ones of yours. I am here as a comfort to them and a reminder to you. The Devil has no power over the truly faithful.

"As long as I am able, I will record the progress of this scourge. Search your hearts and your souls for the strength that comes from knowing Him and His love. It is the one weapon that can defeat what evil has brought down upon us.

"Pray for me as I pray for you. Together, with God's help, we will overcome and survive this plague until God sees fit to relieve me of this burden. God bless you all."

Patrick stopped the camera and clicked off the lights. The blessed darkness dropped over her like a cool blanket and Mother closed her eyes.

She felt the ministration of one of her faithful straightening and smoothing her bedclothes.

Rest now, Mother. You did well.

Did that voice belong to her water bearer? Or God?

She heard the shuffle of feet as her deathbed audience filed out of her room. She had a chance, before blessed sleep spirited her away, for one fleeting thought.

Where will I wake up tomorrow? In heaven? Or, still trapped in this flaming hell?

Chapter Fifty-Three

ENLIGHTEN ME

T wo nights in the woods did nothing for their personal hygiene or their hunger pangs. B barely felt the discomfort, however. Relieved that El's interventions with Nicole had brought the woman back from the brink, B took every opportunity to sit by her friend and will the woman's strength to return. She held Nicole's hand, talked to her, watched her sleep.

El appeared completely unfazed by his actions over the past two days. Weakness he'd shown right after healing Nikki, the slight tremor in his hands and a tendency to nod off, had disappeared by the next morning. He claimed the scene at the stadium drained him but that he felt fine now. Whether he did or not, Beatrix couldn't say.

They'd been hiding out under the pines and hickory trees ever since.

Thank god they'd found a partial case of bottled water in back of the van. Several forays to their old campsite had found it deserted but with several welcome luxuries; two folding chairs and a sawed-off tree stump, a couple of tarps, a discarded pot, a half box of instant cocoa packets and, the Eureka find so far, a Costco-sized plastic jug of individually wrapped jerky sticks.

They made their new camp deeper in the woods, putting the blue van between them and the road for extra cover.

"Water's getting low." El's voice came from the passenger window in the van. He'd adopted the van as his private comfort zone, leaving fresh air and the two found chairs to she and Nicole. "Have to do something pretty soon."

Beatrix looked over at him and nodded, silent. She'd not quite forgiven him for hesitating over Nicole. She walled off his thoughts and spoke with him sparingly. She figured the less she traded words with him the better off they'd both be. No sense letting loose something they may both regret later.

"How's Nicole doing?" he called.

"Come see for yourself."

"I'm getting stronger every minute, El," Nicole called. "Thank you. I know what it cost you and I want you to know that I am so grateful—"

El interrupted her by popping open the van door and sliding out. He walked over and squatted on his haunches before them. "Listen guys, I'm serious about the water, okay? I'm thinking I might make a run for supplies."

"Has that big head of yours sprung a leak?" B grabbed his chin and lifted his head for emphasis. "We are the most wanted people on the planet at the moment and you want to go traipsing along in the crowd like nothing's happened?"

"I don't want to, I need to. Besides, I can scrounge up a disguise from what we have here. No problem. While I'm at it I'll bring back some food and I'm taking orders. Nicole? Anything you've been jonesing for? Cheetos? Oreos? A Big Mac?"

"All of that," Nicole said. "And fruit. I could sure go for a crisp apple."

El stood and held B's hand in his. They stood silent for a few seconds until she pulled her hand away and shoved it into her back pocket.

"Long as you're listing off the basics," she said. "Toilet paper is number one."

He grinned and made a checkmark in the air. "Got it."

She called to his back as he headed for the van. "Goes without saying to be extra careful."

He waved a hand in answer.

"I mean it, El. No taking stupid chances like you do."

He turned at that and raised his eyebrows. "Who, *moi*?"

Beatrix watched the back end of the van snake through the trees. The red lights flashed a couple of times and the string of what-if's cranked up in her head. What if he has a flat? A cop spots him? That dumb wig slips? Some gun-toting *bad* Samaritan blows him away? Or, more likely, he pulls some half-baked stunt like only he can dream up?

The van's brake lights winked out and she heard tires spin as he pulled out onto the road.

She went back to her seat beside Nicole and reached for her friend's hand.

#

The parking lot of Grab 'N' Go had three cars in it and El pulled to the last spot on the far end. He backed in and sat with the engine idling, checking the road, the surroundings, being sure. In the mirror his disguise gave *half-assed* a bad name but it would have to do. They needed water, food, basic comforts; enough to give them breathing room to make a plan. Hiding out from the world in the piney woods outside Atlanta might look good in a movie. In real life it sucked.

The electronic chimes *bing-bonged* when he entered the store and El held his breath. Nobody looked at him. The clerk and three other patrons barely noticed the strange dude with pasty white skin in a very bad wig, sunglasses and hoodie. He kept his head down and shook a battered shopping cart free from its lineup by the door. The tiny grocery only had four aisles. It didn't take long for him to choose from their meager selection and fill the small cart with what he could.

Cases of water, toilet paper, snacks, luncheon meats and cheese, apples and oranges, a Styrofoam cooler and two bags of ice. He wheeled his tiny cache of supplies to the front. The same patrons in line hadn't moved. The clerk acknowledged his presence with a nod, not the least bit worried that his cue of shoppers had grown by one odd-looking man pushing an overflowing cart.

El discerned the reason when the clerk thumbed the volume on a TV remote by the register. All eyes, El's now included, stared at the TV mounted high above the cigarette rack. The riveting images on the tiny flat screen held them as surely as a tractor beam from an alien spaceship. Across the bottom of the picture, words crawled by in a repeating rotation.

The images that follow may not be suitable for younger viewers. Please use discretion. Video is from a blog feed posted within the hour of Mother Magdalene from inside the religious compound of In His Name…*The images that follow may not be suitable for young viewers….*

The high quality video looked stark and clear as soap opera footage. A woman in a bloodstained robe lay propped against a bank of pillows, coughing into a hand towel, also tinged with red. Her words came haltingly between ragged breaths. The microphone on the camera picked up every moist wheeze.

"Holy crap, dude, look at that shit," said the young man first in line, wearing a Georgia Tech ball cap. "Think that's for real?"

"Nah," said the man behind him. "They edit this stuff. Probably not even real blood."

The figure onscreen narrowed her eyes and glared into the camera. "My children, I fear that it has come to this and I will not be with you much longer. The evil that those demons spread eats at my flesh even as it burnishes my soul."

Cough cough.

"Satan has done his damnedest to stop us but we will not be turned aside from our mission."

"I assure you, young man," an older woman in front of El stabbed an indignant finger at the TV, "that is Mother Magdalene and she is very much *for real. In His Name* has thousands of followers, more every day, and when that sainted woman dies, it will be a very bad day indeed. For all of us."

On screen, the bed-ridden woman continued: "God will give us strength to purge the devil's spawn from among us and we must not falter. We cannot. Your soul, my soul, will have the refuge promised us by the Lamb of God from the cross. I will be with you as long as I am able, lending support and shining a light on the darkness that has descended upon us.

"Keep your browsers pointed to *In His Name* for I promise you, we are at the vanguard of this contest of good and evil. Join us. Seek out and destroy the evildoers and I in turn will pledge all I have, even to my last breath in this, the only fight that really matters."

The cameraman artfully zoomed in slowly as the feverish woman spoke, ending on her apple red face streaked with sweat and plastered with sticking strands of hair. By the end, the woman's eyes burned glittery hot and commanded the attention of everyone watching before a violent coughing fit seized her and she buried her face in the blood-soaked towel.

The image onscreen quickly cut to a still photo of the front of the *In His Name* compound accompanied by a choral sound track singing Onward Christian Soldiers.

"That is some scary lady. I don't mind saying," said Georgia Tech. "You gonna ring me up or what?"

"Goes with the scary times, guys." The clerk snapped to like a reanimated doll and began scanning the merchandise on his conveyor belt. "Very scary times." He scanned and bagged and made change, adopting the same bored demeanor that no doubt got him through long days at the register. "Thank you for shopping at Grab 'N' Go."

Behind him, the TV flashed *InHisName.com* in bold white letters across the screen before the video ended and the newscast's talking head returned. The newswoman's carefully coifed hair and meticulous makeup presented a shocking contrast to Mother from the video.

No one in line appeared impressed, anxious to get their merchandise and leave. El pushed his cart forward and loaded the belt, aware that the size of his purchase might garner more attention than his appearance. *Nothing I can do about that. Don't want to hurt anybody else tonight but we need these supplies.*

"In related news, our very own CDC right here in Atlanta has reported incidences of a flu outbreak that has the potential to cause great harm. They are asking that people refrain from congregating in large groups and stay away from enclosed public places until we learn more about the contagion. Early reports suggest the spread of this disease may be infecting people far beyond the abilities of the area's hospital Emergency Rooms to treat safely."

The clerk muted the TV with the remote and slid the first of El's items across his scanner. "Now this is what I like to see. A by god Grab 'N' Go shopper. Find everything you need?"

El nodded and adjusted his shades.

The clerk glanced up from his register and stopped. He narrowed his eyes and appeared about to say something.

"Believe that crap?" El jerked a thumb at the TV. "Guess they'll do anything for ratings, eh?"

The clerk scanned the store over El's head and must have realized they were alone. He flew through the rest of El's order and bagged it in record time, snatching the bills from El's hand and jamming them in the drawer. He managed all of it without once meeting El's eyes.

"Keep the change," El said and piled his bagged purchases into the cart. He felt his heart pounding on the side of his neck and resisted the impulse to scurry out the door. He even managed a whistle as he wheeled his supplies toward the van.

Cargo stowed and key in the ignition, he cranked the engine and pulled away. Through the glass doors he saw the clerk on his cell phone gesturing wildly. El stopped in the parking lot, broadside to the storefront, and revved his engine. The clerk looked up, saw him and quickly put down his phone.

El turned the wrong way out of the lot, expecting the clerk to report everything to the cops. He looped and backtracked and took every side street that looked promising, weighing the extended time he spent on the streets with the need to cover his tracks.

When he turned in at the dirt road and snaked his way back under the trees to their camp, he took his first deep breath in forty-five minutes.

Beatrix ran up and yanked open his door.

"Any problems?" she said. "Anybody see you?"

"B," he said. "You wouldn't believe it. I walked in, loaded up my cart, and made it all the way to the checkout counter before I noticed."

"What?"

God, she looked so cute with her mouth open like that.

"Noticed what, El?" She followed at his heels as he went around to the back of the van and began to unload.

"Everyone in the store, including the checkout guy," he stopped and presented her with the giant package of toilet paper, "had white canes and guide dogs."

"You asshole."

"Did anyone see me? Of course they saw me. *Did they recognize me* is the question."

"And?"

"Maybe." He shrugged. "I took the long way home, made sure no one followed. Important thing is, you and Nicole are safe."

"What do you mean *you and Nicole* are safe?"

He shrugged. "Figure of speech. Anyway, I'm thinking it's time to come clean."

That puzzled her. "El, what do you want to tell me?"

"Not me. *You*. Remember? The Council? The Given Goal? What happened at the stadium? You were going to enlighten me after we got Nicole back? Who I am. What I am. All that."

"Now?" she said. "I'm not sure Nicole needs to hear—"

"Quit stalling. And Nicole's seen more than enough of our shit. Whatever you have to say she can handle."

Nicole patted B's arm and nodded. "He's right, girl. Don't mind me."

Beatrix rose and paced back and forth, wringing her hands. "Fine. But don't interrupt me. Even if you disagree or you think I'm nuts, keep your trap shut."

"Agreed." He zipped his lips and tossed away an imaginary key.

"Most important thing first. We're different—"

El snorted and she glared at him.

"But we're human. Not aliens, gods, or demons. Not some weird race or anything. The way we see us, we're what humans are supposed to be like, *will* be like, after evolution does its thing. We got a head start on it is all. With a little help from a twelve-month gestation period—and the flu."

El squirmed but held his tongue.

"I told you way in the beginning, and you saw proof in my

papers, that I'm older than I look. Most of us are. A few as old as a hundred. Do the math and you'll land around 1918. The time of the First World War and the flu outbreak some think actually ended it."

"The Spanish Flu?" Nicole asked.

Beatrix nodded. "The same. We don't know how or why—sorry, I don't have those answers. Our best guess is the virus mutated peoples' DNA. Introduced a very rare, very recessive gene into the population. The ones it didn't kill, it altered. Some women, not many really, carried babies in their wombs for a full twelve months instead of the normal nine. We've researched this and found plenty of records proving that."

El couldn't contain himself any longer. "Baloney. My mother wasn't alive in 1918."

"No, but that gene was, *is*. Trace her family tree and I guarantee someone in her past survived the Spanish Flu. When you get the time, look it up, and now, if you please? Shut up and let me finish."

He crossed his arms and looked pained, but stayed quiet.

"If you hit the genetic lottery and your mother and father have the gene, they'll have a baby with a funny shaped head, crappy white skin and later on, certain um, *talents*, no one can explain.

"We don't all have the same skills. And they're not developed to the same extent. The Speaker, for example, has most every known skill and his power is at a very high level. I'm not bad, but not near as developed. Smith and the others on The Council are about the same."

"Okay, The Council. Really? What's the deal—"

"Jesus, El. You promised."

"The Council came about because what do people do to things they don't understand?" She stabbed a finger at El. "That was a rhetorical question. Back in the day, until we learned to blend in and stay under the radar, people like us, who acted and looked like us, were rounded up, put in institutions, stoned, beaten, even killed. We had to do something.

"Once several of us realized we were not alone in our *predicament*, that there were others like us, those early people banded together. For protection, they adopted certain rules, certain ways of acting. Didn't always work but it kept a lot of us alive. We got better and better at hiding in plain sight.

"First order of business became searching out our brothers and sisters. To help them and teach them what they were. What they could do. Like I tried to do for you, El.

"Second, and this is a big one for us, we made it our goal—our *Given Goal*—to be able to come out to the world and live as we were meant to. Without fear. That goal has yet to be realized."

Once again, El couldn't hold back. "Thanks to your almighty Council back at SunTrust Stadium, you made it a whole lot tougher."

She glared at him and continued. "Best way to get people comfortable with something is make it familiar, non-threatening, normal. Patient ones among us lobbied to wait and let time do its job. Another faction, call them the impatient ones, grew tired of waiting and decided to hurry things up a bit. The Speaker came from that camp and SunTrust Stadium was his brainchild.

"It took years of planning and searching for the right pieces to be put into place. We needed our most highly developed people. Enough of them so that, when linked—we discovered how linking could magnify our powers several decades ago—we would be able to do what needed to be done.

"We also needed The One." B stopped and drank from a water bottle. "Over the years, The One developed into The Speaker's pet theory. He believed that one day, one of us would come along so strong, so highly developed, that he or she could serve as the lightning rod for his plan. The Speaker tried. He wanted it to be him, but hard as he tried, he didn't have the juice. Then you came along."

"Yay for me."

"Sorry, El. But you did everything right. My god, you have such power, you don't even know. The Speaker knows and I wouldn't be surprised if he's not a little afraid of you. You did everything you could to show off to the world."

"I did not."

She mimed a headline across her chest. "The Amazing El? Really?"

"Okay. Maybe."

"I know you didn't plan it, but your *lifesaving miracles* going viral played right into The Speaker's plans." She shook her head. "My god, all those people gathered in one place, open and receptive to what you had to offer? He had to be salivating at the opportunity you handed him on a silver platter."

"Opportunity for what? I still don't get that—"

"The flu, genius. Remember?"

His wrinkled brow said he didn't follow.

"How do we make sure the Given Goal happens? How do we speed things up so we can all come out of hiding?" She looked at him, willing him to come up with the answer on his own.

It took him a second. "Oh my god."

"Now you get it?"

"Make more of us," he said. "*That's* the Given Goal? We infect a bunch of people who show up to be healed and make them sick instead."

B nodded. "The Speaker's grand plan to speed up evolution. We can make people well. Millions of people have seen you do it. We can also make them sick. Not something most of us are particularly proud of."

El slapped his forehead. "Infect people with the Spanish Flu and they'll spread it like in 1918. Genes will get altered. More egg-headed freaks with abilities get born."

"Bingo. Humanity evolves faster and the world ultimately improves and gets better. That, in its purest form, is the Given Goal."

"Kick Darwin in the ass and speed up evolution? That is insane and your Speaker is a certified psychopath."

"He's your Speaker, too El."

"Hell he is. Oh, Jesus. Oh, Jesus." El tramped up and back, mimicking B's pacing earlier. "You're wrong. Don't you see? You can't kill millions of people to breed a bunch of super humans. Someone already tried. Remember that one, B? You were probably a teenager then."

"It's not the same, El."

"It's exactly the same."

El continued walking and talking to himself. She tried to break in on his thoughts but he'd grown way too strong for her. Much stronger, she sensed, even than The Speaker.

He stopped and looked up as if checking something in the clouds. He must have gotten the right answer because he set his lips in a line and grinned tightly at her.

"Sorry about this." He stepped close and planted a kiss on her lips. "Been wanting to do that for a while. Take care of Nicole. There's something I gotta do." He hugged her tight and hurried to the driver's side door of the van.

"El? What the—? What's going on in that big ugly head of yours?"

"I figured out a way to make things right," he said. "Or not. Don't wait up." He started the van and put it in gear. B promptly stepped around to the front of the car and put her hands on the hood.

El felt her next move and snuffed it out before she mustered the force she needed. *Nice try, B.* He sent the thought to her and shoved the van into Reverse.

Before he pulled out onto the highway he stopped and toggled the NAV system. At DESTINATION, he selected Points of Interest and began clicking letters from the onscreen keyboard.

Didn't take long. His selection appeared after the second word.

In His Name

Distance 28 miles.

Time to destination, 41 minutes.

Begin driving on the indicated route.

Probably his imagination, but the female, android voice coming through the speakers might have contained a tiny bit of breathless anticipation.

"What do you know that I don't?" he asked.

Continue driving on the designated route.

Chapter Fifty-Four

IN HIS NAME

E l slowed the van and eyed the traffic ahead. Wouldn't do to get caught up in bumper to bumper traffic this far from his goal. He reached over into the glove compartment and extracted the rock Nikki had rescued from the stadium. *I've got plans for you.* He kissed it and slipped it into the front pocket of his sweatshirt.

News crews parked outside the closed iron gates and at least two helicopters buzzed overhead. Camera crews, an assorted crowd of onlookers, and more than a few uniforms milled about in a shifting, nervous mass of people. Placards and signs poked above the crowd waiting to be discovered on the evening news, their positions evenly divided:

We Love You Mother
Take Me Satan
Jesus Is God
Evil Is Just An Opinion

"We could have done without the dang crowd," El muttered.

He pulled off the road and took a parking place about a quarter-mile from the front gates. El opened the door and got out. The whup-whup-whup of a chopper overhead and the muted white noise of the distant crowd were the first things to grab his attention.

He crooked the side mirror and bent over to check out his reflection.

Nothing like making a dramatic entrance.

He flopped back the hoodie and snatched the wig and sunglasses off his head.

Felt good to get the damn things off. He didn't blame the *impatient ones* for wanting to live their lives in the open, in peace. Except the assholes went about it in such a way that every overcooked egghead in the world could now expect to be shot on sight.

Someone had to do something or they'd be exterminated, special powers or not.

He scratched fingernails across his bald white head and squared his shoulders.

This is for you and Nicole, B. He sent the thought out with such force that B couldn't miss it. When her immediate reply hit him—EL. YOU STOP WHATEVER YOU'RE—he closed off contact.

No room for distractions, now.

Eldridge—The Amazing El—Montcalm approached the seething crowd ahead with all senses on full alert. The brown crabgrass on the road's shoulder crunched as loud as potato chips. The roil of colognes and perfumes mixed with sweat from the scores of individuals wafted to him like flower overload in a greenhouse. And the sun on his pale skin seared hot as any desert sky. Every pore on every square inch of his body tingled with an electricity he'd only felt a few times before. The last time being on stage in SunTrust Stadium linked by hands to The Speaker and the entire Council.

But, he was alone now. Even though that power unfolding inside him had never stopped growing, from the first telekinetic pencil push in his bedroom to the destruction of a stadium, he had not truly tested it on his own. The El today felt radically different, *stronger*, even than yesterday's El. He prayed it would be enough.

As he walked, getting closer to the crowd ahead, he pressed outward; testing, feeling the tremendous presence of the force inside him, stretching it like a balloon one breath away from bursting.

He got within ten feet of the crowd's fringe before anyone recognized him. An overweight woman in a floral print dress stopped wrestling with her homemade poster—*Evil Walks Amung Us!*—shrieked and leveled a pointing finger.

Others beside her turned to see why and reacted in various ways. He felt fear and curiosity in equal measures but friend or foe they generally adopted the same wide-eyed, open-mouthed response to his presence. The effect rippled across the crowd like shockwaves in a pond.

Still, he kept coming.

His strategy, if it could be called that, consisted of walking straight, keeping his eyes fixed on the compound's distant front gates, and not reacting until he had no other choice.

An Atlanta police officer, dripping sweat in his half-fastened riot vest and helmet, forced El's hand by clawing the Glock from his holster and leveling it in a two-handed grip. At least the man had the wherewithal to not discharge his weapon in the surging landscape of bodies.

El could not depend on the man's reticence continuing, however. He reached his left hand, palm out, toward the man, made a fist and yanked downward, hard. The pistol in the police officer's hand clattered to the ground.

El continued walking.

The thick miasma of noise in front of him; people shouting, squealing, car horns blaring, bullhorns calling nasally instructions that no one paid attention to, the choppers overhead, it all built until the sheer volume of it all beat at him with physical force.

He made no outward sign that he heard a thing, much less let it stop him.

He pushed past the shrieking poster woman and several others until the thinner fringe became simply *crowd*.

He strode purposefully into the heart of it.

Immediately in front of him people parted to let him by. Some jumped back as if he carried leprosy. Others held their pieces of pavement until the very last moment, backing off enough to allow him to pass within inches of touching them.

But they *didn't* touch him. No one laid a finger on him.

As he walked, head up, looking neither right nor left, the bubble of invincibility continued to push out ahead of him, as did the silence.

The noise that beat on him in the beginning had largely died to a murmur by the time he made the center of the mass of people. Soon the only noises to crack the shell of silence were rustling feet and the odd radio chirp from the black-uniformed police officers dotted through the crowd like raisins.

Quiet reigned. El so wanted to stop right there and take advantage of it; assure everyone they had no reason to fear him, that he was harmless and on a mission of compassion and mercy.

He dared not do any of that.

The thrall he held over the mass of people stayed in effect right on up to the compound's wrought iron gates. He marveled at his hold on the milling crowd. The strength inside felt as if he'd linked with B and Smith and maybe one or two others from The Council. It swelled like a massive, contracting muscle and damn it felt strong and hard.

The automatic front gates to *In His Name* gleamed in brilliant white abstract swirls. Where the two gates met in the center, a ten-foot gold figure of Jesus, arms spread wide in welcome, smiled down upon his flock.

El turned his back to Jesus and faced the crowd.

The people froze in place, all eyes riveted on him, their faces an equal mix of hate and wonder.

When he knew for sure he had them controlled, El turned back to the gates and mimicked Jesus's pose, raising his arms and spreading them wide.

The iron gates vibrated and shook in place, hinges clanking, until with a loud bang and a clang, they creaked open. El shouldered through before the gates had a chance to open fully and they began to close again once he stepped clear.

The two halves came together with another loud clang and Jesus once again stared down on his flock. As if released from restraints, the crowd assumed its previous shouts and wild gestures. Noise returned as if cranked up on a dial.

El smiled to himself and started walking up the winding approach to the massive white marble building that dominated the compound's architecture. A little bit Roman, a lot Greek Parthenon with a dose of Babylon temple, the thing positively defined gaudy. As he walked, he looked up on the whitewashed walls flanking the compound and noticed video cameras spaced at regular intervals. They tracked him as he approached.

Good. Least they'll see me coming. Or will they? Sure hope this monument to excess has a doorbell.

He needn't have worried. Five steps up; he topped the generous front landing when one side of the massive double doors swung open on silent hinges.

The sounds from outside faded as he stepped inside and shut the door behind him.

A young woman in a plain white robe held a lantern. Yellow glints from the dim light sparkled in her eyes as she backed away from him.

"Bright light hurts Mother's eyes." She lifted the lantern in explanation. "We who are left use these to get around, out of respect." She turned without another word and headed off down a darkened hallway, her bare feet silent on what looked like polished marble tiles.

El followed, unsure of what else to do.

A long walk later, the hallway dead-ended into another wide hall. To the left, a warm glow leaked around the corner, as if spilled from the beams of many lanterns like the one held high by his escort. To the right, darkness. His greeter stopped short and faced him.

"Can you really do what they say you can? What it says on the TV? I need to know before we go any further."

"TV says a lot of crazy things. Most not true."

"Oh." The young woman's shoulders slumped. "I thought, I prayed—"

"What's your name?" El said.

"I am Sister Evelyn."

"I am El—Eldridge. But, I like El." He offered his hand and the young woman flinched before clasping it then clung to it tightly.

"So, can you? Mother is very ill."

"I came here to see what I could do. I won't really know until I see how—"

"She says you are the devil. Most believe her. Some of us don't know what to believe." She yanked her hand back. "No one knows you're here or that I went out to get you."

"How did *you* know—?"

"I'm the only one left on security watch. I saw you on our monitors." She twisted a fistful of robe in her free hand. "Once we turn that corner, there will be no going back." She looked at him and cast her eyes to the floor. "So you know, however it goes, I will tell everyone you cast a spell on me to come let you in." She shrugged.

El leaned close on his way by her. "It'll be our secret Sister Evelyn. And so *you* know, I am not the devil. At least I don't think I am." He squared his shoulders and stepped up to the corner ahead.

The flickering golden light gave him an idea. He looked back at the young woman. "You might want to stay here."

If they're going to act like superstitious sheep, let's give them something to believe in.

He waved a hand in the air before turning the corner and in an instant, the flickering lights ahead of him winked out. Cries of consternation and worried shrieks pierced the blackness.

He pushed through the crowd, steadying several panicked bodies as he passed, until he judged himself well placed in the midst of Mother Magdalene's flock.

"Enough," he roared. He waved his hand one more time and one-by-one the lanterns nearest him bloomed into life. The awakening lights spread in an ever-widening circle of brilliance.

"Oh, dear god it's him."

"Mother protect us, the demon is set upon us."

"We are doomed."

"How did it get in?"

Several in the crowd shut their eyes and began mouthing prayers over clasped, shaking hands.

El crossed his arms and tried not to smile. Absurd as their reactions seemed to him, he'd best not treat them lightly.

He raised his arms and tamped down their rising hysteria with a placating gesture. "If I could have your attention please? Would everyone please quiet down? I am not here to harm any of you—HEY!"

Silence reigned but for a few mumblings from several still locked in their prayers.

"How many here think I am a demon or the devil himself?"

After a few pregnant seconds, more than half of the crowd raised hesitant hands.

"I see. How about the other way? How many think the opposite. That I could be an angel?"

No hands.

"Oops. Had to try. Got to give me that. What about this—how many think I could be a normal guy with creepy white skin and a funky-shaped head who happens to be able to do some things you can't?"

This one took longer, but several brave souls thrust up hands.

"Okay. That's what I'm talking about. We have a chance here. Is one of you in charge?"

Several in the crowd made way for a cadaverous man with a sullen look. He eschewed the robes most wore, choosing an open-collared tunic over pressed blue jeans. El noted the red welts of scars slashed across one side of his neck and face and the wooden cross hanging on a thong around his neck.

"They seem to think that's me," the man said.

El stepped forward and extended his hand. "My name's El," he said.

Those crowding in behind the man backed up a step. The man stood his ground and raised his chin. Black eyes glinted gold in the lantern light. He glanced at El's hand and crossed his arms.

"You're not welcome here. This is a godly place. We serve the Father and the Son and follow in the footsteps of Mother Magdalene who lights our way."

Emboldened by the man's attitude, heads in the crowd nodded.

"Amen, Brother Bernard."

"You speak the wisdom of Mother."

"We are with you, Bernard."

El drew his hand back and scratched his head. "I'm betting your name's Bernard."

"You need to leave, devil." Bernard crowded closer and sneered. "Your powers are useless in this sanctuary of faith."

"About that. First off *Brother Bernard*, I'd prefer it if you got out of my face." El made a shooing motion with his hands and Bernard slid backward a couple steps unbidden. "No need to be uncivil. My parents raised me with a faith as strong as yours and truth be told this whole devil demon thing really upsets my mom.

"Second, I can see you have a good thing going here, Bernard. I wouldn't want to mess that up. But you are not who I came to see. Or is it whom? I can never get that right."

El cast his mind beyond the crowd, probing hallways and rooms, feeling his way. The thick walls slowed him a little—*Dang place is built like a fortress*—so he amped up his push.

He found her, behind the crowd of her faithful, far down at the end of the hall in a room off to the left. Sickness clung to Mother Magdalene like a sour stench.

He looked toward her room, over the crowd's heads. "Hello, Mother," he murmured. "So sorry we have to meet this way."

"El, you idiot. What the hell are you doing?"

"Hello, B. I'm kind of busy right now."

Damn. That last hard push must have made it easy for her to find him.

"This is not going to end well. You are in no shape for this."

"Better hope so. I need to make things right. For all our sakes."

"No. NO, EL!"

"Thanks for everything, B. I mean it. I—well you know how I feel about you. Probably always have known. Take care of Nicole."

He closed B off. She fought him hard, pushing with a force he'd never felt from her, but he had to do it.

"Whew, man." He massaged his temples. "Women. Am I right, Bernard?" El winked at Bernard's puzzled expression and pushed past him, heading for Mother Magdalene's room.

Part way down the hall, El passed a mural of the crucifixion. He paused to take it in. The artist had taken extra time to paint in the bloody details of the brutal act: Jesus' face contorted in agony, blood dripping from the crown of thorns and the cruel nails in wrists and ankles. To add a touch of realism, Mother apparently had someone construct a dim-lit wall cutout with ancient sledge and square-head nails on a thick slice of timber. Beside those, a small silver box glinted in the light of many lanterns. Above the cutout, a hanging Roman shield with crossed spears completed the display.

Mother Magdalene definitely has issues.

He shivered and hurried on, anxious to get past that grotesque mural and finish what he'd come there to do. The crowd followed timidly, either in awe or from fear, El didn't care which. The doorway to Mother's room loomed a few steps ahead and he paused. The shuffling and murmurings of the crowd behind him quieted. In the relative silence of the hallway the room ahead harbored the absolute hush of the grave.

He stepped up to the threshold and opened the door. The stench hit him first. The coppery decay of exsanguination and the sweet stink of disease smacked him in the face and he breathed open-mouthed to compensate.

Four candles divided shadows in the room, their flickering more than adequate to reveal the huge iron bed, dominated by a wrought iron headboard, inlaid wooden crosses lent it a frantic pattern, as if the more crosses, the better the sleeper's chance at making it into heaven.

El recognized the figure in the center of the bed from the TV even with her hair askew and cheeks sagging in deathly repose. Mother's eyes were closed and her mouth slightly agape. Eyelids flicked over restless eyeballs and the jaw twitched in spasms.

Sitting beside the bed in a straight-backed wooden chair, the young woman who'd let him in reached into a white porcelain basin on a side table and squeezed a cloth semi dry. She folded it and blotted the ailing woman's forehead.

"Sister Evelyn," El said. "I didn't see you make your way down here."

"Private passageway. Didn't want to be a part of whatever the others may have had in mind for you." She gently tucked and patted the covers underneath Mother's chin. "I see you got through them in one piece."

El waved a dismissive hand. "They're good folks. Misinformed is all. Like the rest of the world."

The young acolyte picked up a walkie-talkie from the nightstand and thumbed the button. "We're getting close Patrick. She doesn't have much time now."

"Patrick?"

The girl shrugged. "Mother's video guy. She left strict instructions for us to capture her final moments." Sister Evelyn jerked a thumb at a camera and tripod in the far corner of the room. "She said history would thank us."

A bookcase on the sidewall swung inward a foot and a man in creased blue jeans and a pink golf shirt slipped into the room. He stopped short when he spied El. "You," he said.

"Me." El smiled. "Relax, Patrick."

The man's eyes widened and he paled.

"No, I didn't read your mind." El pointed at the walkie-talkie in

Evelyn's hand. "Sister Evelyn called your name, remember? Welcome to the party. I won't bite—nor will I send you straight to hell."

The man stiffened.

"Okay, sorry. I might have read you a wee tiny bit." El chuckled to relieve tension in the room. "I'm messing with you guys, all right? I do that when I get nervous. And yes, see? I'm nervous, too."

El stepped up to the bed and walked slowly around it. He made note of the dark red stains in uneven patches like thrown cups of paint, some wetter than others.

"I wanted to clean the sheets and blankets," Sister Evelyn wrung her hands. "She wouldn't let me."

"You've done an amazing job Sister Evelyn," El said. "I know Mother appreciates everything you have done for her."

An abnormally deep breath raised the covers higher than usual, followed by a ragged wheeze.

"You're right, Sister Evelyn. She doesn't have much time." EL looked at Patrick. "How are you fixed for batteries? Got plenty?"

The video man nodded. "Dual redundancy, always. Spare camera too. Mother insisted on it."

"Good man."

El heard a slight cough behind him and turned to see Bernard in the doorway. Over the man's shoulders, people in white robes jostled back and forth trying to get a better look.

"You have no right," Bernard's upper lip curled. "This is holy ground and you're not fit to—"

El raised his hand and the man's speech stopped abruptly. His mouth worked and his jaws moved, but no sound uttered forth except a constricted squeak.

"Sorry, Bernard," El said. "I heard you the first time. I need quiet so I can concentrate. Do all your weeping and gnashing of teeth later. Mother and I would appreciate it." He walked over to the doorway and the people backed off. "That goes for all of you," he called. "Please. Let me do what I can to help her. Hate me out loud all you want, but hate me later."

El returned to Mother's bedside and sat on the edge of the bed, pushing at the woman's sickness, probing for weaknesses. He traced his hands in the air above her form, along one side and down the other. Searching, sensing, he needed to find the sick woman's light in the darkness billowing around her.

He allowed himself a quick glance at Patrick in the corner. A tiny red light glowed on the camera like the tip of a cigarette in the shadow.

282

Showtime.

El swiveled around and spoke loud so the people clustered in the hallway outside could hear. "I know you all want to help. The best way you can help is through prayer." He saw eyes widen and heard whispers as people in front shared his words with those in the back. "Mother and I would sure welcome your prayers right about now." He held up a finger. "*Silent* prayers."

He stood and wiped his palms on his jeans before peeling back the soiled bedclothes to expose Mother from head to toe. Gently, he crossed her left and then her right arm over her chest and straightened her head.

Let's do this.

El moved around to stand at the foot of her bed. Pushing, feeling with his mind, he quivered in a surge of confidence. Faint as this woman's life light had become, covered over by swirling, fluttering blackness, he tapped into it easily. The tenacious strength in this woman would not be denied. When his light contacted hers he received a jolt of pure energy that rocked him.

Whew.

He took a moment to orient himself and, much like he'd done earlier with Nicole, he crawled up on the bed and lay down on top of Mother. He summoned the reserves in his inner light, stoking them to match and align her fierce brightness with his.

While he still had the strength, he propped up on hands placed outside her shoulders and gazed down upon the face that had vilified him on TV screens across the world. So much hate in this woman, so much fear.

El looked toward the camera he knew was watching. "It's time, Mother," he said. "As it is written, a time to build. Time to cast away stones." He reached inside the pocket of his hoodie, closed his fist around the chunky piece of granite and placed it on the pillow beside her head. "Time to heal." He bent and kissed her on the forehead. "I understand and I forgive you, Mother. I pray God can forgive me."

The exertion set him back a bit as the swirling moths of black oblivion fluttered about with renewed energy. His arms quivered as he lowered and raised his form over hers, using the changing distance to bring her life force back into sharper relief.

His light pulsed with every beat of his heart and he concentrated, hard, to shift her heartbeat to his. Where the two lights overlapped, the combined brilliance flashed through his entire body and he felt flickering heat tickle his insides, a portent of what lay ahead.

Mother's light shone brighter with every passing second and El felt every thud of her heart like a physical blow. The thuds grew harder and more pronounced until his life and hers merged in perfect harmony and their heartbeats had no separation.

He held his position over top of her until both arms quivered with the strain and he collapsed. Pressed against her like an uncomfortable lover, he felt the inevitable drain of his force as it moved from him to rebuild and strengthen hers.

Damage from the disease had to be repaired and the disease banished from every muscle, organ, every hidden shadow. Not until then would she be safe. Not until then could he rest.

El persevered though every cell in his body cried out for him to end this. It was too much. It drained him too low. But this one, *this one* he wanted more than any of the others, more even than Nicole. He needed it to show the world, prove to the world he and his kind were no monsters and certainly no demons.

El soon knew every inch of Mother, every cellular nook and cranny. Healing her on the micro level showed him more of her than the most sophisticated high tech scans.

He saw inside her skull and all around the clenching muscle of her heart. He felt the solid weight of her bones and touched the vital life growing in her womb.

This last made him smile and gave him the strength he needed to roll aside and get off the woman he'd brought back from death's door. She was still weak, though much stronger than he at the moment, and needed to breathe in clean air and expel the dank staleness hidden in the tiniest, most stubborn air sacs deep in her lungs.

He lay beside her and watched her chest rise and fall, higher than before and with renewed vigor. Good thing. She breathed for two, now.

He grinned to himself. The pregnancy was so new, Mother herself may not even know about it. But he did. He also knew the identity of the father. He propped up on one elbow and turned toward the doorway.

"Bernard, you sly dog. You're going to be a dad—"

The tip of the ancient Roman relic pierced El's chest before he could finish. At the other end of the spear, Bernard's face contorted with his effort to shove it home.

Dimly, in the distance El heard screams that barely registered while he fought the blazing pain blooming in his chest.

Too weak, too weak.

The blackness he'd fought in Mother rushed at him from all sides; eager to exact its revenge? Or is this merely nature's way without judgment, without motive?

He closed around the pumping wound in his chest to contain the pain of it, if only for a moment. The spear fell away and he looked up to see Bernard stagger backward into the waiting arms of the crowd. After what seemed an eternity, El turned to the woman beside him. Her breathing came easy and full as he pulled himself forward and up close to her one last time.

He tenderly brushed a stray lock of hair off her warm forehead. It left a faint bloody streak and he kissed her one last time. He bent and whispered in her ear, "Congratulations, Mother. You're going to have a beautiful baby girl."

Mother's eyes flew open and stared into his a full second, before her face wavered and the blackness closed in on him for a final time.

#

The crowd outside, oblivious to the goings-on inside the compound, paid scant attention to the figure of a pale young woman in a hoodie hastening through their midst. She pushed and sidestepped, moving forward, always forward, with nimble deceptive speed.

People closest to the In His Name gates finally took notice when the giant figure of Jesus began to vibrate. His outstretched arms seemed to be a plea for help as the gates began to part. The tortured squeal of uncooperative metal caused many to plug their ears.

Several of the nearby protesters would later claim they heard the young woman say, "Pardon me, Jesus. But I'm in a hurry," as she placed a hand on either side of the vibrating gate and shoved. The two gate halves flew open faster than their mechanisms could handle. The left gate drooped on bent hinges. The right gate clanged wide and immediately, black smoke billowed from its severely damaged control box. Orange flames licked from its top and distracted some from following the figure of the woman as she bounded up the front steps.

Eyewitness accounts differed on what happened next. Some said the huge front doors to the compound bowed outward, cracked and then split into pieces. Others said the massive slabs of wood literally exploded outward, blasting a shower of smoke and splinters back at the crowd.

However it happened, the slight young woman in the hoodie disappeared inside before the first splinters hit the ground.

A few minutes later, no witness timelines came close to agreeing on exactly how long, a crowd of white-robed *In His Name* believers surged through the shattered doors. They screamed, they shouted. Several fell to their knees with hands upraised, sending loud prayers to the heavens. Many exited the building and staggered down the steps with shiny swathes of brilliant bloody red splashed across their robes.

That started the stampede and all those who'd assembled outside the compound gates turned and ran with predictable results. The first to stumble and fall were the clumsy and the slow. They were the first to be trampled and most certainly the first to sustain serious injury. Remarkably however, outside of those and several broken bones, no one in the crowd died that day.

Chapter Fifty-Five

WE'RE ON

Nicole Charbonneau sat back in the soft leather chair and submitted to the makeup artist's quick touchups. The woman had already spent fifteen minutes on their host, Wanda Weathers. Nicole's book hit the bestseller's list two weeks ago and she'd chosen Wanda's Weather Report for her first live interview.

"You about ready Ms. Charbonneau?" Wanda fixed Nicole with a stare that oozed practiced sincerity.

"Call me Nicole, please."

"That man with the headphones is going to count us down and when the red light goes on *we're* on. Look at me, not the camera. Pretend we're two old friends discussing the weather, yes?"

"I'll try."

"That's my girl."

Three. Two. One—

"Good morning, my pretties." Wanda addressed the camera and pressed her palms together in orchestrated excitement. "I have a treat for all of us, today. The first ever interview with the young woman at the eye of the storm in all the headlines for over a year now—Nicole Charbonneau. Good morning, Nicole, and welcome to the Weather Report."

Nicole smiled and took a sip from a nearby water glass. *Darn throat picks now to dry up on me?*

Concern flickered across Wanda's face for a nanosecond. She went with the flow like a pro. "I know how hard this must be for you, and I want to give you every opportunity to give us your point of view of the events."

Nicole found her voice and wheezed, "That's all in my book."

"Of course." Wanda held up a copy of *Overcooked* on cue. She mugged for the camera. "She signed it for me, guys and everyone in the audience gets a signed copy as well. But we're interested in the real stuff you know, what's not in the book. Especially now."

"You mean especially now, because of all the births?"

Wanda nodded. "They hadn't happened when you wrote this. If my math's correct."

"We knew they would, though."

"We?"

Nicole shifted in her chair. "Mothers carrying their babies to twelve-month terms—being *overcooked* is what they called them. The births of extraordinary, beautiful little boys and girls. They may look a bit … different." Nicole chuckled. "El used to say he had creepy Casper skin and a freakish fat head—"

"Yes, yes. But how do you explain that some mothers, when faced with giving birth to what some have called monsters, reportedly killed their offspring?"

Nicole squeezed her hands together, her knuckles white. She answered in an even tone, "How do you explain murder, Wanda? Fear? Hate? Ignorance? I choose ignorance, because I can do something about that. That's why I am here today. To tell you," she turned and looked straight into the camera, "and all you out there, that El and the others who look like him were and *are* the opposite of monsters."

"All those people they killed at the stadium in Atlanta—"

"Not their intent. The people you saw on stage in Atlanta were a desperate splinter faction. Their plans went a little … haywire."

Wanda raised her eyebrows. "A global plague—some are calling it Spanish Flu II— resulting in ten thousand deaths and counting, worldwide panic, riots, murder, mayhem. *Haywire* is not the word I would use."

"You are right." Nicole sat forward in her chair. "Tragedy is the better word. The deaths of those people in Atlanta, certainly. The fatalities from the flu, also tragic. I guarantee, those tragedies ate at my good friend Eldridge Montcalm more than any of you. I am sure by now everyone here—and out there—who hasn't been living under a rock has seen the terrible, over-analyzed footage?"

"Thank you for that segue Nicole. Perfect timing." Wanda twirled her finger in the air. "Can we roll that last Mother Magdalene video please?"

Nicole closed her eyes and let the images play out on the monitors without her. She'd seen them. The Internet and TV regurgitated them ad nauseam. El assessing a deathly ill Mother Magdalene. His climb onto the bed and his struggles to heal her. The cowardly asshole Bernard thrusting that Roman spear into El's side. She knew from the gasps in the audience when they reached that part of the video.

"Production, can we replay that last part again, please?" Wanda called. "Can we zoom and freeze that? Good. Nicole?"

Nicole sat with her eyes clenched.

"Nicole, I know how hard this is."

"You cannot begin to know how *hard this is*." Nicole spit the words through gritted teeth.

Wanda placed a hand over her heart. "I'm sorry, truly. But people have been asking and I don't have the answers. None of us do. Please, for your friend El's sake."

Damn woman sure knows which buttons to push. Nicole opened her eyes.

The image on the monitor showed a close-up of El's face. Thankfully, they'd zoomed in tight. She saw El's beautiful visage and that look. Of course, the look is what they all wanted to know about.

Wanda cleared her throat and said softly, "Thank you, Nicole. The expression on your friend El's face, can you explain it?"

"You can't? I should think it's pretty obvious."

"But, he's been mortally wounded. He has to know he's dying. Every expert we've brought in to examine the video footage agrees. That spear, the location, the angle, by all accounts a killing stroke."

"What is your point?"

"Ms. Charbonneau, your friend looks remarkably at peace, relieved even. He stares at the man who's killed him for the longest time. And that last part, before he turns to kiss Mother Magdalene and whisper in her ear? He actually smiles."

Nicole sat forward, desperate to make them understand. "That is the El that I knew; generous, kind, loving. Gifted beyond any of our comprehension. The things he could have done for us, if we'd let him."

"But—can we get back to that spear for a moment?"

Nicole grimaced. "You saw him save a woman who called him terrible things. She called him a demon, the devil. And she wasn't alone in that. Many of you used those very same words. When evidence shows, *this* videotaped evidence, El as quite the opposite. You all heard him forgive that woman. Saw him return the very same rock she felled him with. It still had his blood on it."

"Yes, yes Ms. Charbonneau. I believe your friend's blood was *also* on the same spear used to kill another man in that compound? How do you explain that? His name, um, I believe—"

"Bernard." She sighed. "They called him Brother Bernard."

Wanda picked up a clipboard and flipped through several pages. "Ah, here we are. *A woman waded into our midst like an avenging angel, flinging people aside like rag dolls. She looked like one of those devils. Big head and white skin* . . . I'll read one more. *The woman never uttered a sound, even when she stabbed Brother Bernard with the lance. Again and again. Her face stayed neutral and calm like she was cutting out coupons. Blood's flying everywhere, spraying us, and she's silent. I'll never get over the horror of that day.*

Wanda tossed the clipboard aside with a self-righteous air. "Cutting. Out. Coupons."

Nicole said nothing, trying to look concerned.

"Someone took that same spear we see on the video and, unfortunately, we don't know who or how because the video does not show us. But plenty of witnesses report that a female with features similar to your friend stabbed Brother Bernard several times. In fact, ran him through and through until whomever that murderer was, apparently got tired and ended their attack by stabbing the man under his neck and lodging the tip of the spear in the poor soul's brain."

Nicole fought to keep any hint of a smile off her face. "Yes. Poor soul."

"Then flings the bloodied body of the dead man into the faces of the assembled crowd of church members." Wanda paused for dramatic effect. "*Do you know who killed Brother Bernard?*"

"I wasn't there."

"Perhaps the crazy woman we catch glimpses of later on in the video? The one who cradles your dying friend in her arms?"

"Again, Wanda. I wasn't there."

"Forward to that scene, please. There—"

Nicole didn't need to look at the video. She'd replayed it a hundred times. B with El's head in her lap, smoothing his hair, bent over his bloody form rocking and sobbing. The scene ends when Beatrix's tear-streaked face looks straight into the camera. She narrows her eyes and after that, no more video.

Wanda nodded at the screen. "That young woman and your friend seem to have disappeared from the murder scene. How is that possible? There are many theories as to how they escaped and where they went. "

"I've heard them, yes."

"Do you know where they might be?"

"Once more, Wanda. I wasn't—"

"I know, I know. You weren't there. Let's try an easy one. Do you know what your friend El whispered to Mother Magdalene after his stabbing?"

"That I do know."

"Finally."

Nicole leaned forward. "But it's private. I suggest you ask Mother Magdalene."

The interviewer squirmed in her seat. "The woman has gone into hiding and will not respond to inquiries. The key figures in this entire tragic affair seem to have vanished."

"You want to talk about tragedies?" Nicole stabbed a finger at the monitor. The image of B cradling El clenched her heart. "*That* is the greatest tragedy in a long string of them. Where do the tragedies stop Wanda? How about right here, right now? When I think about the loss of El and all he could have given to the world I want to cry. That's all I have to say. We're done." She removed her headset and stood, dropping it on her chair.

Not to be overshadowed, Wanda stood as well. "From the reports of all the unnatural births and scores of new big-headed babies being born around the world, I would say he's given us quite a lot."

Nicole halted her walk off and turned back. The studio mikes picked up her retort. "I would reflect on that if I were you, Wanda. And so we're clear, there's nothing unnatural about those beautiful new babies." She shrugged and stared into the camera. "They're only a little, as my friend El would say, overcooked."

THE END

Dear Reader,

I am honored that you took the time to read this novel and I sincerely appreciate your carving out valuable time from your life to devote to El and me. What began as an idea for a short story morphed into a full-fledged novel over the course of several years and it became a true labor of love. I had a blast writing this book and I hope you had as much fun reading it.

Every novel I write tends to become my new best favorite and this one is no exception. But I do have another novel coming up—the follow-up to THRUTHELIGHT.COM. It is nearing completion and so I expect that EARTH WITCH may unseat OVERCOOKED later this year. Keep tabs on it by signing up: https://www.markmcwaters.com.

As I sit typing this it is 2021 and the pandemic is showing encouraging signs that it may be slowing down. Please stay safe. And if you feel so inclined, I would be grateful if you left a review. Reviews are the Holy Grail for us authors. In a very real sense we owe our livelihoods to them. Thank you once again.

Sincerely,

Mark

ABOUT THE AUTHOR

Mark lives in Mount Dora, Florida with Bentley, the world's smartest Westie. After a long and successful career as an advertising copywriter and creative director he has focused his gift for making up stuff. Today he is following his bliss as a storyteller. He reads stories, writes them, and shares his love of them with others who have the same passions. It is a blessing he appreciates more with each passing day. Check out his novels and short stories on Amazon and at MarkMcWaters.com. If you like this book, please leave a review on Amazon. He will be forever grateful) no matter how many stars you bestow. If you would like to get in touch with Mark he answers all emails at: mark@markmcwaters.com.

Made in the USA
Columbia, SC
18 April 2021